Romantic Suspense

Danger. Passion. Drama.

Colton Mountain Search
Karen Whiddon

Defender After Dark
Charlene Parris

MILLS & BOON

Karen Whiddon is acknowledged as the author of this work
COLTON MOUNTAIN SEARCH
© 2024 by Harlequin Enterprises ULC
Philippine Copyright 2024
Australian Copyright 2024
New Zealand Copyright 2024

First Published 2024
First Australian Paperback Edition 2024
ISBN 978 1 038 90558 1

DEFENDER AFTER DARK
© 2024 by Charlene L. Lokey
Philippine Copyright 2024
Australian Copyright 2024
New Zealand Copyright 2024

First Published 2024
First Australian Paperback Edition 2024
ISBN 978 1 038 90558 1

MIX
Paper | Supporting
responsible forestry
FSC® C001695

Published by
Harlequin Mills & Boon
An imprint of Harlequin Enterprises (Australia) Pty Limited
(ABN 47 001 180 918), a subsidiary of HarperCollins
Publishers Australia Pty Limited
(ABN 36 009 913 517)
Level 19, 201 Elizabeth Street
SYDNEY NSW 2000 AUSTRALIA

Colton Moutain Search

Karen Whiddon

MILLS & BOON

Karen Whiddon started weaving fanciful tales for her younger brothers at the age of eleven. Amid the gorgeous Catskill Mountains, then the majestic Rocky Mountains, she fueled her imagination with the natural beauty surrounding her. Karen now lives in north Texas, writes full-time and volunteers for a boxer dog rescue. She shares her life with her hero of a husband and four to five dogs, depending on if she is fostering. You can email Karen at kwhiddon1@aol.com. Fans can also check out her website, karenwhiddon.com.

Visit the Author Profile page
at millsandboon.com.au for more titles.

Dear Reader,

Once again, I was fortunate enough to return to writing about the Colton family. This time, the story combined several of my favourite things—mountains and dogs! I was thrilled to write a story about Della Winslow, a search and rescue volunteer and dog trainer in the beautiful state of Idaho. Pairing her with former playboy turned FBI agent Max Colton was a lot of fun! Throw in the huge Colton family, a small town and a serial killer on the loose, and what a story.

I truly hope you enjoy reading it as much as I did writing it.

Karen Whiddon

Chapter 1

Even the light seemed different up in the mountains. Clearer, somehow. The sunshine and cloudless blue sky made this a perfect summer day. Della Winslow took a deep breath and smiled. She loved the crisp mountain air at this elevation, slightly cool even in August. Keeping a watchful eye on her surroundings, she whistled for her black Lab, Charlie. Though she usually kept him on leash, today she'd been allowing him to range ahead of her on the steep and rocky trail.

Since she'd trained him well, he immediately returned to her side, long black tail wagging. After praising him, she rewarded him with one of his favorite liver treats. This, she thought, was one of the reasons she loved her life choices. Not everyone got to work their passion. Hers had always been training dogs. Today she got to do that and work out as well, combining hiking in the Bitterroot Mountains along with schooling her already very talented search and rescue cadaver dog. She'd been working with him since she'd gotten him as a puppy at eight weeks old. Now two, he'd earned his certification and had accompanied her on several SAR missions, where he'd easily proved his skills.

Specifically, Charlie had been trained to smell decomposition. When working a scene, whether an accident of some sort or an act of nature, his job was to locate anything that had been left by a human body. This could be body parts, including tissue, blood and bone or fluids. He could also detect residue left by a scent, which meant he could tell if a body had been somewhere, even if it had been moved.

So far, she'd been working with him for eighteen months. Luckily, her job as a dog trainer at Crosswinds Training had made it easier for her to teach him, since he often needed to work up to eight hours a day. She'd also had to socialize and desensitize him, getting him used to sirens and flashing lights, since they'd commonly be requested at accident scenes. While she'd trained SAR dogs in the past, Charlie was her first cadaver dog. He'd already been an asset on the one accident scene they'd worked—a train derailment close to Boise.

These days, she spent as much of her time as she could fine-tuning his training. She'd known the instant she'd started with him that his hunt drive, confidence and unflappable nerve would serve him well in search and rescue work.

Today, though, they were mostly focused on fun. Every now and then, she'd call Charlie back to her before letting him roam again. Judging by the way he carried his tail curled over his back, he was thoroughly enjoying himself.

They entered a clearing. Charlie took off again, running in circles around her and panting happily. Smiling, Della watched him, her heart light.

Suddenly, her dog froze. He sat and barked once, looking back at her to see if she'd caught his cue.

Puzzled, she hurried toward him. Charlie had just given the signal that meant he'd found human remains.

As she got closer, she saw them. Bones. Large ones, unmistakably human, protruding from the dirt near the edge of the clearing.

Charlie stayed in place, watching as she circled the area. They both knew better than to disturb anything. Time to call in law enforcement.

Except this high up, her cell phone had no signal. She'd expected that since she'd been here before. A quarter mile back down the trail she could climb up on a few large boulders, and sometimes, if the conditions were just right, she could get a signal. Though the likelihood often ran fifty-fifty, she had to try. After all, the only other option would be to hike back to her vehicle and drive closer to civilization.

Before she left, she had to mark the scene. Digging in her backpack, she pulled out a strip of bright yellow cloth that she sometimes used for sight work. When she'd tied this around the nearest tree, she used her cell phone to take several photos of the area, including a couple of the bones themselves.

Then she whistled for Charlie, and they set off down the trail in the direction of the rock formation. Once there, she climbed up as far as she safely could and checked her cell. Two bars. Enough to call the Owl Creek Police Department and report her findings. If she was lucky, they'd send someone out to investigate right away.

It must have been a slow day in Owl Creek, because by the time Della reached the parking lot, two police cruisers were pulling up. Since the place where Charlie had located the body wasn't accessible by vehicle, all four of the uniformed officers had to hike back up along with Della and Charlie.

Luckily, they appeared to be in pretty good shape. Della kept her pace a little slower than usual, just in case.

By the time they reached the clearing, all four of the officers were only slightly out of breath. Charlie kept pace with Della, watching her every move. Since they had company, she'd given him the hand signal to stay by her side. Now he waited for her to signal him to search.

Once they'd stopped in the middle of the meadow, she pointed to the cloth she'd tied around the tree. "The bones are over there."

Next to her, Charlie quivered with impatience. "My dog is a search and rescue cadaver dog. He found them. And he really wants me to allow him to point them out again."

With a flick of her hand, she sent Charlie out again. He went to the bones he'd found earlier, sat and barked. Once she'd given him his verbal praise, he took off again.

Della stood back and watched while the police officers took photos of the scene. She kept an eye on Charlie, noticing the way he kept moving in circles around the field, almost as if he was actively working a crime scene.

She'd just had that thought when Charlie sat and barked, signaling he'd located something else. Dread coiling in her stomach, she walked over to him. As soon as she reached him, he began pawing at the dirt. She saw the gleam of another large bone and knew.

"Leave it," she commanded, gesturing him back into a sitting position. Then she turned. "He's found another body."

Immediately, all four men hurried over. One took a few more photographs while the other tried to call someone.

"There's no cell signal up here," she advised. "We'd have to walk about a quarter mile back and climb up on that stack of rocks. Even then, it's hit-or-miss."

The older officer, a man whose name tag read Handy, sighed. "I was afraid you'd say that. Now that we have more than one body, we're likely going to have to call in the FBI."

She frowned. "The FBI?"

"Just in case this might be the work of a serial killer," Handy explained. He turned to the others. "Larkins, you come with me. Santis, you and Kinney stay here and make sure nobody disturbs the scene until the FBI can send someone. Put out some crime scene tape or something. Once you're done, we'll all meet up at the squad cars."

"We're going to leave those bones unprotected?" Larkins asked. "What if wildlife comes along or something?"

Handy shook his head. "From the looks of them, they've been here a good while. I'm going to guess any animals have already gotten what they wanted." He glanced at Della. "Are you ready to go?"

"I am," she replied. "Charlie, come." Then, with her dog at her side, she led the way down.

When the call came in from the Owl Creek Police Department, the FBI switchboard operator passed the information to a supervisor, who immediately assigned the case to Max Colton. After all, Max had grown up in Owl Creek and everyone in the office knew his family all still lived there.

Human remains had been discovered by a woman training her SAR cadaver dog on a hiking trail. The police had been out, and the dog had promptly located another buried body, which might indicate a possible serial killer. Which was why the FBI and, now specifically, Max Colton had been asked to step in.

Naturally, Max agreed to take the assignment. Close to home meant he could fit in an extended visit to his family. Despite the fact that he worked about two hours away, with his busy career he found it more and more difficult to fit in a long visit home. With five siblings, he could usually manage to spend time with two or three of them. Maybe this trip, he could see all five.

Since he also had a special fondness for dogs, and in the past had been amazed by the supersmart, well-trained SAR canines, he figured this might be even more of a good fit for him.

Feeling excited and, as his assistant Jack liked to say, pumped, he headed out. In his line of work, he kept a go bag in his truck, so he didn't even need to stop at his apartment before hitting the road.

He made it to the Owl Creek city limits right after lunchtime. Because he hadn't taken the time to eat anything, he made a quick stop in the drive-through of a new burger joint on the outskirts of town. Eating while he drove, he went straight to the trails, wondering if they'd waited for him or if he'd need to round everyone back up.

Two squad cars and an older Jeep Cherokee were parked in the middle of the lot, which meant they'd waited. Several uniformed officers stood around talking to a slender woman with long brown hair that she wore in a thick braid down her back. A large black Lab stood next to her.

Parking, he killed the engine and got out. As he approached the group, he recognized all the officers. One of the benefits of growing up in a small town.

"Hey, Max!" Drew Handy greeted him with a smile. "I kind of figured they'd send you. That's the only reason we waited all this time. We knew you'd rush up here as soon as you got the case."

"Thanks," Max said. "I appreciate that." He glanced around. "I'm guessing they didn't send Fletcher." His cousin worked as a detective for the Owl Creek PD.

"He's off today," Handy replied. "Otherwise, I'm sure they would have."

The woman turned then, smiling, and Max lost all capacity for rational thought. He didn't know her—must not have ever met her, because he damn sure wouldn't forget a woman like her. Achingly beautiful in a natural kind of way, with large brown eyes and a lush mouth. Staring might be rude, but he couldn't seem to pull his gaze away.

Luckily, her dog stood and drew his attention. Long tail wagging furiously, the Lab quivered with eagerness. He was, Max thought, one hell of a good-looking animal. His black coat shone, and his eyes were clear and bright. The woman gave a quick hand signal and the dog sat back down, staying put at her side.

"Hey, there." Crouching to put himself at eye level, Max glanced up at the woman. "Is it okay if I pet him?"

Slowly, she nodded. "Charlie, free," she said, her expression reserved. Immediately, Charlie launched himself at Max, nearly bowling him over. Max laughed, fending off dog kisses and slobber while scratching the gleaming black fur.

"Charlie, heel," the woman said. Her clearly well-trained

dog returned to sit at her side. She waited until Max had gotten back on his feet before holding out a hand. "Della Winslow," she said. "My apologies. He's not usually so enthusiastic about strangers."

Shaking her hand, Max smiled. "No apology needed. I like most dogs and they like me. I'm Max Colton."

The wary look came back into her eyes. "I know who you are." She glanced at the officers, who were all watching with unabashed interest. "I've done some searches with your brother Malcolm. He's a nice guy."

Max nodded. His brother helped run the family ranch and did some volunteer SAR work on the side. "That he is," he replied.

She turned her attention back to the others. "Are you guys ready to hike back up to the site?"

"Yes, ma'am," they replied in unison, grinning as they looked from her to Max and back again. Her creamy skin became pink, but she turned and whistled for Charlie, striding ahead. Max shook his head at the officers and took off after her.

Over the years, with his aversion to any kind of permanent relationship, Max had managed to cultivate quite a reputation as a player. He knew the guys all thought they'd witnessed another hapless woman reacting to his supposed charm, but in fact it was the other way around. For the first time in his life, a woman had rendered Max Colton speechless. The sharp tug of attraction he'd felt had been something he'd never experienced, and he'd dated numerous beautiful women. He couldn't explain it and wasn't sure he even wanted to.

However, Max knew better than to mix business with pleasure. Della Winslow might be gorgeous, but while they were working together, he'd consider her strictly off-limits.

The hike up the path felt good after spending a couple of hours in the car. He'd put on his hiking boots earlier, aware reaching the site would require some effort. Years ago, when he'd lived in Owl Creek, he'd spent quite a bit of his adolescence on these very same trails.

Della led the way, her thick brown braid swinging. Charlie kept pace with her, occasionally ranging a bit ahead, though a single word from her brought him back to her side. They passed the outcrop of giant rocks Max remembered sitting on top of with friends and various dates. He'd felt like the king of the mountain, surveying the landscape and watching wildlife pass below.

"Not too much farther," Della said, glancing back over her shoulder at them.

"We've already taken a bunch of photos." Drew sounded out of breath. "And I'm guessing you'll want to use your own forensics?"

"We'll see." Noncommittal until he got a good idea what they were dealing with, Max shrugged. A lot depended on how old these burial sites turned out to be.

One more turn and they came out into a large clearing. Max spotted a bright yellow strip of cloth tied to a tree. "There?" he asked.

"Yes," Della answered. "Charlie found the first set of bones in that location."

Despite Drew having taken photos, Max pulled out his pocket camera and got to work. "I like to have my own," he explained, even though no one had asked.

As soon as he'd finished with the first grave, Della directed him to the second. He took the photos, careful not to disturb anything, and then met her again. Again, he felt a jolt straight to his midsection, which he managed once more to ignore. "Are you sure there aren't any more?"

The question appeared to startle her. She tilted her head, considering. "I guess we need to ask Charlie," she finally replied.

Hearing his name, the black Lab looked up at her, on instant alert. "Go out," she said, gesturing toward an area with her hand.

Tail curved high over his back, Charlie leaped forward, nose to the ground, intent on his work.

Everyone went silent and watched.

Max had watched search and rescue dogs work before, focused and unflappable in even the most horrific of circumstances. Most of them could, and would, do the same type of work as a cadaver dog if needed, but they specialized in finding signs of life rather than human remains. Cadaver dogs like Charlie received even more specialized training.

As alert as her dog, Della appeared to balance on the balls of her feet, ready to move the second Charlie gave an alert. Max honestly hoped he didn't, because if they found any additional bodies, this case would turn into a major investigation. Which, with four members of local law enforcement present, would be impossible to keep under wraps.

Charlie stopped, sat and barked once. Eyes wide, Della met Max's gaze and nodded. "He's found another one."

Damn it. "Stay put," Max ordered the Owl Creek police

crew. "This entire pasture is about to turn into a crime scene."

Following Della to where Charlie waited, Max looked around. This time, there were no visible signs of a body. "Let him dig," he told Della. "Just enough to unearth whatever he's found, not more."

"He knows his job," she shot back, her voice terse. One flip of her fingers and Charlie began digging.

It wasn't long before he unearthed a dirty and jagged bone. The instant he did, he sat and once again looked toward Della for cues.

Grim now, Max told Della they'd seen enough for now. "I'm going to have to call in a team," he said, speaking loud enough for the others to hear. "We'll bring in our own forensic people too. I'll need you to make sure to mark off as much of this area as you can."

"I doubt we have that much crime scene tape," Drew said. "But we'll do the best we can."

"I appreciate that." Returning his attention to Della, Max thanked her for her help. "Will you and Charlie be available to assist when I get my team in place?"

"Of course," she replied, scratching her dog behind his ears. "That's what we do."

"I'm going to need to hike down back to the rocks so I can make the call," he said. "Once I've done that, I've got a tent in my truck. I figure I might as well spend the night here so I can make sure nothing is disturbed."

Appearing unsurprised, she nodded. "Would you like Charlie and me to stay here with you? We have our own tent."

Of course she did. Working with SAR teams, Della would be prepared for anything. He had to admit, the prospect of spending some alone time with her so they could get to know each other had a lot of appeal. Probably more than it should have.

"I'll leave that up to you," he said. "I've got enough rations to get us through tonight and tomorrow morning. My team will bring more."

Her smile lit up her face. Again, he felt that tug. He swallowed hard, well aware he couldn't let her see how she affected him.

"I travel with rations too," she told him. "And dog food, so Charlie never has to miss a meal."

Aware of the others watching intently, Max turned to them. "The FBI will be taking the lead on this. I need you to keep this quiet for now. No media. Please just keep a lid on this until we figure out what we're dealing with."

All four men murmured their agreement. Though Max knew it would only be a matter of time until one of them told someone, hopefully this would buy him a little time.

"Good. Well, thank you for your assistance with this." He dismissed them with a smile. "I'll walk back with you as far as the boulders."

Della called Charlie to her side, and once again, the small group took off. This time, the hike was silent, everyone apparently lost in their own thoughts. Finding a mass burial ground tended to have that effect on people. And unfortunately, that was what this site was becoming. With the discovery of three bodies and who knew how many more, they likely had a serial killer on their hands.

As soon as they reached the towering rocks, Max and Della stopped. The policemen continued down to the parking lot. While Della gave Charlie some water, Max climbed to his former adolescent perch and checked his phone. Two and a half bars. Enough of a signal to make a call or two.

Once Max had outlined the situation to his supervisor, Brian Mahoney, and listed who and what he needed, he waited, watching Della interact with her dog below. A moment later, Brian returned to the line and informed Max that everyone would be on their way first thing in the morning. He'd have his entire team assembled by lunchtime. And yes, they'd all be prepared to camp as long as necessary.

Thanking the man, Max ended the call and climbed back down. Della looked up from her dog and smiled, her brown eyes bright. Mouth suddenly dry, Max wondered if he'd ever get accustomed to the gut punch of her beauty.

Della turned away, appearing completely unaware. "Let's go get our gear and establish a campsite."

Back on solid footing, he fell into step alongside her. "Yes, we've got to make sure we pitch our tents on safe ground." By which he meant not on top of any buried bodies.

"True." Nodding, Della smiled up at him again. This time he braced himself and, to his relief, was able to smile back. He counted it as a small victory. Once his team assembled, he knew he'd be too focused to pay much attention to a random physical attraction.

When they reached the lot, all the squad cars were gone.

"How long do you think you have before one of them alerts the media?" Della asked.

He grimaced. "I'm just hoping for enough time to get the full scope of the situation. The FBI will want to issue an official statement, but not until we have all the facts."

"People will panic once they know we have a serial killer in Owl Creek."

"I know." Pressing the key fob, he unlocked his truck and reached into the back seat, where he kept all his gear. He unloaded it all, looking up to see Della doing the same thing at her Jeep. Charlie sat quietly at her side, watching her.

"Are you sure you want to do this?" he asked, shouldering on his pack and grabbing his duffel. "You don't have to. You can always go home and come back tomorrow."

"It's all good." She loaded up quickly, clearly an expert in the art of packing. "If I'm on-site, Charlie and I can get an early start. Just in case there turn out to be more."

More. Damn, he hoped not. Finding three unmarked graves was bad enough. Any more than that and they'd have a potentially catastrophic situation on their hands. At least he knew his team would be busy getting data before coming this way. They'd look for reports of missing women, because most likely that was what these remains would turn out to be.

"Are you ready?" she asked. The question made Charlie stand, his tail wagging.

"Sure." Once she'd reached him, they went back to the trail. This time, he felt glad he'd packed a satellite phone in his gear. He even thought he might have remembered to charge it. At least with that, they'd have a way to communicate with the rest of the world.

Charlie led the way up, staying fairly close and glancing back often to make sure they followed. Once again, Max found himself enjoying the exercise, the fresh air and the company. He liked that Della apparently didn't feel the need to fill the silence with small talk.

"Do you have the resources for relatively quick identification?" she asked, after they'd passed the rocks. "I know sometimes that sort of thing can take time, especially when some of the bones have been there awhile."

"We do." He smiled. "It still takes longer than what you see on TV, but we're pretty fast. We're the FBI, after all."

Her eyes sparkled as she met his gaze. For a second, he could have sworn something arced between them. A kind of connection, almost as real as a physical touch. But then she looked away and the moment vanished. Which was a good thing, he supposed. He was about to be much too busy, and professional, to be making goo-goo eyes with the SAR handler.

They reached the clearing. The wind had picked up a little and even in August it carried a definite chill. Instinctively he eyed the sky for signs of a gathering storm, but the perfect blue dotted with fluffy white clouds allayed his fear. A peaceful summer afternoon with a breeze, nothing more.

Della had Charlie perform a search of the area where they'd decided to pitch their tents. Max watched, fascinated, as Della controlled exactly where she wanted Charlie to search. She used a combination of vocal cues and hand signals, all of which Charlie clearly understood.

After a few minutes with his nose to the ground, the talented dog returned to Della's side and sat.

"This means he didn't find anything," Della said. "So it's safe to get busy setting up camp."

They each tended to their own tents. They placed them side by side, almost touching. That way they'd have easy access to each other in case some sort of emergency arose. Standard protocol when in the wilderness, especially in small groups. It didn't help that all he could think of was how close she'd be sleeping in the tent next to him.

He gave himself a mental shake. This nonsense needed to stop. They were two professionals working a potential crime scene, nothing more.

"Firepit here?" she asked, already digging out a spot in the dirt. "I'm pretty sure we can gather enough rocks to make a perimeter."

"I can do that." He'd also noticed the rocks scattered around the edge of the clearing. Almost like markers... No, that was what they had Charlie for.

In a few minutes, he'd gathered enough good-sized rocks to ring their makeshift firepit. Despite the constant pull of physical attraction, he felt comfortable around Della and her dog. He actually looked forward to getting to know her better. In a purely work-colleague type of way.

Once they had the pit ready, they each went off to gather wood, making several trips. Since it hadn't rained in a good while, they found lots of dry timber in manageable sizes and hauled it back to the campsite.

"I have an old newspaper," she said. "I forgot to take it out of my duffel after my last rescue mission. I'm thinking we can use it to help get the fire started."

"That'll work," he replied, refraining from asking her

why she didn't read her news on her phone like everyone else. But then again, she likely went to remote locations like this one, where phone reception was spotty to non-existent. So a physical newspaper made sense.

Watching him as if she could read his thoughts on his face, she shook her head and went into her tent to retrieve it. Handing it to him, she went to take care of her dog while he worked on the fire.

It wasn't long until he had a good-sized blaze going. Just in time, since the shadows were lengthening, and it would soon be dark.

This was one time where he was glad his reputation from the old days in Owl Creek apparently hadn't preceded him. Though they were alone in the woods, isolated from civilization, Della treated him like a work colleague. Nothing more, nothing less. Which was exactly as it should be.

If only he could get himself to regard her the exact same way.

Chapter 2

Della loved dogs more than people, as evidenced by the fact that she'd made training and working with them her life's work. Training search and rescue, drug detection and various other law enforcement canine officers had long been her passion. When Sebastian had added basic manners classes at Crosswinds, at first she had been ambivalent. Now she found she quite enjoyed it. Helping teach their owners how to communicate with their pets had also been unexpectedly rewarding. In all, she lived her life exactly the way she wanted to.

Her friends might be few, but the friendships were deep and long-lasting. When she dated, she made sure to keep things casual. She'd never been one to picture herself settled down and married with a couple of kids. In fact, she didn't really want that. She enjoyed the freedom of her current lifestyle and the opportunities for travel her work with SAR brought.

In short, she considered herself happy. Vibrantly alive even. The last thing she wanted or needed was to be attracted to Max Colton, a man everyone used to consider Owl Creek's major player.

Over the years, she'd heard the stories. He'd left swaths of brokenhearted women pining after him. *Love them and leave them* appeared to be Max Colton's mantra and Della had privately wondered how he'd managed to hook so many women. After all, his reputation surely preceded him. These chicks had to know what they were up against. Maybe they hadn't cared or they'd harbored some delusional belief that they'd be the one to change him.

She couldn't fault his choices. Like her, he appeared to live life exactly on his own terms. All the women throwing themselves after him had puzzled her. Perhaps they liked the challenge of pursuing the truly unattainable.

At any rate, Della had never understood why. Until today, when she'd come face-to-face with the man and felt a bone-deep longing the likes of which she hadn't believed was possible. She'd wanted to run, to hide, and she'd also wanted to jump his sexy-as-hell, bad-boy bones.

Quite the paradox and completely unlike her. Luckily, he didn't appear to feel the same tug of attraction as she did.

After he'd gathered the rocks, he went back for enough dry wood to use for kindling. Glad to be busy, she did the same.

While he worked on getting the fire going, she put out food and water for Charlie. Tail wagging, he gulped down his kibble, drank and then curled up on the ground near her.

Once Max had flames crackling, he dropped down to sit on the ground. She hesitated, even when he invited her to join him with a tilt of his head and a half smile.

She felt a moment of panic. What would they talk about? How much could they actually have in common, this wealthy playboy turned FBI agent and a free-spirited dog trainer?

In the end, she decided none of that mattered. At this moment in time, they were coworkers, nothing more.

As she lowered herself to the ground near, but not next to, him, he smiled again. "Tell me about what all goes into training a search and rescue dog."

So she did. She told him about how she'd begun working with Charlie as a puppy, the socialization work she'd done, taking him around fire stations and police stations so he'd get used to sirens and flashing lights. The obedience training they'd started on day one, all with the same positive reinforcement she taught in her classes at Crosswinds Training.

"That's my day job," she said, feeling relaxed and happy, and wondering if she'd prattled on for too long.

"I'm impressed." He sounded as if he meant it. "Not everyone gets to work doing something that they love."

While she'd talked, the fire had burned down to nearly embers. "I think it's time to turn in," he said.

Checking her watch, she was surprised to realize it was nearly eleven. "I agree." She pushed to her feet and stretched. Charlie eyed her but made no move to get up.

"Come on, boy," she said. "It's time to go to bed."

Charlie got up and came to her side. "See you in the morning," she told Max, and she and her dog went inside her tent.

She'd laid her sleeping bag out earlier. Crawling inside, she motioned to Charlie to join her.

As she settled into sleep, she found the sounds of wildlife comforting rather than frightening. Wolf howls, thankfully in the distance, made her tilt her head and listen. As long as they weren't visited by a bear, she'd be fine.

Sharing her sleeping bag, Charlie lifted his head a few times and sniffed the air, but he didn't appear worried. She laid her cheek against his head and gave him a gentle kiss. If he wasn't, she wasn't. She went to sleep with a smile on her face.

In the morning, she woke early and checked the time on her fitness tracker. Even at home, she made a habit out of watching the sunrise while sipping on her coffee. She signaled Charlie to be quiet and opened her tent flap. The sky had lightened enough that she could see, though the sun hadn't yet made an appearance over the horizon. Together, she and her dog went into the woods to make their morning toilet.

Back at camp, she added some wood to the still-smoldering embers, and once she had a decent-sized fire going, she washed her face with cleansing wipes and brushed her teeth. Then she got some water boiling to make coffee. While she waited, she glanced at Max's tent, which was still closed. Too bad, because she'd kind of wanted to watch the sunrise with him.

The instant the thought occurred to her, he popped his head out of his tent. With his tousled hair and early morning stubble, he looked even sexier than he had the day before. She swallowed hard. "Good morning," she said, her voice bright. "Are you a coffee drinker?"

"I am." Smiling lazily at her, which made her insides twitch, he stood. "I even brought my own cup. I'll be back in a moment," he said, before disappearing into the woods. Charlie watched him go, tail wagging lazily, but made no move to leave Della's side. It took every ounce of self-control she possessed not to keep her gaze locked on Max's very fine backside as he walked away.

Honestly. She rolled her eyes at herself. She wasn't sure what had gotten into her, but it was nothing that hard work wouldn't take care of. The FBI team would be there soon. That should be enough of a distraction to set her mind straight.

She had the coffee ready by the time he returned. He went to his tent and brought out his mug, and once she'd filled it, he sat down on the ground next to her.

Her first sip had her sighing in pleasure. Even instant coffee tasted amazing when made over a campfire. They sipped in silence while the sun colored the sky red, orange and pink. Charlie got up and circled a few times, before lying back down and heaving a contented sigh.

"Look at him," Max said. "I swear he looks like he's grinning."

"That's because he is." She laughed. "He's a very expressive dog."

"I should check in with my team." Max stood. "Much easier now that I have my sat phone."

While he did that, she fed Charlie and made herself a second cup of coffee, which she drank slowly. She needed to eat something too. She wasn't sure what kind of rations he'd brought, but she ate a protein granola bar and some of her favorite smoked beef jerky.

Emerging from his tent, Max appeared to be chowing down on his own protein bar or something.

"They're on their way," he announced, coming closer to use the last of the water to make himself a second cup of coffee. "ETA about ninety minutes."

Impressed, she checked her watch. It was barely seven thirty. "Wow, they sure got an early start."

He shrugged. "They're pretty fired up. It's not every day we get a case like this, and local too. That's the best part of the job. Assembling the evidence and using it to catch the bad guy."

"Are you going to meet them at the lot?" she asked.

"I am." He eyed her. "Are you okay with holding down the fort alone?"

His question made her laugh. "I am. Remember, Charlie and I were out here on a solo hike when we found the first set of remains. We'll be fine."

"Just don't get started without me."

She wiped out her cup and stowed it back in the tent. "Do you want to search a little more now?"

His gaze sharpened, but he shook his head. "Honestly, I do. But we'd better wait for the team."

"I understand." The proximity to him, the constant buzz of sexual tension and the prospect of the day that lay ahead of them had her practically vibrating with energy. Maybe she shouldn't have had that second cup of coffee.

Not wanting to stand around doing nothing for an hour and a half, she whistled for Charlie. "We're going to go for a walk."

"Can I come?" he asked. "It feels better to keep moving instead of just sitting here waiting."

"Sure."

They took off on the narrow, Charlie in the lead, with Max bringing up the rear. She knew exactly where she wanted to go. It had in fact been her intended destination yesterday, before Charlie had made his gruesome discovery.

"Do you have a route in mind?" Max asked from behind her.

"I do," she replied, without turning around. "I often come up here when I need to be reminded of my place in the universe. Have you ever been to Owl Falls?"

"I have." His voice sounded hushed, which told her the falls gave him the same feeling it did her. Reverence for the beautiful countryside in which they lived. A sense of peace and wonder and, often, simple joy at being alive.

The falls weren't easy to get to, which made for a challenging hike. She knew better than to come alone if there was even the slightest possibility of the weather changing, and considered walking here off-limits in the fall, winter and even spring. August with the higher temperatures seemed like the perfect time.

"Not many people hike up that far," he said. She liked that he didn't sound at all out of breath.

"I know. And it's best to go in teams, since some of the footing can be treacherous. But I've been hiking up there since I was a teenager, sometimes in groups and more and more often, alone. I'm always extremely careful."

"I believe you," he said.

Something in his voice made her turn to glance back at him. Because of this, she almost lost her footing, but after a stumble or two, she regained it. Luckily, without incident. Cussing her own carelessness, she resolved to not let him be such a distraction. She knew better.

Following the stream, they continued to climb. The physical exertion made talking difficult, which she liked.

As usual, Charlie led the way, carrying his tail curved over his back. He was such a happy dog.

They heard the roar of the waterfall before they saw it. She knew that around the next bend in the trail, it would come into view. Most people stopped there, admired the sight, took their photos and hiked back down. Not many continued to climb the rocky and sometimes slippery path to the top of the falls. She and Charlie had gone up there numerous times. She guessed she'd see what Max wanted to do.

They made the turn and she stopped, gazing up at the water cascading down. From here, the summit appeared unreachable, though she knew better.

Whistling for Charlie, she took a seat on one of the large rocks near the bank of the river. The sun felt warm on her skin. Charlie bounded back to her, then went carefully down to the edge of the water to get a drink.

"I could look at that all day," Max said, shading his eyes with his hand as he looked up at the falls.

"The view is even better from the top," she said, watching him to see his reaction.

"I imagine it is," he replied. "Unfortunately, I think we need to head back. By the time we get to camp, we'll need to hike to the parking lot to meet my team."

Surprised, she glanced at her watch. He was right. As usual, when she got out in nature, she tended to lose track of time.

Giving the waterfall one last look, she nodded. "I agree. I can always hike out here another time."

"Maybe I can go with you?" he asked. "I've never been up there. I'd really like to go."

She concealed her astonishment by turning her attention to Charlie and ruffling his fur. "Sure," she replied. "We'll have to do that sometime." Vague and noncommittal. That way neither of them had any expectations.

"Cool." Turning, he glanced at her. "Are you ready?"

"I am. Let's go."

They made it back to their camp without encountering any obstacles. Once there, Max checked in with his team via his sat phone before joining Della at her seat near the front of her tent. Apparently, all the exercise had worn Charlie out, because he'd gone inside and curled up to take a nap. Which was good, as she'd want him rested so he could work with the team once they arrived. In fact, she could go for a short nap herself.

"They should be here soon," Max said. "I'm going down to the parking lot to wait for them."

She nodded. "Charlie and I will be here when you all get back."

"Sounds good." Pushing to his feet with a fluid kind of grace that she again found attractive, he took a swig of water from the canteen. "Once we have everyone here, we'll get to work."

Staying seated, she watched until he disappeared out of sight. Then she crawled into her tent and joined her dog, figuring a quick nap would do her good.

Now that he knew who the Bureau had decided to send, Max felt really good about this team. Caroline Perrio, forensic pathologist and crime scene investigator, was one of the best in the business. Max had worked with her on a couple of cases before. The other two team members, Theo Darter and Chris Everitt, were both experienced agents. While on-site, Max would be designated special agent in charge, though that real title went to his boss, Brian Mahoney. Brian had elected to remain at the office in Boise. No one minded, as Brian wasn't a fan of nature or the outdoors. Max would provide daily reports as needed.

None of the team had worked with Della and Charlie before, though Caroline had heard of her work in SAR. They all seemed eager to meet Della and see Charlie in action.

Once at the lot, which was still empty except for his truck and Della's Jeep, he took the opportunity to sit in his vehicle and charge up his phone. Here, he got a halfway decent signal, so he was able to check his email and scroll through his social media feed.

By the time the team pulled up, he'd gotten thoroughly caught up and kind of wished he hadn't. There was something to be said for unplugging for a longer period of time.

Max helped unload their vehicle, a Bureau-issued white windowless van that looked like it belonged on the other side of the law. They were all excited and chattered happily, eager to start the investigation. While Max appreciated their enthusiasm, as they hiked up toward the campsite he found himself longing for the peace of Della's quietness.

"It's just up ahead," he said, when he could finally get a word in. And that seemed to only be because everyone except Caroline was out of breath.

"We don't hike much," Theo said when he caught Max eyeing him. "We'll be fine."

"As long as we can rest a little once we get there," Chris chimed in. Tall and lanky, he wore a Colorado

Rockies baseball cap that looked like it had seen better days.

"Rest?" Caroline teased. "I want to get right to work. I can't wait to watch Della and her dog in action."

Again, Max appreciated Della. Clearly, she hiked often. The two of them had kept up a brisk pace and neither had seemed to mind.

"It's sure pretty out here," Theo said, gasping for breath. "Do you mind if we take a break for a minute?"

"It's not too much farther," Max replied, reluctantly slowing and then stopping. Slightly red in the face, Theo bent over, hands on his knees, chest heaving. Next to him, Chris gave his coworker a sympathetic smile, though he also appeared grateful for the break.

Only Caroline looked visibly impatient. She shifted her weight from foot to foot, making Max wonder if she planned to forge on ahead without them. He wouldn't blame her, but he wanted them all to arrive at camp at the same time.

Five minutes dragged, but finally he made a show of checking his watch. "Are you good to go?" he asked Theo. "It really isn't too far away."

The other man nodded, and they took off again.

Another turn and they could make out the two tents pitched at the edge of the meadow.

"It's pretty remote up here," Theo mused. "I'm guessing that's why the killer decided it would be a great place to bury his bodies."

As they drew closer, there was no sign of Della or Charlie, and Max felt a twinge of concern. He hoped they hadn't gone off on another solo hike.

The others were chattering again, commenting on

everything from the size of the clearing to how close the tents had been pitched together. Theo, ever the practical one, had already begun laying things out in preparation for setting up two additional tents.

Caroline had already wandered over to look at the first set of bones, crouching on her haunches to study them. Despite all the photos they'd already taken, she had her camera in hand and was snapping some more.

Just then, Charlie bolted from the tent, barking an alert, though his tail wagged furiously. A moment later, Della peeked her head out and quieted him. "It's okay, boy," she said. "We're about to go to work." Judging by her tousled hair and sleepy eyes, she'd just awakened.

"Did you take a nap?" Max asked, smiling. The team went quiet, looking from Max to Della and her dog. Caroline pushed to her feet, smiling.

"I did." Covering her yawn with her hand, Della emerged. "It was supposed to be a short one, but clearly I overslept." She looked from one person to the next, her expression friendly. "I'm Della and this is my canine partner, Charlie."

"Hi! I'm Caroline Perrio." Hand outstretched, she approached Della. "Forensic pathologist and crime scene investigator."

After the two women shook hands, Max performed the rest of the introductions, unable to help but notice the way both Theo and Chris reacted to Della's beauty. Theo's pale skin flushed while Chris simply flashed Max a knowing grin.

Oblivious, Della told them the timeline of Charlie's discovery. "Max seems to think there might be more graves. I'm hoping he's wrong, but that's Charlie's area of expertise. Just let me know when you're ready for him to work."

"We will." Caroline glanced at Max. "I'd like to work on the three known graves. I'll need to prep them so they can be transported back to my lab." She pointed at Theo. "I'll need your help."

Theo nodded. "No problem."

"Perfect." Beaming, Caroline spun around and went back to the first set of bones. Theo trailed along after her.

"Okay, then." Max rubbed his hands together. "Why don't we see if Charlie can find anything else."

Eyes bright, the dog watched him, almost as if he understood everything Max said.

"We'll start over on this side." Della pointed. "And work our way back toward the areas where the first three graves were located."

Noting her phrasing, Max nodded. Like him, he suspected Della had a gut feeling they'd find more bodies hidden in this clearing.

"Are you ready?" Della asked. When he nodded, she quietly ordered Charlie to go to work. Even Caroline paused to watch the skilled dog work.

In less than five minutes, Charlie sat and gave his signal, a single bark. Della praised him, and she and her dog waited while Max and Chris hurried over.

The two men dug, using the small, blunt shovels the team had brought along for that purpose. Less than three inches under the topsoil, they found another set of bones.

"Damn it." Max shook his head. "I wonder how many more are out here."

Tongue lolling, Charlie watched him.

"Mark this one too," Max told Chris. "We might as well see how many more the dog finds."

"We're going to need more people," Caroline piped up. "And depending on the end total, another transport van or two. Three is about the maximum I can move in the single van we have."

Max rubbed his eyes. Expression grave, Della watched him. She knew, he realized. Somehow, just like him, she knew that they were going to find some sort of killing field here. What had formerly appeared to be an undisturbed, peaceful meadow would be forever tainted.

Uncharacteristically silent, the rest of the team suspected too. Their somber faces gave testimony to their feelings.

"Go ahead—send Charlie out," Max said.

In the next ten minutes, Charlie signaled twice more. Six bodies. Knowing he needed to make a report immediately, Max got out his cell phone and called his SAC.

"Are you effin' kidding me?" Brian asked. "Six?"

"Yes, sir. And there might be more." While Max fervently hoped they'd found all the graves, he had no idea how long the killer had been dumping his prey here. If not for Della taking a hike with her SAR dog, none of these would likely have ever been discovered.

"The media is going to have a field day. You know how they like to sensationalize serial killers." Brian exhaled loudly. "We need to keep a lid on this as long as we can. I'm going to have to bring in more people."

"And Caroline says she needs more transport vans. All these remains have to go back to her lab so she can ID them."

"I'll work on that." Brian sighed. "I'll give you a call once I have an ETA."

"Thanks." Max ended the call. "Brian's sending a couple more vans," he said. "He wants an update with the total once we're done."

"We'll need them for sure," Caroline replied, looking up.

Max walked over, checking out the fourth set of bones, which Chris still worked carefully to uncover. A gleam of something caught his eyes. "What's this?" he asked, pulling a bit of silver metal from the dirt. "It looks like a necklace. Some sort of wolf."

Several feet away, Della froze. "Let me see it," she said, hurrying over. "I need to know if there's an inscription on the back."

Max handed it over, noticing the way her hands trembled. She turned it to see the other side, and her expression crumpled. She let out a cry, so full of pain she might have been mortally wounded. "Angela," she said, gasping for air. "Oh, Angela."

Max took the necklace from her unresisting fingers. He turned it over and read the inscription carved into the back. *To Angela, from Della. Forever family.*

Della swayed. Afraid she might go down, Max pulled her close, supporting her with his arm.

"You knew this person?" he asked, frowning.

"Yes. Angela is...was...my cousin." Della's voice broke. Taking a deep breath, she leaned on Max and continued. "She went missing two years ago, in Kalispell, Montana. None of us ever gave up hope that we'd find her." She shuddered, her gaze unfocused, looking inward. "And now I have. She was killed."

As the enormity of the realization washed over her, Della seemed to shrink in upon herself. Shuddering, she turned away from the others, pressing her face into Max's chest. He held her close while she cried, great heaving sobs that she clearly tried to muffle.

Damn it. He hadn't expected this case to turn personal.

Wanting to give her some privacy, the rest of the team moved away. They gathered around one of the other graves and got busy working to clear dirt from the bones.

Standing motionless, Max tried to offer what comfort he could while poor Della mourned the loss of her cousin.

Though he'd only just met her, Max held her while she wept. Charlie, clearly worried about her, came over, sat down with his body pressed against her leg and whined. Despite her obvious pain, Della reached out blindly and laid her hand on the dog's head. This quieted him. Max wished he could do something similar for her.

After a few moments, Della seemed to get her emotions under control. Her shuddering quieted. She straightened and took the necklace out of Max's hands and moved away, avoiding eye contact. Charlie followed, sticking close to her side.

As if by mutual agreement, everyone stopped what they were doing and silently watched as Della and Charlie disappeared into her tent.

"That's awful," Caroline murmured. "What a horrible way to find out what happened to your cousin."

Max nodded. "It is. And even though she's tentatively identified the body, you'll still need to get a positive forensic ID."

"Of course." Caroline nodded. "Everyone, let's get back to work."

They worked for several hours, painstakingly unearthing the bones. During this time, Della did not emerge from her tent. When Max finally called for a break, Caroline came over and touched his arm. "Should you check on her?" she asked.

"Should I?" He shrugged. "She kind of seemed like she wanted to be left alone. Honestly, I can't blame her."

Caroline met his gaze. "I guess I was just thinking that since you two appear to be close, you'd be best able to offer her comfort."

"Close?" The description unsettled him. "I just met her yesterday."

"Oh. Wow." Now Caroline appeared flustered. "I'm sorry. I just assumed..."

For some reason this irritated him. Despite keeping his dating life low-key for the past several years, he couldn't escape his reputation. "Don't assume. The last thing I think Della would need or want right now would be me intruding on her personal grief."

"Maybe not." Caroline shrugged. "I know if it was me, I'd want to be left alone." Turning, she walked away.

This should have made him feel better. Truthfully, he'd been wishing he could figure out something to help Della. While it was true that he barely knew her, there'd been some sort of instant and intense connection between them. What that might lead to, if anything, he had no idea.

Naturally, he'd never admit such a thing to anyone, ever. Men like him—practical, grounded and focused on their career—weren't the type to experience more than a flash of sexual attraction. Lust, he could deal with. Anything more than that, and he'd always back the hell off. Relationships simply weren't his thing. Never had been.

He could—and would—concentrate on the case. After what had happened today, Della would likely ask for someone else to take her place if they needed any more search and rescue work. And he wouldn't blame her. When things became too personal, the professional aspect tended to fall by the wayside.

For now, he'd give her space, let her come to terms with what had happened to her cousin and, when she felt ready, figure out what she wanted to do going forward.

And most important of all, he'd keep his hands to himself from now on. No matter how tempting he found Della Winslow.

Chapter 3

Doubled over in grief inside, while trying to act normal on the outside, Della didn't know what to do with herself. She needed to scream, pound a pillow—something, anything—to release the awful pain building inside of her.

Charlie nudged her hand with his nose, intuitive as usual. She wrapped her arms around him, burying her face in his fur, and cried. Patient and loyal as always, he stood still and offered comfort the only way he knew how—by being there.

When she'd cried herself out, she wiped her eyes with the backs of her hands and kissed the top of Charlie's head. She felt slightly better. Instead of wanting to rage against the injustice of it all, she felt hollow. Drained. She needed to think.

The tent wasn't big enough to pace in and damned if she could go back out there and face the FBI agents just yet. They were all professionals, here to do a job. Meanwhile, she could hardly catch her breath. A hundred things ran through her mind as she struggled to process the information that her beloved cousin Angela had been murdered. When and how, of course she wanted to know that. But she also wondered how to find the words to tell her aunt and uncle, Angela's parents. Like Della, they'd refused to abandon hope that Angela would be found.

When they learned the truth about what had happened to her, they'd be devastated. And Della knew she had to be the one to tell them. News like this couldn't come from a stranger.

On top of all this, Della had to face the fact that she'd fallen apart while on the job. As someone who prided herself on her composure and professional demeanor, she'd found herself taking comfort from Max Colton, the stud of Owl Creek. Sure, he was a dedicated FBI agent, she reminded herself, but that didn't help. She figured she probably needed to apologize to the entire team.

Just not right now. Her emotions were too raw.

Charlie, the best dog ever, stayed close to her. She kept her hands tangled in his fur, stroking him. He snuggled close, offering comfort the only way he knew how.

Outside, the steady sound of the others working made her feel even worse. Briefly, she considered making a run for it, leaving her tent and heading for her Jeep in the parking lot with her dog. But she'd never do something like that. Not only did she have a reputation to consider, but she'd agreed to perform a service working with the FBI.

She owed Angela, and all the other nameless women buried here, to have their identities discovered and their killer found and brought to justice.

Oddly enough, it was this last thing that helped her the most. She might not have been able to save her cousin, but she sure as hell would play a part in finding out what had happened to her.

Aware she looked like a mess, she brushed her hair,

used a disposable wipe to clean her face and crawled out of her tent. She had to face the team sooner or later. Might as well get this over with.

From the looks of things, they were taking a break. Everyone sat together on the large rocks that ringed the edge of the clearing. They all had water and various snacks. Without exception, they went silent the instant they caught sight of her.

"Della." Caroline stood. "I was just about to come check on you and make sure you're okay."

"Thanks." From somewhere, Della summoned up what she hoped resembled a smile. "I'm still processing. I wanted to apologize for breaking down back there."

"Don't." Caroline shook her head. "We all understand and sympathize with you. Any of us would have had a similar reaction, making a discovery like that."

Nodding, Della took a deep breath. She desperately wanted to get back to normal, even if it was only temporary.

"Would you like some water or a snack?" Caroline asked. "We brought plenty of food."

Della gratefully accepted a bottled water and a small package of cheese crackers. She took a seat on a vacant rock, watching Charlie as he cozied up to Theo, hoping to score a handout for his own snack.

"Watch that one," Della called. "He'll take that chip right out of your hand if you let him get too close."

Theo laughed, but he moved his bag of chips a little farther away from Charlie. The others began talking among themselves again, and the warmth of the sunlight made Della feel a bit better.

A shadow blocked out the sun. Della looked up. Max.

He stood in front of her, gazing down at her with an inscrutable expression.

"Walk with me?" he asked. Despite everything, her heart skipped a beat.

Aware of everyone watching them while pretending not to, she nodded and stood.

Charlie, ever vigilant, immediately came to Della's side.

"He doesn't like to let you out of his sight, does he?" Max commented.

Swallowing past the lump in her throat, Della touched her dog's silky fur. "He's a good boy," she said.

When they'd gone far enough from the others that they could no longer be seen or heard, Max stopped. "Are you going to be all right to continue with this investigation?" he asked, the tone of his voice both concerned and businesslike. "None of us would blame you if you'd prefer we call in someone else."

Though it shouldn't have, it felt almost as if he'd slapped her. "I appreciate your concern, but I'm a professional," she replied, lifting her chin. "And Charlie's the best in the region. We started this case, and we'll finish it, thank you very much."

He watched her, unsmiling, that blue-eyed gaze of his searching her face. If he'd considered overriding her protests, he must have thought better of it, because he simply nodded. "Then let's get back to work. We've got several other agents joining us, so there'll be quite a few extra tents pitched here overnight."

Relieved, she whistled for Charlie. Once he'd rejoined her, she turned and made her way back to the others, without looking at Max again.

By the time she reached the clearing, everyone else had already started working again. Della found herself avoiding Angela's final resting place, helping Chris unearth a different set of bones.

"They're all female," Caroline said. "Which is not entirely unexpected, but in case any of you wondered. I'll know more once I examine them in the lab."

Della sent Charlie out to look again, working each part of the meadow in sections so they wouldn't miss anything. Never happier than when he was working, Charlie took his job seriously. He was very thorough and wouldn't move on until he'd finished.

Once she'd cleared one area, she marked it with a can of spray paint, putting large *X*s on each corner. Then she moved on to the next section.

When Charlie didn't find any more remains, Della breathed a sigh of relief. Six, then. Six was bad enough. But she was infinitely thankful there weren't more.

As she worked, both with and separate from the others, the sun felt warm upon her skin. The breeze picked up, coming down from higher elevations, which gave it a bit of a chill. All in all, if it had been under any other circumstances, it would have been perfect weather. Closing her eyes, Della put her head up and inhaled, hoping the fresh scent of the mountains could help cleanse some of the darkness clouding her soul. She couldn't believe her bright, vivacious cousin had been killed. Though distance had separated them once Angela moved to Montana, they'd managed to stay in touch. They'd joked that no matter how much time passed between conversations, they always picked up as if only a few minutes had passed.

When Angela disappeared, every time her phone rang, Della had always hoped it would be her. Saying she'd lost track of time, or she'd gone on a wonderful new adventure and just realized they needed to catch up.

Damn, Della was going to miss her. So, so much.

Tears pricked at her eyes. Her throat clogged and she choked back a sob. Not again, not here, not now. Later, she'd figure out a way to properly mourn. She squared her shoulders and sent Charlie out one more time, even though they'd already cleared every area.

"Are you all right?" Max asked. Somehow, he'd walked up behind her without her noticing.

She nodded. "I am. Thank you for asking." Inwardly wincing at how formal she sounded, she waved her hand at the field. "Charlie didn't find any more. So unless the killer has another burial ground somewhere else, six bodies appears to be it."

His gaze searched her face. "That's a relief." He took a deep breath. "Listen, I'm really sorry about your cousin."

As she looked up into his light blue eyes, everything else faded away. "Thank you."

Charlie came up and nudged her hand. Dizzy, she turned her attention to her dog. "Good boy, Charlie. Let's go get you some water."

And then, as if a simple glance hadn't rocked her to the core, she turned and walked away.

The rest of the crew arrived before dusk. Max and Theo went down to meet them. Aware they'd need a safe place to pitch their tents, she had Charlie do a search of the area on both sides of the existing three. He sniffed around but didn't signal, which was not unexpected but still came as a relief.

"Nothing, huh?" She scratched behind his ears in his favorite spot. "Good dog!" She tried to keep her voice cheerful, since Charlie reacted to her sorrow. Tail wagging, Charlie grinned up at her, though she suspected she didn't fool him. He knew her too well.

Caroline and Chris continued to work, talking quietly as they cleared dirt away from bones. Della went over to watch, Charlie close by her side. She took care not to venture too close so she wouldn't accidentally disturb anything.

"This is so sad," Caroline said, glancing up at Della.

"It is." Once again, Della found herself blinking back tears. "I'm sorry. I'm not usually so emotional."

"Don't apologize." Voice fierce, Caroline sat back on her heels. "I can't imagine how you must feel. If it had been me, I don't know what I would have done."

At a loss for words, Della nodded, hoping the simple gesture conveyed her thanks.

"I'm excellent at my job," Caroline continued. "So believe me when I say that I'll do everything in my power to make sure the killer is caught. Hopefully, that will give you some small measure of peace."

Retribution. "I want him brought to justice," Della said. "He needs to pay for what he's done. After he faces down the families of all his victims."

"Agreed." Caroline brushed a stray strand of hair away from her face. "Would you like to help me? I could use another set of hands."

Relieved to have something to do, Della immediately knelt in the dirt. Caroline handed her a pair of gloves and waited while Della put them on. Then Caroline showed her how to use a tool that looked like a miniature trowel to carefully unearth the bones from the earth and use a soft brush to clean them.

Normally, handling a deceased person's bones might have creeped Della out. But now all she could think about was that everything she did right in this investigation would bring the FBI that much closer to finding Angela's killer.

"Easy," Caroline cautioned, making Della realize she'd gotten a bit too impatient. "We don't want to break anything. I need the bones as intact as possible."

Nodding, Della slowed down. The work, the sheer physical act of digging in the earth, and then sifting dirt away carefully using a brush, helped time pass. At one point, she realized she kept watching the path, waiting for Max to return with the new members of the team.

"He's really a good agent," Caroline commented, making Della realize the other woman had noticed. "And easy on the eyes."

This last made Della smile. "There's a reason he's considered the playboy of Owl Creek."

Caroline's eyes widened. "He *is*?" she asked. "I had no idea."

"That must mean you're not from around these parts."

"True. I grew up in Denver. I moved here for this job." Caroline glanced back at the trail, as if she expected Max and the others to show at any moment. "But I've worked with Max on a couple of cases, and he's nothing but professional at work. People talk, though, and I know some of the guys envy him since he often is seen with beautiful women. He seems to do a lot of casual dating, and I've never gotten the sense that he goes around deliberately trying to break hearts."

Della considered Caroline's words. "You're right," she conceded. "I shouldn't have repeated old gossip. After all, it's been years since Max Colton lived in Owl Creek. I'm sure he's changed."

"Were you speaking from experience?" Caroline asked, watching Della closely.

Horrified, Della shook her head. "No, not at all. I'd never even met him before this case. Can we please pretend I never said anything?"

"Of course." Caroline got back to work. "And now I'm going to speak out of turn, so feel free to ignore me. I couldn't help but notice the way the two of you look at each other. Just remember, you can't always hold someone's past against them."

Max walked a few paces behind Jake and Ed. Without exception, both new male agents did a double take when they first caught sight of Della. She and Caroline both looked up and smiled when they approached, but immediately went back to working in the dirt. Either Della had gotten so used to men staring that she didn't react, or she was oblivious to her effect on them. She barely acknowledged their presence, though Caroline appeared to be having difficulty keeping from cracking up laughing.

Normally, Max would have found this sort of thing amusing. Now, though, he found himself clenching his teeth and biting back a sarcastic comment.

Since the light was fading, they decided to start fresh in the morning. Everyone gathered around while Jake and Ed pitched their tent.

"Somehow, I thought they'd send more people," Caroline commented.

"Two vans, two drivers," Jake shot back, clearly overhearing. "What more do you need?"

Caroline laughed. Theo and Chris joined in, ribbing the newcomers, claiming they'd gotten here late so they could avoid work. Even Max found himself smiling, glad that the team had developed an easy rapport.

Della kept to the edge of the group, quietly observing everyone. Charlie stayed close to her side. Ever since she'd discovered her cousin's body, her dog had seemed to sense she might need him. Max envied that. Many times over the course of his adult life he'd badly wanted to get a dog, but the long hours he spent working had always been a deterrent.

Once the tent had been pitched, the others gave Jake and Ed a quick tour of the site. While they did that, Max gathered more kindling for the fire. It didn't take long before he had a good-sized blaze going.

"Perfect for burgers," Jake announced. "Since Ed and I stopped at the store on the way up, I thought you all might like something a little better than the usual nonperishable rations."

"I could just hug you!" Caroline said, and then did exactly that. "Did you think to bring paper plates and buns and all of that?"

"We did." Grinning, Jake and Ed gave each other a high five. "We've been on several of these overnight cases before."

In addition to the meat, Ed had brought a cooler full of beer and soft drinks. The atmosphere lightened considerably as everyone relaxed. Jake started grilling the hamburger patties over the fire and people cracked open their drinks of choice.

Even Della appeared to perk up at the easy banter among the team. She didn't say much, though she accepted a diet cola. She looked up once and met Max's gaze, making him realize he might be watching her too closely.

He knew his team had noticed it too. He'd worked with all these agents before in some capacity or another. And, despite the fact that he did his damnedest to keep his personal life private, every single one of them had given him grief about his reputation as a player.

At least in this situation, they knew better than to say anything. Della had been through a lot, and everyone knew she'd be well within her rights to leave now that her dog had completed the search of the field. Then again, they'd only had time to partially excavate three of the graves. She might decide to stick around until they'd completed the task, but he doubted it.

In fact, he imagined she'd hightail it out of there at first light. And he wouldn't blame her. What he didn't understand was why the notion of her leaving made him feel so hollow. Likely because he felt responsible for everyone on his team, and despite the fact that she didn't work for the Bureau, she'd come in and assisted after finding the first grave.

Burgers were passed out and everyone ate. Darkness came as suddenly as if someone had flicked a switch, and stars looked like strands of diamonds in the cloudless night sky. Though the temperature had begun dropping, as it always did in the mountains after dark, it was still comfortable. If not for the circumstances, it would have been a perfect August evening.

"Where do you think the killer came from?" Della asked softly from beside him. "This isn't exactly an easy location to reach, especially dragging a dead body."

He braced himself for her reaction. "It's likely they were alive when he brought them here," he said.

Her eyes widened. "You're saying he killed them in this meadow?"

"Most likely." Noticing how she swayed, he reached out and grabbed her arm. "But we don't know that yet. Caroline will be able to tell us a lot more once she can examine the bones in her lab."

Ever respectful of Della's feelings, the team talked about everything but their findings. But finally, Caroline brought up her concerns. "There's another, smaller clearing just past that group of trees," she said, pointing. "It's too dark to see it right now, but I think we should have Charlie check that out too in the morning, just in case."

Della nodded. "We'll check it out at first light."

"Thanks." Caroline stood, stretching. "It's been a long day and it's likely going to be an even longer one tomorrow. I'm going to turn in."

After she disappeared into her tent, Theo and Chris made their excuses and did the same, followed by Jake and Ed. Which left Max and Della alone in front of the campfire, with Charlie stretched out close by.

Max wouldn't have minded getting some rest himself, but no way would he leave Della by herself. If she needed to talk, he'd provide an ear. If not, he could give her space too.

Staring into the fire, she didn't seem to be aware of his presence. They'd stopped adding wood and were letting it burn low, though the flames still provided enough light to make shadows dance around the darkness.

"Do you think he's still out there, killing women?" she asked, her voice low and intense.

Scooting closer, so they could talk without keeping everyone else awake, Max grimaced. "I think it's likely. However, a lot of that depends on what forensics reveals. If all these bones are pretty old, then whoever killed them might have moved on to another location."

"Will you be able to find out their identities?" she asked. The moonlight bathed her in soft silver, making her pale skin and long brown hair appear to glow. Again, he found himself marveling at her beauty, wondering how it was that she seemed completely unaware of it.

Realizing she'd asked him a question, he tore his gaze away and collected his thoughts. "As far as identifying them, I'd say yes. Caroline's really good at this sort of thing. And since we don't have any reports of missing women from Owl Creek, it'll likely turn out they came from somewhere else."

Like her cousin had. Though she didn't say this out loud, he could see it in her face. She looked away, stared at what remained of the fire, before directing her attention back to him.

"But he brought them here to kill them. Somehow, these women trusted him enough to travel to this remote location with their murderer."

Her tortured expression told him she was picturing her cousin.

"That's only a theory," he said, lightly touching her arm. "We're only at the beginning of this investigation. Lot of possibilities are going to get tossed around."

She turned to face him, her full lips slightly parted. Her gaze swung to his, the fire making flickers of gold in her eyes. At that moment, he would have given anything to chase the sadness from her face.

Somehow, they came together, mouth upon mouth. Kissing hungrily, urgently, with reckless abandon. He lost himself in the velvet sensation of her, desire searing his veins. Hands tangled in her hair, he crushed her to him.

Fully aroused, wanting her more than he'd ever wanted anyone, he forced himself to pull back. Inhaling the sweet scent of her, he brushed her brow with his lips. They were both breathing heavily and neither of them spoke.

After a moment, Della pushed to her feet, quietly called her dog and disappeared into her tent. Leaving him staring after her, aching with need and full of remorse.

Max sat by himself for a while, watching the fire burn down to embers, aware he'd need to apologize to Della in the morning. That kiss never should have happened. And he needed to make sure it never happened again.

That night, alone in his tent, he slept restlessly, tossing and turning on the uneven ground. It had been a long time since he'd burned for a woman like this. Usually, he was able to get it out of his system quickly so he could go on with his life. But none of the women he dated were like Della.

In the morning, he woke up to the sound of the others making breakfast. He got up, stiff and sore, and ambled out to greet everyone before going into the woods to take care of his morning toilet. When he returned, Theo handed him a large mug of coffee with a knowing smile, which Max ignored.

Della came sauntering up the path, Charlie close by her side. She smiled at everyone, including Max. "Good morning," she said.

Theo offered her coffee, but she lifted her mug to show him she already had some. "When did you even get up?" he asked.

"A little before sunrise." She wrinkled her nose. "You all were still asleep. Charlie and I walked to one of my favorite vantage points to watch the sun come up."

Among the food items that Jake and Ed had brought were doughnuts. "Carbs for energy," Ed chirped, passing them around.

Once everyone had eaten, Della announced she and Charlie were going to check out that smaller clearing now. "Hopefully, we won't find anything."

Whistling for her dog, who bounded over to her side immediately, she told him to heel.

"Do you mind if I come with you?" Max asked, keeping his voice casual.

Her gaze flashed to his. "Not at all."

With Charlie prancing between them, they walked toward the area.

Heart in his throat, he tried to find the right words. "I need to apologize for last night," he said, deciding he might as well be direct and up-front.

She glanced sideways at him. "No. You don't. You didn't take advantage of me, if that's what you're going to say. I'd honestly find that insulting. I participated equally. Was kissing on the job site inappropriate? Probably. And yes, we need to make sure it doesn't happen again."

All he could do was nod.

"There," she continued. "Have I covered everything you were going to say?"

He couldn't hide his amusement. "You have. And much more succinctly than I would have."

"Good. Then can we forget about it and get this area checked out?"

"Yes, we can."

Fascinated, Max watched while she gave Charlie the command to work. Nose to the ground, the Lab set off, carrying his tail in a happy curve over his back. Intent on her dog, Della seemed to be holding her breath. Hoping, Max guessed, that Charlie didn't find anything. After all, six bodies were more than enough.

A second after Max had that thought, Charlie sat and barked once. Max's heart sank.

Della glanced at Max, clearly stricken. "Another one," she said, her voice raspy.

Feeling grim himself, Max looked over at his team. Without exception, they'd all stopped what they were doing to watch Charlie work.

At Max's signal, Caroline got to her feet. She hurried over, followed by Theo. "I was afraid of that," she said. "Now we have seven."

"I don't understand." Della looked from one to the other. "Why over here? Why deviate from the other area?"

Max shrugged. "We can only guess." He hesitated, and then continued. "I'm thinking it's possible he started here. This one might have been his first victim."

"And then he realized he needed more room," Caroline finished for him.

Expression horrified, Della swallowed. "In my years volunteering for SAR, I've worked natural disasters. But never a murder scene with multiple bodies, all killed by a sick serial killer."

Max heard the part she didn't say. And never, ever with one of her loved ones being one of the victims. He watched as she squared her shoulders and took a deep breath. Then, praising Charlie, she sent him out to search again.

Luckily, the dog didn't turn up any more remains.

"I need to call this in," Max said. He hurried back to his tent, where he'd left the sat phone. Though it was still early, he knew Brian would want to be updated.

"Seven bodies?" Sounding nearly as horrified as Max felt, Brian cursed. "I've had people running reports on missing women from the area and have only turned up one. Not seven."

"I'd suggest expanding. Maybe make it statewide." Max thought for a second. "You might even do the tristate area."

Brian cursed again. "Tell Caroline I'm bringing in a couple more people to help her. We need to get ahead of this before the media does. The last thing we need is to start a widespread panic."

Max agreed. "We're hoping to start moving the bones out today," he said. "The only other people who know anything about this are the Owl Creek police officers who called us out. And at that time, there was only one body."

"Good. Let's try to keep a lid on this for as long as we can."

Promising to try, Max ended the call.

Chapter 4

With her work done, Della began packing up her things in preparation to head back to town. She had an afternoon and an evening dog training class to conduct at Crosswinds, so she needed to get home and shower.

Saying her goodbyes to the team, she smiled as they all thanked her and praised Charlie for his good work. Max offered to walk her to the parking lot and, ignoring the knowing looks of the others, she accepted. She resolved to keep things between them strictly businesslike.

Like the others, Max thanked her. "I really enjoyed working with you," he said, sounding sincere. Even though she doubted he was referring to the kiss they'd shared, Della felt her face heat.

"I enjoyed working with everyone too," she replied, purposely making generalities. "Please keep me posted on this case." She took a deep breath, then lifted her chin. "Also, I plan to notify my aunt and uncle of Angela's passing myself, so don't send someone official to do that, okay?"

"I'll make sure to notify the proper channels." He met her gaze. "That's going to be tough. Are you sure you don't want to wait until we have an official, positive ID?"

She grimaced. "I might. Just in case that's somehow

not her. Even if I think that I already know the truth, I don't want to give them wrong information. But they deserve to be told as soon as possible, once it's confirmed."

"I understand." The warmth of his gaze felt like a physical touch. "And I agree that you should wait. Just in case. And I'm just putting this out there, so you know. When the time comes, if you'd like me to go with you and lend you support, just say the word."

Touched, she wasn't sure how to respond. While this was a family matter, she knew she'd welcome his strong shoulder to lean on.

Except for one small thing. His reputation would precede him. If she showed up at her aunt and uncle's house with Max Colton, the playboy of Owl Creek, they'd think she'd lost her mind. Of course, once she delivered the awful news about Angela, whom she'd arrived with wouldn't matter.

She said none of this to Max, however. "I appreciate that," she replied simply. "You've been more than kind."

Which was the understatement of the year. She felt her face heat again. Luckily, Max wasn't watching her.

They'd reached the parking area. When they got to her Jeep, Max helped her load up. Panting, tail wagging happily, Charlie jumped up into the back seat, ready to go.

"Thank you again," she said, feeling awkward as she turned to face Max. "And I'd really like to remain as much in the loop as possible about this case."

"I'll make sure to do that." Expression intense, he met her gaze. "Della, I'm going to figure out who did this. I promise you that."

Believing him, she nodded. "If I can help in any way, feel free to reach out to me."

"I'll likely do that. I'm sure I'll have some questions about your cousin. I'll definitely be in touch." Reaching into his pocket, he pulled out a business card and handed it to her. "Here's my number if you need me for anything. Please don't hesitate to call."

"I won't." Since there was nothing more to say, she pocketed the card, smiled and got into her Jeep. "Take care," she said, waving as she started the engine and drove away.

Now she understood, she thought, eyeing Max in her rearview mirror until she made a turn and could no longer see him. For as long as she could remember, she'd heard stories of the legions of brokenhearted women Max Colton left in his wake. Until this very moment, she'd wondered what could make someone abandon all reason and set themselves up for heartbreak. Now she knew.

When she pulled into her driveway, she felt a sense of relief at the sight of her familiar home. She'd grown up in this house, the only child of a single mother. After a brief stint in Boise, Della had returned to help care for her mother through her long battle with pancreatic cancer. A fight her mom had ultimately lost.

Having Aunt Mary and Uncle Alex, and of course Angela, next door had been a lifesaver through it all. Now, as she looked at the house next door, the knowledge that she had to go over there and tear apart her family's world sat like a lead weight in her stomach.

Maybe, she thought, she should do as Max had suggested and wait until they had a definitive medical ID. After all, what if some other woman had stolen Angela's necklace?

Hefting her backpack and duffel bag out of the Jeep, she called Charlie, and they went into the house. She was well aware she might be indulging in a bit of self-delusion. Nonetheless, her decision made her feel slightly better.

Once she'd received official notification, she'd break the news to her aunt and uncle. Until then, she'd keep it to herself.

A hot shower and a change of clothes made her feel better. She had back-to-back classes to teach tonight, the first one a basic manners class and the second, advanced manners. Now that Crosswinds' owner, Sebastian Cross, was about to become a family man, he'd decided to branch out and offer classes to the general public. Before, Crosswinds had only focused on training search and rescue dogs. Now they'd expanded, with Della teaching most of the classes. She'd learned only the most dedicated dog owners who completed the first class followed up by taking the second.

But for those who did, the possibilities were endless. They could train their dog in obedience, agility or rally, among other things. Sebastian had hired a couple more trainers who specialized in various dog sports, even bringing in one from Denver. Crosswinds had a well-respected name among law enforcement agencies for their SAR dogs. Soon, if Della had her way, they'd also have a presence in the competitive world of dog sports. Watching her manners clients go on to other things and succeed made Della truly happy. She honestly loved her job, and there was nothing else, besides search and rescue work, that she'd rather do.

Since she had a little bit of time before she had to go

to work, she went ahead and made lunch, saving half of it to eat for dinner later. Charlie had curled up in his dog bed and gone to sleep, clearly exhausted after his busy couple of days.

Della puttered around the house, doing a load of laundry and tidying up. To her dismay, her thoughts kept returning to Max Colton and that amazing, sensual kiss.

She couldn't wait to go to work. Keeping busy should help her get her thoughts back on track.

Though she usually brought Charlie to work with her, tonight she decided to leave him home. He'd definitely earned a night off. Her first class would all be people and dogs new to the training center, so while she covered the basics and assessed each pair, she wouldn't need Charlie to demonstrate anything.

When she entered Crosswinds Training, Pepper greeted her. One of the employees who worked in the retail store, Pepper also handled registration. "You've got a full class tonight," Pepper said. "Nine dogs and owners."

"Awesome. I'd better go get set up. They should start arriving soon."

As the dog training area filled, Della saw she had a good mixture of breeds and ages. She'd worked with some of the younger dogs in puppy kindergarten a few weeks ago.

In the first class, she went over the curriculum, passing out worksheets for what she expected them to do at home and a list of supplies they were going to need. "Get some high-quality dog treats," she advised. "Something that's just a step above what they get at home. Personally, I like to use liver treats."

She then had each client walk their dog around the

middle of the ring to give her an idea of what, if any, training they might already have received. As usual, she made detailed notes.

A few of the clients lingered after she'd dismissed the class, which wasn't unusual, especially since she'd told them to come to her with any questions.

The first one, a young woman whose dog wouldn't stop jumping on her, asked for advice about how to stop that. Della gave her some exercises to try at home.

The second man had attended her puppy class with his bloodhound, Rolo. He just wanted to tell Della how well Rolo had been doing, and that he was hoping to move on to obedience trials. She smiled, petted the adorable droopy-eyed dog and told him she'd see him next time.

The last individual, a man with a young Rottweiler, hung back until everyone else had left. During the class, Della had noticed him staring at her, which she'd found slightly off-putting, but she put it down to first-class nerves. In dog training, they all knew they were actually teaching the humans, not the dogs. Once the people knew what to do, their pets learned how to follow.

"I'm Hal," he said, holding out his hand. "Hal Murcheson." After they shook hands, he continued holding on for a heartbeat too long, which forced her to tug her fingers away. Meanwhile, his Rottie kept pulling on the leash, clearly anxious to leave.

"What can I help you with, Hal?" she asked, keeping her voice pleasant.

"I was wondering if you'd like to go out and have a drink sometime." His friendly smile didn't match up with the way he focused his gaze intently on her chest.

"Oh, that's so nice of you," she replied, on familiar

ground since this happened occasionally. "But I don't date clients."

Almost on cue, the Rottweiler barked and made another lunge toward the door. Hal yanked him back and told him no, before refocusing his attention on Della.

"Then maybe I'll have to drop out of your class," he teased. "Though Marco here could use some training."

"That's what I'm here for." Checking her phone, she glanced toward the retail area. "Now, if you don't have a training-related question, I have another class starting in fifteen minutes. I need to get ready for it."

"Do you mind if I watch?"

"I'm going to have to say yes, I do mind. For these types of classes, especially on the first night, I don't want any distractions. I suggest you take Marco home and start working on some of the things I touched on in class."

For a moment, she thought he might continue to push, but to her relief he nodded and left, Marco pulling hard all the way.

"You all right, hon?" Pepper asked. "I couldn't help but notice what happened."

"I'm fine." Della shook her head. "He wanted a date, but I'm hoping now that I turned him down, he'll focus on training his dog."

"He's new to Owl Creek, he said. Just moved here for work." Worry still shone in Pepper's eyes. "I'll watch and make sure he doesn't come back. I'd hate for him to try and follow you home."

"Aww, I appreciate that, but I'm sure it'll be fine." Della touched Pepper's arm to reassure her. "Every now and then, I get a client who's a bit overly enthusiastic. It's been a while, but I know how to handle it."

"I'm still going to keep an eye out," Pepper replied.

The next class, Advanced Manners, contained people and their dogs who had recently passed the previous Basic Manners class. Many of them were eager to show Della what they'd been working on and how far they'd come.

"I'm proud of you all," Della said, meaning it. One of her greatest joys was seeing how far her students and their owners could go if they tried. She passed out the new curriculum for the next six weeks, and then they got started.

By the time she'd finished up with that class, Della was more than ready to go home and rest. After the last client had left, she wandered into the store to purchase some treats for Charlie.

"You look tired," Pepper chided.

Since Max had asked Della to keep the investigation under wraps, she couldn't share details about what she and Charlie had been doing for the past couple of days. "I've been busy," she responded. "I'm sure I'll feel better once I get some sleep. I need to check the schedule while I'm here." The two Manners classes were only held once a week, but if enrollment warranted, she'd sometimes have another on Wednesdays. They must have gotten a lot of sign-ups, because she had a full class for Wednesday evening. She'd only be working those twice a week for the next six weeks, which was a good thing. Well-trained humans made for well-behaved dogs.

"Looks like you'll have lots of time to train Charlie along with the other six you've been assigned," Pepper said, reading over her shoulder. "Speaking of Charlie, why didn't you bring him tonight?"

"He got a lot of exercise this weekend." Della smiled. "We hiked up to Owl Falls."

"Oh, fun." Another customer came in, pulling Pepper's attention away from Della. "See you later."

As a precaution, Della scanned the parking lot before walking outside. Not that she thought Hal would have returned to try to press his luck, but better safe than sorry. After all, Angela had always seen the good in everyone, and she'd lost her life.

Grief slammed into her, making her gasp for breath. *Not yet*, she reminded herself. Not until she had an official, positive ID. Until then, she'd simply hope the grave belonged to some other unfortunate soul.

After Della left, Max had hiked back up to the crime scene, using the alone time to try to figure out why he felt so attuned to her. No, he'd decided, he'd call his feelings *protective* instead. That had to be it. One of the reasons he'd gone into law enforcement had been a deep-seated desire to protect the public. And watching Della, a capable and confident woman, discover the body of her own beloved cousin had stirred up every protective instinct he possessed and then some.

Did that explain why he'd kissed her? If he really wanted to mess with his head, he could convince himself of that too. But he'd never been in the habit of indulging in self-delusion, so why start now?

Della's beauty attracted him. Plain and simple. But since she clearly wasn't the type of woman willing to settle for what little he had to offer, he'd need to rein himself in.

When he reached the site, he found everyone hard

at work. Entire skeletons had been carefully unearthed and Caroline had begun preparing them for transit back to her lab.

"We should have most of them out of here by tomorrow afternoon," she said cheerfully. "I've got my two best assistants on standby, and I've heard they're sending me a few more people to help out in the lab."

"How long do you think before you're able to start getting IDs on them?" he asked.

She shrugged. "It depends what I find on each victim and also what's in the database. Some of them were disturbed by animals and, quite frankly, we're lucky it wasn't worse."

Caroline took a deep breath. "But I'm going to start with Della's cousin first. I want to be able to confirm for her that this is actually Angela Hobbs."

"I appreciate that. She's decided to wait until she has official confirmation before telling her family."

"I agree." Caroline shook her head. "I've been working for the Bureau for nearly twenty years. This is the first time I've ever been involved in a case where one of the team found a murder victim who was a member of their own family."

Remembering the stark pain in Della's beautiful eyes, the jagged control she'd tried—and failed—to exert over her emotions, he grimaced. "Definitely a tough time," he said, meaning it. "Even more reason to catch this guy."

They worked until dusk and then ate another meal around a smaller campfire. This time, they ate out of cans. The mood was more somber, the knowledge of the seven shallow graves weighing heavy on their minds.

They all retired early, planning to rise with the sun.

One more night in the tent. Bright and early the next morning, Max helped as the team carefully transported the remains down the path to the vans, one by one.

By the time they'd gotten the seventh victim securely loaded up, it was early afternoon. "Let's get the camp broken down and head out," Max decided. "We can grab something for lunch on the road."

Perspiring, grateful for the slight breeze stirring the trees, everyone packed up their tents. Max made sure the fire was completely out, pouring water just in case any embers still smoldered.

They debated whether or not to leave the crime scene tape. Since Charlie had made it clear they'd found all the graves that were there, Max didn't want to provide an easy target for the media to photograph.

"What about the killer?" Theo asked. "If we leave it, he'll know we're on to him. But if we take it, he might just bury another victim after we're gone."

Max gestured around the field. "All of his graves have been disturbed. He's likely going to figure that out whether there's crime scene tape or not. Let's take it down."

After making sure they hadn't left anything in the clearing, they hiked again back down to the vehicles. Caroline had decided to wait, watching over everything, she'd said.

By the time Max put his truck in Drive, following the vans down the mountain, a bone-deep sort of weariness had set in. The others would go back to Boise, but Max had to head out to Owl Creek. His family owned Colton Ranch. It had been started by his father, Buck, and managed by him along with Max's two older brothers, Greg and Malcolm. Their sister, Lizzy, lived in town and worked as a graphic artist.

In addition to them, Max had six cousins who also lived in Owl Creek. His uncle Robert and Robert's oldest son, Chase, had founded Colton Properties. Fletcher had gone into law enforcement, and Wade was Special Forces in the Marines. Ruby had gone to veterinary school and started her own veterinary practice in town, Hannah had a catering business, and Frannie, the youngest, owned and managed a bookstore/café.

With such a large family, the only way they could all get together when Max happened to be in town was to schedule a sit-down dinner. Mama Jen, Max's aunt, usually organized something.

This week, they were all meeting at a restaurant in town. Everyone had agreed to attend because in addition to catching up with each other, they were meeting their half siblings for the first time.

The story could have been a soap opera. Max's mother, Jessie, had left her husband, Buck, and had an affair with his brother, Robert. The two of them had built a house near Boise and together they'd had two more children, Nathan and Sarah.

Robert hadn't completely abandoned his wife, Jenny, along with their six children, not in the same way Jessie had ditched her entire family. But Robert had been a distant and often absent husband and father. Buck had helped Jenny with her brood of six, and Jenny had helped him with his four, and as a result the kids were more like siblings than cousins. Ten. A huge family, by any standards.

And now there were two more. Once Robert had

passed away, the rest of the story had come to light after his funeral. Max and his siblings had wondered if their mother, Jessie, would actually make an appearance at the service. They weren't even sure they'd recognize her if she did, they hadn't seen her in so long. And like Max, the others felt a lot of resentment and simmering anger at her for what she did. Nothing like a mother abandoning her children to instill a deflated sense of self-worth.

His father had tried to bolster their self-esteem, but Buck was a cowboy through and through, and not much good with emotional stuff. If not for Mama Jen and their extended family of cousins, Max suspected they'd likely all have amounted to nothing. As it was, Max himself shied away from commitment. He blamed his demanding career, but part of him never wanted to risk feeling abandoned again.

Shaking off the past and the unsettling memories, he thought about the case. He'd never worked a full-on serial killer case before, though of course he'd studied all the big ones during his time at Quantico. He knew enough to understand that seven bodies might only be the tip of the iceberg. A very real possibility existed that the murderer might have other burial grounds in different locations. He hoped not, but couldn't discount the notion altogether.

As he continued to drive north, the landscape flattened, the craggy peaks and evergreen trees giving way to rolling hills of fertile grass. When the first herds of cattle came into view, the part of Max that would always be a rancher came to life. One more turn and then the ranch spread out ahead of him. The red-and-white wooden house matched the large barn. In the distance he could see the bunkhouse where the ranch hands lived. A smaller guesthouse, barely visible past the private garden, was where Max's oldest brother, Greg, lived.

Home. A rush of happiness filled him. Visiting Colton Ranch helped put the rest of his life in perspective. Eight hundred fertile acres filled with cattle and horses brought the kind of peace city life couldn't buy. At least as far as Max was concerned. He suspected his father and brothers might think otherwise, since keeping the place running was their job.

Driving through the gates, Max parked in front of the garage. Though he'd called his dad to let him know about his visit, he knew no one would be inside the house at this time of day. Too much to be done. He remembered it well.

Once inside, Max carried his stuff upstairs into his old bedroom and immediately jumped into the shower. He figured his father and brothers were likely out working cattle, so they wouldn't be back at the house until later.

After his shower, he toyed with the idea of taking a nap, but felt too keyed up to possibly sleep. He couldn't stop thinking about Della Winslow. He wondered what she was doing, how she was holding up. He couldn't forget how soft her lips had felt when they'd kissed. In fact, he found himself almost wishing he had a dog so he could sign up for one of her classes.

Ridiculous. And unlike him. They'd worked together on a case. He'd promised to keep her posted. He'd offered support when she'd suffered a horrific loss and experienced unimaginable pain. True, she might be gorgeous, but he knew lots of beautiful women. He'd touch base with her soon.

Taking a seat at the huge handmade oak kitchen table, he opened his laptop and logged in to Wi-Fi. Within minutes, he began filling out his initial report. Tedious and time-consuming, the task made him lose track of time. When the creak of the back door made him raise his head, the sight of his aunt made him grin.

"Mama Jen!" Jumping to his feet, he rushed over and wrapped the older woman in a hug, lifting her off her feet. "I'm so happy to see you."

Once he'd set her down, she beamed back at him. "I heard you were coming for a visit. Buck asked me to come over and make a special dinner, just for you."

Hearing her say that made him feel like a kid again. Despite often seeming emotionally distant, Mama Jen had been more of a mother to him than his own ever had. Just thinking of her cooking made his stomach growl.

"What are you making?" he asked, letting his eagerness show. "I could really go for some smothered steak."

"That's exactly what I was thinking! With mashed potatoes, gravy and green beans. And those biscuits you love so much."

He hugged her again. "Thank you. I can't wait. Who all's coming?" Usually when Mama Jen cooked, he knew to expect a crowd.

"Just you, your dad, Greg and Malcolm. Lizzy couldn't make it."

"What about the cousins?" Her children.

She tried for a laugh but ended up frowning instead. "I invited them. Chase claims he's too busy, Fletcher too. Wade is working. Ruby says she's too tired. Hannah and Frannie made plans with Lizzy. Girls' night out, they say.

They all said to tell you hello and that they'll see you at that dinner when you meet your new half siblings."

Since no one had communicated a date, time or place for that to him, he was surprised. When he said as much to Jenny, she shook her head.

"Thursday night," she said. "At that new barbecue place in town. Back Forty, I think it's called. Seven o'clock."

"Wow." He shouldn't have been surprised that Jenny knew all the details. After all, she was the glue that held the entire family together. "Are you coming?" he asked.

"Me?" She snorted. "So I could meet the children of my cheating husband and my own sister? Hard pass."

He couldn't blame her. "I get it. I'm not even sure I want to go myself."

Though she shook her head, she refrained from commenting. "I'd better get to cooking," she said instead. "Buck and the boys are always starving when they come in from working cattle." Despite working part-time as a nurse, Jenny always enjoyed making the family a good meal.

"What can I do to help?" he asked.

"Nothing." Like she always did, she shooed him out of the kitchen. Jenny didn't like anyone getting in her space when she created her masterpieces. Though she wasn't a gourmet cook, everyone in the Colton family considered her comfort food better than anything made by a fancy chef.

While she puttered around doing her prep work, Max continued filling out reports, which he despised. Although he knew they were a necessity, he always found the paperwork time-consuming and tedious. Somehow, working on them in his family home made them feel less like work.

He'd just finished the last report and closed his computer when the back door opened, and his father and brothers came stomping into the kitchen. They smelled like cattle and horses and sweat, the aroma of Max's childhood. Bickering lightly among themselves, they stopped short when they caught sight of Max and Jenny.

"Damn, I forgot," Buck said, rushing forward and sweeping Max up in a bear hug. "Good to see you, son."

"It's good to be here." Max barely got the words out before his dad released him and Greg and Malcolm tag-team hugged him. Of the three of them, Malcolm was the tallest, but only by an inch.

"Been too long," Greg said. "Let's go get cleaned up and then we'll catch up over dinner."

While the boys took off for the showers, Buck went into the kitchen and spoke quietly to Jenny. The two of them had been close for years. When Max had been younger, he'd wished his dad would marry Jenny, so they could all be one big happy family. It would have been a sort of poetic justice, since the two brothers had clearly married the wrong sister.

These days, Max had a different philosophy. Buck and Jenny seemed happy with things the way they were. And if they were good, so was Max.

Greg returned first, his hair still damp from the shower. Breaking off his conversation with Jenny, Buck excused himself and went off to clean himself up. Jenny watched him go and then returned to cooking.

A few minutes later, Malcolm joined them. "How do

you two feel about meeting Mom's other two kids?" he asked, cutting right to the chase.

Max and Greg exchanged glances. "I'm not looking forward to it," Max admitted. "How about you?"

"I think it'll be fun," Malcolm replied, his eyes twinkling. "I mean, it's always been kind of a Colton thing, having such a big family. I like the idea of adding a couple more."

Greg eyed him. "I wonder if our mother actually stuck around for them. It kind of sounds like she did. Which might not actually be a good thing, you know?"

Max did know. They all did. It hadn't been easy for any of them to get over having their own mother abandon them. If not for Jenny stepping in and trying to fill in the gap, he often thought the family would have fallen apart.

"The past is the past," Malcolm pointed out, as if he knew what Max had been thinking. "All we can do is move forward."

"We know." Greg and Max spoke in unison.

"Dinner is almost ready," Jenny chimed in. "Would one of you boys go check on your father?"

"No need—I'm here." Buck grinned. "Let's eat."

Chapter 5

The next morning, Della woke shortly after sunrise. She'd slept deeply and felt well rested, ready to take on a new day. With a new attitude. Though she suspected she might be giving in to self-delusion, until she got the official notice that the body in the grave definitely belonged to Angela, she'd decided she wouldn't allow herself to dwell in the deep, dark recesses of grief. All these years, she hadn't given up hope, and while finding the necklace she'd given her cousin was certainly damning, she'd simply move in a place of hope until she knew differently.

That decided, she had a leisurely breakfast and then she and Charlie went for a walk. The cloudless sky and light breeze made for perfect walking weather, and she let Charlie sniff to his canine heart's content.

When they returned, Charlie went and got his favorite toy and amused himself by tossing it around in the living room. With the entire day free, Della decided to take him out to Crosswinds and work on more training.

Not many people realized how many hours of work went into training a search and rescue dog. She'd started Charlie young, taking him everywhere she went and working on his socialization skills. She also had to get him desensitized to loud noises, so they made trips to the police station, the fire department and anywhere they heard sirens. In addition to that, they'd begun work on basic training. Charlie had been around more dogs and more people than any other dog she'd owned.

Taking him into work on her day off was one of her favorite things to do.

Putting a well-trained canine through his paces was one of the great pleasures of Della's life. Over the years, she'd worked with lots of dogs, some belonging to others, and some to her. She'd met good ones, bad ones and many in between. And there'd never been a dog like Charlie. The instant she'd met the young black Lab in the shelter, they'd locked eyes and she'd known he was meant to be hers. They shared such a close bond instantly, which made working with him a thing of beauty.

Even her coworkers at Crosswinds remarked on it. The owner of the dog training facility, Sebastian Cross, often used her and Charlie for advertising videos and promotional material. And in an environment of accomplished and certified dog trainers, she and Charlie had become minor celebrities. Sometimes, when she was putting her dog through his paces, she'd look up to find a small crowd had gathered to watch.

Today was no exception. For fun, she was letting Charlie run the Agility course, one of his absolute favorite nonwork activities next to Dock Diving. Everything had been set up for a level one class later that afternoon, so Della put her dog through the course. He loved running through the tunnel, up the ramp and back down, but most of all, he adored jumping over jumps. His movements were poetry in action. He soared over the obstacle, his tail curved high over his back. As soon as he'd run the course, he came trotting over to her, panting happily.

When they finished, she looked up and saw a couple of her coworkers admiring Charlie. Then she noticed Max Colton standing near the doorway, watching her intently.

As before, her first glimpse of him sent a jolt through her system. More than merely handsome, he radiated a kind of quiet confidence that she found more than attractive. In fact, she'd venture to view it as dangerous.

Mentally shaking her head, she took a deep breath and tried to act normal. "Hey!" She greeted him with a friendly smile and walked over. Ignoring the wide stares of the others, she watched as he bent over to pet Charlie. "What brings you out this way?"

Meeting her gaze, he appeared to lose his train of thought. She thought about teasing him, but then, as she realized he might be here on official business, her smile faded. "Did you get confirmation of identity? Is that why you've come?"

"No, it's too soon for that." Lightly touching her arm, he shook his head. "I'm sorry. I didn't mean to make you think..."

"It's okay." Now she felt awkward. "You will let me know as soon as you find out, right?"

"Yes, I will." He took a deep breath. "Actually, I came by to see if you wanted to have lunch."

He couldn't have shocked her more. "Lunch? With you?"

One corner of his mouth kicked up in amusement, sending another jab to her stomach. "Yes. Grab a sandwich or something? You know, that thing friends sometimes do."

Friends. Right. She wasn't sure whether to be flattered or insulted. But since she truly had no interest in becoming romantically involved with a man like him, she thought they actually might be able to become friends. Once she got past this ridiculous attraction, that was.

She looked down at her dog to give herself time to gather her thoughts.

"We'd need a dog-friendly patio," she said, stroking Charlie's head. "Which means we'll have to go to Tap Out Brewery."

"I love that place," he replied. "Are you able to leave now?"

"As a matter of fact, I am." Since her coworkers' stares felt like they were burning holes into her back, the sooner, the better. "Charlie and I just finished up and I'm done for the day."

"Great." They walked outside together. He'd parked his truck next to her Jeep. "Want to ride together? I can bring you back to pick up your vehicle."

"I'll just follow you," she said. "That way I can go home after we eat."

Driving into town with Charlie sitting happily in the back seat, she tried to quash a buzz of unfamiliar excitement. She hadn't really thought this through, she realized. Once people saw her and Max Colton together, the rumor mill would go into overdrive. And since they couldn't yet discuss the case, they'd have no choice but to let people think whatever they liked.

Maybe people would realize Della wasn't Max's type. Over the years, he'd been linked up with a number of beautiful women, all of them with blond hair and blue eyes. Della's light brown hair and ordinary brown eyes were about as far as one could get from that.

Oddly enough, this made her feel better. Surely anyone with a propensity to gossip would take one look at her and realize she wasn't in Max Colton's league.

As they pulled into the parking lot, she supposed she should be glad it was nearly one, toward the end of the noon lunch rush. A popular place to have lunch or an early dinner, Tap Out would be quiet from about two until five. After eight at night, and during any kind of sporting event, the brewpub was packed, with a rowdy atmosphere.

"They have the best chicken tenders," Max said, taking her arm. This startled her and she gave him a quick glance, which made him let go.

"Sorry," he muttered. "Old habits."

Instead of going in the front door, they went directly to the patio. There were quite a few patrons enjoying the nice weather, and even a couple of other dogs. Charlie wagged his tail happily, but ever obedient, he stayed by Della's side.

The waitress came to take their drink order, bringing Charlie his own bowl of water. They both ordered a Tap Out Lager, smiling at each other over their menus.

Their beers came quickly, and they both ordered lunch. Max went with the chicken fingers and Della got a flatbread pizza. The waitress promised to bring the food out as soon as it was cooked and disappeared.

Della took a sip of her beer and sat back in her chair.

"Tell me about Angela," Max asked. "What was she like?"

Della sighed. "You would have loved her. Everyone

did. She was bright and funny and beautiful, from the inside out. Let me show you." Reaching into her purse, she pulled out a wallet, opened it and extracted a photo. "This was taken the last time she visited Owl Creek. Maybe two months before she disappeared."

In the picture, Della stood side by side with Angela, a taller woman with purple-and-blond hair. Arms around each other, they beamed at the camera, the affection between them clear and vivid. Looking at it made Della's throat ache. Swallowing, she handed it over to him. "Isn't she beautiful?" she asked.

He studied it a moment in silence. "She's pretty," he replied, handing the photo back. "You know, in my opinion, I've never met another woman who could hold a candle to you. But I have to admit your cousin comes close."

Blinking, Della tried to process what he'd just said. Then she realized he had to be acting from habit. Once a playboy, always a playboy.

When she didn't respond, he took a sip of his beer. "What was Angela doing in Kalispell?"

Relieved to be back on familiar ground, she put the photo carefully back into her wallet. "She went there to start her own hair salon with one of her friends from cosmetology school. They'd had their grand opening and seemed to be doing well."

"Did she go to cosmetology school here in Idaho?"

"Yes, in Boise." She sighed. "Angela had a real talent with hair. She could make anyone look good, no matter how old or how young. I always intended on making the trip there to see her in action and get my hair done. Now I wish I had."

Max must've seen her blink back tears, so he gave her

a moment. Composing herself, she took a sip of her drink and shook her head. "Damn, I'm going to miss her. I kept hoping she'd simply gone off on one of her epic adventures and lost track of time. Though it wasn't like her not to keep in touch, none of us knew what else to think."

"Did you notify the authorities?"

"Yes. Her parents filed a missing person report. Her business partner did too. Because Angela was dedicated to her work and to the business." Della's voice broke. To cover, she took another sip of her drink. Despite vowing not to give up hope until Caroline weighed in, she wasn't in the habit of living under delusions.

"Her apartment looked like she intended to return," Della continued. "Her parents—my aunt and uncle—went out there. There wasn't anything missing. Even her luggage was still in the closet, which kind of negated the whole gone-on-a-trip theory."

Again, Max gave her a minute, which she appreciated.

She refused to cry in front of him again, so she blinked several times and then grimaced. "The family all went into panic mode. Except me, because I knew that wouldn't help her. I helped contact every friend she'd ever had—at least the ones that I could reach or that I knew about. I made sure to be there for my aunt and uncle. And I refused to give up hope. They did too."

She bowed her head, lost in emotion. "Thanks for listening to me," she said.

"No thanks necessary. I'm really sorry everything played out the way it did."

On the patio at Della's feet, Charlie stretched out, clearly enjoying basking in the sun. Every now and then, he'd raise his head and look up at her, as if wanting to make sure she was okay.

"You're a good boy, Charlie Black," Della said. "The best dog ever."

The waitress arrived with their food just then, a welcome relief. Concentrating on her lunch gave her time to collect her emotions and regain some of her composure.

They ate in a kind of companionable silence. She liked that Max didn't feel the need to fill the quiet with small talk or seem to expect her to.

She glanced up at him, only to find him watching her, his expression intense.

"Are you okay?" he asked.

Considering his words, she finally nodded. "I think I will be. But I'm really going to miss Angela." She pushed her plate away. She'd managed to eat about half of her pizza and would take the rest home to eat later.

"When was the last time the two of you spoke?" he asked. He'd demolished his meal and leaned back in his chair, his eyes locked on hers.

Something in his light blue eyes made her yearn to lean across the table and touch him. Instead, she focused on his question. "She and I spoke a couple of days before she disappeared. She'd recently joined a new church and seemed excited about the new friends she'd made."

"A church?" His gaze sharpened, though his tone remained casual. "Were you able to reach out to them and see if they knew anything?"

She grimaced. "That's just it. We couldn't. Angela was pretty vague when she talked about them and none of us knew to press her. Even Karyn, her business partner, didn't know much about Angela joining a church.

We didn't even know the name of it or where it was located."

"That's odd," he mused. "Though it might not mean anything. Then again, I've learned the hard way that sometimes the smallest clue could be the missing link."

"We told the police about it when we filed the missing person report," she said. "They didn't seem too concerned."

"Probably because there isn't any real reason to be. It's just another clue. She might have met someone at this church, though, maybe a friend who might know something that might help."

"I thought of that," Della admitted. "But since Angela didn't give me very much information and she'd just started going there, I didn't think much would come of it."

"You're probably right," Max replied. "For now, I'll just add that information to my file."

"Do you mind if we change the subject?" she asked. "I still am dreading the moment when I have to go let Angela's parents know." Pushing to her feet, she handed him Charlie's leash. "Would you mind watching him while I go to the ladies' room?"

"Not at all," he responded. Charlie sat up when she walked away, but when she gave him the hand signal to stay, he didn't follow.

Forcing himself to tear his gaze away from Della as she walked away, Max managed to smile when the waitress walked up. He took care of the bill and left a generous tip.

While waiting for Della to return, he petted Charlie.

The black Lab seemed to like the attention, leaning into Max's touch. As Della strolled across the room toward them, Max realized he didn't want the afternoon to end yet. He wondered if she'd be willing to continue hanging out on the patio, enjoying the nice weather. Since the restaurant wasn't crowded, he knew they wouldn't mind.

She sat down and took a sip of her half-finished beer. "Are you ready to go?" she asked.

"Not until you are," he replied. "I'm actually liking getting to pet your dog."

As if he understood, Charlie whined, making Della laugh.

"I've got nowhere urgent to be," she said, surprising him. "As long as we can talk about something other than the case."

"I can do that." He found himself telling her about his mother carrying on an affair with his uncle.

"She deserted her children?" she asked, her eyes wide. "That's unreal."

"I know. And my uncle basically deserted his family too. But my aunt Jenny and my dad pitched in and worked together to make sure we all had good childhoods. When we all get together, it's like one huge family." He smiled. "My cousins are more like siblings than anything else."

"I'd heard the stories," she admitted. "Your family kind of owns most of Owl Creek. I went to school with some of your cousins, and your sister, Lizzy, was a couple years ahead of me."

Della finished her beer and shifted in her seat. Max had emptied his glass too. The waitress noticed and reappeared, asking if they wanted another.

"Oh, no, thank you," Della said.

Max declined also and the waitress moved away.

Afraid Della would push to her feet and start to leave, Max continued talking. "It gets even more bizarre," he said. "As I'm sure you've heard, my uncle Robert recently passed away."

She nodded. "Yes, the funeral was a big deal in town. It's all everyone talked about." She took a deep breath. "I'm sorry for your loss."

"Thanks." Watching her closely, Max grimaced. "I know how people in Owl Creek gossip about my family. So even though we tried to keep it quiet, I'm guessing you heard about what happened after the will was read."

"No." She shook her head. "Whatever you did must have worked, because no one's said anything."

Glancing around to make sure no one was close enough to overhear, he leaned toward her. "We've all just learned we have a couple of half siblings."

Della's mouth dropped open in shock. "What?"

"Yes, two more Coltons. A brother and a sister. All the rest of us kids are supposed to have dinner Thursday night at that new barbecue place in town and meet them."

"Back Forty? I've been wanting to try that," she said, clearly still mulling over what he'd said.

She had other questions, he could tell. He saw it in her face. And he also realized that as distractions went, this particular topic of conversation obviously did the trick. The sadness had receded from her eyes, replaced by curiosity. He liked the way her brown eyes glowed.

In fact, he liked everything about this woman.

"Would you go with me?" he asked, surprising himself. "I really could use the support."

Head tilted, she studied him. "Are you sure you want to bring a friend to something like this? It seems more like it should be a family matter, don't you think?"

"Maybe." He shrugged. "Maybe not. I'm sure some of the others will bring friends. It's all going to be very informal."

Since she still didn't appear convinced, he admitted the truth. "I'm not sure I even want to go, to be honest."

She caught on right away. "It's not their fault, you know. Whatever your mother did to you and your brothers and sister, it had nothing to do with them."

"I'm aware. It's just we didn't even find out about them until after the funeral, after the will was read."

"They didn't come?" She gaped at him. "To their own father's funeral?"

Now he wanted to change the subject. Instead, he tried to steer the conversation back on track. "Will you come with me? Or at least think about it? I really could use the support of a friend."

"Friend? Is that what we are?"

Her directness was refreshing. Another thing to like about her.

"I'd like to think so," he answered. He didn't feel like he had to give his "I'm not looking for a relationship" speech, because other than that one accidental kiss, he hadn't given her any indication he'd be romantically interested.

Even if he was.

The second the thought occurred to him, he shut it right down.

She laughed, the light sound easing some of the tightness in his chest. "I like that. Friends. And you know what? I think I will. It might do me good to get out and be around people who don't know me. What time do you want to pick me up? Or would you rather I meet you there?"

"I'll pick you up at six thirty."

"Okay." Her eyes sparkled as she got to her feet. "I'll text you my address." She typed and his phone pinged. "There. It's a bit out of town, but not too far from Crosswinds."

Tamping down his regret that the afternoon had ended, he stood. Following her and Charlie outside, he watched while she loaded the dog up in her Jeep and turned to face him.

"Thanks for lunch," she said. "I enjoyed it."

"Me too." He would not kiss her upturned face. He absolutely would not. Because he suspected if he did, she wouldn't go to dinner with him Thursday. And he realized he desperately wanted to see her again.

He stood outside his truck and watched until her taillights had disappeared. Then, shaking his head at himself, he got in, started the ignition and drove back to the ranch.

Once there, he set up his laptop in the large dining room. He had two back-to-back online meetings scheduled for that afternoon. Both were about the serial killer case. The first call would be between Max and Brian, discussing how to manage the media. The FBI would soon be releasing an official statement. They didn't want to cause a mass panic, but they had a duty to let the public know.

Caroline would be conducting the second one, briefing the team on her findings. He strongly doubted she'd be able to positively ID Della's cousin's remains. Even if she did, the official statement by the Bureau wouldn't identify anyone, pending official notification of the victims' families.

The family he was most concerned about was Della's. The anguish he'd seen in her expressive brown eyes would haunt him for a long time. Actually, he wished he could be with her when she learned the truth, though he suspected deep down she already knew.

Since Caroline had promised to call Della as soon as she knew, he decided he'd try to check in with Della later, to see if there was anything he could do to help. For now, he had work to attend to, for which he was deeply grateful. He needed to get his mind off Della Winslow and back where it belonged. On his job. This case.

Brian sent the link for the meeting and Max clicked on it. A moment later, his boss's face filled the laptop screen.

"Good afternoon," Brian said, his expression uncharacteristically grim. "I've had my assistant busy drafting the press release. I thought we could go through it and get everything fine-tuned. I'm going to have a tentative story 'leaked' to the press later today."

Which meant that would give the media time to have a feeding frenzy, complete with various possible scenarios and speculation. The local Owl Creek police would direct all questions to the FBI. Eventually, Brian would schedule a press conference and release the official statement.

Max and Brian tossed phrases back and forth, using previous statements made by other state FBI divisions when addressing their own serial killer investigations. Finally, they settled on something both of them liked and ended the call.

With thirty minutes to go until his second meeting, Max used the time to make a glass of iced tea and grab a couple of the homemade chocolate chip cookies Mama Jen had left behind. His dad and his brothers were still out working the ranch, so he had the house to himself.

Growing up, he'd been required to help out around the place. After he got home from school, he'd had to come home, change and head to the barn, to help muck out stalls, exercise horses or help with the feedings. He hadn't minded, though even then he'd known that he wanted something different than a life spent tending horses or cattle.

With two older sons already committed, Buck had been much more lenient with the younger two kids, Max and his sister, Lizzy. They'd been allowed to pursue their own interests and Buck had given them his enthusiastic support over their choices. When Max had gone to Quantico, Buck and Jenny had even thrown him a going-away-slash-celebratory party.

Checking his watch, Max took a seat and opened his laptop. A moment later, he found the meeting invite and clicked on it.

The second Zoom call brought the entire team back together. Though Brian had scheduled the meeting, he quickly turned it over to Caroline to brief them on her findings.

"I've successfully been able to identify four of the remains," she announced. "Using DNA and cross-referencing missing person reports with a narrow focus on females between the ages of eighteen and thirty, we had a resounding success. As for the other three, my forensic team is still working on those."

A series of photos appeared on the screen. "These are the victims, along with their name, age and last-known address at the time of their disappearance. We have not yet been successful in finding anything that might link them together."

Everyone fell silent as they studied the photos. All young, all pretty. Max focused in on the first one. Angela Hobbs. Della's cousin.

Though his throat had briefly closed, Max managed to find his voice. "I assume you've started the process of locating and notifying next of kin?"

Caroline eyed him, her expression sympathetic. "Yes. I'll be doing that once we finish this meeting."

And Della was by herself. Then and there, Max knew he'd be heading out to her place as soon as he could. Locating her text from earlier, he put her address into his GPS. Twenty minutes, if he drove fast. He toyed with asking Caroline to wait, to give him a head start, but didn't want the gossip mill to go into overdrive.

For now, he needed to force himself to pay attention to the rest of the meeting.

"These young women are from all over the tristate area," Caroline was saying. "Though Angela Hobbs grew up here in Owl Creek, at the time of her disappearance, she was living in Kalispell, Montana." Caroline used a pointer to highlight each woman's profile. "The others came from Idaho, Wyoming and Utah."

"Idaho?" Max asked. "But not Owl Creek?"

"No. Pocatello." Caroline shook her head. "The question is, what did they have in common?"

That was what they needed to look for. The single

common denominator that might lead them to the reason the killer had targeted these particular women.

Unfortunately, at this moment they had nothing.

"Theo, you and Chris start working on the ones from Wyoming and Utah," Brian ordered. "Jake and Ed, help them. Max, I want you to check out the two from Idaho, especially the one who grew up in your hometown. I want each of you to dig into their backgrounds, talk to their friends and family, learn their hobbies. There has to be something similar that each of these women did or knew."

"And I'll continue to work to identify the others," Caroline said. "Once I have more information on them, I'll get with you all again."

Now that the assignments had been passed out, the meeting ended. Max immediately grabbed his truck keys and headed out the door. He needed to get to Della as soon as possible. He hated that she'd be alone when she learned the news about her cousin.

Chapter 6

By the time Della got home from lunch with Max, she'd received individual text messages from four different coworkers, every single one of them wanting the dirt on how she knew Max Colton and what might be going on between them. Since his reputation preceded him, she supposed she couldn't blame them. After all, she'd worked with most of them for years and they all knew her to be a steady, low-key and down-to-earth woman. Not the type to be taken in by a man who was known for loving and leaving women.

Instead of responding individually, she made a group text and sent out a two-word response. We're friends!

In response, she received a few emojis, exclamation points, and one flat-out declaration that said, When you're up here next, we want details. Again, no more than she'd expected. Heck, she'd have done the same if she'd spotted any of her coworkers hanging around with Max.

The thought caused a twinge of unease, which shocked her. Jealousy? Or just that she didn't like the thought of what—*sharing Max Colton with anyone*? As if he belonged to her or some such nonsense.

Shaking her head at her own foolishness, Della decided to keep busy with some housework and laundry.

As she puttered around the house, Charlie watched from the comfort of his oversize dog bed. He'd had a busy couple of days and had earned his rest. Speaking of rest, she wouldn't mind taking a short nap herself. With one load of clothes in the washer and another in the dryer, now might be the perfect time to do that.

On her way to the bedroom, her cell phone rang. Caroline's number was displayed on the screen, which sent Della's heart rate into overdrive. Taking a deep breath, she answered.

"Good afternoon," Caroline said, her voice soft. "I just finished briefing the team. As promised, I'm calling you to let you know I've identified four of the bodies."

Though she'd expected this, for a moment Della's world spun. She put out a hand to steady herself, gripping the side of her dresser. "Was one of them Angela?" she croaked, suspecting she already knew the answer.

"Yes. I'm very sorry."

"Thank you." Blinking back tears, Della raised her chin and took a deep breath. "Have you determined her cause of death yet?"

"We're still working on that. It's much more difficult at this stage."

When there were only bones. Though Caroline didn't say that out loud, Della knew what she meant. "When and if you figure that out, will you also let me know?"

"Of course," Caroline replied. "Again, I'm really sorry for your loss."

After murmuring her thanks, Della ended the call. Numb, she sat down at her kitchen table. Through the window over the sink, she could see the house next door, where Angela had grown up and where Della had spent as much time as at her own home. Her aunt and uncle still lived there. Now Della had to summon up the strength to go over there and break both of their hearts.

She didn't know how long she sat there, staring into space, lost in her memories and thoughts. But when Charlie nudged her hand with his nose, she blinked and pushed to her feet. Charlie whined, then gave a short bark and hurried over to the front door, his tail wagging.

A moment later, her doorbell rang.

Not really sure she wanted to deal with anyone, she looked through the peephole. Max Colton stood on her doorstep, dragging a hand through his hair, his expression concerned.

At the sight of his handsome face, her heartbeat skipped. Though she wasn't sure why he'd come or even how he'd found her house, she opened the door.

"Max..." she began.

Without speaking, he stepped forward, closing the door shut behind him, and pulled her into his arms. "I'm here," he told her.

Face against his chest, she froze. And then, as the warmth of his strong body seeped into her bones, she heaved a giant sob and began to weep.

He offered her comfort, a silent rock of a man, saying nothing. She didn't know how it was that he'd come to comfort her, but right this moment, she didn't care. He'd understood that some things shouldn't have to be dealt with alone.

Finally, she had no more tears, having cried herself out. Eyes swollen, she stepped away and disappeared into her bathroom to blow her nose and wash her face. She still wasn't entirely sure why Max had come and she half suspected he might be gone when she emerged. Either way, she owed him a debt of gratitude for his unwavering support. She appreciated that he hadn't asked for anything in return.

Instead, he waited for her in the kitchen, one hip resting against the counter. Charlie had taken a seat right next to him, leaning himself against Max's leg for pets. Even her dog loved this man. She eyed him, one part of her thinking he looked too damn sexy for her peace of mind.

Friends, she reminded herself. She needed to remember that.

"Caroline told me she was going to let you know she'd identified the remains," he said. "I wanted to make sure you were all right."

Blinking, she stared at him, her words of gratitude stuck in her throat. Needing a second to compose herself, she went to the fridge and poured herself a glass of lemonade. Without thinking, she got one for Max too. Handing it to him, she sighed. "Thank you. Though deep down inside, I knew this was coming, it's still hard." She glanced at the house next door. "Now I've got to fill my aunt and uncle in."

"My offer to go with you still stands," he said, his sympathetic expression making her ache for another hug. "I'm here if you need me."

Briefly, she considered. "I think it's best if I go by myself. They wouldn't appreciate me bringing a stranger."

"Maybe not." He drew himself up. "But I'm an FBI agent. Eventually, I'll have to speak to them. I can go in my official capacity. It might help."

He had a point. Charlie nudged him and Max bent down to continue scratching behind the dog's ears.

Restless, she went to the kitchen window again to look at the house next door. Two vehicles were in the driveway, which meant both her aunt and uncle were home.

"I want to tell them now," she said, deciding. "And yes, I'd like you to come with me, in an official capacity."

Straightening, he gave a wordless nod.

She marched to the front door, gathering up every ounce of strength she possessed. Though she knew it might be best to call first to let them know she was coming, she felt strongly that they'd hear something in her voice and know. No way she wanted them to learn their daughter's fate on the telephone. They deserved better than that.

With Max right behind her, she crossed the distance between the two houses. Stepping up onto the front porch, she rang the bell. A moment later, her aunt answered the door, her expression puzzled.

"Della?" Her gaze swung from Della to Max.

"Aunt Mary, this is Max Colton with the FBI," Della said, her voice trembling only slightly. "May we come in?"

At first, her aunt appeared puzzled. But then she jerked her head in a quick nod and motioned them past her. "Let me call your uncle," she said. "Please, wait in the den."

Instead of dropping down onto the sofa as she would normally, Della stood, twisting her hands nervously.

"Do you want me to tell them?" Max offered. "In my official capacity, of course."

Tempting as the offer might be, Della had never been a coward. "I'll do it."

"Just stick to the facts," he advised. "It'll be easier on them that way."

"What's going on?" Uncle Alex demanded as he entered the room. "Mary tells me you brought an FBI agent here? Do you have news of Angela?"

Could she do this? Trying to speak past the ache in her throat, she nodded. "I do. And I'm afraid it's not good."

Somehow, she managed to relay what Caroline had told her. She left out the fact that she and Charlie had been the ones to find the body, or even that they'd found six more unmarked graves.

"But who killed her?" Aunt Mary asked, seemingly unaware of the tears streaking down her face. Uncle Alex had covered his face with his hands to hide his emotions but lifted his head at the question.

At a complete loss for words, Della looked toward Max for help.

"We're working on finding that out," Max replied. "As soon as we know anything, I promise we will inform you." He took a deep breath. "For now, I'm afraid I have to ask you to keep this quiet. We'll be holding a press conference about the entire situation soon. Until then, if you could keep this under wraps, we'd appreciate it."

Uncle Alex's gaze narrowed. For a moment, Della thought he'd protest, but instead he simply bowed his head. "We've got to notify our family and her friends. Can we do that?"

"Yes, of course," Max responded.

"Thank you for letting us know." Voice wooden, Mary turned and walked out of the room. A moment later, her husband followed.

Aching, Della wished there was something she could say, something she could do, to help ease their pain. Instead, she knew she'd have to let them deal with it however they chose.

"Come on," she said quietly, touching Max's arm. "We can show ourselves out."

Back in her own kitchen, Della realized she had no memory of how she'd gotten there. Charlie rushed over, tail wagging, and she dropped to the floor and buried her face in his fur.

She didn't cry. She had no more tears left inside of her to shed. Instead, she held her beloved dog and took comfort from his unwavering devotion.

Instead of leaving, Max took a seat at the kitchen table. He waited quietly, both giving her space and lending his support, if she needed it.

She appreciated him more than she could say.

Finally, she got up and went to let Charlie outside. As if he understood, the dog took care of his business quickly, bounding back to the door to indicate he was ready to go in.

When they returned to the kitchen, Max still waited.

Eyeing him, she admired his patience, the way he managed to emit both an aura of stillness and a readiness to spring into action if needed. Now she finally understood why so many other women had been willing to throw themselves at him.

As she approached, he stood. "Della," he began. The intensity in his gaze was her undoing.

Somehow, she wound up in his arms, her mouth on his. Hungry—so, so hungry. His hand tangled in her hair, they devoured each other. This kiss took their first one to another level. Smoldering, intense, almost overwhelming. Each kiss, every touch, set her ablaze with longing. Their tongues tangled, breath intertwined, and she couldn't get enough.

With their clothing an unwelcome barrier between their skin, they tore at each other's shirts, pants and, finally, undergarments. As he stepped out of his boxers, his arousal free, she couldn't stop herself from stroking the physical demonstration of his need for her.

As he pushed into her hands, desire clawed at her.

"Are you sure?" he asked. When she nodded, he bent over and retrieved a condom from his jeans. She helped him tug it on, each movement arousing her to a fevered pitch.

When they'd finished, they kissed again. Body tingling, she throbbed with an ache to take him inside of her. Somehow, they made it to the living room and fell naked onto the sofa. Limbs entangled, wrapped around each other, she pushed him back and climbed on top. As she took him deep inside, his body filled her velvet softness, and she arched back and let out a moan. All the superlatives applied—eroticism brought to vibrant, immediate life with every movement.

Nothing gentle about this. She demanded and he gave. Everything, all at once. Electrified, the tension built in her. She burned. And yet she needed more.

Then, just as she almost reached the apex, he rolled, pinning her beneath him. "Not yet," he rasped, even as she bucked against him. "Just. Give me a minute."

She could feel his heart thudding against her skin. Somehow, shivering, she held herself still. When he began to move again, each slow stroke an exquisite form of torture, she writhed beneath him. Using her body, she tried to urge him to go faster. She burned for him. When he finally let go of his restraint, she met him stroke for stroke. Raw possession. And this time, when she reached the peak, she toppled over it. Explosive pleasure clawed through her, like nothing she'd ever felt before.

A moment later, he shuddered and let go. They held on to each other while his body bucked and hers clenched.

He slid his hand along the curve of her hip, tucking her body into his. They lay together while their heart rates slowed and their breathing got back to normal.

Finally, he raised himself up on one elbow and smoothed her hair away from her face. "You're so beautiful," he said.

She made a face. "So are you."

"I'm serious." He kissed her neck, right below her jaw, which made her shiver.

"As am I." Because she knew she ought to move, she shifted away and began gathering up her clothes from the floor. He watched her for a moment while she got dressed, then sighed and did the same.

"No regrets." She hadn't meant to say that out loud, but when she saw his startled expression, she realized she had.

"Right," he replied. He frowned and then took a deep breath. "Listen, we can still be friends, right?"

Chest aching, she slowly nodded. "Of course."

Silently thanking him for the reminder, she walked to the front door and held it open. "Give me a call when you hear something on the case."

"I will," he replied. "And don't forget dinner Thursday."

As friends. No way was she going to allow this man to break her heart. She had too much sense for that. "Of course."

Head spinning, his entire body buzzing, Max hurried to his truck. Instead of feeling sated after that amazing round of lovemaking, he craved more. He'd successfully fought the urge to ask her if he could stay. For the first time in forever, he'd longed to spend the night with a woman tucked up against his body.

Not just any woman. Della.

What the hell was wrong with him? Not only would getting involved with her be the height of unprofessionalism, but her personal involvement with one of the victims could jeopardize the entire case.

Also, if he were completely honest, with his reputation as a player, he didn't want the folks of Owl Creek to make wrong judgments about Della's character. She didn't deserve that. All the other women he'd dated had known up front what they were getting into. The rules had been agreed to by both parties. He and Della had never discussed anything other than the fact that they were friends.

Friends. Most people might find that insulting. Normally he would, especially around a woman as sexy as her. But he genuinely *liked* Della Winslow. Sure, he also desired her, but from past experience he knew finding a woman he enjoyed being around outweighed any rush of passion. He'd also learned it never worked out trying to have both.

As he started the truck and drove home, he wondered what the hell he was going to do. He hadn't meant for this to happen, and clearly, neither had she. But damn, he refused to regret it. Because no matter how he tried to spin it, he'd never experienced this kind of connection with another woman. He kind of doubted he ever would again.

Snorting at his own uncharacteristic train of thought, instead of driving directly back to the ranch, he decided to stop in town for a drink. By now, Tap Out Brewery ought to be hopping. He figured he'd see if he could snag a seat at the bar, have a beer and do some people-watching. Maybe that would help clear his head.

Briefly, he considered calling one of his cousins, like Fletcher, who worked as a detective for the Owl Creek Police Department. But then Fletcher would want to discuss the case, and Max wasn't in the mood for that. No, it would be better to go alone, have his drink and try to unwind.

He had to circle the packed parking lot several times before he lucked out into a space when someone left.

Once inside, he had to shoulder his way through people to get to the packed bar. Surprised to see a couple of empty stools, he took one. The bartender caught his eye and motioned that he'd be over as soon as he could. Since there were only two behind the bar, Max figured he might be in for a bit of a wait. However, he had his beer in less than five minutes. Grateful, Max took a long drink and then surveyed the room. He always found people-watching entertaining.

"I hear we're having a news conference tomorrow." One of the cops who'd originally been at the meadow dropped into the seat next to him. "To talk about that mass grave site up in the mountains."

Max eyed him, drawing a blank when he tried to remember the guy's name. Luckily, he'd spoken quietly, and no one else appeared to have heard.

Apparently realizing this, the man stuck out his hand and Max shook it. "Ryan Larkins," he said. "Owl Creek PD. I work with your cousin Fletcher. We've been getting calls all day about a potential serial killer and were told to refer all of them to the FBI. Everyone says the FBI is going to talk about it officially tomorrow."

Max didn't bother to say his own name since Ryan clearly remembered it. Since the story would have just been leaked to the press, Max wondered if Ryan knew this for a fact or was simply fishing for info.

"Are we?" he asked casually, taking a long drink of his beer. "I haven't been informed if that's the case. But then again, I'm not part of the PR department, so I'm not involved."

Larkins nodded and ordered his own beer. While he waited for it to arrive, he turned and eyed Max. "What did you all find in that meadow? Must have been something interesting, if there's a need to brief the general public. I heard there were several more bodies."

Beginning to regret his impulsive decision to stop here, Max shook his head. "I'm sorry, but I can't discuss an ongoing investigation. You'll have to wait for the news conference, like everyone else."

Ryan's eyes narrowed. "Come on, Max. I'm not just a citizen. What's the big secret?"

He should have called Fletcher. If his cousin had been sitting here with him, he bet this guy wouldn't have been so inquisitive. "Sorry. I seriously am not at liberty to give you any information. I would if I could."

Though Ryan didn't appear convinced, he nodded. His beer arrived and he took a huge gulp, wiping his mouth with the back of his hand. "You can tell me," he finally said, his beefy face reddening. "We're both in law enforcement."

"I really can't." Infusing his voice with regret, Max drained the rest of his beer. He motioned to the bartender and closed out his tab. "Sorry," he told Ryan. "I've got to run."

Ryan's eyes narrowed further, and for a moment, Max thought there might be a fight. To his surprise, he clenched his fists, realizing he'd actually welcome that. Clearly, he needed to blow off some steam.

Instead, the other man backed down. "Have a good night."

Max nodded. There were lots of other ways to blow off steam. He kept a workout bag in his trunk. He could head to the gym, change and lift weights plus do some cardio. Breaking a good sweat would definitely help him release some of his pent-up tension. But then again, having mind-blowing sex usually took care of that too. Since he'd definitely just done that, he didn't understand his current mood.

Fletcher called when Max was getting into his truck. "Want to meet up for a beer?" Fletcher asked.

"I'm just leaving Tap Out," Max replied. "I ran into one of your officers. Ryan Larkins."

Laughing, Fletcher took a moment to speak. "Did he try to interrogate you? He's been bugging the heck out of me to find out what's going on in the investigation."

"Yep," Max admitted. "I barely stopped myself from getting into a bar fight with him."

"I can imagine. And I'm guessing you don't want to go back inside and wait for me."

"Nope," Max replied. "Sorry, but I'm heading back to the ranch."

"Are you going to be at the presser tomorrow?" Fletcher asked. "They've requested that I appear and stand near the police chief and the mayor to represent Owl Creek PD."

"I haven't been asked to be there," Max replied. "At least not yet. I didn't even know there was anything scheduled for tomorrow. I'm guessing my boss must be driving up to do it."

"Isn't that kind of weird?" Fletcher asked. "You're already in town since you're actively working the case. I'd think they'd want you involved."

"I'm just glad they don't. Giving public speeches has never been one of my favorite activities."

Fletcher laughed again. "I hear you. See you Thursday?"

"I'll be there. I'm looking forward to trying a half rack of ribs."

Once the call ended, Max eyed his phone and realized he'd missed several calls and had a couple of voice mails. All from his SAC Brian. With all the noise inside the bar, he hadn't been able to hear it ring. There was even a text from Brian, asking Max to call him ASAP.

Max had a sinking feeling that this would be regarding the press conference tomorrow. Though there was always the chance that they'd learned something new regarding the investigation. Before he even got a chance to return the call, his phone rang again.

"Brian," Max began. "Sorry I missed you. What's going on?"

"I'm driving out to Owl Creek in the morning," Brian said. "We're holding a joint press conference with OCPD. I've shared my PowerPoint presentation with you. I need you to take a look at it and let me know if there's anything you'd like to add or change."

Relieved, Max agreed to do so as soon as he got back to the ranch.

"Also," Brian continued, "I'm going to need you to meet me at the police department headquarters tomorrow around ten. The presser is at eleven."

"I'll be there," Max promised. He should have seen this coming. Since Brian had placed Max in charge while in Owl Creek, there was no way Brian would brief the media without him.

Back at the ranch, he walked inside the house and realized he'd interrupted dinner. His father and two brothers were in the middle of their meal, which consisted of leftovers from what Jenny had cooked the previous evening.

Max made himself a plate and sat down to eat. Luckily, his family wasn't into small talk, so he was able to finish his meal and head up to his room. He heard the television come on downstairs, which was good. It meant no one would be disturbing him.

The next morning, Max put on his best suit and tie. Glad his father and brothers were already out working on the ranch, he eyed himself in the mirror. Sometimes, FBI agents got to wear their Bureau windbreakers over slacks and a shirt. Brian had decided this was not one of those times.

Driving into town, Max arrived at the police station thirty minutes early. Despite that, Brian was waiting for him on a metal bench out front, drinking a large to-go cup of coffee. The various news crews had already started setting up out front. In addition to the local stations, Max recognized a couple of reporters from national news. Luckily, no one knew him or Brian, so they were left alone. For now, at least. That would definitely change once the presser started.

"Morning," Max said, dropping on the bench next

to his boss. Brian also wore a dark suit along with sunglasses that screamed *federal agent*.

"Nice town," Brian commented. "I've never made it out this way before."

"It's a popular tourist destination," Max pointed out. He pulled his own sunglasses from his pocket and put them on. "Are we having this thing outside?" he asked.

"We are." Brian nodded. "That way there's more room for both the news crews and the citizens. The mayor tells me he's posted notices all around town, in shop windows, as well as on the city's social media. He expects a large turnout."

Sure enough, people were already filling up the lot and parking in the street. Since Max recognized many of them, he was especially glad he'd put on the sunglasses. They may not completely hide him, but at least they'd give people pause while they tried to figure out his identity. Of course, once everything started, they'd recognize him for certain.

Finally, the police chief emerged, accompanied by the mayor, Skipper Carlson. Though Chief Stanton wore his uniform, the mayor had chosen a dark suit as well. A retired ski instructor, Skipper usually went around town in jeans, a T-shirt and motorcycle boots. Max thought he cleaned up well. A couple of junior staffers came out with them, also dressed up. They carried a microphone, speakers and a wooden podium that had seen better days. They got all this set up and did a couple of "Testing, 1-2-3"s on the mic.

Meanwhile, the crowd of townspeople continued to grow. Max recognized Angela's parents, though he saw no sign of Della. Too bad. He should have asked Brian to have Della and Charlie there to represent the SAR team who'd made the initial discovery. Too late now.

Several other police officers emerged from the building, most of them in uniform. Max's cousin Fletcher came with them. There was no sign of Ryan Larkins, which made Max smile.

Brian took one last deep gulp of his coffee and stood. "Showtime," he murmured. "Let's go."

Joining him, Max kept his gaze fixed straight ahead. Since it seemed half of Owl Creek was here, not to mention all the news teams, he needed to project the stereotypical image people associated with an FBI agent. "Let's do this," he said.

Chapter 7

Della watched the press conference on her television, along with everyone else in town who didn't attend in person. Gossip had run rampant through all the shops and restaurants. Crosswinds hadn't been immune. Since no one knew exactly what the topic would be, imaginations ran high. Her aunt and uncle apparently hadn't discussed Angela's death with any of their friends or acquaintances in town, because no one came up to Della with expressions of sympathy.

The FBI had decided to hold the news conference with very short notice, likely to keep gossip from reaching a fevered pitch. It had only been announced yesterday afternoon. She imagined some of the major news outlets had done a bit of scrambling to get their reporters into town on time.

Della had briefly considered making the drive into town to see everything in person, but in the end, she'd decided against it. If they mentioned anything about Angela, she'd likely lose her composure. The last thing she wanted was to have a meltdown on live TV.

Plus, since it was Wednesday, she'd be working at Crosswinds tonight. Her coworkers would already have too many questions because they'd have figured out that she and Charlie had been the ones to find the graves.

And since the identities of some of the victims had been released, they'd know her cousin Angela had been one of them.

Her aunt and uncle had called her the minute they learned of the news conference. "Is it true?" Aunt Mary had asked. "There were other women killed? Angela wasn't the only one?"

"Yes. There were six others," Della had replied softly. "That's why the FBI has taken over. They're working the case as a probable serial killer."

Aunt Mary had gasped. "Why didn't you mention this before, when you told us about Angela?"

"Because the FBI asked me not to." Della's gut had clenched. "They've promised to find the killer."

"They'd better." For a moment, her aunt had sounded furious. "Before Alex gathers up all his friends in this town and they go out and find him themselves."

The mingled anger and pain in her aunt Mary's usually calm voice had made Della's chest hurt. She stared at the TV, wondering if she'd be able to see them.

As the camera panned out over the crowd, Della spotted her aunt and uncle, standing front and center. Uncle Alex had his arm around Aunt Mary, almost holding her up. Several of their friends surrounded them, clearly there to offer their support.

It looked like a large portion of the town had turned out for this event. Judging by the variety of the rumors being bandied about, Della wasn't surprised. They'd flown fast and furious, beginning the moment the press conference had been announced. No doubt everyone wanted to find out which of those rumors were true. Della couldn't blame them, though she knew everyone would be shocked once they knew the truth.

When the camera returned to the group near the podium, Della spotted Max, wearing a dark suit and sunglasses. He stood next to another, shorter man similarly attired. If someone had asked for a couple of actors to portray FBI agents, the two of them would have made the cut.

The mayor stepped forward and spoke into the mic. He too had dressed with care, forgoing his usual casual Western attire for a suit and tie, though he still wore a black cowboy hat. He began by welcoming everyone, though he wished it was for a better reason. He then introduced chief of police Kevin Stanton and turned the microphone over to him.

Clearly working from a script, the police chief read from a paper. He detailed how a search and rescue canine and handler had happened across remains buried in a shallow grave while hiking. He didn't mention Della and Charlie by name, though she knew everyone in town would guess it was her.

"We called in the FBI," Kevin said. "And now Special Agent in Charge Brian Mahoney will discuss what they've found."

While the SAC spoke, Della watched Max. He stood ramrod straight, staring directly ahead, his handsome face expressionless. When several in the crowd gasped at the words *serial killer*, he didn't physically react. Inwardly, she suspected he was wincing.

Ending the speech with the usual platitudes, Brian told the crowd that they had no reason to panic. They were currently working all leads and this killer *would* be apprehended.

She wondered if he'd take questions from the towns-people or the reporters. Apparently not, as he'd already turned away. Several reporters shouted out to him, though he didn't acknowledge any of their requests. Along with the mayor, police chief and Max, he disappeared inside the police station. The camera followed them until the doors closed behind them.

A reporter appeared on the screen, her blue eyes sparking with excitement. When she began talking, Della grabbed the remote and clicked the television off. She'd seen enough.

When her aunt and uncle arrived home next door, she saw them pull up in the driveway out her kitchen win-dow. Watching as they got out of the car, she realized they both looked like they'd aged twenty years since she'd given them the awful news.

They'd also been avoiding her. As if they felt she was somehow responsible.

Shaking off the thought, she waited until they'd gone into the house before calling Charlie. Another new Man-ners class tonight. This time, she'd bring her dog to work with her and let him demonstrate.

Once she got to Crosswinds, she managed to dodge people until right before her class started. Sebastian, the owner, even popped into her work area, but once he saw her students had already arrived, he left. Della figured he was just as curious as everyone else.

She was busy with back-to-back classes, and the time flew. The students were all focused and respectful, which was good since she didn't have to deal with another Hal.

She dreaded seeing him again at the next class and actually found herself hoping he wouldn't show up. Sometimes students dropped out after one or two classes, deciding training their dog was too much work.

As soon as her second class ended, she and Charlie hurried out to her Jeep. By some miracle, no one stopped her. With Charlie in the back seat, she pulled out of the parking lot and headed home.

A few miles in and she began to suspect someone might be following her. A black Honda with black rims. Hoping she was wrong, she made an abrupt right turn without signaling. The Honda did the same.

Maybe just coincidence. However, until she knew for sure, she wasn't going home.

Another right turn. The Honda followed. Now heading back the way she'd come, she passed the turnoff to Crosswinds and kept going toward downtown Owl Creek. She could either pull into the police station parking lot or one of the well-lit gas stations. She'd decide once she got there.

As she drove, she kept checking her rearview mirror, hoping the other vehicle would turn off and disappear. No such luck. She had no idea why anyone would want to follow her, unless it was some overzealous reporter in search of a story. Which made no sense. She hadn't been mentioned by name in the press conference. No one would have any reason to wish to interview her.

Ahead, she saw the sign for the Chevron station. Impulsively, she turned in, pulling up to one of the pumps like she meant to fill her tank. To her shock, the Honda did the same, parking at the pump right behind her.

She swore under her breath. Instead of getting out of

her vehicle, she pulled forward into one of the parking spaces near the entrance. Then she hopped out, grabbing Charlie's leash and bringing him with her. She hurried into the store, where she could ask for help.

As she yanked open the glass door, someone called her name.

Turning, she saw Hal Murcheson getting out of the black Honda and waving at her.

Jaw clenched, she continued on inside the store. At least there were several other customers, plus two cashiers behind the counter. The pumps were busy and people were buying snacks or drinks. She found a spot close to the exit, near the cashiers, and turned to face the door.

Undeterred, Hal followed her inside. "Hey, Della," he said. "I thought I saw you leaving Crosswinds. I've been trying to flag you down since then."

"Flag me down?" she asked, crossing her arms. "No, you weren't. I'd like you to explain why you've been following me."

She'd spoken in a loud enough voice to draw the attention of several customers. Hal noticed this too. He came closer. Too close, which forced her to take a couple of steps back to escape him.

"I just wanted to say hello," he said, smiling. "I actually waited for you to finish up at Crosswinds, but you didn't see me. That's why I had to follow you."

"You didn't *have* to follow me," she insisted. "Do you have any idea how badly you frightened me?"

Right then, Charlie growled. She looked at her dog, the one who loved everyone, and realized he'd gotten to his feet. Hackles up, he'd bared his teeth, clearly intent on protecting her.

"I swear, I didn't mean—"

"Go away, Hal." Interrupting him, she tried for her most intimidating stare. "If you don't leave right now, I'm going to have to call the police."

A large college-age kid stepped up, accompanied by one of his friends. Both of them towered over Hal and Della. "Ma'am, is this man bothering you?" the kid asked.

"Yes, he is," Della replied.

"Back off," Hal said, sneering at the kid. "This doesn't concern you."

Della whipped out her phone. "I'm calling 911," she warned.

"Why?" Hal asked quickly. "Just because one of your students happened to run into you at a gas station? That's a little ridiculous, don't you think?"

"You just admitted that you were following me," she replied. "Either you leave, or I'm calling the police."

"Fine." He threw up his hands. "I'm going. I'll see you next week in class."

"No, you won't. You're not welcome back at Crosswinds. I'll make sure you get a full refund of whatever you paid."

Eyes narrowed, he glared at her. "You can't do that. I'm a paying customer. I haven't done anything wrong."

"You're stalking and harassing me. I don't have to put up with that."

By now, a small crowd had gathered. The two teenagers who'd originally sprung to her rescue appeared ready to escort Hal out if needed.

The front door opened and a uniformed police officer came inside. "I got a call about a disturbance here."

Relieved to see it was one of the men who'd initially responded to her discovery up in the meadow, Della quickly filled him in on the situation. Even if she couldn't remember his name, she knew he recognized her. As she explained, Hal tried several times to interrupt her. Each time, the officer asked him to be quiet.

When she finally finished, both the teenage boys and several other customers backed her up.

"I didn't do anything illegal," Hal said, his sullen expression matching his voice. "I'm taking one of Della's dog training classes and I got a little excited to see her outside of the school."

The policeman shook his head and she finally caught sight of his badge. *Santis.* "I'll need to see some identification," he said. "Your driver's license, please."

Though Hal appeared as if he wanted to protest, he finally reached into his back pocket, extracted his wallet and his ID, and handed them over. Santis studied the ID for a moment, and then, instead of giving it back, he asked Hal to come with him out to his cruiser. "I need to put this into our system and make sure you don't have any outstanding warrants or anything," Santis said. "Shouldn't take too long."

"Is this really necessary?" Hal asked. By now, the bystanders had wandered off to pay for their own purchases or go home.

"Yes, it is. Please come with me, sir." Officer Santis then turned to Della. "You can go ahead and leave now, Della. I'll make sure this man doesn't follow you."

Della thanked him and hurried back out to her Jeep and loaded Charlie up. She got in and backed out of her space, but when she reached the road and turned in the direction of home, she realized she'd started shaking so hard she could barely grip the wheel. Even though she knew Officer Santis would still be detaining Hal, she couldn't stop looking in her rearview mirror.

By the time she pulled into her driveway, with her heart trying to pound its way out of her chest, she was on the verge of a full-out panic attack.

Telling herself she'd be safe once she got inside, she opened her door, got out and grabbed Charlie's lead. Together, they rushed for her house. Though her shaking hands fumbled with the key, finally they made it inside. She closed and locked the door behind her. Then she pulled out her phone and dialed Max's number.

Max had started researching churches in Kalispell when his phone rang. Seeing Della's number come up on his screen made his heart skip a beat. Figuring she was calling to discuss the press conference earlier that day, he answered.

"Max, I need your help." Voice flat and shaky, Della didn't sound at all like herself.

Alarmed, he asked her if she was all right.

After a long silent pause, she exhaled. "No. Is there any way you can come over? I can text you my address if you don't remember it."

He didn't even hesitate. "I've got it. Sit tight. I'm on my way."

Closing his laptop, he snatched his keys up off the dresser and rushed through the living room, where his father had some old Western movie on. "I'll be back later," Max said.

Buck simply grunted, barely looking away from the TV.

Though he drove safely and carefully, Max broke every speed limit between the ranch and Della's house.

When he pulled up and parked, he felt relieved to see her Jeep was the only vehicle in the driveway. He wasn't sure what he'd expected—reporters harassing her, maybe—but since that didn't appear to be the case, his worry ratcheted up a notch.

As he sprinted up the sidewalk, the front door opened. He rushed inside, pulling her into his arms as soon as she shut the door.

"Della?" Cradling her, he realized her entire body trembled. He kissed the top of her head and held on to her, wishing he could give her his warmth or his strength or whatever it might be that she needed. "What the hell happened?"

Haltingly, she explained, her voice muffled since her face was still pressed against his chest. As she told him about the man named Hal, his shock turned to fury.

When she finally finished, most of her tremors seemed to have subsided. Gently, he steered her over to the couch. When she sat down, he went with her. Hip to hip, one arm still around her shoulders, she leaned into him. He tamped down his rage since none of that was directed at her. It was a good thing this Hal person wasn't here right now, because Max didn't entirely trust himself not to inflict some serious bodily harm. Which, as an FBI agent on assignment, would not be a good thing to do.

Charlie, viewing this as an invitation to join them, jumped up next to Max and nudged him with his head.

"Not now, Charlie," Della said. "Get down."

A good dog, Charlie instantly complied, tail wagging.

Seeing the bond between Della and her dog made Max want one of his own. If only he didn't spend such long hours at work, he would have gotten a dog years ago. Maybe someday.

"Charlie was with me in the Jeep," Della continued. "If anything happened to him because some guy decided to stalk me, I could never live with myself."

"I assume you've talked to Sebastian and made sure that person is banned from Crosswinds permanently?" Max asked.

"Not yet." She swallowed. "But I will. I'm not as worried about what might happen while I'm at work. He followed me after I left. I think he's trying to find out where I live. I can't be afraid to be alone in my own home."

He agreed. "Would you like me to have a word with him? Or with Fletcher, since he's a detective with OCPD?"

"Officer Santis was called out and had a talk with him already," she replied. "Honestly, I don't think any of that will make a difference with this guy. He seriously doesn't seem to think what he's doing is stalking or even wrong. And since he hasn't made an actual threat, I don't have enough to request a restraining order."

"Which might be a good thing, even though it might not seem like it," Max said. "Restraining orders don't always work. Sometimes they have the effect of enraging the person they're taken out against. I've seen it happen."

She groaned. "Great, just great." She went quiet for a moment and then sat bolt upright. "What if Hal's the one who killed all those women?"

Pulling her back to him, he kissed her cheek. "I promise we'll check him out, okay?"

"But you don't think it's likely. I can tell by the tone of your voice."

Surprised that she could read him so well, he nodded. "Whoever this killer is, he's been stashing bodies up there for a good while. Your cousin disappeared two years ago. Caroline said some of the remains have been there even longer. A guy like that isn't going to risk drawing attention to himself like Hal did."

Her gaze locked on his, she finally nodded. "Then why is Hal bothering me? I don't get it."

Unable to pull his gaze away, he grimaced. "Probably because of the way you look. You're beautiful, you know. Hal's probably never seen anyone who looks quite like you."

To her credit, she didn't disparage her looks or try to pretend she had no idea what he meant. "I've been told that before," she said. "But honestly, that sort of thing is subjective. I don't care about how I look. What should matter is the fact that I've worked hard to get to do what I do. I've gotten every dog training certification possible. I'm good."

Her confidence made him grin. He liked seeing this side of her.

She took a deep breath before continuing. "Actually, you know what? Without bragging, I have to say I'm excellent. I like helping people with their dogs, almost as much as I enjoy training for search and rescue work."

"I can tell you do," he said. "You're an actual example of someone working their dream job."

This comment made her go still. "Thank you," she said. "But if you can see that, why can't people like Hal? How I look should have no bearing on anything. I wear very little makeup on purpose and I keep my hair in a ponytail ninety-nine percent of the time. Just because someone might think I'm pretty doesn't give him the right to harass me."

"Agreed," he told her. "Men like him have no concept of how women should be treated."

"Exactly! It shocks me that someone with a dog could come to my class, supposedly to help them both learn how to communicate better, and then act like that."

"I'm sorry this happened to you," he said. "Hopefully, he'll have realized you're not interested and will leave you alone."

"Possibly." She didn't sound convinced. "I feel sorry for his poor dog."

Of course she did. He had to say, he'd never met a woman like Della Winslow. Again, he felt that tug of attraction, so much more than mere sexual desire.

Something must have shown on his face.

"What?" she asked. "Why are you looking at me like that?"

"Like what?" he countered, though he knew.

"As if I just spilled something all over myself."

He laughed. That did it. He could no more stop himself from kissing her than he could keep from breathing. The instant his mouth touched hers, she wrapped her arms around him and kissed him back.

"This," she breathed, her lips still against his. "I needed this."

Addictive, he thought, and he was powerless to stop himself from drowning. Reckless now, he didn't care about anything other than her.

They made it to her bedroom this time, shedding their

clothing as they went. He managed to put on his condom, though his hands shook so badly she had to help him. Her mischievous grin only aroused him more.

Kisses again, urgent and open-mouthed. And hot. So damn hot. Wrapped around each other, they fell onto her bed, she laughing, he trying to keep from losing control too soon. No other woman had ever affected him this way. Never.

Raw and powerful, his naked need fed off hers. And when they came together, their lovemaking was every bit as electrifying as it had been the first time. Maybe even more.

Della. Moving together, her body tightly sheathing him, he called out her name right before he fell into the abyss. She, clenching around him, pulled him back out and into the light. They came together, all at once, and collapsed at the same time. He held her while their breathing and heart rates slowed. She curled into him, drowsy and content, and he kissed the top of her head. Her scent, vanilla and peaches, enveloped him. He felt as if he could lie there and hold her forever.

In the other room, Charlie barked, reminding them that reality still waited. Della stirred, turning in his arms to smile up at him. With her drowsy eyes and tousled hair, her beauty awed and humbled him.

Damned if he wasn't about to get himself into deep, deep trouble. He needed to change his way of thinking. Because once this case was over, he'd be going back to his sterile apartment in Boise and living his life like he had before. Without her.

The thought shouldn't have brought him pain. He

hadn't known her long enough to get too attached. Especially since he didn't do relationships. At all.

But yet again, as he got up off the bed and out of her arms, got dressed and prepared to leave her, instead of feeling sated, he only wanted more.

Yep. Definitely deep, deep trouble.

Unaware of his thoughts, she propped herself up on one elbow and watched as he dressed. The sexy little smile on her beautiful face had him aching to gather her close again. He managed to resist. Even when she stood, the sheet falling from her delectable curves, and wore her clothes with her gaze trained on him, he didn't move.

She showed him out, standing on her toes to press one last kiss on his mouth, before locking the door behind him. Dazed, he walked to his truck, climbed in and started the engine.

All the way home, he tried reasoning with himself. Temporary infatuation, that was what this had to be. Nothing more. Eventually, he'd get Della Winslow out of his system and both their lives would return to normal.

Or would they?

When he got back to the ranch, the last thing he felt like doing was talking to his dad and brothers. Instead of going into the main house, he headed out back to the shed where he stored his woodworking tools. His workshop, the one place on the sprawling ranch that belonged only to him. When he needed to think, whether about a case or something more personal, he'd found the best way to get through his unsettled emotions was to work with wood. He loved everything about the process, from the designing to the carving, the sanding and building and staining. Over the last several years, as he'd honed his skills, he'd gotten really good. He'd made quite a bit of furniture, well enough that one of the shops on Main Street allowed him to display several pieces for sale. He liked to have a decent inventory so he could keep them restocked when they sold, which they did quite often. Every time he came back home, he made time to work on a few things.

Today, he'd work on his favorite—and bestselling—piece. His oversize rocking chairs. He had several in various stages and decided to focus on the ones that were basically finished, except for needing paint or stain. Painting always soothed his soul, which was exactly the kind of thing he needed right now.

The white ones were the most popular. He'd made the chairs in several styles, from modern farmhouse to rustic and sleek modern, to round things out.

He'd also made a few side items, small tables to go alongside the chairs. He'd started work on an ambitious new piece, an outdoor sectional that he'd only just begun putting together.

Grabbing a can of white paint, he got busy. Anytime his thoughts strayed to Della, he redirected them to the case. While the killer had apparently been getting away with this for several years, now that they were on to him, he'd eventually make a mistake.

Also, Max couldn't shake the seemingly random information that Angela had joined a new church right before her death. Once interviews were complete with some of the other victims' family members, they'd know if there was a connection.

For several years, there had been rumors around Owl Creek about some kind of church called the Ever After

Church. Since there wasn't any kind of actual church building, Max guessed maybe they met in individual homes. Which would mean their congregation remained relatively small. At one point, Sebastian Cross, the owner of Crosswinds Training, had been approached by a member of the Ever After Church. This man, Bob, apparently quite wealthy, had tried to buy Crosswinds and the land around it for the church. Sebastian had turned him down, the same way he'd refused to sell to other interested parties over the years.

Since then, Max hadn't heard of any other attempts by the church to purchase land or buildings. Which meant there was one more thing he needed to look into. Tomorrow he'd check property tax records for the county. While the connection might currently seem tenuous, it wouldn't hurt to have all the information in case something developed.

Naturally, thinking of Crosswinds brought Della to mind. Again. He shook his head, wondering why he couldn't seem to get her out of his system. He wasn't even sure he wanted to.

That thought shocked him. While he couldn't deny the strength of the attraction between them, he wasn't in any kind of a position to even attempt to begin a relationship.

But then again, wasn't that what he'd done?

After that thought, no amount of painting could settle him down. Disgusted, Max finished painting the chair he'd started and cleaned everything up. He'd better start worrying about the family dinner tomorrow night. While he was glad he'd invited Della, bringing her with him to something like this meant he'd have to convince his entire family that they were just friends.

Even worse, he'd need to convince himself.

Chapter 8

After Max left, Della went to the front window and watched as he got into his truck. She stood there until his taillights faded into the night. Then she turned and smiled at her dog, who watched her with his head tilted, his tail wagging slowly.

"You like him too, don't you, Charlie?" she asked. "Come on, boy. Let's go outside and then we'll get on the couch and watch some TV."

Charlie barked as if he understood.

A mess of conflicting emotions, Della hoped getting back to routine might help her feel…normal. Once she'd taken care of her dog, the two of them settled onto the sofa and she turned on the television. A crime drama had just come on, one that she normally watched, so hopefully she could get lost in the show.

But she couldn't shut off her mind. She couldn't stop thinking about everything.

Her joy at the burgeoning feelings Max brought was overlaid by her ever-present grief at the loss of her cousin. There was the mystery of who'd killed Angela and wondering if Owl Creek had a serial killer walking among them. Add in the fact that she now had a stalker, and she felt overwhelmed. It was too much. Part of her wanted to run; the other part knew she had to stand her ground and fight for justice for her cousin. And possibly reach out and grab a chance at happiness for herself.

She must have fallen asleep on the couch, because the next thing she knew, she woke up to the sound of Charlie snoring, his furry face a foot or so away. Chuckling, she shook her head and checked the time: 1:00 a.m. She grabbed the remote, turned off the television and whistled for Charlie. Then she and her dog went to bed.

Thursday morning dawned bright and sunny. Sunlight streaming through her bedroom window woke her. She got up, carried her coffee out to the back porch and settled gingerly into her ancient patio chair to watch Charlie play in the yard.

The sun on her skin felt warm, the coffee tasted delightful, and her dog had always been all the company she needed. But she couldn't stop thinking about Max. Not only the explosive and passionate lovemaking they'd shared once again, but the other connection they seemed to have. She didn't think it was all one-sided, but then again, his reputation preceded him.

And tonight, she'd agreed to accompany him to a family dinner. As his *friend*. What the heck had she been thinking?

But hearing him talk about his family and the circumstances behind their meeting tonight, she'd known he needed her support. And she'd be there to give it, no matter how anyone else might view her being in attendance.

Finishing her coffee, she called Charlie inside and made herself an egg-white omelet. After breakfast, she showered and got dressed. Still feeling unsettled and restless, Della decided to go into town and do a little retail therapy. Though she wasn't a big shopper, every now and then she liked to buy a few small items to spruce up her house or something new to wear. Since tonight she'd be meeting Max for dinner with his family, she felt like a new outfit might be in order. At the very least, maybe a new pair of earrings or a necklace.

As she got ready to go, Charlie waited, watching her. When she'd finished, he went to the front door and barked. Tail wagging, panting eagerly, he clearly expected her to take him to Crosswinds to train, like they did most days.

"Not today, boy," she said, petting him. "It's going to be a day off for both of us. But if you're a good boy while I'm gone, I just might bring you something from that dog bakery in that pet store downtown."

Charlie barked again, as if he understood. He went and curled up in his oversize dog bed and watched her as she made herself a large cup of coffee to go.

There were only a couple of stores downtown that sold clothing. She decided she'd check all of them out before stopping at her favorite place, a resale shop tucked away on a back street where she'd found some fabulous clothes in the past.

Walking down the sidewalk on Main Street, she skipped all the stores where she usually shopped for things for her home. Today would be one of the rare days where she concentrated only on herself.

She found a beautiful pair of silver earrings in one of the tourist shops. A good start. She purchased them and browsed through the clothing racks, which consisted mostly of souvenir T-shirts. Not what she needed.

The next shop was a place she'd purchased clothes from before. Since she'd decided to wear jeans tonight, she needed a new shirt. However, the instant she walked inside, she caught sight of a soft pale green dress in a baby-doll style that she knew would be flattering. The first thing she noticed when she picked it up was the pockets. And it was in her size. Even better, the price seemed reasonable. Though she didn't need it for the barbecue dinner tonight, surely there'd be another occasion where she could wear it.

Max came instantly to mind, which made her blush. Shaking her head at her own foolishness, she carried the dress over to the changing room to try it on.

It fit exactly the way she'd known it would. Twirling in front of the full-length mirror, she felt pretty in a way she had never felt before.

He'd called her beautiful. Over the years, other men had paid her compliments. She'd paid them no mind, certain they'd all had ulterior motives. But Max, who admittedly was one of the most handsome men she'd ever met, had meant it. As corny as it might sound, she'd seen his reaction to her appearance in the depths of his light blue eyes.

She took off the dress and put her own clothes back on. Then, before she could talk herself out of it, she went to the counter and paid.

After that, she went to the resale shop, but nothing there caught her eye. Surely, she could find something in her closet to wear along with her favorite pair of jeans. Max had said the dinner would be casual, after all.

Back at the house, Charlie greeted her and then, after a quick trip outside, curled up in his bed to resume his nap. Nerves still humming, Della did some housework, wishing she could stop feeling so nervous. This wasn't a big deal. Just dinner with a friend and his family. But for whatever reason, it felt like more.

That afternoon, she must have changed her outfit six times, trying for the right mixture of casual but not too much so. Since the dinner would be held at a barbecue place, she'd decided on jeans and boots. It was deciding on the right top and accessories that had her wavering between frustration and indecision. Worse, she didn't know why she cared so much. Max would definitely make sure his family knew that she was just his friend, not a date.

Except this felt like a date. More than a date. A take-your-girlfriend-to-meet-your-family kind of thing. She wasn't Max's girlfriend, though, no matter how much it felt like she was.

Finally, she chose a pretty black shoulder-less top, her new dangly silver earrings and several silver bracelets. That done, she took care with her makeup. Usually, she went with the bare minimum, going for a natural look. Tonight, she tried for more of a glam look, using the eye-shadow techniques one of her girlfriends in college had taught her. When she'd finished, she peered at herself in the mirror, added some neutral lipstick and smiled.

Then she got dressed, choosing a pair of black boots with a slight heel. She'd barely finished adding her jewelry when the doorbell rang.

The sound made her heart stutter in her chest. Though she knew she shouldn't, she secretly hoped her appearance would knock Max Colton's socks off. This despite the fact that they'd agreed they were only friends and occasional coworkers. Who'd made love twice now and probably would again. She knew that she shouldn't harbor this secret desire to wow him, but she did.

Hurrying to get the door, her boot heels clicking on the hardwood floors, she took a deep breath before turning the handle. Charlie, who'd heard the doorbell, pranced around her in excitement, his tail wagging furiously.

She opened the door, and her heart stuttered as she took in Max, his broad shoulders filling her doorway. Tonight, he'd gone with a Western shirt and jeans, along with a pair of brown ostrich-skin boots.

"Come on in," she said, stepping aside so Max could enter. Next to her, Charlie sat waiting, panting happily as he waited for Max to notice him.

But Max didn't budge. Instead, he stood frozen, staring at her as if she'd suddenly grown two heads.

Sudden insecurity grabbed her. Maybe she'd overdone it. Perhaps she wasn't as great at putting on makeup as she'd thought. Could her outfit be too much, or too little, or...?

"You look gorgeous," Max said, his voice raspy. He finally stepped inside, closing the door behind him, all without taking his eyes off her. Charlie barked happily, butting Max with his head so he'd pet him. Absently, Max reached down and scratched her dog behind the ears, still staring at Della.

She stared back. Her entire body felt warm and tingly. He'd said *gorgeous*. Better than *beautiful*. Though she'd never really cared what she looked like, tonight she did. She'd take it.

More grateful for the compliment than she should have been, and wondering where the weird insecurity had come from, she finally managed to break her trance. Looking away, she smiled and thanked him. Max smiled back and ruffled Charlie's fur, continuing to scratch him behind his ears. Charlie leaned into him, clearly in canine heaven.

Warmth spread through her, watching as her beloved dog thoroughly enjoyed Max's attention. Charlie liked him, and if there was ever a good judge of character, it was Charlie. Prior reputation or not, her instincts said Max was a good man, a kind man and, more importantly, her friend. Charlie's approval simply confirmed it.

Time to reclaim her sense of self and stop all this nonsense clattering around inside of her head. Charlie glanced at her as if he agreed, his long tail still wagging.

"Are you ready?" she asked, once Max straightened. "I've been dying to try that barbecue. When they first opened, it was so crowded, with over an hour's wait. I decided to try it later, once the novelty had worn off, but I haven't managed to make it in yet."

Still staring at her, he finally blinked. "I haven't been there either. Honestly, a barbecue place seems like an odd choice to meet two new half siblings, but what do I know?"

She kind of agreed with him there. "I'm thinking whoever chose it is trying to go with a casual atmosphere."

"Maybe so." He held the door open for her and then waited while she locked it. When they reached his truck, he did the same.

Once he'd started the engine, he turned and looked at her. "We reserved an entire section of the restaurant," he said. "Even so, it'll likely be crowded. I just wanted to warn you."

"Thanks. I figured. Since you have two families coming, one with six siblings, one with four, plus add in their spouses or dates or whatever, as well as the two newcomers, who also probably wanted to bring support, it only makes sense."

He nodded. "Yep. No reason to be nervous."

Confident Della had returned, thank goodness. "I'm not. I went to school with some of these people, you know. Since my boss, Sebastian, got engaged to your cousin Ruby, I'm sure he's going to be there. I've also worked with others at Crosswinds. And Malcolm and I have done a couple of search and rescue operations before. So we're not all total strangers. It's inevitable that we'd know each other, especially in such a small town."

"True." As he watched her, his gaze had darkened. "Damn, I'd like to kiss you right now. But I don't want to ruin your lipstick."

Heat flooded her. Taking a deep breath, she leaned forward, keeping her eyes locked on his. "I have the lipstick in my purse. I can always touch it up."

Instead of waiting for him to follow through, she pulled his face down to hers. If she'd needed a reason to question why she felt they were more than merely friends, this would be it. This soul-searching electricity that flared between them every time they touched. And the instant their lips met, neither of them seemed to be very good at maintaining control.

The realization that her aunt and uncle next door could walk out at any moment and see her making out with the notorious playboy Max Colton was the only thing that made Della pull back. Heart racing, desire turning her body to a puddle of need, she sat back in her seat and stared at him.

Chest heaving, pupils dilated, Max seemed to be having just as much difficulty reining himself in. "Damn," he managed. "If this dinner wasn't so important to my family, I'd say forget about it and take you back inside to finish what we just started."

She gave a strangled laugh. "None of that," she said, though she secretly wanted to do the same. "Plus, there's always afterward."

Since making out with Della like a randy teenager in the front seat of his truck had damn near decimated him, Max knew he had to get his arousal under control before walking into the restaurant and facing his family. He glanced sideways at Della. Her swollen lips and tousled hair gave her the appearance of a woman who'd been thoroughly kissed.

Then she mentioned what they might do after the dinner, and now making love to her was all he could think about. Judging by her flushed complexion and dilated pupils, she felt the same.

They'd need a little bit of time to get their composure together. While he didn't want to be late, he also didn't want anyone in his family to know he and Della had been kissing. If they figured it out, the teasing would be unmerciful.

"Are you okay?" Della asked, her voice a little unsteady. "Maybe we should drive around a few minutes before we go in?"

Her comment, oddly enough, helped defuse some of his tension. "My thoughts exactly," he replied. "We've just got to clear our heads."

"I know what would help. Classic rock," she said. Reaching for his radio dial, she glanced at him. "Do you mind if I change the station?"

Curious, he shrugged. "Do your thing."

With a few turns of the knob, she put the radio on 96.9 The Eagle, Boise's classic rock station. The Rolling Stones came on, singing about "Satisfaction." Without hesitation, Della turned up the volume and began singing along, slightly off-key.

"Come on," she urged, elbowing him. "It'll help get your mind off other things."

What could he do but join her?

To his surprise, by the time they reached the restaurant, his almost painful arousal had subsided, and he felt...normal. Happy even. He didn't even feel the need to drive around the block a couple more times.

Pulling into the parking lot, he turned the volume down. "Thank you," he told her. "That really helped."

Her infectious grin had him smiling back. "Music helps almost anything."

He found a spot next to a sleek Mercedes and parked. They were only ten minutes late. Perfect timing, since he hadn't wanted to be the first one there nor the last. By now, he figured about half of the group would have arrived, with the rest of them straggling in over the next ten or fifteen minutes.

"Let's go," he said. Jumping out, he hurried over to the passenger side so he could help her down.

She took his arm and lifted her face to sniff the air. "That smells absolutely amazing. Nothing like some good smoked brisket."

Leave it to her to focus on the food. And she was right—the aroma coming from the place made his mouth water.

Side by side, they walked to the door. Once he opened

it for her and they were in, she slipped her hand into his. Enchanted way more than he should have been, he followed the sign toward the back part of the restaurant where his family had reserved a private room.

A quick scan of the people there told him his new half siblings weren't yet in attendance.

The first people he spotted were his cousin Ruby and Della's boss, Sebastian Cross, standing very close to each other. Max had never seen a couple more meant for each other than those two. Ruby gazed up into Sebastian's rugged face with an adoring look, totally engrossed in whatever he had to say.

Grinning, Della dragged Max over. "Sebastian! And Ruby! It's so good to see you. Have you eaten here before?"

The two turned, Sebastian smiling. "Della! I didn't know you'd be here." And then, as he realized she and Max were holding hands, his smile faltered, and he frowned. "May I have a word with you privately?"

Though Della's smile wavered, she agreed. "Excuse me one minute," she told Max. "I'll be right back."

When she and her boss moved away, Ruby crossed her arms and glared at him. "I went to school with Della Winslow," she said. "She's a good person. I like her."

Pretending not to understand the warning note in her voice, Max nodded. "I like her too."

"You know what I mean," Ruby continued. "She's not your usual type. If you think you can treat her the same way you have the others, you can't. You'll break her heart."

With that, she spun on her heel and stormed off, back to where Sebastian appeared to be lecturing Della.

When Ruby reached them, Della made her escape, hurrying back over to Max.

"Whew." Shaking her head, she took his arm. "Ruby looked pretty intense. What was that all about?"

"Ruby wanted to warn me not to hurt you," he replied. "And judging from the way Sebastian is glowering at me, he said something similar to you."

"He did. He's like family to me. He's always been a little overprotective, but he acts like he's really worried about me being with you. I tried to tell him that we're only friends, but he didn't seem convinced."

Likely because they'd been holding hands. Though tempted to reach for her hand again, he didn't. Instead, he kept her arm tucked into his.

"Well, let's not let those two ruin our evening," Max said. "Come on. Let me introduce you to the rest of my family."

Though he should have known it was coming, the way his family gave him and Della strange looks hurt Max's feelings. Sure, she wasn't his usual type of date. Those women had been placeholders, he realized. He'd purposely dated women who didn't expect anything but a good time, and once he gave them that, they went their separate ways.

But Della... They were *friends*, he reminded himself. Not dating. Because he definitely didn't want to think about why being with her felt a million times better than any other woman.

His cousin Fletcher had his arm around Kiki Shelton, a vibrant, dark-haired woman who was the perfect counterpoint for the more serious Fletcher. Kiki and Della appeared to hit it off right from the start, chattering happily together while more and more family members arrived. Listening in, Max realized Kiki had a foster dog named Fancy and she'd been training her at Crosswinds. Since talking about dogs was one of Della's passions, the two women had lots to discuss.

The restaurant had set up three long tables each with about ten chairs. Patrons had to go up to the front counter, grab a plastic tray and order their meal. Their choices were sliced and dished up right in front of them and placed on a plate. Once they'd paid and gotten their drink, they carried the tray to the table to eat. Someone went around with a basket full of rolls. If it tasted as good as it smelled, they were in for a treat.

Max ordered the brisket, and after a moment's hesitation, Della did the same. For his two sides, he chose potato salad and pinto beans. Della got macaroni and cheese and green beans. They both got iced tea.

As soon as they'd taken their seats and unloaded their trays, a strange hush came over the room. Max glanced up and realized Nathan and Sarah Colton, his mother and Uncle Robert's other two children, had arrived. Though he'd suspected his mother wouldn't come, nonetheless he was relieved when he didn't see her. Since Jessie hadn't bothered to make contact with any of her other children for years, why would she suddenly care to do so now?

"Welcome!" Since she hadn't yet gotten her food or taken a seat, Max's sister, Lizzy, greeted them. She'd come alone and, smiling, led Nathan and Sarah around the room, introducing them to their half siblings. Max had a moment to consider how strange they must feel, knowing some were related to their mother and others to their father.

When Lizzy reached Max and Della, she eyed Max. "Are you here with Della?" she asked, her brows raised.

"I am." Keeping his smile firmly in place, Max turned to Nathan and Sarah. Nathan towered over his sister, but they both had the exact same smile. "I swear I've seen you before," Max commented to Sarah.

"You probably have," she replied, her green eyes twinkling. "I'm a librarian. I work in the main branch of the Boise Public Library."

"That must be where. I live in Boise." Max shook her hand before eyeing her brother. "And I understand you're in law enforcement."

"That's correct." Unlike his sister, Nathan Colton appeared slightly uneasy. "I've heard you're with the FBI?"

"I am."

Lizzy tugged Sarah away, leaving Nathan to follow.

"We'll talk more later," Max said, watching as Lizzy introduced the two to more of his family members.

"That didn't seem so awkward," Della mused. She picked up her fork and dug in.

A moment later, Max did the same. Though the meal had cooled slightly, the tender brisket had a wonderful smoky flavor. "This is really good," he said.

"Yes, it is." She nodded. "You sound surprised."

Since he'd just taken another bite, he chewed and swallowed before answering. "I wasn't sure what to expect. Idaho isn't exactly known for good barbecue."

They finished their meal, talking in between bites. All of Max's earlier apprehension had vanished, mostly due to how comfortable Della seemed. Anytime one of his cousins stopped by, she seemed to instinctively know exactly the right thing to say.

Max couldn't help but notice his oldest brother stayed far on the other side of the room. Greg seemed intent on inhaling his food. Malcolm walked in, spotted Della and made a beeline toward her.

"Hey, Max," he said, then turned his attention to Della. "I heard you and Charlie were the ones who made the discovery up on the hiking trail."

"We were." Smiling up at him, she stabbed the last bit of her green beans and popped them in her mouth.

Suddenly, Malcolm seemed to realize Della had come with Max. Eyes narrowed, he looked from one to the other. "How do you two know each other?" he asked. Then, before either of them could respond, he answered his own question. "Let me guess. This is the case that brought Max home."

"Bingo," Max replied. He fought the urge to put his arm around Della's shoulders, aware he had no right to feel so possessive. However, watching her smile at his brother brought on a flash of jealousy so strong he frowned.

Malcolm, somehow seeming to sense this, grinned. "Take good care of her, little brother," he teased. "Della is pretty damn special."

Then, before Max could respond, Malcolm walked away.

Expression bemused, Della watched him go. "What was that all about?" she asked. "I get that you have a reputation, but why is everyone so worried about me? Not only can I take care of myself, but we've told them all that we're just friends."

He managed a casual shrug, pretending to be wounded. "I don't know what you've heard about me, but it's likely not true."

This made her laugh. "You forget, I've lived in Owl Creek my entire life. And while you graduated high school the year before I started, your reputation precedes you."

For the first time in his life, he found himself regretting the way he'd avoided any kind of long-term relationship. But then again, maybe there'd been a reason. He doubted he could have gotten to this point in his career if he'd allowed himself to get bogged down. Now he had to wonder if any of it had been worth it.

"Hey, Max, do you have a minute?" His cousin Chase, CEO of Colton Properties, dropped into the seat across from him. Chase glanced at Della and smiled. "In private, if you don't mind."

Della stood. "That's my hint to make a trip to the ladies' room. Gentlemen, please excuse me."

Max watched her as she walked away. When he looked back at Chase, the other man shook his head. "Man, you really have it bad."

Since he suspected his cousin was right, instead of responding to this, Max asked what Chase needed.

"I have some issues going on with Colton Properties," Chase said. "I don't really want to go into detail, but I'd like to have a security team take a look at my system. Since you're with the FBI, I figured you might have a recommendation."

"SecuritKey is the best in the industry," Max replied. "They're pretty exclusive. They don't even advertise, but I can put you in touch with the owner. Her name is Sloan Presley."

"Thank you." Chase looked past Max and smiled. "Della's coming back. She's a keeper, you know." With that, he stood, clapped Max on the shoulder and rejoined the small group at one of the tables.

"Is everything okay?" Della asked, sliding back into her chair.

Instantly, the annoyance he'd felt from Chase's last comment vanished. "Never been better," he replied. "Let's go talk to Nathan and Sarah one last time and then we can go."

Smiling, Della came with him, though this time she didn't hold his hand. He couldn't help but wish she would.

Standing close to his sister, Nathan looked up when the two of them approached. Sarah's smile faltered around the edges. She looked exhausted. Even Nathan had a bit of fatigue around his blue eyes. Initially, Max hadn't wanted to like either, but Sarah pulled on his heartstrings and Nate seemed like an upstanding guy.

"We'll have to get together again sometime," he said, clapping his new half brother on the back. "Like you can probably tell, we're all open to expanding our family. The only stipulation is you should know I have no intention of meeting with our mother."

At the mention of Jessie, Nathan's smile vanished. "That's good, because I doubt she wants to meet with you either," he said, grimacing.

Despite everything, hearing that hurt more than it should.

As if she sensed this, Della slipped her hand into his.

Chapter 9

"That was something else," Della said. Never had she been so glad to leave a restaurant. She hadn't known she could feel so protective toward Max, but she did. Though he hadn't outwardly reacted to his half brother's statement, she'd seen the flash of pain in his eyes. When she'd taken his hand and squeezed, he'd held on tightly as if she was some kind of lifeline.

No matter how awful they might be, she suspected no one ever outgrew the need for their mother. Even Nathan and Sarah had looked pained when they'd talked about their mother.

"I left home as soon as I could," Nathan had continued, apparently oblivious. "She's always been pretty awful, as I'm sure you know."

"I do," Max had agreed, still clutching Della's hand. He gestured around the room. "We all do."

"Well, she's gotten worse ever since she joined that weird church," Sarah had interjected. "You can't even talk to her now."

At the word *church*, Max had tensed. He'd asked a few more questions, but as soon as he learned Jessie had joined the Ever After Church, he'd been ready to go.

He was unusually quiet as he drove her home, and

Della figured he needed time lost in his own head. When they finally pulled up into her driveway, he leaned over and kissed her on the cheek, clearly distracted. "Thanks for coming with me," he said. "I really appreciate it."

"Did you want to come in?" she offered, even though she felt pretty sure he didn't.

"Not this time." He shook his head. "I can't help but feel there's something I'm overlooking. I need to investigate how far that church has reached."

"The Ever After Church?" For years, fringe members had been hanging around town. There'd been rumors they wanted to build an actual physical building, maybe even some sort of compound, but nothing had ever come of it. At least not that she knew of.

"Yes." His clipped answer made her study him. As she realized what he might mean, she sat up straight.

"Are you thinking they might have had something to do with Angela's—and others'—murder?" she asked.

"I don't know. But I'm sure as hell going to look into it." Meeting her gaze, he grimaced. "Any other time, you know I'd come in. But I'm looking at several hours of computer work, and you are way too much of a distraction."

This made her smile. She leaned over and kissed him softly. "Another time, then."

"Definitely." He checked out his fitness tracker watch. "I've got to go. I'd like to get started on it right away."

She opened her door. "Thanks for inviting me," she said. "I had a nice evening. I'll talk to you later. Please, if you learn anything interesting, let me know."

"I will," he said, waiting until she'd reached her front door and unlocked it before putting his truck in Reverse.

After watching him drive away, she went inside. Charlie danced around, greeting her as if she'd been gone for days instead of hours. She got down on the floor with him, returning his affection as effusively as he gave it.

Once she'd let him out and back in, she went to change into her pajamas and wash off her makeup. She'd enjoyed the evening more than she'd thought she would, at least right up until the end, when Nathan had made that offhand comment to Max. Growing up in Owl Creek, she knew most of the Colton family by sight. Despite being legends around town, especially because of Colton Properties, she found them surprisingly down-to-earth.

And while there definitely had been a bit of dysfunction there, relating to Jessie and Robert Colton, she couldn't exactly blame them. Anyone would be bitter after being ditched by a parent. Parents weren't supposed to abandon their children. The one thing kids should be able to count on was their mother or father's unconditional love.

Though she was enough of a realist to understand this wasn't always the case, it tore at her heartstrings to know Max and his siblings had never known what she had. She missed her mother still, with every fiber of her being, and she'd always be grateful to have had that kind of maternal love.

She and Charlie settled on the couch to watch a movie. Charlie was one of the few dogs who watched television with her. Snuggling into her side, he kept his eyes fixed on the TV until he finally grew tired and dozed off.

Though tempted to text Max since she couldn't stop thinking about him, she didn't. Instead, she finished the movie, took Charlie out once again and went to bed.

The next morning, she had a full day scheduled at Crosswinds. She wanted to get in there early, since she needed to fit all six of her charges in, plus make time to train Charlie.

When she woke, the first thing she did was check her phone. No message from Max or anyone else. Chiding herself for acting like a teenager with a crush, she drank her coffee while she got ready. She made herself a protein smoothie to go, and she and Charlie got on the road shortly after sunrise.

The orange-and-pink sky lightened her heart. She arrived at Crosswinds, parked and hurried inside with Charlie.

After placing Charlie in a sit-stay, Della went back to get one of the newer dogs she'd started training, a Belgian Malinois named Beth. Beth was young, barely nine months old, but she'd been started on basic obedience training and the myriad of desensitizing and socialization work required of a good SAR dog.

Beth had a bit of a reactive personality, but once she settled down and got to work, Della was able to get her to focus.

She'd been training in the ring thirty minutes when she looked up to find Sebastian standing near the entrance to the ring, watching her.

"Do you have a minute?" he asked. "When you're all done, of course."

Hoping he wasn't going to lecture her on Max Colton again, she nodded. "I'm just about finished with Beth here. Let me take her outside and I'll be right with you."

Clearly tired, Beth had just started to pant. Della knew

if she had pressed her too much longer, the young dog would shut down.

After taking Beth outside, Della returned her to the kennel. Of the ten dogs currently on the property, she worked with six while Sebastian took the other four. Between those and her new classes for the general public, she kept busy. Of course, if she got called out on a SAR mission, her boss would have to take over everything until she got back.

When she returned, Sebastian had taken a seat in the small office they both used for paperwork. "Pull up a chair," he said. "I'm wondering how you've been holding up since your cousin's death."

Unbidden tears filled her eyes. Blinking them away, she dropped into a seat. "I'm doing okay," she replied. "The FBI has promised to keep in touch with any new info regarding the case."

"FBI being Max Colton?"

Deliberately holding his gaze, she nodded. "He's a good guy, Sebastian. I promise."

"I never doubted that. He's just not your type."

Della bit back a retort and nodded instead.

"I'm aware it's not any of my business," Sebastian continued. "But you're like a sister to me and I'd hate to see you get hurt."

"I know." She smiled. "And I appreciate that. But since we've already had this discussion, do you mind if we don't do it again?"

This made him chuckle. "Point made." He took a deep breath. "I also wanted to ask how the classes are going. I heard there was an incident with one of the clients?"

"I can't believe I forgot to tell you." She relayed everything that had happened with Hal. "While I feel bad for his dog, I don't want him back on the property."

Grim-faced, he nodded. "I one hundred percent agree. I'll take care of it. And, please, let me know if this man bothers you again."

"I will. Since I have classes again tonight, I'm hoping he doesn't show up. Pepper did call him and let him know his class fee would be refunded since he's now banned from the premises."

Sebastian nodded. "All I can say is after what happened before, we are definitely prepared to deal with someone like him this time."

Della knew he referred to a few months ago, when it seemed like Crosswinds had been under attack almost constantly. "Thank you."

"One of my dogs is being picked up by his new handler later today," Sebastian said. "I'll be spending the afternoon working with them before they head back to Denver. I can take over one of your dogs once Silver is gone."

"That would be great," she said. "If you don't mind, would you take Chadwick? He's the newest and I've barely started training him." She laughed. "There aren't enough hours in the day sometimes."

"I'll take him," Sebastian said. "As a matter of fact, I can start working with him right now."

Thanking him, Della went to get her next dog. She knew her limitations and tried to stick to four dogs before lunch, and if she felt up to it, she did a little light work with some of her new ones.

After an hour of ring work with her next dog, Della decided to take an early, and long, lunch. She took Charlie home and scarfed down a quick sandwich. Then, with a little extra time on her hands, she decided to go into town and do some purposeful shopping.

Though her budget didn't allow for many extravagances, she usually allowed herself to buy one decorative or household item each season. For summer, she'd planned to purchase a few pieces of outdoor furniture, specifically chairs and possibly a small table to put in between them.

Now here it was actually August, and she hadn't been able to find anything she liked that she could afford. "Champagne tastes," she told herself. She hadn't been able to stop thinking about the handmade rocking chairs she'd seen for sale in a shop downtown called Angus's Whatnots. The sign on the display only said they'd been crafted by a local artist, which actually endeared them to her even more.

What she liked best about them was their quirkiness. They were big and clunky, yet sleek and well-made. The ones she wanted had been stained a dark mahogany and she could just picture one on her back porch.

Since they were a bit pricey, she told herself one was all she needed for right now. Once she had it, she could sit out on her back patio and rock while she drank her coffee. And she could finally get rid of the beat-up old chair she'd gotten at a garage sale.

Decision made, she hopped into her Jeep and drove into town. She could only hope the one she wanted would still be there, because the salesperson she'd talked to had mentioned the chairs were extremely popular.

To her relief, it appeared several of the white painted chairs had sold but the two dark-stained ones were still there, along with a small table clearly built to sit in between them.

Exhaling, she checked the price tag again, just in case they'd gone on sale. Nope. Still the same price, just high enough to make her feel a teeny bit nauseated. "You get what you pay for," she muttered under her breath and turned to head up to the counter to make her purchase.

The teenager working the register grinned when she told him she wanted to buy one of the chairs. "They're pretty popular," he agreed. "How many do you want?"

About to say just the one, she considered. "How often does the person who makes them bring in new inventory?"

"When stock gets low," he answered. "My dad owns the store and he likes to keep more of the white ones around, since people seem to want those the most."

"I want the dark brown," she said. "Just one. And I'll take the little table too." The last had been an impulse, but it felt right.

"Only one?" the kid asked, clearly dismayed. "Most people buy two."

"I just need one, thank you."

He shrugged and rang her up.

She managed not to wince when she heard the total. "Here you go," she said, counting out cash and handing it over.

Brows raised, he recounted it before putting it into his register and giving her the change. "Not many people pay with cash these days," he commented.

"It's how I roll." She only used credit cards in an emergency.

"Do you need some help loading it up?" he asked.

"Yes, please." She hadn't thought about what she'd do once she got home. Hopefully, she could manage to wrestle the thing from her Jeep and onto her back porch. She wasn't sure about navigating the stairs, though. Maybe she'd call Max and see if he could help her.

Once he'd carried the chair and small table out for her and loaded them into the back of her Jeep, she realized she could actually fit the other chair if she wanted to buy it. For whatever reason, she kept picturing sitting out on the back porch with Max, each of them in their own chair. She had enough cash with her to cover it.

"You know what?" she said. "I just decided. I'll take the other matching chair too."

Instead of reacting with surprise, the kid fist-bumped the air. "Yessss! I knew it. Come on back inside and let me ring you up, and then I'll bring it out for you."

Once everything had been loaded up into her Jeep, Della thanked her helper and got in to drive home. She didn't want to think about how she'd get all this unloaded and up to her porch. While she supposed she could always call Max, part of her wanted to surprise him with the chairs. After all, she'd bought the second one because she could so easily picture the two of them sitting out there with their morning coffee.

Since the furniture took up so much space and blocked her view out the back window, Della didn't notice the vehicle following her until she turned into her driveway and it did too. Parking right behind her, it blocked her in. A black Honda with black rims. Hal's car.

Heart pounding, she made sure her doors were locked and got out her phone in case she needed to call 911.

Hal got out and sauntered over. Expression amused,

he motioned for her to roll down her window. When she shook her head, his gaze narrowed, and his smile vanished.

"Get out of the car," he ordered. "Now."

"Go away," she responded, desperately trying to figure out what to do now. She couldn't help hoping when he saw she wasn't receptive, he'd simply leave.

When he turned and went back to his vehicle, she held her breath. But instead of getting in and driving off, he retrieved what looked like a metal baseball bat and came back. He rapped sharply on the driver's-side glass.

"Don't make me have to break your window," he said, his confident smile chilling her to the bone.

Even so, a flash of anger mixed in with her fear. "And then what?" she asked, speaking loud enough so he could hear her. "Once you take out your frustration on my Jeep, what are you planning to do?"

"What I should have done the first day that I met you," he answered. "Make you mine."

Heart pounding, fingers shaking, she dialed 911. As she did, he raised the bat and shattered her window.

The night before, Max had gone down a rabbit hole with the Ever After Church. After leaving Della's house, he'd driven straight to the ranch and holed himself up in his room. After hours scouring the internet as well as accessing FBI data on the church, he hadn't come up with anything concrete that might have tied them to the serial killer.

He'd gone to bed with a headache and his eyes burning. When he got up in the morning, later than he usually did, all he could think of was Della and the way he'd brushed her off the night before.

The house had been empty, since no self-respecting rancher ever wasted a sunrise.

Since he had a Zoom meeting scheduled with the team at ten, he had enough time to grab a shower and down a couple of cups of strong black coffee before sitting down with his laptop and logging in to the meeting.

First, Caroline gave her report on her efforts to identify the last three bodies. So far, she hadn't met with any success. She'd even scoured missing person databases looking for anything that might be close enough.

"What about you, Max?" Brian asked. "Any new leads on your end?"

"Della said Angela had mentioned joining a new church," Max said. "But no one seems to have any concrete information on it. We don't know what it was called or where it was located. I've kind of wondered if there was any connection with the other victims, though the distance might rule that out."

"With Angela in Montana and the others from other places in the tristate area, the possibility of them all belonging to the same church is a long shot," Brian mused.

Max took a deep breath and then told them about the Ever After Church. "It seems to bear a lot of similarities with a cult."

Brian nodded. "Continue to dig on that one. It's all we've got right now, and the media is really putting the pressure on us. I even took a call from Senator McCutchin the other day, wondering how close we are to catching this guy."

Everyone looked grim.

"Caroline, have you found any other possible connections?" Brian asked.

"Other than the various physical similarities—age, gender and build—no," Caroline replied. "We've got all of them but those three identified and next of kin has been notified. I'll email you all the list and last-known locations."

"Thank you," Brian said. "As soon as we have that, the team can begin the interview process. I'll be assigning each of you some to work on."

Max cleared his throat. "I'd like to deal with all the ones who lived close to Owl Creek," he said. "Since I'm already here."

Brian nodded. "Done. I'll give everyone their assignments once I review Caroline's information." He took a deep breath. "I don't have to remind you all that we have a ticking clock on this case. We need to catch this killer as soon as possible."

They went over statistics, discussed the various missing person databases and the ongoing search for various police reports mentioning attacks on women by unrelated men. Brian had assigned Theo and Chris to sift through those.

After nearly ninety minutes, the meeting wrapped up. As soon as he clicked *Exit*, Max closed his laptop and phoned Della. When she didn't answer, he left her a message, asking her to call him. Just in case, he also sent a text. He figured she was working at Crosswinds, and it would make sense for her to mute her phone when training dogs.

He stood and stretched, checking his phone one more time, even though barely a minute had passed. He wasn't usually so impatient, but he found himself longing to see her.

As a matter of fact, he might as well just head on over there. Ever since she'd told him about that former client stalking her, he'd been uneasy. A bit worried too, though hopefully the guy had taken the hint and would now leave her alone. Still, it wouldn't hurt for Max to check on her. Maybe he could take her to lunch so he could explain his abrupt departure last night. Just the thought of seeing her again immediately lightened his mood.

On the way, Max even considered stopping in town and getting Della flowers. Damn, he had it bad. He ended up shelving this idea. If he were to show up at Crosswinds with a bouquet for her, that would certainly start the gossip mill up again.

When he pulled up in the parking lot, he didn't see Della's Jeep. Parking, he tried calling her again. Still no answer. He sent another quick text just in case, but nothing.

As he was debating whether to go inside and ask, Sebastian walked out. Max got out of his truck and met the other man halfway. "Any idea where I might find Della?" he asked.

Sebastian smiled. "She said she was going to take a long lunch and maybe do some shopping. I'd check town first. Have you tried calling her?"

"I have, but she's not answering. She also hasn't responded to my texts." He shrugged. "I can't help but worry. She told me about that former client who was stalking her."

Now Sebastian's smile turned into a frown. "Yeah, I called that guy and banned him from Crosswinds. To make sure there's no misunderstanding, I even refunded his class fee."

"Thank you." Max nodded. "I guess I'll head into town and see if I can meet up with her."

"Knock yourself out," Sebastian said. "Listen, Ruby says you're a good guy. But I want you to know that I consider Della family. Don't do anything to hurt her, or you'll be answering to me."

Solemnly, Max nodded. "I won't. And I appreciate you for saying that. It's good to know she has so many people in her corner."

The two men shook hands. Then Max got into his truck and drove into town, hoping he'd be lucky enough to find Della.

Up and down Main Street, looking for her Jeep, he began to feel a little bit stalkerish himself. Still, he couldn't seem to shake the feeling that something might be wrong.

After making one final pass by the shops, he decided to head to her house. Maybe she'd done some whirlwind shopping and gone home to take a nap. Though that didn't explain why she wasn't answering her phone or his texts.

On the way to Della's place, two Owl Creek cruisers came up behind him, lights flashing and sirens blaring. He pulled over and they blasted on past.

Were they heading to her house? Heart pounding, Max pulled back onto the road. Stomping the accelerator to the floor, he followed the flashing lights all the way to Della's house.

Sure enough, both police cars pulled up in front of her place. Max parked right behind them and jumped out, flashing his FBI badge so they wouldn't attempt to make him leave. Her Jeep sat in the driveway, blocked in by a black Honda. Then he saw the glass on the pavement and realized the driver's-side window had been shattered.

His heart stuttered in his chest. He wanted to bellow her name but knew better. All he could think about with every ragged breath was that Della had to be okay.

"We received a 911 call from this location," one of the uniformed officers informed him. "The caller didn't identify herself, only started screaming."

Max cursed. "Anything else I need to know?"

"That's all we have."

Drawing his gun, Max gestured at them to do the same. "This is a personal friend of mine. A man has been stalking her and I suspect that might be his vehicle back there."

They approached the front door with their weapons drawn. One of the officers broke away and headed around toward the back. The fence gate was locked, however, so he didn't get very far.

Taking the lead, Max tried the front door. Unlocked. As he stepped into the foyer, he heard Charlie. The dog seemed to be alternating between growling and snarling.

"FBI," Max called out. "Della, it's me. If you can, let me know you're safe."

A second later, Della came around the corner. Disheveled, with darkening bruises around her throat, but alive. She was carrying a metal baseball bat.

"He's in there." She pointed toward her living room. "Charlie's keeping him down."

Max motioned to the two officers. Moving together, they turned the corner, where they found a bloody man backed into a corner, hands up, guarded by a ferocious-looking Charlie.

Della called her dog to her. The instant Charlie left his post, the intruder stood up. "I demand you arrest her," he said. "Her dog attacked me."

"Inside of her own home," Max pointed out, throttling the urge to put his hands around this man's throat the way he'd clearly done to Della. "I'm guessing you must be Hal?"

Though surprise flickered across the other man's face, he slowly nodded.

"Della?" Without turning to look at her, Max kept his gaze and his gun trained on Hal. "Please tell us exactly what happened here."

"Charlie's hurt," she said. "That man—Hal—followed me again. This time, I didn't notice him right away. After he blocked me in my own driveway, he broke my car window with his bat. He dragged me out of the car, choked me and forced me into the house." She took a deep, shaky breath. "But he didn't count on Charlie. I was able to get this baseball bat away from him, but not before he used it on my dog."

Tears streaming down her face, she knelt and began gently running her hands over Charlie's thick black fur. Tail wagging, he licked her face. He didn't yelp, not once.

Max inclined his head toward the police officers. "Go ahead and arrest him."

"For what?" Hal asked, his defiant expression aligned with his suddenly combative posture. "She invited me in here and then set her dog on me. If anyone should be arrested, I'd think it'd be her."

Ignoring this, one of the policemen began reading Hal his rights, while the other one cuffed him.

Hal began shouting curses, calling Della every vile

name he could. Shaking his head, the officer turned and marched Hal out the door, with the stalker cursing at Della the entire time he was led away.

"Is Charlie okay?" Max knelt down next to the two of them.

"I don't know," she replied, still silently crying. "I want to take him into the vet just to make sure. Will you call Ruby and see if she can fit him in?"

"Give me a minute," Max said. Instead of calling, he sent his cousin a text asking if he could call her. Ruby responded almost immediately, saying she'd just finished with a patient and yes, he could, if he made it quick.

Once she answered and he explained what had happened, Ruby asked to speak to Della. Passing the phone over, he listened while Della answered a few questions.

"Hold on," Della finally said. "Let me try." She stood and moved toward the door. "Charlie, do you want to go outside?"

Though the dog briefly struggled to get up, once he did, he didn't appear to be limping. Della relayed this information to Ruby. Then thanked her and ended the call.

"She said to bring him in. She'll squeeze him in for an appointment."

"Let's go," he said immediately. "I'll drive you. We can't take your Jeep with all the glass inside."

"You're right and thank you." She nodded, wiping at her eyes with her hands. "Do you mind lifting him into your truck? She doesn't want him jumping."

"I don't mind at all." He went to her and pulled her in for a hug. "And after we get Charlie taken care of, you need to have someone look at your throat."

Though she started to protest, something in his expression stopped her. "I'll think about it," she finally said. "Now let's go get my dog checked out."

Chapter 10

Never in her life had Della known such stark and outright terror as when she'd watched Hal swing that bat at Charlie. Roaring her outrage, she'd launched herself at him then, determined to protect her dog at all costs.

Hal had appeared equally determined to cause serious canine injury.

But, focused on defending her, Charlie had won out. He'd pounced on the intruder, teeth bared. While Hal tried to protect himself from the onslaught of both of them, Della had been able to wrest the bat away. Only then had she called Charlie off. She didn't want her dog to kill the man, after all.

"Are you all right?" Max asked again, while he drove. She appreciated that he not only tried to hurry but made sure Charlie wasn't thrown around in the back seat. Della was sitting back there with him, needing to be with her dog.

Instead of answering, Della spoke another truth. "I'd rather have been the one to have gotten hurt a million times over. I don't know how I'll live with myself if I allowed that bastard to cause Charlie serious injury."

Max nodded. "I get that. But go easy on yourself. From what I can tell, Charlie did his best to defend you too. I think you both did an amazing job protecting each other. And I know Ruby will get Charlie fixed up as quickly as she can."

Blinking back more tears, Della continued to stroke her beloved dog's soft fur. Charlie was panting more than he usually did, which she knew could be a sign of pain or distress.

Once they reached the vet clinic, Max parked. He came around to the back door and reached inside. But before he lifted Charlie, he eyed Della. "Do you want me to carry him inside or would you rather see if he can walk?"

She swallowed hard. "Carry him, please. I don't want him to hurt anything else."

Once inside, one of the vet technicians named Maria stood waiting. "Ruby told me you were on your way. Come with me," she said, showing them to an exam room.

Max placed Charlie gently on the metal table. Charlie lifted his head, wagged his tail, but made no effort to sit up. The already hard knot inside Della's stomach twisted. She brushed away more tears—stupid things—as she stroked her dog and promised him that he'd be all right.

The back door opened, and Ruby rushed in. "I'm between patients," she said. "I've informed them that we have an emergency."

Bending down, Ruby spoke softly to Charlie, letting him know that she was there to help him. After asking Della to describe exactly what happened, she listened quietly.

"That's horrible," she said, once Della finished. "I'm going to feel all over Charlie to see if he exhibits any pain or if anything seems broken. Is he walking okay?"

Again, Della felt tears threaten. "I'm not sure," she

replied, twisting her hands. "Everything happened so quickly."

"I see." Ruby looked to Maria, who'd remained in the room. "Please hold him while I perform the examination. Della, I'll need you to step back."

Though she wanted to argue, Della knew better. She moved a few feet away, far enough that she wouldn't interfere with the exam, but close enough that she could comfort Charlie if needed. Max moved closer and put his arm around her shoulders. Grateful, she leaned into him, glad of his strength.

Eyeing Della, Charlie lay still while Ruby gently ran her hands all over him. He grunted once and yelped when she touched his shoulder.

"I'd like to get some X-rays," Ruby said, once she'd finished her exam. "Honestly, I don't think anything is broken, but we won't know for certain without some images. Is that okay?"

"Of course," Della answered.

"I'd like to see him walk as well." Ruby looked at Maria, who nodded and then lifted Charlie off the table and placed him on the floor.

Still panting, Charlie shook himself and wagged his tail.

"Come on, you handsome boy," Maria crooned. Ruby watched intently as Charlie glanced back at Della as if needing her permission.

"Go, Charlie," Della told him. "I'll be right here when you get back."

Charlie blinked and then followed the vet tech out of the room.

"It looks like he's moving okay," Ruby commented. "We'll bring him back once we're done."

The minute the door closed behind them, Della turned her face into Max's chest and held on for dear life.

"You've got this," he said. "Charlie's got this."

With his muscular arms wrapped around her and his familiar scent filling her nostrils, Della managed to reach a feeling of calmness. Charlie hadn't seemed seriously injured, and when Hal had swung the metal bat at him, Charlie hadn't yelped.

A short while later, Ruby returned. "No broken bones," she said, smiling. "And all his vital organs appear intact. We did a sonogram also. He might have some bruising. He might be stiff or sore, so I'm giving you some meds he can take."

Maria appeared with Charlie. Tail wagging furiously, her good boy hurried over to Della, nudging her with his nose as if telling her he wanted to go home now.

"If anything changes, give me a call." With a friendly wave, Ruby went on to her next patient.

At the front desk, Della paid, and then the three of them left. When they reached Max's truck, Charlie jumped right in without any help. This made Della's heart happy.

Once in the truck, Max eyed her. "Now that we've gotten Charlie checked out, how about we do the same for you? I don't like the look of those bruises on your neck."

"I'm good." She waved away his concern. "They're just bruises, and they'll fade with time. He didn't hurt me anywhere else."

Though Max didn't appear entirely convinced, he

didn't argue with her, for which she was grateful. Instead, he took them home.

After they pulled up at her driveway, Della carefully kept Charlie away from all the broken glass. Inside, he went to the back door, signaling he needed to go out and do his business. Once she'd let him take care of that, he went straight to his favorite dog bed and curled up in it with a loud sigh.

Max watched him, grinning from ear to ear. "I'm so glad he's going to be all right."

"Me too." Suddenly exhausted, all Della wanted to do was go lie on her bed and sleep. But she needed to call Sebastian and let him know what had happened. She wouldn't be going back to work today. She needed to rest and try to get over the shock.

Before she could dial his cell, Sebastian called her. "I just talked to Ruby," he said. "She filled me in. Are you okay?"

"I'm fine," she sighed. "Physically. Mentally, I'm going to need a little bit of time to decompress. Max is with me, so I'm not alone. But there's no way I can come back to work this afternoon. If I were to attempt to work with any of the dogs, they'd sense what a mess I am."

"I agree," Sebastian answered. "Why don't you take a couple of days off? I can cover your classes tomorrow."

Though that sounded like heaven, she didn't want to foist all her work on her boss. "I appreciate the offer. We'll see how I feel tomorrow and go from there. I'll be in touch."

"Sounds good. Take care of yourself." Sebastian ended the call.

A wave of exhaustion hit her. She felt dizzy, not like

herself, and she guessed this must be a reaction to the trauma she'd suffered.

"Come here," Max said, pulling her close and steering her over toward the couch. "You look like you need to sit down."

Grateful, she dropped onto the cushions, with him right beside her. Laying her head on his shoulder, she closed her eyes.

Then she remembered her new outdoor furniture and sat up.

"What's wrong?" Max asked, concerned.

"I bought a couple of rocking chairs and a little table earlier. The store loaded them up in my Jeep for me, but with all the excitement..."

"I'll unload them for you," he said, pushing to his feet. "Where do you want them?"

Try as she might, she couldn't seem to summon the energy to join him. "Are you sure? They're pretty big and bulky. I was planning on putting them on my deck."

He smiled. "I can handle it. You just sit and rest."

Too tired to argue, she nodded and closed her eyes again.

She must have drifted off to sleep, because the next thing she knew, Charlie's barking startled her awake. She bolted up in a panic, once again feeling hands locked around her throat. Except she was alone. Even Charlie's barking had come from the backyard.

Wondering if Max had left and forgotten to let Charlie back in, she went to her sliding patio doors and opened them. Her new rocking chairs were in place on the deck, with the small table right in between them.

Spotting Max out in the yard playing with her dog

made her catch her breath. She watched silently while the two of them enjoyed each other's company, oblivious to her presence. She appreciated the way Max took care not to let Charlie do anything too strenuous. They simply walked the perimeter of the yard, Max talking and Charlie watching him, head cocked, as if listening intently.

She walked over to one of her new chairs and sat. Rocking back and forth, she felt a deep sense of contentment. While she knew it would take a while to recover from the trauma of being attacked, she also counted her blessings that she was still alive. Her cousin hadn't been so lucky.

This made her wonder. Had Hal been involved in any of the other women's murders?

"Hey!" Max waved as he noticed her. "I'll be right up."

Though there were steps outside leading up to the porch, Max brought Charlie into the house through the downstairs back door instead. A few minutes later, the two of them walked out through the slider and joined her.

"Nice chairs," Max said, grinning. He dropped into the one next to her. Charlie came over and sat at her feet, laying his head in her lap.

"Thanks," she replied. "I've been eyeing them for a good while. I finally bit the bullet and purchased them."

His grin widened. "They didn't tell you anything about who made them?"

"No. Just that it's a local." Perplexed, she gazed at him. "Do you know him or her?"

"I do." Still smiling, he nodded. "These are my chairs. I make them. Making furniture has been my hobby for years. It's how I relax. My family lets me keep all my tools and supplies in one of the outbuildings on the ranch."

Stunned, she stared. While they hadn't known each other very long, this completely surprised her. "You're very skilled," she finally said, meaning it. "I'm guessing you must come home to Owl Creek frequently, because the guy working in the store said these chairs sell well and he's constantly replenishing his stock."

"They do." He ran one hand down the arm of the chair, a pleased expression on his face. "I love making them as much as I love working for the FBI. Sometimes even more, I think. It's certainly less stressful."

They fell into a companionable silence, rocking slowly, with Charlie asleep and soaking up sunshine at Della's feet.

This, she realized. The longer she sat, the more her tension seeped away from her. She felt…safe. And happy. Being here with Max brought the kind of contentment one could only find with the right person.

Absently, she reached up and touched her throat. Wincing at the tenderness of her bruises, she thought of how differently that situation might have gone. "Thank you for everything," she said, her voice quiet. "The police got here quickly, but I was very glad to see you."

He met her gaze. "You did a good job protecting yourself."

Again, she thought of how close Charlie had come to getting injured. She shook her head. "Charlie did most of the work. I'm just relieved he's all right."

"Me too," he said.

She took a deep breath, aware she might be making

a big leap without any evidence but needing to get it off her chest.

"You know, ever since Hal attacked me, I've wondered if maybe he was involved in any of that mess up in the meadow."

"Me too."

This surprised her. "I'm glad I'm not the only one."

"You're not." He grimaced. "After I leave here, I plan to stop by the police station and have a word with him. Right now, we don't have anything to tie him to the murders, but I'm going to ask that they hold on to him as long as possible."

The thought of Hal being released made her shudder. "I bet they'll give me a restraining order now."

He nodded. "I'm sure they will. Though, honestly, since you've pressed charges, I plan to let Hal know we'll be watching every move he makes."

"The thing that bothers me the most," she said, "is that Hal now knows where I live. The thought of him hiding here waiting for me to get home…"

"You need an alarm system."

She didn't want to point out that she couldn't afford one. "Not here, not in Owl Creek. This isn't the kind of place where we need such things. Until recently, no one even locked their doors."

"I know. But times change." He checked his phone. "I have contacts. I'll take care of getting something installed."

"But…" she started to protest, but he cut her off with a quick kiss.

"Della, let me do this for you. Please."

Relenting, she agreed, aware she'd be paying him

back. "Nothing too expensive, okay? And the sooner, the better."

For an answer, he kissed her again.

Though he hated to go, Max knew he couldn't stay at Della's all day. After one final kiss, he got to his feet and looked at her, drinking in the beauty of her dozing in the sunshine in one of the chairs he'd made with his own hands.

He could get used to days like this. The thought no longer felt as shocking as it once would have. Which might mean he was ready for a change.

Seeing the furniture he'd made in the back of Della's Jeep had brought all kinds of tender feelings to the surface. On top of getting to her just in time to keep that man from seriously hurting her or her dog, the myriad of emotions felt almost too much for him. Working in law enforcement, he'd long ago learned how to remain detached and impartial. But not this time. Not when Della and Charlie were involved.

He wasn't sure he trusted himself to be around this Hal guy right now. Which was partly why he'd hung around Della's house. He needed to get a grip on his rage and regain his professional detachment.

Sometimes he wished he could build furniture for a living. Once, after a particularly disheartening case, he'd even run the numbers. He'd have to ramp up production and increase distribution to more than just Owl Creek, but it could be done. It was an option he always kept in the back of his mind.

But for right now, he needed to get his act together and question Hal.

After he'd called Owl Creek PD and heard the particulars on Hal, he'd gotten permission to come in and question the man himself. On the way, he'd phoned the team and given them and Theo the information. "Find out anything you can about this guy," he'd said. "See if there's anything that might tie him to those bodies in the meadow. And see if he's a member of the Ever After Church. My contact at the local PD says he's mentioned his church a few times."

"The what?" Theo had clearly never heard of them. Max had filled him in, saying he was operating off a hunch. One that might not even pan out.

"I'll get back to you," Theo had promised before ending the call.

Max parked outside the police station and walked inside. They'd already put Hal in one of the interrogation rooms in preparation for Max's arrival. He'd also been told, confidentially, that the judge was out on the golf course and couldn't be reached to come in and make a decision about Hal's bail. Any delay was a good thing, as far as Max was concerned.

Before turning the doorknob to enter, Max took several deep breaths. He needed to remain objective. Especially since every time he thought of this man with his hands around Della's throat, a red haze of rage clouded his vision.

Professional and detached, he reminded himself. Then he stepped into the room.

Looking up, Hal blanched when he saw Max. Wearing his street clothes, he sat in one of the hard plastic chairs behind a polished metal table. He didn't speak, just continued to stare sullenly.

"Good afternoon," Max said, pulling out the chair across from Hal and sitting in it. "I have a few questions for you."

"I want an attorney," Hal replied, sneering. "I've already told them I'm not answering anything without a lawyer present. You're wasting your time."

Staring at Hal, Max fought for control. The idea that this man had put his hands around Della's throat made Max see red. Despite his best efforts, fury pushed him back up out of the chair. "You…" He bit out the word. For the first time in his career, he teetered on the edge of acting unprofessionally. Somehow, he managed to rein himself in.

"Enjoy your stay," he said and let himself out.

All the way back to the ranch, he let his anger simmer. Though he kept telling himself that Hal would eventually pay, knowing how close he'd come to hurting Della made Max feel ill.

He'd just turned down the ranch drive when he slammed on the brakes. He didn't want to go home. Not now, with all these things bottled up inside of him. He couldn't talk to his dad or his brothers about what had happened today. They'd not only never understand, but they'd think Max had lost his mind.

Before he had time to rethink or reconsider, he made a U-turn and headed back the way he'd come.

The sun had begun to set, though it wasn't dark yet. The orange-and-red sky promised a warm day tomorrow. Gazing at it, he felt a sense of hope. As he neared his destination, his mood continued to lighten.

It wasn't until he'd pulled up in Della's driveway that he realized he should have called first. After all, she'd clearly been exhausted and the last thing he wanted to do was wake her.

This indecisiveness wasn't like him. Ever since he'd met Della, she'd occupied his thoughts constantly. He craved her, cared about her and quite honestly believed he could be falling in love with her.

The notion didn't terrify him the way it once might have.

Staring at her house, he realized she might not feel the same way. Or even close. They'd agreed to be friends, and even though they'd moved into the *with benefits* area, she'd given no sign of becoming emotionally entangled.

Which meant his unannounced arrival at her house might be problematic.

Calling himself a fool, he shook his head and decided he'd better leave.

Just as he put the truck in Reverse, the front door opened, the porch light turned on, and Della came flying down the sidewalk. He shifted into Park, killed the engine and opened his door. Jumping out, he met her halfway across the lawn. Grinning, feeling like he was in a greeting card commercial, he scooped her up in his arms and lifted her.

She clung to him, murmuring his name over and over. Then he kissed her, right there in her front yard, uncaring who might see.

Still locked together, they stumbled back toward her house, with Charlie barking happily.

Inside, Max kicked the door closed. She broke away, gazing up at him with wide eyes. "What are you doing here?" she asked, breathless. "You seem...unsettled."

His heart skipped a beat.

"I wanted to check on you and make sure you're all right."

Truth, but not all of it.

She seemed to sense this, because she continued to watch him, letting him work out what else he wanted to say.

"Plus, I went and saw Hal at the police station. He refused to speak without an attorney present." Swallowing, he gave her the rest of it. "Della, I almost lost it. When he eyed me with that smug smile, I wanted to come up out of my seat and make him pay for what he did to you."

She stared.

Pacing now, he dragged his hand through his hair. "If I'd acted on impulse, it would have been the end of my career. I'm an FBI agent. People in my position don't lose control like that."

"But you didn't." She touched his arm. "And Hal is still locked up. I'm pressing charges. I just hope they managed to delay getting a judge to agree to bail."

"They did." Smiling, he pulled her close again. "I was told the judge was playing eighteen holes of golf and couldn't be reached today. Which means he'll stay locked up for at least tonight."

"Oh, thank goodness." She sagged against him. "I appreciate you telling me that."

For a few heartbeats, they simply held each other. He breathed in the light vanilla-and-peach scent of her, marveling at how perfectly they fit together.

"Was that the only reason you came by?" she finally asked, her arms still wrapped tightly around him.

"No. I also came by because I missed you," he admitted, feeling she'd understand. "Were you asleep?"

"No." She shook her head. "I feel too restless for that. I was just about to get on the treadmill," she said.

Pulling back slightly, she reached up and kissed him again, the kind of lingering, deep kiss that promised more. "But now another kind of physical activity seems more likely."

The shiver of raw desire that went through him made him shudder. "You've got that right," he murmured.

Shedding their clothing as they went, they made it to her bedroom. Naked, they fell onto each other as if it had been weeks since they'd come together, even though it had just been days.

He couldn't get enough of her, it seemed. And she apparently felt the same way. Their lovemaking was fierce and wild, yet tenderness came through the passion.

After, neither seemed in a hurry to get out of her bed.

"You mentioned a treadmill," he said, drawing lazy circles with his finger on her bare arm. "Do you have one or do you go to the gym?"

"I have one." She sighed. "I usually only use it in bad weather. I like to run and try to get in a few miles every day if possible. When I don't run, I hike. Charlie enjoys going with me and that way we both get exercise."

Lost in thought, she looked down at her hands. "Though with the whole Hal thing, I don't feel safe. Which I hate. So I thought the treadmill would have to work for now."

"I run too," he said, though he hadn't for at least three months. "Or I used to. I've been meaning to get back in shape. Maybe we can go together, though you'll have to be patient with me."

Hope blossomed in her eyes. "That would be awesome," she breathed.

"You say that now," he teased. "You may not think so if I end up slowing you down."

Lightly, she punched his arm. "If you do, I'll whip you into shape in no time."

This made him laugh. "I bet you will."

Charlie barked, reminding them of his presence. Della grabbed a long T-shirt and shorts, slipped her feet into flip-flops and took her dog outside.

When she returned, she asked him if he wanted to watch a movie. Since he didn't want to leave her yet, he agreed.

Della handed him the remote and told him to pick something. She had all the streaming services, so he easily found an action-adventure flick he'd been wanting to see.

The scent of buttery popcorn filled the air, making him smile. "Movie night done right," she called from the kitchen.

"Do you need any help?" he asked.

"Nope. I'll be out in a moment."

Charlie emerged, tail wagging. He hopped up onto the couch and made a couple of circles before settling into what appeared to be his spot at one end.

This, he thought. If he'd been asked to describe the perfect domestic situation, this would rank up there at the top. Della, Charlie, a comfortable couch and a good movie. He couldn't think of anything better.

When Della returned, she had a huge bowl of popcorn and two bottles of cold beer. Setting everything down, she dropped onto the sofa next to him and eyed the TV.

"I've been wanting to see that," she said, smiling. "And

kudos to you for not sitting in Charlie's spot. Though I'm sure he would have let you know, he always sits there every night."

This made him smile. "I'll keep that in mind for next time."

She smiled back. Watching them, Charlie thumped his tail, as if he understood.

Max put his arm around her shoulders. She snuggled close. Clicking the remote, he started the movie. For the first time in years, he felt at home. His sterile apartment in Boise had always been simply a place to sleep, and despite growing up at the ranch, his lack of ranching ambition had always made him feel like an outsider.

Here, he felt like he could stay. Even if he knew he'd have to return to Boise once this case had closed, he decided to enjoy the feeling while he could.

Though the movie was entertaining, he found his attention straying to Della. Unaware, she ate popcorn while focusing on the TV.

Unable to help himself, he placed a soft kiss on the top of her head. Though she smiled, she barely looked away from the movie.

Debating whether to try harder to distract her, he couldn't suppress a groan when his cell phone rang. Though sorely tempted to ignore it, he didn't dare, since they were in the middle of an important case.

Shifting his weight away from her, he answered. An unfamiliar voice on the other end identified themselves as Officer Fuentes with the Owl Creek Police Department.

"We have an injured woman we are transporting to the hospital in Conners," the officer said. "Before she lost consciousness, she claimed she was kidnapped by a man who tried to strangle her. We're thinking there might be a tie to that serial killer case you're working."

Chapter 11

Della watched Max's expression change as he listened to his caller. Alert, she straightened and paused the movie, wishing she could hear the other end of the conversation. Somehow, she sensed the call might be related to Angela and the other women's cases.

"I'm on my way," Max said, ending the call. When he met Della's gaze, the stern FBI agent was back.

"What's going on?" she asked, her heart rate increasing.

"I'm heading to the hospital in Conners," he replied. "An injured woman was found who claimed she'd been kidnapped and strangled. Owl Creek PD thinks this might be tied to our serial killer." He took a deep breath. "Do you want to go with me?"

"Yes." She didn't even have to think before responding. Conners was a good forty-five-minute drive. Since Owl Creek didn't have an actual hospital, everyone had to travel to Conners. "Let me take Charlie out real quick and then we can head out."

After she'd taken care of her dog, she followed Max to his truck. He wasn't talking much, clearly lost in his own thoughts. Briefly, she considered asking him if he was sure he wanted her to go but decided against it. She really didn't want to give him the opportunity to change his mind.

Jaw set in a tight line, Max looked furious. Every choppy movement he made spoke to an inner anger that he seemed to be unable or unwilling to express.

"Are you okay?" she finally asked. "I'm a bit worried about you."

He glanced at her, a sharp slice of his gaze, before returning his attention back to the road. "Not really," he answered. "In fact, I'm pretty damn pissed that this guy got the opportunity to attack someone else."

"At least she survived," she pointed out. "It could have been worse."

"True. But he has to know we've discovered his burial place. Not only has everything been disturbed, but the news has been blasted all over the state. I figured he might lie low for a while. I'm actually surprised he attacked someone right now, with all the media attention on this case."

"But he failed," she said. "Luckily for this woman, and for us. She survived. And now she might be able to describe him, giving you the break in the case you needed to find and arrest this person."

"True," he replied, but he didn't sound convinced.

She thought of Hal, with his leering smile and his hands around her neck. "I was sure Hal had something to do with this. But I guess this latest development means it couldn't have been him, since he's still locked up."

"I thought the same thing," he admitted. "But I want to call Owl Creek PD and make sure he's still in custody. I didn't think to ask earlier."

Using his truck's Bluetooth, he placed a quick call

and learned that yes, Hal Murcheson was still a guest of the Owl Creek jail.

"Well, that settles that," he said, once he'd disconnected. "It couldn't have been Hal who attacked this woman." He glanced at her and the still-visible bruises on her neck. "Though I can't entirely rule him out on the others. Once he gets lawyered up, I'm going to put him through some pretty intense questioning. I've already got the team working on determining his whereabouts for the last couple years."

"Good thinking. But are you saying there might be two men going around and murdering women? Like a team?"

He shrugged. "Anything is possible and stranger things have happened. All we know for sure is that Hal didn't attack this one particular victim. I'm interested to get her description of her attacker. I hope she got a good look at him."

"Me too." Della nodded. "Did they say what kind of condition she's in?"

"No. Only that she gave a brief statement before she lost consciousness." He shot another quick glance her way, and then he kept his attention on the road. He drove competently and efficiently, although he couldn't help but exceed the speed limit. His rage seemed much less palpable, though she suspected it still simmered under the surface. She couldn't blame him. Every time she remembered how she'd felt, about to black out as Hal tried to choke the life from her, she alternated between terror and fury.

They made it to the Conners city limits in just under forty-three minutes. "Not bad," she remarked, itching with impatience. She could only hope this woman would survive. And that she'd be able to give a decent description of the man who'd attacked her.

"We haven't had any leads at all, until now," Max mused, pulling into the hospital parking lot. "If this case turns out to be related, this could be the information we've been waiting for."

"What do you mean, *if* this case is related?" Della glanced sideways at him, feeling queasy. "How can it not be?"

"You never know. Like I said, I felt pretty confident that Hal would turn out to be involved. And while we haven't entirely ruled him out, the fact that this latest attack happened while he's still in custody makes his involvement much less likely." He sighed. "And though it's entirely possible that there might have been two men killing these women, everything we know of serial killers tell us they operate alone."

"I'm still trying to wrap my head around all of this. Are you saying there's a possibility that the attack on this woman might not be tied to the murders in the meadow?"

He grunted. "There are so many variables. This—or Hal—could be an isolated incident. We need something to tie one of them to the murders."

"Like what? DNA?"

"I know Caroline would love to have some DNA to work with, other than the victims. But with the weather and wild animals, she said she was lucky to be able to identify the remains."

Della didn't bother to hide her frustration. "I'm still going to hope that this victim can tell us something that might help give you a break in the case. I need this killer to be caught. I want this over."

"I get that." He touched her shoulder. "But we want to make sure and put the right person behind bars."

"True." Refusing to allow her nervous energy to deflate, Della waited until he'd parked and killed the engine before jumping out of the truck. She kept close to Max's side as he strode into the hospital lobby. For whatever reason, she found herself continually checking over her shoulder, as if someone might be watching her.

At the information desk, he flashed his badge and was directed to the ER. There, the triage nurse smiled at him before pointing toward the back. "She's in ER room 8," she said.

After being buzzed through the double doors, they walked down the hallway, past the nurses' station. As they turned a corner, they encountered two uniformed Owl Creek police officers, standing outside of one of the rooms. Room 8.

Della recognized Officer Santis, the one who'd come to her aid at the gas station. He inclined his head in a nod when he saw her, but like his partner, he focused his attention on Max.

"What's the status?" Max asked, his voice stern.

"The doctor is with her now," Santis replied. "We've been told that she's stable, but still unconscious at the moment."

"Not critical condition, then?"

"Not that we've been told." Santis glanced at his partner, who nodded. "I got a quick look at her. She had a lot of blood. The bruises on her throat are pretty bad, but the doc says she has some internal injuries. He thinks she might have been beaten with something. They're getting some imaging done in a few minutes."

Hearing about the bruises, Della's hands involuntarily went to her own throat. And hearing this poor woman might have been beaten with something, she kept thinking about Hal and his metal baseball bat.

Seeing this, Max squeezed her arm. "We'll wait here with you," he said, offering her comfort.

The two officers nodded.

"Do you want her placed under guard twenty-four seven?" Santis asked. "We can call in reinforcements if you'd like. That way we can take shifts."

Max considered. "I'm not sure that's necessary, but let me think about it for the long term. For now, I'd like you to stay."

"We can do that." Officer Santis nodded. "I'd like to get my hands on the guy who did that to her. She looked pretty badly beat up."

Della swallowed hard. Her heart ached for this woman she didn't even know. Especially since she'd recently had a similar experience. It could very likely have been her who'd ended up in the ER.

The doctor came out of the room. Once again, Max flashed his FBI identification and asked for a word with him. The harried doc nodded but gestured at the two uniforms. "I've already shared everything I know with them. Maybe they can fill you in?"

"They have," Max replied. "I'll just ask you to update me once you have the imaging results."

"That I can do. Now, if you'll excuse me…" And the doctor rushed off.

As soon as the doctor left, a nurse appeared, directing

them to a small seating area between the nurses' station and the rooms. "If you'll wait here, I'll send the doctor to speak with you as soon as he knows anything."

They sat. Though the policemen eyed Della, they didn't question her presence. Which was good, since she didn't have any professional reason to be here. She didn't want to admit the truth—that she was only keeping Max company.

She badly wanted to ask Max the reason he felt this woman needed to be placed under guard, but figured it was something she'd need to wait to find out until they were alone.

Time dragged, as it always seemed to do inside a hospital. Della took to scrolling on her phone while Max stepped outside to make a phone call. The two police officers talked quietly among themselves, occasionally glancing at Della. Finally, Santis cleared his throat and addressed her.

"How are you holding up?" he asked. "I heard that guy who followed you to that gas station assaulted you."

"I'm doing okay," she said, realizing as she spoke that she actually was. "Just relieved he's still behind bars. I'm definitely pressing charges. Though all of this brings it all back up."

He gave her a sympathetic smile. "I imagine it does. I'm sorry."

Max returned and dropped back into the chair next to Della. "I filled my SAC in on what's happened," he said. "He definitely wants me to question this woman when she wakes up."

"Does this woman have a name?" Della asked softly,

directing her question to the policemen. "Do either of you know it?"

Officer Santis nodded. "Maisy," he replied, consulting his notes. "She didn't have any ID on her, so we weren't able to get a last name before she lost consciousness."

"Were you able to get any kind of a statement?" Max asked.

"Not yet. We did take one from the woman who brought her in. She happened to be driving by when Maisy came stumbling out of the woods, all bloody with torn clothing."

Again, he glanced at his notes. "The woman who brought her here is named Regina Quinten. She said that Maisy was able to tell her that she'd been attacked and that was it. Ms. Quinten asked her name, and Maisy got out that much before she went unresponsive."

"Did you get contact information for this Regina Quinten?" Max asked.

"We did." Officer Santis wrote something on a piece of paper and handed it to Max. "Here you go."

"Thanks."

"No problem." The officer closed his pad and sighed. "That's the extent of what we know."

"Thank you." Max looked thoughtful as he studied the sheet of paper.

A moment later, the doctor returned. Della saw him first, and since she met his gaze, he made a beeline over to her. Max looked up and stood, so of course Della did too.

"We've finished running her tests," the doctor said, his smile tired. "She has a couple of broken ribs, but that seems to be the extent of it. I took a quick peek at the

MRI, and though I still need a radiologist to evaluate it, there may be some soft-tissue injuries. She appears to have been severely beaten in addition to the nearly successful attempt to strangle her."

"Is she going to be all right?" Della asked.

The doctor nodded. "I believe so. She's conscious. We'll be admitting her so we can keep an eye on her, so she'll be transferring to a regular room." He looked at Max. "I know you have to question her, but please take it easy. I'll allow her to have one visitor, but you'll need to keep it short."

Without waiting for an answer, the doctor turned on his heel and hurried away.

Della looked up at Max. Again, his tight jaw and remote expression told her he'd retreated inside himself. She wanted to tug on his arm and whisper to him to please be gentle, but truthfully, there was no need. She knew he would.

Entering the small ER exam room, Max stopped just inside the doorway. Despite the fact that the medical staff had gotten Maisy cleaned up, the bruises on her face, throat and arms looked pretty horrific. The pale-blue-and-white hospital gown did little to hide how badly she'd been battered. Her short blond hair had bloody mats and appeared to have been hacked off with a dull pair of scissors or a pocketknife.

She looked up when he came in, her pale blue eyes clouded. Most likely she'd been given some medication to help with the pain. She attempted a smile, though her swelling must have made that painful, since it faltered and quickly turned into a grimace.

"I'm Special Agent Max Colton with the FBI," he said, approaching her bed and showing her his badge. "I know you are feeling pretty awful, but would it be okay if I ask you a few questions?"

She started to nod, but then apparently thought better of it. "Go ahead."

"Let's start with your full name."

"Maisy Pederson," she replied. "I'm twenty-two, and I work as a barista in a coffee shop in Boise while attending Boise State University."

Max noted this down. "Are you originally from Boise or somewhere else?"

"I grew up in Boise," she said. "I still live at home with my parents." For a moment, she appeared concerned. "Has anyone contacted them? I need to let them know that I'm all right."

"We'll have you do that in just a little bit," Max said. "First, can you tell me what happened?"

"I'm... It's all so weird. I've always sung in our church's choir. A week ago, after the service, a man approached me. He said I sang like an angel and asked me if I'd consider singing at his church. It had some weird name, which made me very uneasy."

"A church?" Keeping his expression impassive, Max struggled to contain his excitement.

A nurse interrupted, bringing a plastic pitcher of water and a plastic cup. "Here you go, sweetie," she said, setting them down on the tray near the bed. "You can have a little water now, but don't overdo it."

Once she'd gone, Max went over and poured half a glass for Maisy and handed it to her. She accepted it with shaky hands, took a few small sips and then put the cup back on her tray table.

"You can't remember the name of that church?" Max asked her. "It would be very helpful if you could try."

She sat still for a moment, her forehead wrinkled in thought. Finally, she sighed. "I'm sorry, but I can't."

"Was it the Ever After Church?" he asked, needing to know.

"Maybe," she replied. "But I can't be positive."

This time, Max had to work to hide his disappointment. He hadn't been able to shake the idea that the Ever After Church might be involved in all of this. He just needed some proof.

Maisy fell silent, apparently lost in her own thoughts. Max gave her a minute, aware she likely was in a lot of pain.

"Can you give me a description of this man?" Max asked, pen poised.

"He looked...ordinary," she finally said. "Brown hair, brown eyes, not too tall or too short. Just like someone you'd never take a second look at."

Max nodded. "Any idea of his age?"

"Older than me?" She grimaced and then blanched because apparently even that small movement hurt. "I'm bad at guessing age. I'd say mid to late forties. He seemed...nice. I was definitely wrong."

"How'd you go from being asked to sing in a church choir to being beaten and attacked?" he finally asked, as gently as he could.

Her gaze met his. She shuddered. "He told me I could think about it and asked if I would walk with him to his car, so he could get some literature about the church for me. I guess I'm too naive, because I did. He told me to go ahead and sit in the passenger seat while he put together some papers for me."

Hands shaking, she reached for the plastic cup of water and took another small sip. "I sat down, because it was windy and my skirt was blowing around. He got the papers together and sat in the driver's seat. Then he grabbed me by the back of the head and held something over my mouth and nose. I don't know what it was, but it made me pass out."

"Chloroform," he guessed.

"Probably." Her voice wavered. She swallowed and visibly struggled to compose herself. "Anyway, when I woke up again, he'd parked at the base of one of the hiking trailheads. My head was pounding and I felt nauseated. He told me we were going to go for a walk." She swallowed hard. "I knew if I walked up that trail with him, I'd never make it out alive."

Smart woman. Max nodded in approval.

"I thought about running," she continued, "but when I got out of the car, I could barely stand. He got behind me, prodding me with some kind of metal thing, like a police baton."

That was new. Thinking of Hal, with his metal bat, Max made a note. Coincidence? Maybe. Or maybe not.

"I played up my dizziness," Maisy explained. "Made it look like I was more out of it than I was. Stumbled and staggered and fell back toward him. It might have been reflex, but he caught me." Her eyes drifted closed.

Max coughed, hoping she could stay awake long enough to finish making her statement. "Then what happened?" he prodded.

Her lashes fluttered, but she finally reopened her eyes. "I grabbed the metal stick and swung." She slurred the last word as she fell back asleep.

The monotonous beeping of the machines was the only sound in the room. Max found them reassuring, because he knew if something had gone wrong, they would have sounded an alert. Aware he'd get nothing else from this woman for a while, he turned to make his way back to the waiting area. He wanted one of the uniformed officers stationed outside her room at all times.

When he reached the waiting room, he found Della sitting next to Officer Santis. "Where'd your partner go?" Max asked.

"Men's room. He'll be right back."

"Okay. Since you're here, you can take first shift. I need a guard posted outside Maisy Pederson's room twenty-four seven."

"I can do that." Santis pushed to his feet. "I take it you have reason to believe there's a credible threat?"

"I do. She wasn't able to give me much of a description. From what she told me, it's a miracle she made it out alive."

"I'll go do first shift starting right now."

"Thank you." Max passed Santis his card. "My cell is on there. Call me if you need anything."

Accepting it, Officer Santis nodded. "Will do."

"We'll wait for your partner and let him know what's going on. After that, Della and I are going to head out."

Watching while the young police officer went to take up his post outside ER room 8, Max turned to Della. "Are you ready to go?"

Expression pensive, she shrugged. "I really was hoping I'd get to talk to Maisy. Since I've recently been through something similar, even if it wasn't as bad, I really think I could get her to open up to me."

He considered. "She's out of it right now. How about we come back tomorrow morning, once she's been moved to her regular hospital room. I'm thinking once she gets some rest, she might have clearer memories. All she was able to give me so far was pretty vague."

"I'd like that," Della said. "And you're right—it is late. We could all use some sleep."

The other police officer appeared, looking remarkably alert. Once Max filled him in, he nodded and went down the hall to consult with Santis.

"Come on," Max said, taking Della's arm. "Let's go."

Walking outside into the well-lit parking lot, Max glanced up at the crescent moon. Here, the stars were still visible, though not as bright as they were someplace more remote, like the ranch. Or the campsite near the awful meadow where the killer had buried the bodies.

Just the thought brought a wave of exhaustion. He yawned, covering his mouth with his hand. "I'm more tired than I realized," he said.

They reached his truck. Once he'd unlocked it and they both got inside, Della touched his arm. "You're welcome to stay with me tonight," she offered. "I know it's a bit of a drive out to the ranch."

Touched, he nodded. "I'd like that."

"Me too." Her soft smile had him leaning over to kiss her cheek.

At her house, he parked behind her Jeep. "The insurance company gave me the number of a place to call to get my windows replaced," she said. "I just haven't had a chance to do it yet. It's some kind of mobile place, so they come out to your place of work. Which will be perfect."

Opening the front door, they were greeted by an ecstatic Charlie, bounding around them, tail wagging. Della made him sit before she began petting him. "You're such a good boy," she praised.

When she'd finished loving on him, Charlie came over to Max and nudged him with his nose. Max obliged, scratching the Lab behind his ears.

Satisfied, Charlie walked away and went to get a drink of water.

"Is he always this happy to see you?" Max asked, bemused, following Della into the kitchen.

"Yep. That's the thing with dogs. It doesn't matter if you've been gone a few minutes or an entire day. They greet you as if they haven't seen you in forever." She picked up Charlie's water bowl and carried it to the sink to rinse it out and refill it.

"I like that." Max came up behind her and wrapped her in his arms. "And I like you."

At his words, she went still. Then, shutting off the water, she turned to face him. "I like you too."

He kissed her then. Heat erupted between them, just as it always did. He took her hand, intending to lead her toward the bedroom. "Wait," she said. "Let me put Charlie's water bowl back down. I don't want him to get thirsty."

In that moment, he thought he couldn't love her more.

Later, as they cuddled together with the sheets still tangled around them, she sighed. "Do you think I'd be allowed to visit with Maisy tomorrow? I'd really like a chance to talk to her."

Curious, he nuzzled her neck. "If she's well enough, I can make that happen. Any particular reason why?"

"I can relate to what happened to her, in a way that no one else can. Not only did something similar happen to me, but my cousin lost her life at the hands of that same person."

Though he wanted to caution her about jumping to conclusions, he decided not to. While they didn't *know* with certainty that this incident was tied to the serial killer, it likely would turn out to be.

"Could we go first thing in the morning?" Della pressed. "I have to be at Crosswinds by nine."

"You're going back to work?" he asked.

"Of course. There are several dogs there waiting for me to work with them. Sebastian can't train his and mine. There aren't enough hours in the day."

"I get that," he told her. "But are you feeling well enough?"

His question made her laugh. "We just rather energetically made love. I'm surprised you even have to ask that."

She had a point.

"We'll run by the hospital first thing in the morning," he agreed. "I got a text that she's been moved to room 5128."

They fell asleep in each other's arms. Just before he drifted off, he realized he'd never been happier.

The delicious smell of coffee brewing woke Max. He stretched, momentarily disoriented. Then, realizing he'd spent the night with Della, he grinned.

She showered while he drank his coffee. When she emerged, dressed with her hair in a long braid, she walked over and kissed his cheek. "Your turn. I put a towel and washcloth on the bathroom counter for you."

Thanking her, he took a quick shower. Wishing he'd brought a change of clothes, he dressed in the ones he'd worn the day before. "We'll grab something for breakfast on the way to the hospital," he said.

They were out the door barely an hour after he'd first opened his eyes. He'd never known a woman able to get ready so fast. Including his sister.

Grabbing a couple of breakfast sandwiches on the way, they ate them as he drove. He pulled up to the hospital entrance and found a parking spot close to the door. Another bonus of arriving so early, he thought. Smiling at Della, he told her this meant today was going to be a good day. It had to be.

She seemed to share his buoyant mood. Linking her arm with his, she smiled broadly as they walked into the hospital lobby.

They barely made it past the information desk before the power went out, plunging the hospital into darkness.

Chapter 12

"Wait here." Jerking his hand free from hers, Max sprinted for the stairs.

Since there was no way Della intended to do that, she ignored him. The windows let in enough light that she could see. Though she hadn't been running in a few days, she was in excellent shape and easily caught up with him.

He shot her a look but kept going. So did she.

"The emergency generators should be kicking on," she said. "I don't understand why there's a delay."

Just then, the lights flickered on as if someone had heard her. They came on, went out and flickered a few times.

Despite the dark, Max located the door to the stairwell and wrenched it open. He'd gotten out his phone and used the flashlight on it to help him see. Taking the stairs two at a time, he barreled to the fifth floor. Della stayed right on his heels.

Meanwhile, the lights continued to flicker on and off.

"Backup generator problems," Max said. "They should have that fixed soon. Too many patients depend on electricity."

She nodded. "I wonder what happened."

"I'm betting this wasn't an accident." Barely out of

breath, he opened the door to floor 5. "Good thing I asked Owl Creek PD to place Maisy under a twenty-four seven guard."

Startled, she followed him down the hall. "You think this is related to her?"

"I do."

Though she still didn't fully understand, she stayed close as they rounded the nurses' station. The lights had now come on and remained steady.

They rounded the corner, and Max cursed as he spotted the empty chair in the hall outside of room 5128. "Where's her guard?"

As he started toward the room, a gunshot rang out. It sounded like it had come from inside.

Della froze.

"Get down!" Max said, drawing his gun. "Della, take cover."

Since she'd already instinctively ducked, she went all the way to the floor and crawled over to hide behind the nurses' station. Shaky, heart in her throat, she watched Max advance toward the room.

"FBI!" he called out. He entered the room with his weapon still drawn.

Della hated that she couldn't see him.

"Put the gun down," Max ordered. "Right now."

Shaky, Della tried to breathe. The gunman, still inside the room. Max in danger. Where were the police? Hands shaking, heart racing, she stayed down, on the other side of the counter. She hadn't expected this. She wondered if there was anything she could do to help, but she didn't want to get in the way.

Seconds ticked by. Only seconds, though they seemed like minutes.

Then another gunshot. Just one.

Who'd been shot? Max? The intruder? Agonizing over the uncertainty, she drew a ragged breath.

A uniformed police officer came tearing around the corner, focused on room 5128. He momentarily paused when he caught sight of her but drew his pistol and continued toward the room.

"Owl Creek police," he called out. "The hospital has been placed on lockdown. Come out with your hands up."

"All clear," Max said. "Max Colton with the FBI here. It's okay to come on in."

Relieved to hear his voice, Della got to her feet. Her legs were so weak it took her a moment to stand.

Another policeman ran up and joined the first one inside the room.

Slowly, people began to appear. First the nurses, three or four of them, cautiously gathering nearby. Several curious patients appeared in their doorways, peering down the hall but too afraid to leave their safe spaces.

One of the cops came out of the room and stood guard in the doorway. He shook his head as Della approached. "Ma'am, I'm going to have to ask you to stay back."

"I understand." Still, Della tried to see around him, needing to put her eyes on Max.

"Della, don't come in here," Max said, apparently having heard the officer. "The coroner is on the way. I'll be with you as soon as I can."

Stunned, Della stepped away. If they'd called the coroner instead of medical personnel, that meant someone hadn't survived. Who'd been killed? The shooter or Maisy? She didn't know. At least Max had spoken to her and let her know he was okay.

Though she had no business behind the nurses' station, Della found a chair and dropped into it. More people arrived, security people as well as police officers. The hallway near room 5128 got more crowded.

Time slowed to a crawl. And Max remained inside the room. She glanced at the wall clock and realized there was no way she'd be making it into work on time.

Resigned, she sent Sebastian a text, letting him know she was at the hospital and promising she'd be there as soon as she could.

Sebastian instantly texted back. Della! Are you okay?

After she explained she'd been visiting someone and would fill him in on the details later, he sent her a simple thumbs-up emoji.

Finally, Max emerged, disheveled. He appeared to have shut down. She understood. Sometimes closing off emotions was the only way to survive. He might be an experienced FBI agent, but shooting someone must have affected him. She could only hope the man he'd shot would survive.

"Are you all right?" she asked, her heart going out to him.

"Not really." Grim-faced, he took her hand. "Let me get you to work. I've called this in, but I still need to fill out a report. There's always a ton of paperwork."

Suspecting sympathy would be the last thing he'd want, she waited until they were inside the truck to ask him what had happened. She knew better than anyone how talking could help.

A muscle worked in Max's jaw. "The officer who

was supposed to be guarding the room went to investigate when the power cut out. The instant he left his post, the shooter saw his opportunity and slipped inside the room. We got there right after that, apparently. But we were too late."

"He killed Maisy?" she asked, aghast. "Did he also cause the power outage?"

"Yes, he did. Both things." Max backed out of the parking space and headed toward the exit. "She didn't deserve this. None of it. She survived a brutal attack only to be murdered in the one place she should have been safe."

"Oh no." Della covered her mouth as she blinked back tears. "I'm so sorry. But why? Why would anyone do such a thing?"

He glanced at her and grimaced. "Because now she won't be able to testify against the man who attacked her."

Shocked despite everything, she took a moment to process this. "That would mean the man who killed her had something to do with her attack."

"Most likely," Max responded.

Despite all the sadness, her heart skipped a beat at the thought her cousin's killer would be brought to justice. "What about the shooter? Is he in custody now?"

Max barely looked at her. "No. He's dead. He refused to drop his weapon. I had no choice but to take him out."

"He's dead?" She couldn't hide her shock.

"It was him or me." The clipped tone of Max's voice told her he wasn't good with the turn of events either. He hadn't just shot a man. He'd killed him.

Not sure how to comfort him, she went with the only

thing she could think of. She reached out and squeezed his shoulder. "I'm sorry."

Though he tensed, he didn't brush off her hand. "Me too."

Unsure what else to say, she swallowed. Appearing to sense this, Max turned up the radio, just loud enough to make conversation impossible.

Miserable for him, she got the message. When he pulled up in front of Crosswinds, he turned to her before she got out. "I'll talk to you later," he said.

The flinty look in his eyes made her heart squeeze. Aching for him, she kept her chin up. "I'll consider that a promise."

Then, before she could reconsider, she gave him a quick kiss before opening her door and getting out. He drove away without a backward glance. She stood watching until she could no longer see his truck.

Now the exhaustion from the trauma set in. Her legs very nearly buckled, but she held herself straight and managed to make it inside.

Sebastian took one look at her and motioned her to a chair. "Sit," he ordered.

Grateful, she dropped into the chair and put her head in her hands. She took several deep breaths, aware she needed to get a grip on herself. And she had no doubt she would. She was a fully trained search and rescue volunteer and knew how to react to stressful situations.

But what had happened today was gut-wrenchingly different. Immediate. More personal.

"I know you said you were visiting someone in the hospital." Sebastian knelt next to her. "But you honestly don't look good. Want to tell me what's going on?"

She made herself look up. More deep breathing. When she finally felt calm enough, she told him everything, though she left out the part about Max spending the night at her house.

Sebastian listened, one brow raised. When she finished, her voice finally trailing off, he shook his head. "What I don't understand is why Max Colton is involving you in any of this. He put you in danger by allowing you to accompany him to the hospital."

"He didn't *allow* me to do anything," she retorted. "I asked to speak with this woman. I thought I might help her, since I recently went through something similar."

Sebastian considered. "Of course you did," he finally said. "You have a huge heart. But the fact that Max asked for the police to guard the hospital room tells me he was worried there might have been trouble."

"There shouldn't have been." She tried not to think of how terrified she'd been that Max would get hurt or worse.

"Hey, does that mean the guy who attacked you was killed?" Sebastian asked.

"No. Hal is still locked up at Owl Creek PD. It wasn't him."

"Seriously?" Sebastian shook his head. "Then who was it?"

"Now, that I don't know. I'm guessing I'll find out soon enough."

Feeling slightly better, she pushed to her feet. "I'd better get to it. I've got a lot of work to do. Those dogs won't train themselves."

As she headed toward the kennels, Sebastian kept

pace with her. "How's George doing?" he asked. "Austin PD has been asking for a report."

Thinking of George, an incredibly smart Belgian Malinois, she grinned. "We're working on scent training," she said. "You're definitely welcome to stay and watch."

Sebastian smiled back, clearly relieved at her return to normalcy. "Usually, I'd love to. But I've got my own training to do. I have an appointment to take Clyde down to the fire station. We're working on noise desensitizing."

"Have fun." She gave him a cheery wave before grabbing a leash and collar and going to collect her first dog of the day.

Three hours and three dogs later, Della decided to take a break for lunch. Though she didn't have her car or anything to eat, she was hoping she could talk one of the women working the store into bringing her back something.

Luckily, Pepper was just about to leave for lunch. Della handed her a ten and asked her to bring her back something. Eyeing Della with concern, Pepper agreed and left.

Since it would be close to an hour before Pepper came back with food, Della decided she might as well go ahead and get in some training with her next dog. A young female German shepherd, Zsa Zsa had completed the first part of her training with Sebastian and was now ready to work with Della.

Responsive and eager, Zsa Zsa was an absolute joy to work with. Della took her around out back, where they'd set up an obstacle course of sorts. Della had continued Sebastian's work training the dog on hand signals, and today's task would be locating—and signaling—one particular item among various items Sebastian had buried. These things had been treated with various scents like lavender, lemon, peppermint and chamomile. Once Della let her know which scent she needed to locate, the dog set off. One at a time, Zsa Zsa made short work of finding each item. When she'd completed the work, in record time, Della gave her a piece of her favorite treat, a smelly liver bite, as reward.

Proud and tired, Zsa Zsa went back to her kennel run, where she immediately sprawled out for a nap, panting happily. Della watched her for a moment, and then returned to the office area. Pepper should be back any moment now with food.

Della opened a can of sparkling water and took a long drink. She considered texting Max but decided to leave him alone for now. In attempting to deal with the shooting, he'd retreated inside himself. She wished he'd let her help him, but she figured he'd reach out when he was ready. Since he hadn't said he'd be back to take her home, she wasn't sure if she'd need to find her own ride or not. She'd figure that out when the time came. Right now, she was doing her best to avoid thinking about what had happened at the hospital. If and when she allowed herself to break down, the only person she wanted to be around was Max.

Killing another human being had a way of shaking anyone the hell up, no matter how seasoned an FBI agent or police officer they might be. Even if doing so had been in self-defense.

After dropping Della off, Max released his iron grip

on his emotions. He hadn't wanted her to see him lose his composure. Hell, he didn't even want to look himself in the mirror right now. He'd gone over the scenario in his mind a hundred times and couldn't see any other possible result. It truly upset him that he hadn't been able to save Maisy. She hadn't deserved any of this. Once again, pure evil had won.

Even knowing all this, something had broken inside him and would take a while to heal. No matter how he spun it, a man had died by Max's hand. Pending ID, they'd be looking for something to tie the guy to the serial killings. If they didn't find anything, they'd be right back where they'd started, with no leads and nothing to go on.

He was in such a foul mood he actually contemplated making the two-hour drive to Boise, to deal with the paperwork in person. But that wouldn't make the tedious chore go by any faster and would add four hours of drive time to an already long day.

Instead, he found himself back at the ranch, glad his father and brothers were out working the land. The last thing he wanted would be to have to make nice with anyone, even his own family.

Especially his family. They were practical and down-to-earth. He suspected they'd never understand how shaken he felt. Taking a life wasn't something he or any other agent he knew took lightly. Even if he knew with certainty that man would have killed him if he hadn't taken the shot.

It had happened before, once. Judging by that experience, Max knew he just needed time to sort out his complicated emotions.

Except this time, he'd involved Della. The realization that he might have placed her in danger weighed equally on his mind. When she'd asked if she could speak with Maisy, he'd been touched by her desire to help. And while he'd asked the police to place a guard outside the room, he hadn't really thought anyone would try to harm a bedridden woman inside of a hospital. He should have known better.

It had all gone south and turned into one giant cluster. Right now, he couldn't stop blaming himself.

Grabbing a can of cola from the fridge, he sat down at the kitchen table and opened his laptop. Even on the best of days, he found doing the endless paperwork annoying, and today would be no exception. In fact, it would be worse. For the first time since this case had begun, they'd finally gotten a break. But young Maisy, who'd been lucky enough to get away, hadn't managed to make it out alive. Not only would she not be able to testify, or pick her assailant out of a lineup, but she wouldn't ever be able to enjoy all the life experiences that growing older brought.

Halfway through the multiple forms, Brian called. Max had left him a terse message on the drive home, filling him in on the details of what had happened.

"I've spoken with police chief Stanton," Brian said. "He wants to hold an immediate presser and announce that we've neutralized the serial killer. It will help all the citizens of Owl Creek—and the tourists—regain their sense of safety."

"But we don't know that guy actually was the serial killer," Max protested.

"Who else would he be?" Brian pointed out. "I mean,

come on. Why would this man murder the only woman who managed to escape the serial killer? He didn't want to be identified."

Max's gut twisted. "I really think we need to investigate this more. We need something that actually ties him to those women we found up in the mountains. Right now, we have nothing."

"I think it's enough." The finality in Brian's tone told Max his SAC's mind was made up. "You know we've been under a lot of pressure to wrap up this case."

"Does that mean you've agreed to do the press conference?" Max asked, though he already knew the answer.

"We've decided to let Owl Creek PD handle that," Brian answered. "They've been instructed not to release any information about you as the agent who took the killer down."

"Thanks." Jaw clenched, Max found himself rubbing the back of his neck. "If it's all the same to you, I'd prefer to quietly continue investigating. I honestly don't believe this was our guy."

Brian went quiet, which was never a good sign. "I'm sorry, Max," he finally said. "But I'm going to need you to stand down and head back to Boise. This investigation has been closed."

"I'm going to have to take some personal leave." Max surprised himself but kept going. "It's been a little rough dealing with shooting and killing someone."

"Understood. How long do you need? A couple of days?"

"Two weeks," Max answered. "I've got some vacation time built up that I'd like to use."

"I know what you're doing here," Brian warned. "And it's not a good idea."

"I don't know what you're talking about," Max replied, even though they both knew he did. "I'm just needing to spend a little time with my family here in Owl Creek."

Brian snorted. "Fine. Just stay away from that press conference. It's this evening at five thirty at the Owl Creek Police Department. They're timing it so it can go live on the local news at six."

Biting back a curse, Max promised to avoid city hall like the plague. Ending the call, he resisted the urge to throw his phone across the room.

They were closing the case. How in the hell did they think doing that without any conclusive evidence would bring justice to any of those poor murdered women?

He had no idea how he was going to tell Della.

Turning his attention back to the reports, he focused and worked with a savage intensity until he'd finished. Since he'd dropped Della off at Crosswinds and she didn't have her Jeep, he needed to find out what time she needed to be picked up.

He sent her a text before he made himself a sandwich. A few minutes passed before she texted back.

Sorry, I was eating lunch. You can pick me up if you want or I can try to find a ride home. I should be finished here around 4.

He sent a quick response, letting her know to expect him then.

Three dots appeared, indicating she was typing. Want

to grab dinner on the way home? I have to eat early, since I've got a Basic Manners class to teach at 7.

Yes! he sent back, liking the way he felt hearing her use the word *home* instead of *my place*. Since he knew Hal would likely be released on bond today, Max intended to go up to Crosswinds with Della. Though he doubted Hal would be foolish enough to try something so soon after being released, Max wanted to make sure to be there in case he did. And then he went to pack a bag, just in case she let him spend the night with her again. He really hoped she would.

He pulled up in front of Crosswinds promptly at four. Della must have been watching for him, because she came out the front door before he'd even had time to shut off the engine.

"Hey," she said, sliding into the passenger side and leaning over to kiss his cheek. "I don't know about you, but today feels like the longest day ever."

"Yes, it does." He studied her. Though she smiled, it didn't quite reach the seriousness in her gaze. "How are you holding up?" he asked.

Looking away, she shrugged. "Okay, I guess. As long as I keep busy, I haven't had time to think too much about it. How about you?"

Instead of answering directly, he told her about his conversation with Brian. "They're having a press conference at five thirty tonight to let the public know they're closing the case."

"Oh, I wish I could see it in person," she said. "But since I need to eat, let Charlie out and go back to work later, I'll have to settle for watching on TV."

Whatever reaction he'd expected from her, it hadn't

been that. "I'm going to keep digging," he said. "I promise you."

Tilting her head, she eyed him. "Why? You don't think the guy you shot was the serial killer?"

"It's possible he was, but there's an equal chance it could have been someone else."

"I get that." She sighed. "And I understand. I hope you're wrong, but I know that you have a job to do."

Though he probably should have shut up right then and there, he owed her the truth. "It's not my job any longer. The FBI considers this case to be closed."

"I see." Her voice wavered, just slightly. "Does this mean you'll be leaving Owl Creek and going back to Boise?"

"Eventually. But I'm taking a couple of weeks off. So you won't be getting rid of me for a little longer."

"That's good." Instead of looking at him, she began doing something on her phone. He couldn't tell if the idea of him leaving bothered her or not. It sure as hell did him. The idea of living two hours away from her gutted him.

They'd pulled into her driveway before he remembered she'd wanted to pick up something to eat. He parked but kept the engine running.

"It's okay," she said, when he reminded her. "I'll just order a pizza. Usually they can get it here in thirty minutes or so."

"Pizza sounds great," he said, killing the engine. "But only if you let me buy it."

Smiling, she shook her head. "I keep the app on my phone. I've already ordered. It will be here soon."

"Will you let me pay you back?"

"Nope." She hopped out of the truck. "But I'll let you pay next time."

Following her inside the house, he didn't comment.

As usual, Charlie greeted them enthusiastically. They all went outside so the Lab could roam around the backyard and take care of business.

"I'll be bringing him into work this evening," she said, still avoiding looking directly at Max. "He'll be doing some basic command demonstrations for the class. He loves that."

The stiffness of her posture told him something bothered her.

"Della?" He touched her arm.

Slowly, she turned her face to look at him. "Yes?"

"What's wrong?"

Instead of answering, she shook her head. "I just need a minute."

Not sure if it was delayed reaction to what had happened in the hospital or something else, he nodded. "Would you like a hug?"

"I would."

He wrapped her in his arms, loving the way she molded her body to his. She held on tightly, and some of the tension seemed to leach out of her.

"Do you want to talk about it?" he asked.

"Maybe later." She stepped away, brushing her hands off on her jeans. "Right now, I really just want to eat. I'm starving."

Once they'd gone back inside, it didn't take long before the doorbell rang, signaling the arrival of their pizza. When Della went to answer, Charlie stayed put. He wagged his tail and watched alertly, but he didn't bark.

A moment later, Della came back with the pizza. "Good boy, Charlie." Setting the box down on the table, she went to get some plates. "I hope you like pizza with everything on it," she said, with a wry smile. "I probably should have asked before I ordered a Supreme."

Suppressing the urge to kiss her, he dropped into a chair. "I'm pretty easygoing with pizza. I like all kinds. I'm particularly fond of Canadian bacon and pineapple."

"Eww." She made a face. "Pineapple does not belong on pizza."

"Have you ever tried it?" he asked.

Taking a seat before answering, she opened the box and pulled out a slice. "No. And I don't intend to. I know what I like."

He reached and got himself two. "So do I," he said, aware she didn't have a clue that he wasn't talking about pizza.

They ate in companionable silence for a few minutes. Then Della grabbed the remote and turned on the news.

Live at the Owl Creek Police Department was emblazoned across the top of the screen. The woman reporter spoke excitedly into her microphone. "We're here at a press conference just called by the Owl Creek police. Word has it that they're about to give us some news on the serial killer."

As if on cue, the camera cut to the Owl Creek police chief standing next to the mayor. For this one, Skipper Carlson had even put on a sports jacket, though he still wore his Wranglers and Western boots. Police chief Kevin Stanton was, as usual, in full uniform.

Struggling to contain his disbelief, Max listened while the events of earlier were described, starting with Maisy's rescue and ending with the killer being taken out by an un-named FBI agent. "While we are thrilled to have brought this case to a close, unfortunately the victim did not survive the shooting."

Following the statement, the reporters began asking questions. Max could hardly stand to listen when he knew damn well there had been no conclusive evidence to link the man who had shot Maisy to the other killings.

"What's wrong?" Della asked, turning the volume down on the TV. "You look kind of angry."

"I am." He shook his head. "I just want you to know I am going to keep investigating this case, even without the Bureau's blessing. I won't give up."

"Thank you," she said. "I'm certain that if anyone can find Angela's killer, it's you."

Chapter 13

Switching off the TV, Della told Max she needed to get ready for work. Instead of taking that statement as a hint to leave, he didn't move. "I hope you don't mind," he said. "But I'm going with you."

Touched, she shrugged. "That's up to you. Too bad you don't actually have a dog. If you did, I bet you'd learn a thing or two."

"I'm sure I will anyway," he replied. "You never know. Someday, I'll get a dog of my own. I'm partial to boxers."

This sent a flush of happiness through her and made her laugh. "Do your research before you get one. Those are a special breed for sure, but they're not for everyone."

"They seem like they'd make good emotional support animals," he said, surprising her. "For times like today, while I'm struggling to process how I feel about taking a life."

Stunned and relieved that he was finally opening up to her, she placed her hand lightly on his shoulder. "Do you want to talk about it?"

"Do you have time?" he asked. "Maybe we should discuss this later."

The rawness of his voice made her eyes sting. "I have an hour before my class starts. But if you'd like my undivided attention, which you definitely deserve, you're welcome to stay the night. That way we can take all the time we need."

Her use of the word *we* clearly didn't escape him. "You need to talk too, don't you?"

"Yes." She kept her answer short and sweet, not wanting to allow all the painful emotions to come flooding back. "But not before I have to teach this class. I can't let myself fall apart right now."

Gaze locked on her, he slowly nodded. "That makes sense. And yes, I'd love to spend the night. In fact, I packed a bag just in case you asked."

Joy knifed through her, both unexpected and welcome. At a loss for words, she simply nodded. Mumbling something about needing to get ready for work, she hurried down the hall.

Inside her bedroom, she closed the door and stared at herself in the mirror. Flushed, almost glowing, she shook her head at her own foolishness. She might as well enjoy Max while he was still in Owl Creek, because he'd made it plain he'd be going back to Boise. She sure as hell didn't plan to tell him how big her emptiness would feel once he'd gone.

She brushed her hair and put it up in a ponytail. The jeans, T-shirt and sneakers she'd put on that morning would be fine. She always looked forward to these classes. Watching that moment when owner and dog finally connected made her happy with her decision to teach.

When she returned to the other room, she stopped and stared. Max had taken a seat on the couch and Charlie had climbed up there next to him. Her dog had his big head in Max's lap, gazing up at him adoringly while

Max stroked his fur. She'd never seen Charlie act like that with anyone else, not even Sebastian. While he was a friendly dog and genuinely enjoyed being around people, he seemed to have taken a real shine to Max.

The sight made her chest ache. If ever anyone should have a dog of their own, Max should.

Catching sight of her, Max smiled. "Guess what? I got a text from Angus at Angus's Whatnots. He's sold out of my handmade patio furniture and wants me to deliver more ASAP."

Thrilled and proud, she grinned back. "I hope you have more made."

"I do. There are several pieces that are ready to go. And I've got more in various stages of production."

"Do you do all of the work yourself?" she asked, genuinely curious.

"I do." Expression pensive, he made a face. "I've realized that little hobby of mine has become something I can't live without." He gave Charlie one final pet, and then stood. Charlie jumped down as well. "Ready to go?"

"Yes." She clipped a working harness and lead on her dog, stifling a yawn with her hand. "You know, I'd like to watch you work sometime, if you don't mind."

On the way out to his truck, he didn't immediately respond. She opened the passenger door and moved the seat up, motioning for Charlie to get in the back. He hopped inside and sat patiently while she secured his harness to one of the seat belt receptacles.

Once she'd gotten Charlie situated, she moved her seat back and climbed in. When she glanced at Max, surprising an intense look of tenderness on his face, she found herself choking up. For no reason at all.

"What?" she asked, making her voice grumpy to hide her emotions.

"You're beautiful," he said softly. "And yes, I'd love for you to come to my workshop and watch how I work."

"Thanks." Buckling her seat belt, she gave herself a stern talking-to. Not only did she have a class to teach, but both she and Max had been through a lot in one day. No need to let things get too heavy.

Max started the engine. But instead of shifting into Reverse, he half turned in his seat so he faced her.

"You're the first person who's ever asked to see how I make furniture," he said, his voice gruff. "My brothers and father barely tolerate me taking space for my little hobby, as they call it. My sister, Lizzy, thinks I just use it as an excuse to have a man cave or something. Other than Angus, who has a vested interest since he gets a cut, no one else pays any attention to it."

"I can tell it's important to you," she said, touched. "Plus, you're so very good at it."

He laughed and finally shifted into Reverse. "Thanks."

They arrived at Crosswinds with fifteen minutes to spare before her class started. Though Della knew arriving with Max would cause a bit of a stir, she realized she didn't care. If her coworkers wanted to gossip about her, so be it. Max might have a reputation around town, but that man wasn't the same person as the man she'd come to know.

None of her class had arrived yet, which meant she'd get a few minutes to set up. With Charlie trotting proudly on her left side and Max flanking her on the right, she waved at the two women at the desk and continued to the working arena. For their part, they both stared. She was sure there'd be questions later.

Putting Charlie in a sit-stay, she started placing the partitions. With a full class, she liked to keep everyone in their own space until their turn came. She had them work their dog individually in the center of the ring so the others could watch and learn.

One by one, her students arrived. A few of the women eyed Max, who'd taken a chair and sat quietly in the corner. He looked big and brooding and handsome. Della truly couldn't blame them. It was all she could do to not stare at him herself. But in her SAR work, she'd long ago learned how to tune out distractions. She'd use every ounce of that training to pretend Max wasn't there.

"Today we are learning one of the most important commands," she told her class. "Recall. If you're going to teach your dog only one thing, this would be it."

Teaching interested students, both human and canine, gave Della a much-needed boost of energy. Charlie seemed to enjoy it too. Holding his tail high, he proudly put himself through his paces on command, demonstrating a perfect recall among other things.

By the time the class ended, she felt much better. Still a tiny bit shaky, but closer to normal than she had been all day.

A few people approached her with questions. She answered them with ease and gave each of their dogs some attention as well.

Finally, the last one left. She and Charlie headed over toward Max. He stood as they approached, the intensity in his gaze sending a shiver through her. Her body instantly responded. Dang, this man sure could get her wound up.

Normalcy, she reminded herself.

"Are you ready to go?" she asked.

"Sure." Cocking his head, he considered her. "Would you like to stop by the ranch and check out my workshop?"

Though he'd made the question sound casual, she knew how important this was to him. Plus, it secretly thrilled her that he'd asked.

"Why not?" she replied. "There's still plenty of daylight left. As long as no one minds if I bring Charlie."

"They won't even know. We'll avoid the house."

"Ah, I see," she teased, telling herself that this didn't sting. "Avoiding the family so they don't ask too many questions. I get it."

Expression serious, he shook his head. "That's not it at all. If you want to meet my dad, we can make a quick stop. You already met my two brothers at the dinner the other night."

Secretly mollified, she touched his arm. "It's not a big deal."

"Good. Because if we go inside, my dad will want to have a drink and talk, and that will easily eat up an hour or longer."

Now she understood. "I get it."

The drive north out to the Colton Ranch didn't take too long. Though Della had lived in the area for years, she mostly stuck to town and the mountain hiking paths. She found herself admiring the landscape, feeling like a tourist. Rolling pastures, herds of cattle and the occasional grove of trees made her feel almost as if she'd traveled to another state.

Finally, they turned off the main road and drove under an arched sign that read Colton Ranch.

"How much land does your family have?" she asked, noticing how the same color and type of fencing stretched as far as she could see.

"Eight hundred acres," he answered. "We farm and raise cattle. Or they do," he amended. "I got away from here as soon as I could. I knew at an early age that I wasn't cut out to be a rancher."

"I get that. While I never even thought about living anywhere else than Owl Creek, ever since I was a little girl, I knew I'd be working with dogs."

Expression curious, he glanced at her. "How'd you get started in all of that?"

"Lots of research on the internet. And I took classes. Some of them I had to travel a good distance for. I took one in Denver. Another in Orange County, California. I worked, I studied, I got my certifications. And I lucked out when Sebastian let me come work with him."

Max nodded. "He's well respected around here." He grinned. "And once he and Ruby marry, he'll be related."

"They're a good match."

"Look." He pointed. "There's the main house."

On a slight rise in the distance, she could see a large red structure. The closer they got, she realized it appeared to be a rustic house that had been made out of a renovated barn.

"It's been in the family for a long time," Max said. "See all those other odd-shaped additions? Those were all rooms that were built later. After my mother left, my dad put in a pool and a guesthouse. My oldest brother, Greg, lives in the guesthouse now."

She nodded. "I'm guessing your father and other brother live in the main house?"

"Yes. And I stay there when I'm in Owl Creek."

They drove slowly past the stately red house but didn't stop. She couldn't help but admire how, despite the bright color, the structure seemed to complement the landscape. The sun had started its journey toward the horizon, though darkness wouldn't come for another couple of hours. This time of day had long been one of her favorites. Backlit by the sun, the bright orange, shot through with pinks and reds, made the sky and the landscape seem to glow.

There were numerous other structures spread out over the rolling pastures.

"That's the guesthouse," Max said. "The main horse barn, and those are storage buildings. My workshop is there, attached to that one."

Enchanted, she waited until he'd parked and killed the engine before jumping out. Then, because she didn't want to seem too eager, she clasped her hands together until he joined her.

"It's not much," he explained as he unlocked the door. "A lot of woodworking tools, wood, paint and stain. I don't use this space for anything other than a workshop."

When he opened the door and turned on the light, he stepped aside so she could enter.

Inside, there were at least ten chairs, several settees and various other pieces in various stages of work. What caught her eye immediately was that he'd made different types of pieces. Some were rustic, like the ones she'd purchased. There were also a few made in a more modern, sleek style.

The area appeared well organized, at least to her untrained eyes. Woodworking machinery took up one entire space, and he'd made what looked like a small painting-booth-type area in the back corner. For a one-man operation, she thought it looked incredibly efficient.

"How long have you been doing this?" she asked, trailing her fingers across the back of one of his unpainted pieces.

"I started in high school," he replied. "Working with wood has always been a way to release tension. Of course, when I was in college, it was much more difficult to get back here and make time for this. Summers were always when I got the most done."

"Wow. That's amazing. These days, with you living in Boise and having such a time-consuming job, how do you find the time?"

Her question made him grimace. "I don't get to do it as much as I'd like. I have a smallish apartment in Boise, so it's not like I can move some of this there to work on."

"These are all so beautiful," she said, meaning it. "I bet you could make a living doing this if you wanted to."

He laughed. "Maybe so, but not much of one. Right now, it's a nice hobby that supplements my income. To make any serious money, I'd have to expand. I'd need more places willing to carry my pieces."

"Or you could rent space and open your own store," she pointed out. "Set up an online catalog and sell that way too."

"Shipping prices would be astronomical," he countered.

Liking the way he didn't entirely discount her idea, she nodded. "True. I'd guess there'd be some people willing to pay it, though. And we get a lot of tourists here, especially in ski season. Something to consider, for some day in the future."

"Maybe," he agreed. "But I like the way you think."

Chest aching, she smiled, wondering if he knew how she'd come to love him, and what the heck she was going to do about it.

Max had never brought a female inside his workshop, not even during high school, when the vast majority of his dating time seemed to consist of looking for private places to make out. Even then, he'd considered his workshop a sacred space. His brothers tended to avoid it, having no time for anything that didn't directly impact the ranch. And his father appeared to have largely forgotten about it, which suited Max just fine.

Now, watching Della as she roamed the small space, her hands caressing the wood, an expression of wonder lighting up her beautiful face, he realized she actually got it. No one in his family understood how happy working with the oak and pine and ash made him.

And her suggestions about growing his business had been spot-on. He'd often wondered what it would be like to have more time to build his furniture, but being an FBI agent didn't allow for him to cut his hours or adopt a flexible schedule. However, by living simply, he'd managed to amass a healthy savings account. More than enough to help him get started.

The fact that he was even considering such a thing would have shocked him any other time. But now...he wasn't sure.

Quite honestly, the thought of going back to Boise and

his empty, sterile apartment didn't sound even remotely appealing. And the fact that the Bureau wanted him to drop this case and pin the blame on someone without a single shred of evidence stuck in his craw.

He had two weeks to run his own investigation, as long as he was careful to stay under the radar. More than anything, he didn't want to let Della's cousin, or any of the women who'd lost their lives to this monster, down. If the man he'd shot actually turned out to be the serial killer, great. If not, Max wanted to make sure the right person was brought to justice.

Even more importantly, he needed to make sure no other woman suffered the same fate.

"Oh, I love this piece." Della's comment brought him out of his reverie. Blinking, he saw her crouching in front of one of his more experimental items. A small corner cabinet, whitewashed and made to look rustic. Inside, he'd placed two shelves.

"How much for this?" she asked, delight filling her gaze. "I absolutely love this, and I know just where I want it to go."

Looking at her, so filled with joy over something he'd made with his own hands, in that moment he knew he would have given her the world.

"It's yours," he said, managing to contain his emotion despite the roughness to his voice. "I'll load it up and get it to your place when I take you home."

She stared at him, her beautiful eyes wide. For a moment, he thought she might protest, but instead she pushed to her feet and rushed to him. Wrapping her arms around his waist, she hugged him tightly.

He never wanted to move again.

"Thank you," she muttered, face pressed against his chest. "How about we load it up and head out?"

"Okay." Kissing the top of her head, for the first time ever he realized he wanted to make love to her here, among all the things he valued. His body stirred and he shifted his stance so she wouldn't feel his growing arousal pressing against her.

As if she sensed this, she raised her head. "Not here. Let's go home."

Home.

Later, while Della showered, Max found himself on her back porch, sitting in one of the chairs he'd made, staring at the moon and stars, so bright in the night sky. Charlie had followed him outside and lay curled up at his feet. Max felt a sense of contentment and rightness that he hadn't ever felt before. As if he *belonged.*

Shaking his head at himself, he pulled out his phone. Though technically he was on leave, he went ahead and left a message for Caroline, asking her to call him when she was back at the office. Though he doubted the body of the shooter had been sent to her, he knew she maintained close connections with other forensic pathologists around the state. He wanted to find out if she'd heard anything about the man he'd shot.

Then he called his cousin Fletcher, who worked as a detective for Owl Creek PD. Despite the late hour, Fletcher picked up on the second ring.

"I figured you'd be calling," Fletcher drawled. "Let me save you some time. We're working on an ID for the shooter you took down. Since it's after hours and everyone has gone home for the night, I'm sure we'll know something tomorrow."

"Thank you." Relieved that Fletcher understood, Max took a deep breath. "I know everyone thinks this guy is the serial killer and considers the case closed. Including the Bureau. But I'm not so convinced. Once we find out this guy's identity, I want to work on a timeline of his whereabouts over the last couple of years."

"You do?" Fletcher sounded surprised. "I thought everyone was in agreement that you'd taken out our man."

Max coughed. "Everyone but me, I guess."

"I'm surprised the FBI is letting you continue to work on this case. From what I was told, they consider it closed. Hell, did you watch the press conference?"

"I did. And the FBI has closed the case." Max paused. "I've actually taken a couple weeks' PTO. I'm looking into this on my own."

"Wow." Fletcher let out a low whistle. "You're that unconvinced."

"Aren't you?" Max countered. "There's no other evidence. None."

"Not yet," Fletcher replied calmly. "But don't you think the fact that he killed the one woman who managed to escape him is pretty damning?"

"Possibly. But alone, it's not enough proof. This could have been an entirely separate, unrelated incident."

"Not everything has to be so complicated," Fletcher said. "You've worked in law enforcement long enough to understand that. Maybe this is exactly what it seems."

"I'd like nothing better." Max swallowed, aware he wasn't getting anywhere. "But would you mind giving me a holler once you have more info?"

"I don't mind at all. As soon as we learn more, I'll let you know."

Ending the call, Max sat for a moment, trying to think. He respected Fletcher's opinion. If Fletcher felt there might be a credible chance that the man Max had shot was the serial killer, it could be that Max was about to keep knocking himself out investigating nothing.

Still, he had to try. He'd long ago learned to trust his gut, and right now every instinct he possessed told him they were blaming the wrong man.

The sliding glass doors opened, and Della stepped outside, her hair still damp. "Hey," she said softly. "I wondered where the two of you had gotten off to."

Charlie wagged his tail but didn't raise his head. Shaking her head at her dog, Della stepped around him and took a seat in the chair next to Max.

"You look perturbed," she commented. "Is everything okay?"

"Just work stuff," he replied, not wanting to rehash the situation.

"I thought you were on leave."

He should have known she'd see right through him. He shrugged. "Just doing a little investigating on my own time. Even though I'm not going back to the office, I still want to be kept updated on the case."

"I get that." Running her hand down the arm of her chair, she stroked the wood. "These truly are beautiful pieces."

Watching her, all he could think about was how badly he wanted those hands on his skin.

As if she read his mind, she got up, took his hand and gave a tug. "Come on. Let's go inside."

The invitation in her voice made his body instantly respond. They barely made it to the couch.

As usual, their lovemaking was intense and tender.

The next morning, he woke up at sunrise. Leaving Della sleeping in the bed, with Charlie curled up at her feet, he headed for the bathroom to take a quick shower.

When he emerged, Della sat up and gave him a sleepy smile. "Morning."

The warmth in her gaze tempted him. But then Charlie barked and jumped down, trotting toward the back door.

"Would you mind letting him outside?" Della asked, yawning. "I'm going to jump in the shower."

"No problem," he said.

After he'd let Charlie out, Max made himself a cup of coffee with the intention of carrying it to the back porch. But before he could even take his first sip of coffee, Caroline returned his call from the night before.

"I hear congratulations are in order," she said by way of greeting. "You solved the case *and* took out the unsub. Way to go, Max."

Try as he might, he couldn't detect even a hint of sarcasm in her voice. He groaned. "Not you too?"

His question made her snort into the phone. "I know you have doubts, as do I, but sometimes these cases have a way of working themselves out. It seems this one did."

"Yeah, maybe so." This time, he knew better than to argue his point. Clearly, he was the only one who felt the case should remain open.

"Caroline, I called you because I need to know everything we know about the man I shot. His name, where he's from and if he has any ties to any local churches."

She went silent for a few seconds. "Are you okay, Max?"

"I'm fine. It's just bothering me that I had to kill him. I would have liked to question him, but…"

"I get that." She sighed. "You are aware that the autopsy will be done by the county, right? The local police resumed jurisdiction at our request."

"I heard," he said. "But I also know all forensic investigators talk. I'd really appreciate you filling me in on anything you might hear through the grapevine."

"You got it," Caroline responded. She hesitated a moment before continuing. "Max, I heard you were taking a short vacation. Is that true?"

He nearly groaned out loud. "Damn, news sure travels fast. Yes, I'm on a bit of PTO."

"We had a team briefing yesterday. That's how I knew," Caroline said. "Brian filled us all in on everything. He told us he didn't include you because you were off."

Which stung. Though Max couldn't really blame him. After all, it sounded as if Max had been the only one who objected to the case being closed so abruptly.

"I'm glad you're taking some time off," Caroline said softly. "Because I think this case might have become too personal to you. A little vacation away from all of this should be a good thing."

"Hopefully so." Before ending the call, he once again extracted a promise from her to call him with any information. "Even though I'm on PTO, I still want to stay informed."

She muttered something noncommittal and said goodbye.

A few minutes later, Della came strolling into the kitchen. "I need to feed Charlie," she said. "Where is he?"

"Outside." He smiled. "I left the slider cracked a bit. I assumed he'll push it all the way open when he's ready to come in."

She froze, then hurried toward the sliding door. "I

don't usually leave him out there unattended. I should have told you that."

Not understanding her concern since her backyard was completely fenced, he followed her out onto the porch.

"Charlie?" she called. "Time to eat. Charlie, come."

Nothing. A quick scan of the backyard revealed no black Lab anywhere in sight.

"Oh no." Della rushed down the outdoor stairs, moving so fast Max worried she'd fall. He hurried down after her, wondering what on earth he'd missed in the scenario.

"Charlie," she called again. "Charlie, come."

But the well-trained dog didn't respond.

A moment later, Max realized why. The side gate had blown open. And Charlie was nowhere to be found.

Chapter 14

No Charlie. Filled with an icy panic, Della found herself struggling to breathe. Panicking wouldn't help anything. If she was going to find her dog, she needed to remain cool, calm and collected.

When she caught sight of the open gate swinging in the morning breeze, she spun to face Max. "How long was he out here?" she asked, struggling to keep from sounding accusatory. "I'm just trying to figure out how far he might have gotten."

"Maybe fifteen, twenty minutes," he replied, looking worried and apologetic. "I'm so sorry. I didn't know. Hopefully, he didn't go far. Do you want to hop in the truck and go look for him?"

"Not just yet." Damned if she wasn't fighting back tears. She cleared her throat. Now was not the time to break down. "Charlie isn't the type of dog to just wander off. He's trained off lead. We also have an emergency recall command that's different than the usual one. I'm going to go out front and try that."

Striding through the open gate with Max right behind her, she looked both ways. Up and down her street. No sign of her beloved black Lab. For a moment, anguish closed her throat. She couldn't lose him. She simply couldn't.

"Della, it's going to be all right." Max touched her shoulder, his voice reassuring. "We'll find him. He can't have gone far."

For one second, she let her shoulders sag. Then she straightened, willing herself to calmness. "You're right. Let me try calling out his emergency command. If he's anywhere within hearing distance, that will bring him running."

She walked out into the middle of the street. Then, cupping her hands to her mouth to amplify her voice, she called out, "Charlie, URGENT! COME."

Certain this would bring her dog barreling toward her, she waited. When she still didn't see him, she took a deep breath and tried again, louder. "CHARLIE! URGENT! COME."

Her words seemed to echo off the deserted street. Still no sign of Charlie. If any of her neighbors were still sleeping, she knew she'd likely woken them.

Next door, the front door opened, and her uncle Alex stepped out. Catching sight of her and Max, he shook his head and went back inside without speaking. Neither he nor her aunt had spoken to Della in days. In fact, it seemed they'd gone out of their way to avoid her.

She was disappointed. But none of that mattered now. She had to find Charlie. "Let's drive around the neighborhood," she said. "If he didn't respond to the emergency recall command, he's got to be out of earshot."

"Come on." They ran for his truck. He started it remotely with his key fob before they were even inside. "Which way?" he asked, backing out of her driveway.

"Left." She pointed. "When we take walks, he likes to visit with a couple of the dogs out in their backyards."

Her voice broke halfway through, but she kept her chin up and her eyes peeled. Max drove slowly down the street. She had her window open, and she leaned out a little bit, scanning the bushes and the backyards for a sight of her dog.

"He's got to be around here somewhere," Max said. "Don't worry. We'll find him."

Instead of answering, she nodded. She didn't tell him it wasn't like Charlie to wander off. Of course, he'd never been tempted by a wide-open gate while unsupervised either.

Still, she couldn't blame Max. He hadn't known.

One time around the block, and still no sign of her boy. The dogs he usually interacted with were outside, standing by their chain-link fences, tails wagging.

"We need to broaden the search," Max announced. "We'll move out another block and go around."

Speechless with worry, she nodded. She had taken Charlie for walks that way as well. "There's a pet llama in a small pasture at the end of the next street. Charlie loves to visit with her."

"We'll stop by there," he said. Still driving slowly, they rounded the corner and headed up in the direction of the llama.

Della leaned out her window, scanning, searching, for even the slightest flash of black fur. Charlie couldn't have disappeared. Unless someone had grabbed him and taken him away in a vehicle.

No. She refused to let her thoughts skitter off in that direction. He'd turn up here soon. He had to.

As they approached the next corner, she saw the llama standing at the fence, staring down the street. Della looked in that direction but didn't see anything.

"Hey, there," she said, using that particular crooning tone the llama had always seemed to like. "Have you seen my Charlie?"

The animal cocked its head, listening.

"Too bad he can't talk," Max said.

They continued slowly past. At the next intersection, Max turned right. "Look!" He pointed.

Two blocks up, on the opposite side of the street, a man walked with a large black dog on a leash. Seeing this, Della felt her heart begin to race. "That looks like Charlie," she breathed.

Max sped up. As they drew closer, Della realized that man had her dog!

"Charlie!" Opening her door, she jumped out of the truck while it was still moving. As her boy fought the man with the leash, trying to get to her, she rushed over.

"Excuse me. That's my dog," she called out, sprinting toward them. The instant he heard her voice, Charlie began to struggle in earnest to break free. Clearly startled, the man let the leash go and took a step back.

With a glad bark, Charlie leaped for her. His entire body quivered, and his tail whipped furiously. Dropping to her knees on the sidewalk, she opened her arms and took her boy in. He was so happy to see her that he nearly knocked her backward with his enthusiastic greeting. He kept licking her face and making soft chuffing sounds as he tried to get as close to her as possible.

Overwhelmed with relief and joy, Della let the tears

fall freely. Charlie tried to lick them away, which made her laugh.

"What's going on here?" Catching up to them, Max addressed the stranger who'd had Charlie.

"I was out walking and found this dog," the man said, sounding bemused. "He came right to me when I called him. I used my belt and managed to get him leashed up. There's a vet's office a few blocks that way, so I was taking him in to see if he has a microchip. That's when you two drove up."

Arms around a still-wiggling Charlie, Della looked up and smiled. "Thank you from the bottom of my heart. The side gate blew open and he disappeared. I can't tell you how much he means to me."

"It looks like he feels the same way about you," the man replied, smiling back. He quickly put his belt back on, buckling it. "I'm just glad it all worked out." With that, he walked away.

Frowning, Max watched him go. "Good thing we came up on him before he made it to his vehicle."

"What do you mean?" Della asked. "He said he was out for a walk."

"Maybe so, but look. He's getting into that Toyota parked under that tree."

Looking up, she watched as the man drove off. "Wow. You're right. I wonder if he was trying to drag Charlie over to his car."

"Maybe so. But I guess it doesn't matter. We got him back."

"Thank goodness." She returned all her attention to her beloved dog.

"Again, I'm so sorry," Max said. "This happened on

my watch. I'd never have forgiven myself if anything had happened to Charlie."

"All's well that ends well. But still, I'm putting a lock on that gate," she vowed. "This can never happen again. Ever."

"I agree." Holding out his hand, Max helped her get up. "Let's head back to the house."

Throat tight, she nodded. As she moved toward the truck, Charlie kept himself close, always with part of him up against her leg.

Once they were all inside the truck, Max started it up and drove back to the house. Della glanced at the dashboard clock, surprised to realize that nearly an hour had passed. Still, they'd started so early that she wouldn't even be late for work.

Neither she nor Max spoke on the short drive back home. When they pulled up into the driveway, she opened the door and Charlie bounded out. She immediately headed around the side of the house toward the still-open gate. Charlie followed, close on her heels, apparently loath to let her out of his sight.

She waited until Max, who came right behind, had joined them before closing the gate. While she didn't have a lock just yet, she knew she could jam something into the hole in the gate handle so the gate couldn't be opened.

"Do you have a bolt and a nut?" Max asked. "That would work just as well as a lock."

She did. After fetching them from the garage, she rigged them up. "Perfect," she said, satisfied. "That gate will be a lot more secure now."

"Look." Max pointed. "Your dog is happy to be home."

Charlie rolled on his back in the grass, all four feet in the air, tongue hanging from his mouth. Noticing them watching him, he jumped up and shook himself, before trotting over to nudge Della's hand with his nose.

"He's definitely coming to work with me today," she said. "I'm not letting him out of my sight."

Smiling, Max nodded. "Do you have to work all day? I was planning to hike back up to that meadow and wondered if you and Charlie would like to go with me."

Though the prospect of going back to the scene where so many women had lost their lives made her stomach churn, an afternoon of hiking and fresh air with Max would be just what she and Charlie needed. She'd like nothing better. But even so...

"I'll have to see if I can shuffle things around," she replied, allowing regret to color her voice. "I've missed so much time already, and if I don't get back on schedule, the dogs I'm working with will get seriously behind." She thought for a moment. "I need to spend at least five hours at Crosswinds. If I get there at eight and skip lunch, I could be done around one."

"That'd work," he agreed, smiling. "And I can bring you something to eat on the drive up to the trailhead."

"Sounds perfect." Giving in to impulse, she kissed him. On the cheek this time, because she didn't want to get distracted by passion. "Now I just need a few minutes to get ready. Since you're picking me up later, would you mind dropping me off?"

"Not at all." He grinned. "Though you really do still need to get that broken window on your Jeep repaired."

"I know." Shaking her head, she led the way into the house. Charlie trotted along right after her, leaving Max to once again take up the rear. Della liked having him there. She felt like he was watching her back.

Pushing away her fanciful thoughts, Della excused herself and went to get ready. She dragged a brush through her now-dry hair and put it into a ponytail. Grabbing her backpack where she kept her hiking supplies, including sunscreen, she hurried back out into the living room, where Max and Charlie waited.

Max had taken a seat on the couch to wait, and Charlie had made himself at home next to him. The two of them huddled together, Charlie's head in Max's lap. Max was so engrossed in petting the dog that he didn't even realize Della had returned.

Only when Charlie spotted her and started wagging his tail did Max turn his head.

"Are you ready?" he asked, his gaze darkening as he looked at her.

Again, she felt that tug of attraction, aching to go to him and kiss him until they were both mindless with passion.

"Yep," she said instead, aware she sounded a bit breathless. "Let's get going. The sooner I can get to work, the better."

Calling Charlie to her, she clipped a lead on his collar. Usually, she just made him heel by her side on the way to her vehicle, but not after what had happened earlier. Right now, she couldn't bring herself to take any chances.

They made the short drive to Crosswinds in a companionable silence, Charlie sitting happily in the back seat. After the hellish way this day had started, this bit of comforting normalcy right now felt like a soothing balm on her nerves.

He pulled up to the front door to let her and Charlie out. "I'll see you around one," he said, leaning over to place a quick kiss on her cheek.

At the last moment, she turned her face, needing his lips on hers. He lingered a moment, before chuckling as they drew apart. The heat in his gaze made her body tingle.

"I'd better get going," she said, slightly breathless again. She grabbed Charlie's lead and waited while he jumped out of the truck. Suppressing the urge to blow Max a kiss, she turned and walked into the building without a backward glance.

With several hours to kill, Max went ahead and called Brian. Still slightly irritated that he'd been left out of the briefing, he figured he might as well get the details straight from his SAC's mouth.

"Max, good to hear from you," Brian said. "Caroline told me you'd called her earlier."

"I did," Max replied, slightly surprised. "She told me you had a team meeting yesterday to fill everyone in on the case. I'm wondering why you didn't include me."

"Because I'd already discussed it privately with you. The case is over, Max. We're considering it closed."

"I know, but I was hoping for more concrete evidence that the man I shot actually *is* the serial killer," Max said. "That's why I called Caroline. I am assigned to this case."

"Was," Brian corrected. "Past tense. Let me say this again." His tone became stern and clipped. "The case is closed. The Bureau will not waste any more time or resources on it. Do you understand?"

Max swallowed, his jaw tight. "Yes. I do."

"Which is why I asked you to drop it," Brian continued. "I know you mean well, but there was a lot of behind-the-scenes pressure on us from high-level government officials. Closed means closed." He took a deep breath. "That's an order."

It took every ounce of self-control Max possessed to not inform his boss that he could do whatever he wanted on his own time. "Understood."

After ending the call, Max allowed himself to seethe for a few minutes. Over the last several years, politics and bureaucracy had gotten worse. Sometimes, it seemed to be less about making wrongs right and more about surface appearances.

Hell, he knew better than to allow his feelings to get hurt. Once upon a time, he would have been able to shrug this off and get on with his life.

Except this time, Caroline was right. This case had become personal. Anytime he thought of Della's grief-stricken face when she'd realized her cousin had been killed, he wanted justice. More than justice. Vengeance.

How could he let this go? But Brian had made it abundantly clear that he had to, or risk losing his job.

Fuming, Max drove back to the ranch. He had a lot of serious thinking to do. And what better place to do it than in his workshop.

Thirty minutes later, after he'd vigorously sanded a new chair he'd built, most of his tension had left him. But he'd also reached a decision. He couldn't give up on the case. Especially since every gut instinct he possessed told him they were blaming the wrong guy. The killer had gone undetected for years, murdering his victims and burying them in shallow graves in a remote location. If he started up again, how long would it take for him to get noticed this time?

He'd decided to make a special batch of chairs to sell in town. Instead of his usual brown, white or black, he wanted to paint them bright colors. He'd bought yellow, red, orange, green and blue paint. Cheerful chairs, perfect for summer. He had a feeling they'd sell quickly.

Lost in his work, when he looked up to check the time, he found several hours had passed. Deciding to take a short break, he went up to the house to grab some water and use the bathroom. He'd have just about enough time to finish painting one more chair before he'd need to get cleaned up and head over to pick up Della.

Time flew, as it always seemed to when he worked on his hobby. Idly, he wondered if it would remain as joyful if it became his full-time job and only income. Somehow, he suspected it would.

His stomach growled, making him realize he'd need to stop so he'd have time to pick up lunch on the way to get Della.

Whistling a catchy little tune, Max quickly changed into his hiking gear. Grateful for the bright blue cloudless sky, he locked up and got in his truck, heading for Crosswinds. On the way there, he stopped by Burger Barn and picked up a couple of meals, including a special burger only on a bun for Charlie.

The prospect of a hike with Della and her dog felt like exactly what he should be doing on such a perfect afternoon. A trip to the meadow would definitely help him get his thinking straight. He'd been ordered to drop his investigation. Seeing the burial ground once again might help him decide if he could.

When he pulled up in front of Crosswinds, Della and Charlie came right out. Her bright smile immediately lightened his mood.

She let Charlie in first. The black Lab hopped into the back seat, clearly comfortable and relaxed. Della grinned and ruffled Charlie's fur. "Spoiled boy," she said, without a hint of regret in her voice. "Such a good dog."

Damn, she was beautiful. Max could barely tear his gaze away from her. Her smile widened again as she met his gaze. "Hey," she said, her voice soft.

When she got into the passenger seat, she leaned over and kissed him, a quick brush of her lips across his. Just that light touch had him instantly craving more.

To cover, he cleared his throat. "I brought lunch."

"That smells amazing," she said. "I'm starving."

"I hope you don't mind, but I got a plain burger for Charlie," he told her. "I don't know if you let him eat that kind of thing, but I thought he might like it."

"How thoughtful." She kissed him again, as if doing so was the most natural thing in the world. "I don't usually, but every once in a while, he can have a treat." Reaching into the back seat, she ruffled her dog's fur. "Is it okay if we eat on the way? I'm too hungry to wait until we get there."

"Sure." He felt tongue-tied, something he'd never been. "How about we chow down here? It'd be easier for me than trying to navigate some of those winding roads with a burger in one hand."

"Sounds good." With a shrug, she grabbed the food

bag. First, she handed him his burger and fries, then carefully unwrapped Charlie's. Breaking that burger into small pieces, she fed them to the eager dog, one at a time, placing each piece on one of the paper napkins. Only once Charlie had gobbled down his meal did she get her own.

Max ate quickly, barely tasting his food. He tried not to stare, but the way she practically inhaled her meal had him transfixed, somehow.

"What?" she finally asked, smiling slightly as she popped the last of her fries into her mouth. "I was hungry."

"Me too," he managed, using his thumb to gently brush a crumb from her lips.

"Thanks," she said, clearly oblivious to the way she affected him. "Let's go. I'm definitely ready to get up in the mountains."

"Are you?" he asked, starting the engine and shifting into Drive. "I worried it might be too much for you."

"Thanks." She thought for a moment. "While I confess I'm not sure how I'll handle seeing that field again, getting up in the higher altitude is always good for my soul."

"Me too."

Della seemed pensive as they drove. She looked out the side window, watching the landscape. Max managed to keep his gaze on the road.

When they turned into the trailhead parking area, there were only a couple of other cars there. He found them a spot and cut the engine. Charlie sat up in the back seat, tail wagging.

"That's the best part about going hiking on a random weekday afternoon," Della said. "I try to never come up here on the weekends." She grabbed her bag and changed out her sneakers for hiking shoes. Once she'd done this, she grabbed Charlie's leash and they got out of the truck. Max joined them, taking deep breaths of the clean mountain air.

"Let's do this!" Della offered him a high five. Then, side by side, the three of them set off on the trail leading up the mountain.

Every time he came out this way, the beauty of the Bitterroots struck him anew. He'd been troubled, and some of that tension hadn't entirely loosened its grip on him, but he suspected the fresh air and exercise would help.

"Do you want to talk about it?" Della asked, making him wonder if she'd been able to read his mind.

"Just work stuff," he replied. "Trying to figure out some things."

"Okay." She elbowed his side. "Put all of that away for now. It's a beautiful day. It'd be great if you'd enjoy it."

"I can take a hint." Giving in to temptation, he grabbed her free hand. This made her laugh and give his fingers a squeeze.

They kept their mood light almost all the way to the meadow. The sunshine felt good on his skin, but more than anything, he enjoyed being with Della. Charlie too.

As they reached the large rock outcropping that marked the last area for cell phone signal, they stopped. Della gently pulled her hand free. Charlie, still on lead, sat, waiting to see what they'd do next.

"Not too much farther." Expression pensive, Della gazed up at the rock.

He nodded, hoping she'd want to go with him but understanding why she might not. "Do you want to wait here while I hike up there?"

"Of course not. I want to go. It'll be a good training exercise refresher for Charlie. But I have to say, I'm kind of curious about what you might be hoping to find."

Since Max didn't know the answer to that himself, he wasn't sure how to respond. He finally settled on the truth. "I wanted to see it again."

"To see if it affects you the same way?" she asked.

"Not that." He made a movement with his hand. "It will still be disturbing to both of us. How could it not? It's just since we found the woman who escaped, I felt like we had our first actual lead to discovering his identity."

"Which is why he killed her," Della said.

"That's the general consensus."

"But you don't agree?" she asked. "Why else would that man go into a hospital, cut the power, enter a room that had a police guard and kill Maisy? It's only logical to think he was the killer, trying to cover up his tracks."

Pensive, he considered her words. Everyone, including his cousin Fletcher, thought the same way. He didn't understand why he appeared to be the lone holdout, steadfast in following his instincts. Maybe the time had come to admit he might be wrong?

Except what if he wasn't? That could be the kind of dilemma that kept him up at night.

Pushing the thoughts from his mind, he took a deep breath.

"Let's do this."

Because the terrain got rougher the rest of the way, they went single file, no longer holding hands. Della and

Charlie went first, and Max brought up the rear. The knowledge of where they were heading did little to dim the beauty of their surroundings.

When they reached the clearing where the team had pitched their tents, the remnants of the charred logs inside the fire circle had him remembering the first time he and Della had kissed. A quick glance at Della's pink cheeks told him she remembered it too.

Charlie, on the other hand, clearly wanted to surge forward. He stood at full alert, tail high, nose sniffing the air. Max supposed that only the fact that he'd been well trained kept him from pulling on the leash.

"He's ready to go," Della said, her attempt at a smile falling short.

"You don't have to do this," he told her, his voice quiet.

"I know." She grimaced. "But I've never been one to avoid doing hard things. I've revisited this meadow more than once in my dreams. Nothing here can hurt me anymore."

Aching with love for her, he started forward. Before, Della and Charlie had led the way, but now Max felt he had to go first. If Della were to change her mind, he didn't want to be in the way.

There, that small grove of trees. Around that, and the field stretched before him. Yellow crime scene tape fluttered in the breeze, still marking the place where so many innocent young women had met a violent end.

Max stopped, inhaling deeply as he took it all in. Della removed Charlie's leash, giving him a hand signal command that Max supposed meant the dog could roam freely.

"I asked him to go to work," Della said, her quiet voice matching the sadness in her eyes. "I know he's already checked and made sure there aren't any other buried remains, but he can always use the practice."

Side by side, they watched as Charlie checked out the area, nose to the ground. He made several circles, each one larger than the last.

"He's very thorough," Max commented.

"Yes."

Neither of them moved while the diligent canine continued searching. Finally, Charlie made it to the perimeter of the meadow, still intently searching.

"Do you call him back to you when you think he's done?" Max asked.

"I can. But in a situation like this one, where there's no danger and not a lot of other people and dogs, he'll return to me to let me know he hasn't found anything."

Sure enough, a few minutes later, Charlie came bounding back and sat in front of Della.

"Good boy," Della said, ruffling the dog's head. She glanced at Max. "I'm really glad he didn't find anything."

"Me too." Now Max forced himself to move forward, stopping to look at each area where the earth had been disturbed. His team had been careful to shovel the dirt back into each grave once the bones had been removed.

Once he'd viewed all of them, he stopped, conscious of Della watching him. Each and every woman who'd died here deserved justice. If the man Max had killed in that hospital room truly was the unsub, then they'd gotten it. If not, until more women were brutally murdered, no one would know the truth.

"Are you okay?" Della finally asked.

Returning to her, he met her gaze. "I'm thinking about leaving the FBI," he said, his heart pounding as he spoke his thoughts out loud. "I can't seem to reconcile myself with the way they're not allowing me to investigate this case. I have to know, beyond a shadow of a doubt, that this serial killer has been stopped. And right now, I don't feel comfortable with everyone believing he has."

Chapter 15

Hearing the anguish in his deep voice, Della's heart ached.

"I owe it to you," he continued. "You and your cousin and all the other victims." Gesturing around the field, he grimaced. "But without the Bureau's support, or that of the police, there's not a whole lot I can do."

She put Charlie in a stay, went to Max and took both his hands in hers. Standing on tiptoe, she kissed him. "You know what? There's no need to risk everything for my peace of mind. While I deeply appreciate you wanting to do that, I finally feel like it's going to be all right. Some questions never find their answer. Since you shot that man who killed Maisy, I can truly believe that Angela's killer is now dead and put my cousin to rest."

Max froze, his blue gaze locked on hers.

She watched several emotions flicker across his handsome face. For a stoic FBI agent, he wasn't all that great at hiding his thoughts, but maybe he only let down his guard when he was with her. The thought sent a rush of warmth through her.

"But…" he began, his brow furrowed.

"No buts." She kissed him again, lingering this time. "Let me have this. Please. It's what I want."

She felt the tension leave him. He pulled her close, slanting his mouth over hers. By the time he lifted his head, they were both breathless. Heaven help her, but she didn't know how she was going to survive once he returned to Boise. It would be like trying to breathe without air.

"Are you sure?" he asked, his voice raspy. "Because I promise I'll drop it if you're positive that's what you want."

"I am." She turned and eyed her beloved dog, who watched them both with his head cocked. "It's time to put this case to rest."

Slowly, he nodded. "Okay. Are you ready to head back down?"

What she really wanted to do was kiss him again. Instead, she ducked her head and murmured her assent. When she lifted her chin again, she realized she felt stronger and more at peace.

Charlie whined, as if to remind her she'd asked him to remain where he was. This made her smile.

"Charlie, *free*," she said, releasing him from his stay. Instantly, Charlie bounded over to her, tail wagging, tongue lolling. She clipped the leash on before glancing at Max. "Let's go."

The hike back down the trail went quickly. By the time they reached the parking area, Charlie had begun panting. She got her water bottle and poured some into the collapsible water bowl she always carried. While her dog drank, she took a few swigs herself. Next to her, Max did the same.

Then they got into his truck and drove back home. When they reached her house and Max parked, she wasn't sure if he planned to drop her off and leave or if he wanted to come in. As she opened her mouth to ask, he kissed her. "Would you like to have dinner with me?" he asked.

"Yes." She made no attempt to squelch the joy that flooded her at his question. "I can cook something if you'd like, or we can get takeout."

"I think we should go to a restaurant," he said, watching her closely, a teasing glint in his blue eyes. "Like a real date. That is, if you're not embarrassed to be seen out in public with me."

She started to protest but settled on a shrug instead. "Because of your reputation? Maybe, but I've always loved to live dangerously."

This made him laugh. "Me too. I'm in the mood for fajitas. Is Mexican food okay with you?"

"Definitely. Mexican food is always a good thing. So is a delicious frozen margarita." Hand on the door handle, she hesitated. "Would you like to come inside?"

"Of course I would, but I've got a few errands to run in town, plus I need to stop by the ranch and shower and change. I'll pick you up in a couple of hours. I'll text you when I'm on the way," he told her, his steady gaze filling her with the kind of warmth that made her long to seduce him.

Instead, she hid her disappointment with a quick nod. "Sounds good. See you soon." Opening the door for Charlie, she held his leash while he hopped out of the truck. Then she and her dog stood on her front porch and watched as Max drove away, taking a piece of her heart with him.

"Della?" Next door, her aunt Mary stepped outside

and walked slowly over, shuffling like a woman several decades older. The change in her appearance shocked Della. In the time since her aunt had learned of Angela's death, she'd seemed to age at least ten years. Sorrow had made deep lines around her eyes and mouth, and she no longer attempted to cover up the gray in her hair. Before, she'd always loved dressing in colorful Western outfits that she'd chosen carefully to match her jewelry. Today, she wore a faded T-shirt and wrinkled khaki capris with flip-flops. She had no jewelry on whatsoever.

Swallowing back the ache in her throat at the change, Della felt her smile wobble.

"Aunt Mary!" They hugged. Della couldn't help but notice how thin the older woman had become. "It's been a long time since I've seen you. How have you been?"

The instant she asked the question, she regretted it. Glancing down at her dog, she saw Charlie waiting patiently to be noticed, slowly wagging his tail.

"Not too well," Aunt Mary replied. "Alex and I are both trying to come to terms with knowing we'll never see Angela again. Knowing that the man who murdered her was shot and killed has helped a little, but not as much as I thought it would."

"That's helped me too," Della said. "But I'd really like to have some sort of celebration of Angela's life, if you and Uncle Alex are all right with that. Angela had a lot of friends here in Owl Creek."

Mary recoiled. "I don't think I can handle that. I know your uncle can't. Maybe after more time has passed. I don't know."

"I understand," Della said, even though she didn't.

"Just let me know whenever you're ready. I'll organize everything."

"I will, dear." Her aunt cocked her head. "I've noticed you've been seeing a lot of that Colton boy."

Hearing Max referred to that way made Della smile. "I have. He's a good guy."

"Is he? I'm sure quite a few other brokenhearted women here in Owl Creek thought the same thing. Please be careful, Della. You've been through a lot. Don't let him take advantage of that."

Unsure how to respond to this, Della managed a nod. "I won't. But for the record, he's not like that."

"For your sake, I hope you're right." Mary hugged her once more before turning and making her way back home. She never acknowledged Charlie's presence, not even once. This too wasn't like her. Her aunt had always fussed over Della's black Lab, even referring to him as her dog nephew.

Charlie dropped his head, his tail going still. Della ruffled his fur and dropped a kiss on his head. "It's okay, boy. She's still going through a lot."

As if he understood her words, Charlie licked her hand.

Della could only hope that someday, after the pain wore off, everything would return to a semblance of normalcy. Her aunt and uncle were the only family she had left, and she'd missed them more than she could express.

"Come on, Charlie. Let's go in."

Once inside her own house, after taking Charlie outside for a quick potty trip, Della jumped into the shower. Max's words, calling their dinner tonight an actual date, kept replaying in her head. She couldn't help but wonder if he'd begun to have the same kind of feelings for her as she had for him.

He'd mentioned quitting his job, which had stunned her. But then she'd realized he'd only said that because he wanted to continue working on the case and the FBI wouldn't let him. Not, as she might wish, because he didn't want to leave Owl Creek and her.

Shaking off her fanciful thoughts, she decided that she'd still make every effort to look her best tonight. She wanted to knock his boots off.

After drying her hair, she used her flat iron to straighten it. Then she sat down and carefully applied makeup. She rarely wore more than mascara, but for tonight she went all out. When she finished, she eyed herself in the mirror, feeling as if she looked like a completely different person. Someone beautiful and sophisticated, like the type of woman who would date a man considered a playboy.

Except in her heart, she didn't feel Max was that person anymore. Or maybe she was too naive to realize the truth. Either way, she knew better than to reveal her feelings. The last time she'd made an attempt to do so, Max had completely shut down. Which hurt, despite her going into this with full awareness that he wasn't the type of man who wanted commitment. Nor had he ever pretended to be.

Which was a shame, since he'd be so damn good at it.

She sighed. No matter what happened between them, even though she knew she'd likely see the last of him in two weeks when he returned to Boise, she was determined to enjoy the time they had left together. And in order to do that, she knew she wanted to knock his socks off on what seemed likely to be their one and only real date.

For tonight, she chose the green dress she'd bought earlier and flirty gold sandals. Long, dangly gold earrings and a few bracelets completed her look. Peering at herself in the mirror, she thought she almost looked like a completely different person. Someone glamorous, nearly beautiful. The kind of woman who would have absolutely no problem waving goodbye to a casual lover.

Even if deep inside her heart, she knew what had roared to life between them wasn't the slightest bit casual.

Shaking her head to clear it, she realized since she'd gotten herself ready, she needed to take care of her dog. Scooping out his usual amount of kibble, she turned to find him sitting and waiting in his usual place.

After she fed Charlie, she poured herself a glass of lemonade and carried it outside on the porch to drink. Charlie came with her, content to lie on the deck in the sun with his full belly.

Lowering herself into one of the chairs made by Max's own hands, she kicked off her shoes. In this moment, life felt good. She'd never been one to want anything other than the path she'd chosen, but right now she ached for a man she couldn't have. He'd return to his life in Boise and she, she'd stay here in Owl Creek, doing the things she loved.

Eventually, she realized she'd get over him. Maybe she'd meet someone else, someone who made her feel close to the same way. A man who'd welcome a simple life in the only home she'd ever known and would want to share it with her.

Except she suspected a part of her would always yearn for Max. That made her sad.

Not wanting to allow her mood to slip into melancholy, she slipped her sandals back on and pushed to her feet. Tonight, she'd allow herself to dwell only in the present. Worries about the future could come another day.

Though the summer days were long, the brightness of the day had begun to soften as the sun began its journey back toward the horizon. Since her backyard faced east, her patio stayed mostly in shadow, though long yellow fingers of sunlight made the green grass appear to glow.

Her phone chimed, letting her know she had a text. Max wanting to let her know he was on the way and would be there in twenty minutes. After sending back a message that she'd see him soon, she called Charlie and together they went inside the house. She finished her lemonade, touched up her lipstick and brushed her hair. She was as ready as she was going to be. Honestly, she didn't know why this felt like such a big deal. They'd eaten together before, even gone to the barbecue place with his entire family. Maybe because, for whatever reason, he'd made a point of calling this a date. A date. Despite the way both of them kept insisting they were only friends, she loved the idea of a date with him.

By the time his truck pulled up in the driveway, she'd managed to calm her racing heart. This was Max, after all, and she looked forward to enjoying some delicious fajitas with him.

She opened the front door, with Charlie beside her. Her dog stood at full alert, his tail wagging furiously.

Carrying a plastic-wrapped sheaf of flowers, Max

hurried up the sidewalk. When he saw her, he abruptly stopped moving and stared. "You look…amazing," he said, his voice husky, his eyes darkening.

As always when he looked at her like that, desire heated her blood. Hoping she wasn't blushing too badly, she tried for nonchalance. "Thanks."

Next to her, Charlie's entire body began to wiggle. He could scarcely contain his excitement. Her dog sure liked this man. Almost as much as she did. The thought made her smile since she considered Charlie an apt judge of character.

Meanwhile, Max continued to stare. Then, apparently remembering the flowers, he cleared his throat. He moved forward again, holding out the brightly colored bouquet. "These are for you."

Another first. There were carnations and roses, lilies and bright yellow daisies that complemented her dress.

"A summer bouquet, the florist said," Max told her. "I hope you like it."

"I do." Accepting the blooms, she motioned him inside. Then, while he bent down to greet Charlie, she took the flowers into the kitchen to put them in a vase.

Breathtaking. Even the flowers couldn't compete with Della. He had to make himself stop staring. Not wanting to gape at her as she left the room, Max crouched down and managed to focus all his attention on Charlie. All wiggles and tail wags, the big black Lab immediately rolled over for a belly rub. While Max gave it, Charlie's head lolled to one side, his tail still going, clearly over-the-moon happy.

"I know the feeling," Max told the dog. "Your mama

sure is something." He could have sworn Charlie winked at him.

The sound of Della's heels clicking on hardwood alerted him to her return.

"He's definitely a fan," she observed, standing in the kitchen doorway. The green dress made her skin appear to glow.

Still gobsmacked and trying not to show it, Max grinned and got to his feet. "The feeling is mutual. You've got a really special dog here."

"Yes. I do."

Again, he fought the urge to stare. "You look... amazing," he finally said. "Actually, you always do, but that dress..."

Her color deepened but she nodded. "Thanks." A hint of a smile played around her mouth. "I chose it because I wanted to knock your socks off."

"Well, it worked," he said, fervently. "If I wasn't starving for fajitas, we'd be staying in instead."

This had her chuckling. "You know, that would also work. But I could eat too."

"Later," he promised. "Are you ready to go?"

Smoothing down her dress, she lifted her chin and nodded. Brown eyes sparkling, she took his arm. As always, having her touch him made him realize they were meant to be together.

He couldn't leave her, wouldn't leave her. He could only hope she felt the same way about him as he did about her. She was everything a man could want in a woman. Tough and yet soft, confident and smart and funny. Not to mention, breathtakingly beautiful. All the different aspects of Della were reasons why he loved her.

That was right. *Loved*. More than he would have ever believed it was possible. At the age of thirty-four, he'd finally realized all the things he'd thought were important weren't. He'd faced the truth. About his lifestyle and career, everything really, but most especially Della and her place in his heart.

After they said their goodbyes to Charlie, he took her arm and escorted her to his truck. A slight movement at the house next door caught his eye and he looked over to see Della's aunt Mary watching from her front porch. Realizing he'd noticed her, she lifted her arm and waved. Smiling, he waved back.

When he got into the driver's seat, Della stared, wide-eyed. "My aunt waved at you."

"She did," he agreed, backing out of her driveway.

"I've been a little bit worried about her," Della admitted. "She and Uncle Alex took Angela's death really hard. I'm hoping now that the killer has been located and is dead, that might help them heal."

Located and dead. Maybe in time, he'd come to believe that as well.

Slowly, he nodded. "I hope so."

"And you're all right with this?" she asked.

"I've decided to let the case go," he replied, aware he wasn't actually answering her question. Since he didn't want her to notice, he kept his gaze on the road. "There doesn't seem to be any point in continuing to beat my head against the wall over something everyone views as over."

Would that be enough? He hoped so. Even though he seemed to be the only person in Idaho who believed the man he'd shot might not be the killer, he'd keep quiet about that and hope he was wrong. Whatever was necessary to bring Della and her family peace.

"Thank you," she murmured, lightly touching his arm. "Honestly, now that it's settled, my family and I can finally put Angela to rest. I'm hoping to talk my aunt into allowing some sort of service, a celebration of life maybe. I think Angela would have liked that."

Changing the subject, they talked about other things. She told him about some of the dogs she was training and the amazing jobs they would soon be headed to. "Law enforcement and other agencies come from all over the country to buy our dogs. Besides working search and rescue, helping these canines realize their full potential is my passion." She sighed.

He'd been that way about law enforcement once. When he'd been much younger. He wasn't sure when his job had started to become a grind or when he'd realized he hadn't made any sort of life for himself outside of work.

Well, all of that was about to change. Both excited and slightly nervous, he couldn't wait to discuss it with Della.

When they reached the restaurant, it looked like half the town had decided to go out for Mexican food. He lucked into a parking spot near the entrance. He hurried around to the passenger side of the truck and opened her door. Smiling, she let him help her out. As she emerged, she flashed a bit of her long, shapely legs, sending a jolt of raw desire through him.

Damned if she wasn't beautiful. Both inside and out.

"I'd like to eat on the patio if possible," she said, slipping her hand into his, sending another flash of heat to his core.

"Sounds good." He gave her fingers a light squeeze.

As luck would have it, there were several open spots on the outdoor patio. It seemed most people, despite the beautiful weather, wanted to wait to eat inside.

After a few minutes' wait, they were shown to a small table in a corner, underneath a large umbrella decorated with twinkling lights. The smell of homemade tortillas and sizzling fajitas filled the air, making his mouth water.

Max pulled out a chair for Della. "I like this," she said, smiling up at him as she sat.

"Me too." He lowered himself into a seat across from her. Being with her made him feel like the luckiest man in the world.

Someone brought them a basket of tortilla chips and two small bowls of salsa. The waitress took their drink orders—a large margarita for her and a Mexican beer with a lime for him—and handed them menus before taking off to help another table.

The only thing that could make this night any better would be learning Della felt the same way about him as he did about her.

"What's wrong?" she asked, tilting her head to look at him. "You seem awfully serious all of a sudden."

"I've been thinking about making some major life changes," he admitted, his heart rate increasing.

"Like what?" she asked.

"I've given the FBI one hundred percent of myself for a long time now," he explained haltingly. "I've shoved everything else to the back burner while I focused on what I thought I wanted."

Sitting quietly, she kept her gaze locked on his and listened. Tonight, in the soft moonlight with a flickering candle on their table, her skin seemed to glow. When he looked at her, he found it difficult to breathe from wanting her so badly.

"At least you love your job," she said, her tone light.

"Loved," he corrected. "Past tense."

She stared. "I'm not sure what you mean. I know you were disappointed when they asked you to drop this case, but..."

"That's only part of it." Heart pounding in his ears, he hoped like hell he hadn't misjudged her feelings. But even if he had, he wouldn't change his decision. He'd finally realized what mattered in life. "I'm ready for a change. Ever since we discussed it, I've been thinking a lot about starting my own handcrafted outdoor furniture business."

"Wow!" She took a sip of her margarita, her gaze never leaving his face. "Full-time? Instead of working for the FBI?"

Slowly, he nodded. "Yes."

The waitress chose that moment to appear, asking if they were ready to order. Startled, Max shrugged. "Beef fajitas, please. Corn tortillas, with refried beans."

"I'll have the same, except chicken instead of beef," Della said.

"Perfect." The waitress took their menus and sailed off toward the kitchen.

Max took a deep drink of his beer. "What do you think?" he asked, glad his voice remained steady.

"I'm surprised," she admitted. "You've always talked like you were super dedicated to your career."

He shrugged. "Now I'm ready to be dedicated to

something else." And *someone else*, though he let that go unsaid, at least for the moment.

Reaching for a chip, she nodded. "Good for you. I've always believed in following your passion. That's why I train dogs. For your furniture business, I know we talked about a few options. What's your plan?"

Trying not to be put off by her brisk, impersonal tone, he took a deep breath. "I've got quite a bit saved up and I'm going to look into opening my own store."

"Oh, really? Where?"

"Here in Owl Creek. I've been looking and there's a perfect place for rent off Main Street. It has space downstairs for both a workshop and a showroom, and there's even an apartment upstairs where I can live."

Were those tears in her beautiful eyes?

"Please tell me the idea of having me around all the time doesn't make you cry," he said, only half joking.

Sniffing, she shook her head. "Actually, it's the opposite. I honestly didn't know what I was going to do once you went back to Boise."

A tentative hope made him catch his breath. "Are you saying you would have missed me?"

"Yes." The simple word carried a weight of emotion. "More than I can say."

Now. Instinct had him leaning forward, reaching for her hand. "Della, I—"

"Here we are!" Their food had arrived. Max let go of Della's hand and sat back, while the waitress placed everything on the table. "Does anyone need another drink?"

"Not just yet," Max managed, gulping beer and trying to regain his equilibrium.

The moment, if that was what it had been, had vanished. They both eyed each other across the table, and then she shrugged and dug into her food. A moment later, he went ahead and did the same. Gradually, his heart rate returned to normal, though he still wasn't sure what to think.

He let her try some of his steak and she shared her chicken. He felt as if they were back on familiar ground.

As they ate the delicious meal, his mood lightened. Her smile, no longer so tentative, lit up her face.

Finally, she leaned back in her chair. "I'm too full to finish. I'll get a to-go box and take the rest of this home."

Eyeing his nearly empty plate, he laughed. "Unfortunately, I demolished mine. I'm guessing you don't have room for dessert?"

She groaned and shook her head. "Heck no. But you go ahead."

Just because he'd been craving them, he ordered the house specialty, a plate of light and fluffy sopaipillas with honey. Even though Della said she was full, she smiled and reached over to spear a couple with her fork. "I can't resist sampling these," she said, transferring them to her plate.

He loved watching her eat. Even full, she approached the dessert with passion, savoring every bite. There was something sensual in watching the way she licked her fork, getting every bit of the sweetness off it.

Once he'd paid the check, he took her arm, and they walked side by side to his truck. Driving home, he made small talk, commenting on the weather, the meal and the moonlight.

"I wonder if anyone will be gossiping about seeing

us together," she mused. "Being that you're the playboy of Owl Creek and all."

The description made him wince. "Former," he corrected. "I *was* that once. Not any longer."

They pulled up to her house just then. He walked her to her door, hoping she'd invite him inside. As she unlocked the door, she turned to face him. For one breathless moment, he thought she meant to kiss him good-night and say goodbye.

Instead, she smiled up at him. "Would you like to come in?"

Relief nearly made his knees sag. "Yes."

The instant the door opened, Charlie came barreling over to greet them. He went from Della to Max and back again, his tail wagging furiously. Della dropped to her knees and gathered her dog to her, murmuring nonsensical sweet talk to him. Max almost dug out his phone, wanting to capture the moment. Instead, he simply watched, grinning like a fool and more aware than ever of where he belonged.

"Charlie needs to go out," Della said. "Would you like to sit on the porch with me, in one of those amazing chairs that you made?"

"Lead the way."

She grabbed them both a couple of bottled waters and they settled in under the stars and full moon. A yellow porch light by the door provided additional lighting, attracting a few fluttering moths. Charlie ran down the steps, spent a few minutes taking care of his business, before coming back up to lie at their feet.

Max sipped on his water and tried to figure out the right words. He might have once been considered a playboy, but back then he'd specialized in avoiding commitment. Now he wanted nothing more.

"What do you think about my plan?" he asked, attempting to sound casual.

"You've got to follow your heart. I'm glad you decided to stay in Owl Creek," she said, the moonlight casting a soft glow on her features. "It'll be nice having you around."

"Are you sure?" he teased, aching to tell her how he felt.

"Positive."

"That's good," he said, smiling. "Because I'm planning to turn in my notice tomorrow morning."

Her eyes widened. "Have you truly thought this through?"

"I have."

Gaze never leaving his face, she nodded. "Then I guess you'd better get busy building those chairs."

Right then, he could have detailed all the various pieces he planned to make, in addition to the chairs. He could have pulled up photos on his phone, shown her the sectionals, the loungers and swings. But there'd be plenty of time for all of that later. Right now, he knew he had more important things to discuss with the woman he loved.

Leaning over, he took her hands. "Exploring a new career isn't the only reason I want to stay in Owl Creek."

"It's not?"

"Nope." Taking a deep breath, he squeezed her fingers. "In fact, pursuing self-employment is secondary. I don't want to leave you, Della. I feel we have a very real chance of making a life together, you and me."

Her cheeks turned pink as she stared at him. Was that confusion he saw in her eyes?

It felt like an eternity passed while he waited for her to respond. Heart thudding in his chest, he began to wonder if he'd misjudged her. Maybe she didn't feel the same way about him.

"Well?" he finally asked, feeling desperate. "Aren't you going to say something? Anything?"

"I..." She pulled her hands free. Which wasn't a good thing. "I wondered if there was anything else you wanted to say. To...you know, clarify things."

Now he was the one confused. "What do you mean?"

"You say you can see us making a life together," she said, leaning forward. "As what? Friends?"

"Friends?" he sputtered. Then he saw the twinkle in her brown eyes. All the tension inside him vanished, replaced with a warm glow. He took her hands again, glad she let him. "I'm following my heart, as you aptly directed. I love you, Della Winslow. Is that specific enough?"

Her laugh made his heart light.

"I love you too, Max Colton. And yes, I definitely will enjoy having you around."

He kissed her then, as best he could from the deep seat of his chair. "I need to make you a love seat," he muttered, once they broke apart. "That way we both can sit together and make out under the stars."

She laughed again. "I have a better idea. How about we go inside and truly celebrate?"

"You don't need to ask me twice," he responded. "I'm already more than ready."

* * * * *

Don't miss the stories in this mini series!

HE COLTONS OF OWL CREEK

Colton Mountain Search
KAREN WHIDDON
March 2024

Guarding Colton's Secrets
ADDISON FOX
April 2024

A Colton Kidnapping
JUSTINE DAVIS
May 2024

MILLS & BOON

Defender After Dark

Charlene Parris

MILLS & BOON

Charlene Parris has been reading books for as long as she can remember and romance stories since high school, after discovering her mother's cache of romance books. She loves smart, sharp-witted, independent heroines; strong heroes who respect them; and of course, happy endings. Charlene writes for the Romantic Suspense line because she loves adding twists and turns to her stories. When she's not writing, Charlene is working her full-time job. And for fun, she reads, walks and is learning yoga.

Visit the Author Profile page
at millsandboon.com.au.

Dear Reader,

Have you ever met someone who knocked you off your feet? I met a famous actor during a film festival in Toronto, and I was stunned—as in, I couldn't speak. He was much more handsome in person and lovely to talk to once I found my voice! But for several seconds, everything and everyone disappeared around me until all I saw was him. My pulse raced, I started sweating (which was embarrassing!) and I was literally shaking with excitement.

For Detective Mark Hawthorne and bakery owner Britt Gronlund, the same amazing thing happens to them. However, Mark is in the middle of a police investigation, and he loses his opportunity to talk to Britt as she disappears into the Friday night crowd. They both regret not making the first move.

Fate gives them a second chance. As Mark canvasses the area for witnesses, he meets Britt again at her bakery and no way is he going to mess this up. Britt doesn't believe her luck when the man who stole her breath away reappears, and as they get to know each other, she senses how they are connected in so many ways.

But as Mark digs deeper into his case, he discovers that Britt is a possible suspect. Oh boy...

I hope you enjoy the story as Mark and Britt conquer their obstacles to get to their happily-ever-after!

Charlene Parris

DEDICATION

To my family, and especially my cousins, Rochelle and Kim, who have cheered me on and demand when the next book is coming out. Gotta love the enthusiasm!

To my darling friend Britt, who is the inspiration for the heroine. Love you! <3

Chapter 1

When Detective Mark Hawthorne stepped out of his vehicle, he looked around in confusion and frustration. "What the hell?"

The crime scene was across the street, within the dark bowels of a construction site. Unfortunately, the area in front of it was filling up with curious onlookers, their cell phones held high and lights flashing as if they'd spotted a celebrity.

"Damn it." He looked at both ends of the narrow two-lane street. The intersections were blocked off with police vehicles and bright yellow caution tape. However, the officers were having a difficult time removing pedestrians who had already wandered over to see what was going on. An ambulance was parked a few feet away.

He jogged to the closest officer, who was yelling into his walkie-talkie. "Detective Hawthorne," he shouted, showing his badge. "Are there more officers coming?"

He waited while the officer finished providing instructions. "They're on the way now. Seriously, I don't know how these people found out about this. I got here five minutes after the call."

Mark swore—social media these days was a pain in the ass for stuff like this. "I'm the lead on this case." He spotted a bright light and the silhouette of a crime scene barrier. *Good, Walsh is here already.* "As soon as your backup arrives, get these people out of here."

He'd been notified of a murder while at the precinct, and despite the gruesomeness of the investigation, Mark was itching to get started. Weeks of working on burglaries, car thefts and other minor cases had started to get on his nerves. He wanted what Detectives Timmins and Solberg routinely got—the meatier investigations, ones that made them really think through the clues until they solved them.

And now he was finally going to get his chance.

He observed his surroundings. The building consisted only of stone pillars, some wooden walls and a roof. A chain-link fence encompassed the site, and its front gate stood slightly open. Barely visible within the semidarkness of the building, he could just make out piles of cut lumber, neatly stacked. "Where's the witness who called it in?" Mark asked the officer.

"Over there, just inside the fence with two of my guys. She's pretty shaken up."

"Okay, let me check in with Forensics, see who the murder victim is first."

"Well, that's the odd thing," the officer said, rubbing his forehead. "There's a victim for sure, but he's not dead."

Mark frowned. "Come again?"

He pointed. "He's in the ambulance getting medical attention. The witness who found him panicked and called it in as a homicide. By the time we got here, the guy had regained consciousness, but he's beat up pretty bad."

Mark pursed his lips, annoyed and relieved at the same time. No one was dead, but bringing in police forces across the region… "Thanks."

As Mark headed in the direction of the witness, he noticed that she couldn't be more than twenty-five. She had taken off her hard hat, a hint that she worked here. She was quite pretty, with light brown hair tied up in a bun and blue eyes. He saw the worry and fear etched in her face. "Hey," he called out. When she turned around, he showed his badge. "Detective Hawthorne. Can you tell me what happened?"

"I'm not in trouble, am I?" she asked. The woman was visibly upset.

He gave her a smile. "Why would you think that?"

"Because I thought I saw a dead body—my God, it scared the crap out of me. I managed to call 911 without screaming into the phone and waited outside." She made the sign of the cross on her chest. "When the ambulance and police arrived, the body got up and started walking toward us. I swear, I thought it was a ghost."

"But he's not, thanks to you." Mark looked around again. Construction sites followed strict rules regarding safety. "How do you think he got in there?"

"Oh, he was inspecting the site and chatting with the supervisor about an hour ago."

Weirder and weirder. "Who is he?"

"Mr. Edward Ferguson."

She said the name like he was supposed to recognize it—he didn't, and shrugged.

She raised her brows. "He's the guy who owns the Mighty Big Bakery chain."

Ah, now he was getting somewhere. Edward Ferguson was a conglomerate powerhouse who owned one of the biggest baked goods store chains in southern Ontario.

"I must have really panicked. Maybe he just tripped

and hit his head on something," the woman said, twisting her construction hat between nervous fingers.

"I'll see how he's doing. You don't have to hang around, but I would like you to come to York Regional Police 4 District tomorrow morning to provide a witness statement." He brought out his business card.

"Of course." As she took the card from him, she smiled, which transformed her face. "You don't seem like a cop."

"I try to display the friendlier side of the force. We're not all monsters."

"No...you're not." She stuck his card into her back pocket. "Maybe when this is over, you can continue showing me your nice side."

Mark knew his eyebrow went up. Did she just ask him out on a date? She didn't seem in any hurry now to leave, but he had to get back to work. "How about you get a good night's rest and I'll talk to you at the precinct at nine tomorrow morning?"

"Works for me. Oh, and in case you missed it, the name's Jenny." She sauntered off.

Definitely an invitation.

He turned his attention to the ambulance, where Mr. Ferguson was reclined on a stretcher. However, as he got closer, Mark noticed that Mr. Ferguson was arguing with the paramedics.

"Listen to me, I told you I'm fine. Now will you let me go?"

Mark watched him, surprised at Mr. Ferguson's attitude. He had been beaten pretty badly, his face covered in bruises and a split lip, but now the man was fighting the people trying to help him.

"Sir, you might have a concussion," a female medic

told him. "At the very least, we need to take you to the hospital for observation…"

"I'm not going to a damn hospital! I need to get back to my office!"

Mark watched the struggle a bit more, then stepped in. "I suggest you do as the medic advises," he said, keeping his voice neutral.

The man glared at him. "Who the hell are you? And do you know who the hell I am?"

"You're Edward Ferguson."

That shut him up for a hot minute.

"And I'm Detective Mark Hawthorne." He held up his badge. "While you have every right to refuse medical attention, I'm afraid you still have to go to the hospital. The police will need the doctor's help in collecting criminal evidence from you." Mark smiled—he couldn't help himself. "After you're done, I'll interrogate you at the hospital for information. Which means you'll need to stay there until I arrive."

Mr. Ferguson mumbled something under his breath.

"I don't know what you're complaining about. York Region's finest is providing you the fast, courteous assistance I'm sure you'd expect," Mark added.

"Fine, I get it." Mr. Ferguson lay back on the stretcher as the medics strapped him in.

Mark rubbed his face with one hand. It had been a long day, and it was going to be a longer evening. But it wasn't an excuse to talk to Mr. Ferguson like that, even if the man had it coming. He'd probably get an earful from the captain first thing Monday morning.

"The sarcasm is strong with you tonight," an amused voice said. Myrna Walsh, the new forensics investigator with his precinct, was a fiery redhead with a personality to match. "For a second there, I thought you were going to describe how the medical staff would poke and prod him. You managed to restrain yourself."

He sighed. "I'm sure Ferguson will give Captain Fraust an earful, followed by her doing the same to me."

"Cross that bridge when you get to it." She glanced over her shoulder. "Looks like we finally have the place to ourselves. Come on, we've got a crime to solve."

"Yeah, let's go."

The construction site was bordered with an eight-foot chain-link fence. A section of it was slightly ajar. Normally there would be a chain and padlock securing the gate after-hours. Both were nowhere around.

Mark pulled on a pair of thin plastic gloves and pulled the fence wide enough for him and Myrna to pass through. She handed him a flashlight, and when they passed beneath the unfinished concrete pillars, he turned it on.

They stood in a wide rectangular area about twenty feet across, while the rest faded into blackness. "The witness said she saw Mr. Ferguson lying where I've set up the screen." Myrna pointed. "How did she even see him?"

"She must have come this way when her shift was over and spotted his body." Mark followed her to the crime site, lit up by the harsh brightness of a portable lamp. Dark stains smudged the concrete flooring, and several unknown items lay scattered around it. "Are you finished?"

"No, I've got a few more things to look over."

"I'll let you get to it. I'm going to walk the perimeter."

"Here, put these on." She handed him a pair of booties.

After slipping on the plastic coverings, Mark moved farther into the building, scanning the ground with his light. This case was his first significant one as lead investigator, but he wondered if he would have even received it if Timmins and Solberg weren't already involved in other projects.

No, he needed to shut that down—it wouldn't do to let his insecurities get in the way. Besides, Timmins told him he could handle this with no problem and had offered his support if Mark needed a sounding board. Still, that little twitch of nagging doubt persisted...

He stopped. Just within his flashlight's field, he spied the chain and padlock. He knelt down and placed a yellow marker by them, then scanned the area with his light. He could just make out several footprints. "Myrna, I found the security chain and padlock," he called out. "Might have something on them. I also see footprints, probably belonging to the construction workers, but no harm in checking them out, either." He pulled out his phone and snapped some pictures, then marked the prints with several of the small yellow cones.

"Okay, I'll get over there as soon as I can." Her voice echoed across the space.

Mark continued his observations, spying more footprints. He placed his markers as he completed his sweep. "What did you find?" he asked as he approached her.

She sat back on her heels. "Well, I'm sure the blood is Mr. Ferguson's, but I took samples from a number of areas just in case we're lucky and some of it belongs to the suspect." She pointed to a piece of wood in a large plastic evidence bag. "That was used to beat him. I found more blood and hair samples, and I'll see if there are any fingerprints I can lift."

Myrna then gestured behind her. "The suspect tried to sweep away his footprints, but he—or she—didn't get it all. I took photos of a distinctive sole pattern. You said you found footprints, too?"

"Near the chain and padlock back there. Might be fingerprints on those as well."

"I'll bag them." She stood. "Other than that, I haven't found anything else, but I'd like to keep the area roped off for another day, just in case."

"You got it." Mark looked down at the footprints Myrna had found. Streaks of dust and debris surrounded the spot where Mr. Ferguson had been discovered, but on the edge of the disturbed space was a very clear shoe print. He hunkered down to take a closer look at it, until he spied a distinctive logo. He whistled. "This should prove interesting."

"What is it?" Myrna asked.

"See the logo? We can narrow down our search based on this."

She frowned. "Really? How? This running shoe is more than just famous, you know. I've seen babies wearing these!"

Mark pointed. "The tread pattern. Shoe size. And because I know this brand makes limited quantities of exclusive editions every year. This footprint is one of them." He pulled out his phone again and took a few close-up shots.

"Are they the same footprints as by the chain and padlock?"

He stood. "Don't know. Finish up what you're doing, then let's check the rest of the perimeter. I also want to talk to the site supervisor."

The supervisor, a man in his late forties, had nothing to offer. "I gave Mr. Ferguson a tour of the premises and provided updates. That took about an hour. He said he was going back to his office, and the last time I saw him, he was heading for the exit."

"You didn't hear anything odd?" Mark asked.

"No, sir, I didn't. So damn noisy around here."

It was late evening now, and dark within the half-constructed building. "Can you take us around the outside of the construction site?" Mark asked. "I'd like to see if there's anything else that's helpful."

"Yeah, sure. Both of you need to wear these." The supervisor gave them hard hats. "Let me turn on the portable light towers first, and I've got a large flashlight. I'll bring that, especially as you both need to watch your footing."

The powerful beam cut through the pools of darkness the light towers didn't reach as they slowly walked along a narrow dirt pathway. "Is Mr. Ferguson okay?" the supervisor asked.

"He's got cuts and bruises. I told him to go to the hospital in case anything's broken." Mark didn't want to say too much.

"I keep telling him he needs to wear the hard hat and work boots when he's here. Sometimes he'll wear them, but those other times…" The supervisor let out a loud sigh. "The man can be stubborn."

"Do you work with him frequently?"

"This is my first job as supervisor with him. He's very smart, but his common sense needs a bit of work, in my opinion."

As they came around a corner, the supervisor stopped. "What the hell is that?"

Mark looked at the red container, its shape immediately recognizable. "You weren't expecting to see a fuel canister?"

"At a construction site? Hell no." The supervisor made a move to reach for it.

"Hang on." Mark looked at Myrna. "Can you see if you can get any prints off that?"

"You betcha." She crouched in front of the fuel can as the supervisor held his flashlight steady. "You think the suspect might have wanted to start a fire in here?" she asked. "Maybe Mr. Ferguson caught him in the act and got beaten up?"

"What?" The supervisor wiped his brow. "Hey, this is getting to be too much."

Mark had to agree. A plan to burn down a building with staff inside had just raised the stakes of this investigation. "We'll take it with us," he said, waiting until Myrna finished her analysis. He grabbed the container with a gloved hand. "We'll check if there are any more, then head back."

Thankfully, there were no more fuel cans, but Mark's sixth sense was acting up. "Mr. Smith, I think it best you give your staff the day off tomorrow. I'd like to check the construction site one more time to make sure there aren't any more of these." He held up the fuel canister. "Or any other viable clues."

Mr. Smith shook his head. "Mr. Ferguson won't like it."

"I'll talk to him. In the meantime, don't let anyone come into work tomorrow. But we'll need you here to escort us through the rest of the building."

"Sure, sure."

Mark handed him his card. "Is tomorrow morning around eleven thirty okay with you?"

"Yeah, I'll be here." They had reached the front gate, and Mr. Smith switched off his flashlight. "I hope you catch the son of a bitch who did this."

"That's the plan. I'll be talking to one of your construction workers tomorrow morning as well at the police station. You and I will do a thorough search of the premises. And see if you have another way to secure the site. The last thing we need is some jerk taking videos of himself at the crime scene."

He paused beside the chain-link fence, uncertainty creeping through his skin, gnawing at his gut. This case had taken an odd twist. A homicide was one thing—catch the killer, throw him in jail, give closure to the family. That might be a bit oversimplified, but that was how it seemed to progress when the other detectives worked the investigations.

But this… Someone had tried to kill one of the biggest store owners in Ontario, and if that gasoline had been spread around and lit, several construction workers might have lost their lives as well. Everyone knew Mighty Big Bakery, and the spotlight would be on Mark, glaring at everything he did until he solved the case. To say that he felt the pressure was an understatement.

"Hey, you okay?" Myrna asked.

"Not really. This investigation is going to be…" He didn't finish.

"Don't sweat it. We'll get it done." She took the fuel canister from him. "I'll do an initial analysis when I get back, see if I can come up with some more answers for you."

He smiled, thinking of a memory. "You sound like Cynthia."

Myrna laughed. "What can I say? Ms. Cornwall is one of the best. She sort of rubs off on you."

Mark talked to the officer in charge about security while watching the few remaining curious bystanders, including a pair of young teenagers. "We can open up the street to traffic," he told him, "but I'd like a rotating shift for tonight. I'm coming back to finish looking around tomorrow." Across the street, he noticed the familiar markings of a television van and groaned. "When the hell did they show up?"

"About ten minutes ago. The interviewer is over there."

The officer frowned. "May as well get it over and done with."

With Myrna gone, Mark felt vulnerable, like a team member had taken a hit and he was left holding the ball. But he refused to let that show. His interview was brief and vague, despite the demands for answers—answers he didn't have and wouldn't provide if he knew. Captain Fraust should be okay with that.

He walked to his car, exhaustion making him drag his feet. It was nighttime now, and the street had been re-opened to traffic. Car lights and incessant honking grated on his nerves until he thought he'd yell with frustration. He would need some serious downtime when this case was over. He hadn't been under the impression that he'd pushed himself too hard, but his brain and body were giving him other ideas.

And yet, a tremor of exhilaration coursed through him. This was his first major case as lead investigator. How could he not be excited about that?

He would have a load of stuff to do tomorrow, but for now, a hot shower and his bed were calling him.

He pulled out his key fob and clicked it, hearing the familiar chirp as his car door unlocked. Halfway across the street, Mark let his gaze scan across the pedestrians as they traveled to whatever entertainment awaited them on a Friday night, until he noticed a woman.

She stood on the sidewalk just ahead of his car, so that he had a full, unobstructed, amazing view.

The first thing that caught his attention was her long blond hair, tied back into a ponytail, although some strands had escaped to frame her face. The color was so striking, it looked like a halo around a pale, serene expression. She was tall—about five feet nine inches—and wearing a pair of slim denim jeans and a white T-shirt that couldn't hide the toned body hidden beneath them.

He couldn't see the color of her eyes, but he felt sure they would either be an icy blue or as green as the British Columbia forests that surrounded his old home. A classic Norwegian princess who literally took his breath away. Mark noticed nothing else—only her.

She remained still, watching him, her arms wrapped around a tote bag, one eyebrow raised. He noticed that she was studying him just as intently but hadn't moved. His feet chose to answer for him, drawing him closer, step by agonizing step. That clichéd phrase of moths being drawn to flame ran through his mind. This beautiful vision, only mere feet away, was a flame that lit up emotions Mark had buried so that he could concentrate on his job and claim back the life his father had taken away.

She made a move as if to turn away, and he stopped, holding his breath. *Please*, he thought. *Just three more seconds…*

The sudden squeal of tires, followed by the loud, blaring sound of a car horn, made him jump, his heart pounding in his chest. He turned to look at the white SUV and the irate driver waving her fist at him. "Get off the street!" she screamed. "What the hell are you doing?"

"Sorry," he called out, and got out of the way. But when he turned back to his dream come true, she was gone.

Britt Gronlund closed the door behind her, then leaned against it, clutching her purse so tight to her chest she was afraid she might have ripped holes in it with her nails.

The front window of her bakery shop was a wide pane of glass, and unable to help herself, she turned toward it, wondering if the gorgeous stranger had possibly followed her. But after a few minutes, she realized it wasn't the case.

She sighed, trying to decide if she'd made the right choice. When she'd noticed him crossing the street, she believed the Fates had something to do with it. Britt had been late getting to the bank, and the long lineup had tested her patience. It also didn't help that the police had closed down her street to do an investigation. When the area finally opened up, she'd quickened her pace, thinking about the things she needed to finish before closing up for the evening.

But when she'd seen him, thoughts of work had flown out of her mind. Britt had no way to describe what she felt when he came toward her. He'd seemed distracted, yet his confident stride and aura made her stand at attention. This was a man few could ignore, including her.

She had stopped and stood at the curb, watching as he dug out a set of keys and automatically unlocked his door. As she frantically debated whether to call out a greeting, he looked up, and their gazes locked on each other.

The intensity in his eyes sent shivers through every part of her, and she'd held her breath. Britt had never believed in love at first sight, but the stranger's continued look woke some part of her that she'd believed dead and gone...

The sudden noise of a car horn had propelled her out of her fantasy. Damn it, why was this happening now when she still had her life to get in order? Any kind of intimate relationship would only stall her goals, and Britt had promised herself that she would come first.

So, with one regretful backward glance, she had blended into the Friday-night crowd, memorizing what little she'd seen of the handsome stranger.

Life must still go on.

Blowing out a frustrated breath, she frowned as she stared at the half-constructed building almost across from her, wondering why the police had felt it necessary to shut down the street. She'd seen the barrier and police officers on duty keeping away the curious. Bright lighting illuminated the starkness of the construction site.

That building belonged to Edward Ferguson.

Pursing her lips, Britt carefully wove between waiting customers to get to her office. Betty and Kevin moved around each other like two dancers as they fulfilled orders for those in line, while other customers sat at a few of the half dozen tables throughout the room. One corner held a dedicated free library, where customers could pick a book and read while enjoying a drink and their favorite pastry.

The pace was steady, and her staff were handling it with their usual efficiency and upbeat friendliness. Britt headed toward the back, passing the door to the large well-stocked kitchen and Jacques, her head baker. He waved at her. "Britt! Did you hear?"

Britt hesitated at the entrance. "About what?"

"The assault across the street." Jacques was an older man in his late forties, and had worked with her for almost three years, helping her build the business from the ground up to where it stood now.

"Assault?" She walked into the kitchen, now curious. "Was that what all the commotion was about?"

"Yeah." He was folding dough. "It was Edward Ferguson."

"No way." The CEO had been trying to buy out her store, and she'd told him, using colorful language, where he could shove it. It seemed like karma had paid him a visit. She allowed herself a tiny moment of petty elation before asking, "Do you know if he's okay?"

Jacques gave her a disgusted look. "Should we care? He wanted to shut us down, *chérie*. He's bought a lot of the small bakeries in Toronto already."

"I know. It's just…well, there are other ways to handle a man like Mr. Ferguson."

"I suppose." He portioned out the dough, placed it on a metal pan and covered it with plastic before sliding it into the huge fridge. "However, you and I know that Ferguson is not the diplomatic type. He's a bully."

"Can't disagree on that."

In her office, Britt turned on her computer and checked her email. They had received orders through the week, but there was always someone who would frantically put in a last-minute request for the weekend. This time, there were two—a small order for tomorrow in the early afternoon, and another larger order for the day after, Sunday morning. Thank God they weren't catering events, or she'd have to decline them.

Britt was proud of the work she'd put into Konditori, her bakery and life's dream. The sudden change in direction had been scary, but in the end, well worth it.

She sent the replies, drew up invoices and made notes. She would need to advise Jacques, of course, and have him bring in Thomas, his assistant. She'd leave messages for Jasmine and Oliver coming in for the weekend shift, and she'd be here, overseeing everything.

It's not as if she had a date or weekend plans, right?

Chapter 2

Mark stood in the hospital room that night, tapping his foot impatiently as Mr. Ferguson continued talking on his cell. Ten minutes had already lapsed, and as the man's voice started rising in irritation, he suspected it could go on much longer.

He moved to stand in front of the CEO. "I need to talk to you," he said loudly. "This is a criminal investigation, remember?"

Ferguson gave him a look, but Mark didn't back down. Finally with a sigh, he nodded. "Look, let me call you back. I don't have a choice—there's a police officer standing in front of me." He clicked off the phone.

Mark chewed his lip in frustration but didn't bother correcting his job title—the effort would have been wasted, and he needed to pick his battles with someone as influential as the man lying in the hospital bed before him. "Thank you," he said, trying not to grit his teeth. "So, give me a rundown of what happened." Myrna had arrived earlier to collect the forensic samples taken by the hospital staff.

Ferguson drank from a glass of water, then lay back down. "I have no idea why this kind of shit would happen to me."

I have a few ideas, Mark said to himself. "It can happen to anyone."

"Not to me."

Mark let that one slide and pulled out his work phone. "I just need to record our conversation so that you don't have to come to the precinct later." He placed the instrument on a small table beside the bed and sat down. "What happened?" he repeated.

Mr. Ferguson rubbed his arm, which was bandaged. "I don't know. I had a meeting with the site supervisor at four this afternoon. I was running late and called him to say I'd be there in another fifteen minutes.

"When I got to the site office, he insisted I put on the hard hat and boots. I took off my shoes, and I remember struggling with the boots. I got ticked off and said let's get on with it."

"Do you remember putting on the hard hat?" Mark asked.

"Nah, hate the damn things. I wasn't going to be there long anyway. We went in and did the inspection. That was it."

Mark leaned forward in his chair. "You didn't see anyone suspicious?"

"I wasn't looking for anyone suspicious," he retorted. "As far as I'm concerned, I'm just there to make sure everything's on schedule."

That sounded like him. "Then what?"

"I went back to the office, put on my shoes and got ready to leave. Said I was happy with the progress, and the supervisor confirmed the store would be ready to open by the end of the year."

Mark nodded, more to himself. It sounded like an ordinary day to the bakery owner. And yet… "How did you get lured back?"

Mr. Ferguson turned his head to look at him directly.

"I was in a hurry and didn't wait for the supervisor. I got to the front gate and saw someone walking to the back with a gasoline container. He wasn't dressed like a construction worker, either, only had on the safety vest and hard hat, and nothing else. I've been in enough sites to know. And the gate hadn't been locked, so I was sure it was a trespasser.

"I ran after him and started shouting. I actually got my phone out to call the supervisor. I could see the guy was scared, but when my phone started ringing—I had it on speaker—he must have panicked. Little prick ran at me and pushed me over, knocked the phone out of my hand. Next thing I know, I'm getting hit with something hard. I started kicking and yelling, and pretty sure I scored a couple of hits."

Mark was impressed—Mr. Ferguson was an observant man. "Did you see his face?"

He nodded. "For about three seconds. I don't think I can identify him. But you managed to find some clues, right?"

"We have some evidence, yes." Mark decided to keep the discovery of the fuel container to himself, along with shutting down the site tomorrow. He had a suspicion the CEO would throw a tantrum, and he wanted to avoid that.

"Good, I want that asshole arrested, you got that?"

Mark got up and retrieved his phone. He had a theory and decided to confirm it. "Do you think you were attacked because of your...business ethics?"

Mr. Ferguson laughed. "People need to understand it's a dog-eat-dog world, son. If you can't keep up, you'll be run over. Anyone who tells you different is lying."

Mark pursed his lips. Of course, he held a different view, but what was the point in arguing it? "The doctor told me you should be able to go home tomorrow. I'll keep you up to date on my progress, but if I have any more questions, I'll let you know."

He walked out of the hospital feeling gross. There was just something about Ferguson that rubbed him in all the wrong ways. It was one thing to say you wanted to beat your competition, and another when you'd do anything it took to climb on top.

It was one of the reasons he had decided on law enforcement. He believed in defending people who didn't stand a chance against men like Ferguson. Bullying and intimidation didn't sit well in Mark's view.

So it was ironic that he had to defend a bully. "Will wonders never cease?" he muttered as he got into his car.

Mark woke and stretched his arms over his head. He heard birds chirping outside his window, and when he glanced at his clock, saw that it was just past seven in the morning.

He grabbed his work phone and checked the timing on the two interviews he had scheduled. Jenny, the construction worker, was at nine, while Mr. Smith, the site supervisor, was at eleven thirty. Myrna had texted him as well, letting him know she had stayed at the precinct until late last night, and would arrive midmorning.

After a shower and shave, he felt human again. But when he opened his fridge door, he swore. He'd forgotten to pick up some groceries last night after being distracted by the Nordic princess.

Damn it, he wished he'd been more on the ball. Mark had been awestruck by the woman's beauty and hadn't gotten his act together in time to approach and maybe say a few complimentary words to her. Bad luck on his part, and the chances of seeing her or having the same spell-bound reaction to another woman again was close to nil.

He slapped the fridge in frustration. He knew that had been a once-in-a-long-time encounter. Maybe, if the stars aligned themselves, he might see her again, but he wouldn't get his hopes up.

An hour later, Mark sat at his desk after grabbing a breakfast sandwich and a large cup of decent coffee from the local takeout store close to the precinct. He read through his notes, though the case was still fresh in his mind. He had an idea of the questions he would ask Jenny, the construction worker, and Mr. Smith, the site supervisor. While he believed Smith would be straightforward, he wondered how Jenny would behave during the interview. It may be a bad habit in his profession, but thinking the worst of witnesses and suspects before they proved their innocence did get him around obstacles. If he fell for her flirting, where would that end up, especially if she was guilty of something?

A phone call from the officer at the front desk confirmed her arrival. Timmins wasn't in the office yet—he had texted, saying he'd be there in ten minutes. Mark grabbed his notepad and headed to the reception area to pick her up. "Good morning," he said. "Thanks for coming in."

"Hey, no problem." She stood, and he immediately noticed that she had put care into her appearance. Jenny wore makeup, had styled her hair in waves that framed her face, and her clothing was more suited for an evening out than a weekend police interrogation. It wasn't hard to put two and two together that she was making an effort to continue flirting with him.

"Come on, we're going to an interrogation room to get a formal statement."

The ride on the elevator was silent. He caught Jenny watching him out of the corner of his eye, but he remained quiet while he led her down the fluorescent-lit hallway and into a barely furnished room. "Have a seat."

She looked around, rubbing her arms. "This looks like a jail cell."

Mark dropped his notepad and phone on the bolted table. "You know what the inside of a jail cell looks like?" he asked. That was an odd statement from her.

"Only from the television shows." She sat down, continuing to take in her surroundings.

"Did you want anything? Coffee?"

"No, I'm good."

He looked at his watch. "Detective Walter Timmins should be here in a few minutes."

She frowned.

"We always need two officers during an interview. Protocol."

"Oh." She sounded disappointed.

That will keep her from trying anything funny.

A couple of minutes later, Timmins walked in. "Sorry I'm late," he apologized, and took the seat at the other end of the small room.

"No problem." Mark lifted his hand toward the camera in the wall to signal he was ready. After introducing himself and Timmins formally and describing the purpose of the interview, he got started. "Can you give me a full rundown of your day up to when you discovered Mr. Edward Ferguson?"

"Yeah, sure." She glanced back at Timmins, then took a breath. "All of us knew Mr. Ferguson was coming by yesterday afternoon at four o'clock. Smith, our site supervisor, runs a tight ship—really organized. Everyone knows what they're supposed to be working on each day. But he wanted me and one other coworker to walk the area and clean up any loose debris, check that everything was in its place, that sort of thing."

"What time did this start?" Mark asked.

"I got to work at my usual time, eight in the morning. I think maybe an hour later?"

He wrote some notes. "And when you finished?"

"The coworker and I started our shift. I was helping with the steel girders on the second floor, but I don't know what my coworker's job was."

"Did you work on that during your whole shift?"

"For the morning, yes, until twelve thirty, then I had lunch."

"Do all the workers take their lunch at the same time?" Timmins asked.

Jenny half turned in her chair. "No, lunchtime is split into two shifts."

"So Mr. Ferguson arrived when all of you finished lunch."

"Well, it's not like he needs us with him while he's inspecting," Jenny retorted. "Mr. Smith was there, and I think he took two of his junior assistants with him."

Mark jotted down the assistants' names—he'd verify that with Smith later. "And after lunch?"

"Got back to work. We were starting the electrical, so I was on hand for that until my shift was over, around six that evening."

"Did you see Mr. Ferguson and your boss at all during the afternoon?"

Jenny shook her head. "Nope. Just kept my head down. We were on a schedule."

"And after work?"

She shrugged. "I headed to the front gate and saw something weird on the ground within the site. That's how I found him."

"It's pretty hard to see that distance when it's dark under there," Timmins stated.

"It wasn't that dark where Mr. Ferguson was."

Mark paused in taking notes. "But it would have been difficult to spot him immediately."

She shrugged. "We're trained to spot inconsistencies. I don't know what else to tell you."

The rest of Jenny's story was almost verbatim to what she'd told him last night.

"Thanks for your help," Mark said, getting up. "If you think of anything else, you have my business card."

"Sooo, I'm not getting arrested for anything?" she said innocently, holding her wrists together.

He almost rolled his eyes, then caught Timmins hiding his face with a hand. His cough sounded suspiciously like a laugh. "No." He opened the door to let her out.

In their office, Timmins mimicked Jenny's failed flirtation attempt. "Are you sure you don't want to arrest me, officer?" Timmins asked, imitating Jenny's voice and doing a bad job of it.

"Knock it off."

"Jeez, you're moody this morning. And I thought your witness might have been your type."

"She's not."

"Yeah, maybe she's too kinky for you."

"You know what? That's kinda unpleasant, coming from you."

Timmins leaned back in his chair. "How's your investigation going so far?"

Thank God Timmins changed the subject. "I have to talk to Myrna to find out what she's discovered, but I'm interrogating the site supervisor at eleven thirty if you want to back me up again."

At the appointed time in the interrogation room, Mark wasn't much further ahead. Mr. Smith verified his assistants were with him when they escorted Mr. Ferguson around the premises. "Did anything seem out of place?" Mark asked him.

Mr. Smith shook his head. "Everyone had been doing a fantastic job, and all on time, too. I gotta say, I'm grateful for this team."

"What time did Mr. Ferguson leave?"

The supervisor pursed his lips. "Between five and five thirty."

So in between the time Mr. Ferguson left and saw the intruder, and Jenny discovering Mr. Ferguson's unconscious body, the gate would have been open. There was about an hour in that time frame where a suspect could have done some serious damage with the fuel canister. Mark wondered if the suspect even knew Mr. Ferguson was on the premises. What if beating up the bakery owner was better than burning down the building?

He jotted down his thoughts. "If you don't mind, Mr. Smith, let me do one more sweep of the building with you before you bring your employees back."

"Yeah, sure."

More than an hour later, Mark was satisfied there was nothing hidden around the construction site that could blow up. The supervisor had given his employees the day off as Mark had suggested. The police tape was still up, and one officer was on duty. After thanking Mr. Smith and watching him head to his car, Mark approached his colleague. "Hey," he called out, and showed his badge. "How's everything?"

"Quiet, which is how I like it. There were some kids hanging around when I came on duty, but they took off."

"I'm pretty sure we've collected all the evidence we need." Mark looked around, thinking he'd need to reconfirm that with Myrna.

"I heard it was some big shot that got beat up. The guy who owns those big-box bakery stores."

Mark nodded.

"Probably had it coming to him."

He frowned. "Why are you thinking that?"

The officer's eyes widened, and his face flushed red. "Sorry, sir, that was out of line."

"Not from what I've heard." No one had anything good to say about Edward Ferguson, and Mark now wondered if there was more to this beating than the CEO was letting on. "Tell me why you said that."

The officer shrugged. "My cousin worked for a well-known chain in the Italian community out in the west end. This guy bought the business and promised my cousin and the other workers they'd have jobs when the changeover was finished." He turned and spat onto the ground. "Lied through his teeth."

That seemed to be a consistent trait of the conglomerate. "I'm sorry about your cousin," Mark told him.

"It's okay. She found a job she really loves now." The officer glanced up at the building. "I guess he's gonna try and force out the couple of little businesses along this street. What a douche."

Mark eyed the stores opposite him—a bank on the corner, a variety store, a small grocer's and, at the far end, a bakery painted bright pink with the word *Konditori* spelled out in dark blue letters above the large window. Several customers waited outside to get in.

He decided to skip the bank and started with the variety store, since it and the other stores faced the construction site. An older gentleman sitting beside the front counter barely spoke English, but after Mark pulled out his badge, the man yelled something, and a young woman appeared from the back of the store. A few questions came up empty.

He moved on to the grocer's, where several employees kept busy stocking produce. This time, he got some interesting information from another older gentleman, who spoke perfect English. "That Ferguson man, he tried to buy the stores on this side of the street," he said, his accent thick but understandable. "We all told him no and to get out."

Mark wrote that down. "He wasn't nice?"

"He has plenty of stores. Why does he want more? I told him to leave us alone and don't come back."

Mark pointed out the door. "But he bought property from someone across the street?"

The old man nodded. "Nice people. Butcher shop, fruit and vegetable grocery, and clothing store that also sold flowers. The grocery and butcher owners sold with no argument. But the lady who sold the clothes and flowers refused. Always busy. But I heard bad things happened to her."

He frowned. "What bad things?"

The man leaned forward, and his voice dropped. "Bad people destroyed her store, tore up the merchandise. Broke windows and painted awful words on the building. I'm sure it was Mr. Ferguson who did this. After two weeks, we found out the owner sold her store. That was late last year. She moved back home to Europe." He frowned. "Now all we see is Mighty Big Bakery. No one is happy."

Mark wandered down the street, thinking on what he'd heard. Ferguson had given the impression he'd do whatever it took to get what he wanted, yet somehow, he didn't get the stores on this side of the street first. He jotted that down, intending to question the CEO about it.

The last store, called Konditori, was a quirky-looking bakery. Inside, the space was well lit and bright. Pale gray walls were the perfect background for the colorful wall art. Tables and chairs made of thick white oak were set up neatly to one side, while a tall bookcase covered half a wall at the opposite end.

Two employees—a man and a woman—were behind the long counter, taking orders and moving around each other with a practiced ease born of experience.

"Welcome to Konditori," the man greeted him with a wide smile. "How can I help you today?"

Mark couldn't resist—the smell of fresh-baked goods surrounded him, making his mouth water. He selected a pastry and a large coffee. "I wanted to ask if the owner was here," he said as he paid for his meal.

"Sure is. She's in the back office."

"Could you let her know that Detective Mark Hawthorne is here? Just wanted to ask if she knows anything about what happened across the street last night."

"You bet. Give me a couple of minutes."

"Thanks." He took his snack to a table nearest the front window. The day was turning out cloudy and gray, and as he watched, the sidewalk glistened from a light sprinkle of rain that sprang up out of nowhere.

From his seat, he had a clear view of the half-constructed Mighty Big Bakery. At this angle, he noticed how large the building was, about a half block in length. When it was completed, it would overshadow the stores on this side. Hopefully, the store owners had a plan for that.

Mark heard a gasp behind him, and when he turned around in his seat...

Oh my God, it's her.

Her golden presence slammed hard into his chest—he was glad he was sitting down. Her thick blond hair was braided today and hung over her shoulder. Instead of the casual look from last night, today she wore wide-legged pants and a loose blouse. But he only noticed these things because he was trained for that.

What held him in his chair was her eyes, so green he imagined that he was swimming in them. The ocean off the British Columbia coast had nothing on this woman's gaze. Sparkling, bright, its depths a tantalizing mystery.

Her eyes were wide with surprise, and while he didn't dare to guess, Mark hoped her thoughts were in sync with his.

The temptation to just sit and look at her was overwhelming. But he finally remembered to get his bearings and scrambled out of his seat. "Hello," he managed to say in a normal voice, although there was nothing normal about seeing her again—someone was smiling down on him today.

She blinked several times, as if refocusing. "Good afternoon."

Her voice only enhanced her beauty. Smooth and low-pitched, it had a European accent that gave her voice a musical lilt. Although it could also be her luscious full lips that made her voice sound so delectable.

Crap, don't stand here staring at her like a drooling twit. Inhaling a deep breath, he held out his hand. "Detective Mark Hawthorne. Thank you for seeing me."

Her handshake was firm and warm. "Britt Gronlund."

He pulled out a chair for her. "Please join me."

As she sat down, her hair brushed against his hand. It was silky soft, almost a caress, and his body tingled with heightened awareness. He took another deep breath to calm himself before sitting down across from her.

But looking at Ms. Gronlund this close increased his urge to talk to her about everything else except work. *One day.* Mark paused, surprised at the unexpected thought.

"I suspect you're here to talk to me about Edward Ferguson?" she asked.

"Yes, that's right." He pulled out his work phone, hit Record and placed it on the table between them. "This saves a trip to the police station," he explained when she glanced down at it.

"Makes sense."

Mark deliberately sipped his coffee, allowing him a few moments to figure out how to start. Her comments had been short and to the point, which wasn't a problem. However, to own a bright, cheery bakery like Konditori, with friendly staff and customers who seemed to know each other, Ms. Gronlund's mannerisms seemed off-balance. Maybe she was nervous.

He held up his cup. "This coffee is amazing. I think I'm wired for the rest of the day."

She smiled, but it didn't quite reach her eyes. "Thank you. It's a special coffee roast I get from my supplier in Ethiopia."

"And the Danish? Was it made fresh this morning?"

Her eyes widened in shock. "How did you know?"

"My family had friends who owned a bakery in British Columbia, and I could guess when they had freshly baked goods ready." He pointed to the store name located above the cashier. "What does Konditori mean?"

She glanced over her shoulder. "It's Norwegian for cake shop."

"I like that. It feels authentic."

She was starting to look more relaxed. "It reminds me of home."

He nodded, then looked around the bakery. There was still a lineup, although he knew at least a dozen people had come and gone. "Is it always this busy?" he asked. "It's what, about two o'clock now? I've never been to a bakery that had so many people in it."

This time, her smile lit up her face. "It's always busy, but especially on the weekends. Customers like to pick up dessert for their weekend events. It makes the days go by faster."

Mark wasn't sure how to take her comment. Did she want her days to fly by because she had nothing else to do? "Sounds like my schedule, sometimes."

She raised an eyebrow at that.

"Speaking of schedules, I don't want to take up too much of your time, Ms. Gronlund. Can you give me a rundown of what you did on Friday?"

Mark loved listening to her voice. She was methodical and precise, describing everything until she reached the evening.

"After I left the bank, the police had stopped pedestrians from entering the street. They mentioned there was a police investigation. A lot of people took alternate routes, but I decided to wait. It gave me a chance to catch up on work emails."

He watched her face, wondering what she would say next. "And when the street reopened?"

"I hurried back to the store, as we were closing in thirty minutes. I'm very strict on that. My employees' well-being comes first, and I wanted them to enjoy their Friday night."

Ms. Gronlund lowered her gaze, as if thinking. But then she slowly propped her elbows on the table, linked her fingers together and rested her chin on her hands. When she looked up, her eyes had darkened. "Then I saw you."

There were no words to describe the strange vibrating pulse that coursed through her body when she saw him.

Britt half suspected that the police would pay a visit to see if she knew anything about what happened Friday night. When Oliver had told her a Detective Hawthorne was here to talk to her, she'd been ready.

She'd stepped out of her office, then slowed to a complete stop. The detective was half turned while looking out the window, and she had a clear view of his profile. A strong square jaw, straight nose and a muscular neck swept up from the collar of his shirt. His hands and manicured fingers were agile as he fiddled with the mug. And despite the looser cut of the shirt, Britt caught glimpses of well-defined muscle beneath the material as he moved.

Her hand came up to her chest, and she released a sigh that was louder than intended. He turned around, no doubt hearing her, then held still.

And Britt experienced the same damn uncontrollable emotions that hit her last night.

When he stood, she almost had to take a step back. There was something about him that demanded respect, but it wasn't threatening, a trait that made her want to know more about him. In retrospect, Britt thought it was his eyes. They were a warm brown with flecks of gold, and she wondered if they changed color depending on his mood. And his voice...deep with a hint of roughness. She could spend all day listening to him recite a damn dictionary.

That in itself excited and scared her at the same time.

Detective Hawthorne had asked for a summary of her Friday activities, which didn't take long to discuss. However, she was more interested in talking about another topic. "Were you at the crime scene last night?" she asked.

"I was." He turned off his phone and stuck it into his pants pocket.

"Do you think it'll be a complicated case?" Britt knew where she was going with her questioning but wasn't sure if the detective would catch on.

"I hope not." He focused his gaze on her. "I'd rather spend my time doing more interesting things."

She licked her lips, a move he didn't miss. "Such as?"

"Getting to know a Nordic princess who ran away from me last night."

Britt frowned. "I'm not a princess. And I didn't run away."

"You didn't stay, either." He tilted his head.

What could she say? "You're right. I had a business to run."

He nodded slowly. "And I should have had the courage to approach you, but I had work to do."

They sat in silence for a few moments, and Britt thought hard about how to ask if he'd like to...oh, she didn't know, go on a date? It had been a long time since she'd been out with a man, and feeling rusty was an understatement.

"However, destiny seems to be in our favor." Detective

Hawthorne reached into his shirt pocket and pulled out a business card. "This is in case you think of anything else you'd like to tell me." He pulled a pen from the same pocket, turned the card over and scribbled something. "And this is in case you'd like to talk about anything other than work."

Britt took the card between two fingers, suddenly realizing that while he was flirting with her, the detective had left the ball in her court. She was liking him more already.

Chapter 3

It was past three in the afternoon, and Mark sat at his desk. His notes, photos and statements were strewn in front of him like so many puzzle pieces. Myrna had arrived at the precinct while he'd been out, and he was waiting for her to give him an update on her findings.

He mulled over Mr. Ferguson's attack and the small amount of evidence gleaned from the man. No doubt the CEO would gnash his teeth in frustration when he learned his newest store was in limbo until tomorrow. Curious, he looked up Ferguson via the internet on his phone and frowned at the information he found.

It seemed like Edward Ferguson took his dog-eat-dog motto to heart. He bought smaller bakeries, independent family businesses, then fired all the original staff and re-modeled the purchases into his design. There had been a couple of lawsuits against him, but with his money and elite law teams, no one stood a chance against the conglomerate.

The CEO knew nothing of compassion.

This case smelled of revenge. To deliberately bring a gas container with the intention of arson was one thing. Mr. Ferguson's beating was another level. He wondered how many people hated the CEO enough to risk being caught and shuddered at the possibilities.

He started to organize his information, moving the pieces around until they resembled a timeline. Mr. Ferguson's and Ms. Gronlund's statements were still on his work phone, and Mark tapped the necessary buttons to transfer them to his computer.

"Hey there." Myrna walked through the open door, her arms laden with several folders and her laptop.

"Hi." He watched as she dumped her stuff on the small meeting table. "How late were you here last night?"

"Oh, until about two in the morning."

"Myrna, you didn't have to do that."

"I know, but I wanted to because I knew it would be quiet. Besides," she added as she opened her laptop, "this case is a big one. You and I need to get a decent report together to present to Captain Fraust first thing Monday morning."

Mark groaned. "I'm surprised she hasn't called me yet."

"Be careful what you wish for, Hawthorne."

He sat opposite her. "We can cross-reference with my evidence," he told her, pointing to his desk. "But I want to find out what you've got first."

She tapped a few keys. "So the blood and hair in the area all belonged to Mr. Ferguson, along with the footprints that led from the site's entrance to that particular spot. I managed to lift the suspect's fingerprints from the fuel canister and the piece of wood used as the weapon. But when I ran the prints through the database, I didn't get any hits. The canister is a common brand sold at Canadian Tire stores—it'll be hard to track down the location that sold it."

"Guess I can't be surprised at that." Mark leaned forward. "What about the sneaker prints?"

"Ah yes, you hit the bell on those. The majority of this

brand's shoes have the recognizable circular pattern on their sole, with the logo located in the middle. This one, however, is different." Myrna turned her laptop so that he could look at the screen. "The distinctive logo is at the top of the sole this time. There's another symbol under the heel of the shoe."

"Yeah, I know this edition. There was a stink a few years ago about that symbol. It resembled an Arabic word."

"And as a result, the company had to stop selling that particular shoe, but not before the initial 225 pairs were sold in Toronto."

Mark knew his brow went up in disbelief.

Myrna nodded. "That's it. We can get a list of buyers."

"That's it? Myrna, that's a lot of customers to get through." Mark envisioned the amount of time and man-power involved in that task. "What if the suspect sold off his shoes?"

"Do you really think that? Those shoes are worth a lot of money, especially after that debacle. I don't think he'd sell them."

"So you know they're men's shoes. Good work."

"Not only that, but we won't have to go through the full customer list." She tapped a couple of keys. "Take a look at that."

He stared at a photo with two different-sized prints. "We're looking for two suspects?" he asked.

"No. These were the only prints in the immediate area."

He thought hard, wondering what the investigator was trying to show him. He pursed his lips and shook his head. "You've lost me."

Myrna grinned. "Our suspect's feet are two different sizes."

The stroke of luck that Myrna provided him had Mark

feeling they would be close to nailing the bastard. "What size are we looking for?"

"That's even better. According to my measurements, he's wearing a size 14 on his right foot, and a size 12 on his left. Average height would range from five foot ten inches to six foot three inches."

So a man wearing two different-sized shoes of a limited edition. How much luckier could they get? "Myrna, I could kiss you."

"Now, now. No office hanky-panky, please." Her grin was contagious.

He parked his car at a lot within the Queen and Yonge Street area, then waited for a westbound streetcar. Checking his searches on his phone, he found most of the hip sneaker stores were in the west end, within a five-mile radius. He could easily walk to about half of them.

The first store was the top hit on his list. A three-story black building, it had a mural consisting of several Toronto Raptors players.

Inside, the white shelves and walls were a perfect backdrop for the sneakers that came in every color. The floor was an ingenious idea—skateboards were displayed beneath a thick plexiglass cover. *Look, but don't touch.*

In the middle of the space were floating glass displays of rare sneakers, caps and T-shirts from some of the most famous brands out there. A security guard stood at the front door, carefully watching everyone.

Mark headed toward the back, where a cashier was ringing through a purchase. As he waited, he checked out the prices on a couple of interesting pairs. "Holy hell," he whispered, and glanced at some of the others. The average price was five hundred dollars and up. It wasn't that he couldn't afford a pair, but he didn't think he'd wear them outside.

When the cashier had finished, he approached her. "Good afternoon," he said, then showed her his badge. "Detective Mark Hawthorne with York Regional Police 4 District in Vaughan."

The woman, in her twenties, with thick black hair tied up in a bun and bright brown eyes, frowned. "I was told the theft from a couple of weeks ago had been resolved."

"No, this isn't about that." He pulled out the picture of the footprints from the crime scene. "Someone was assaulted, and I recognized these prints from a limited edition that got backlash because the symbol resembled a holy Arabic word."

"Yeah, I heard about that. It was before I started working here." She leaned forward. "You're looking for a guy who owns these?"

"Yes, and in particular, the person who bought a size 14 right foot and size 12 left."

"Wow, different foot sizes. I've heard of that, too, but it's rare. Give me a second."

He waited as she typed, but in a few minutes, she shook her head. "We don't have a sale like that in our records," she told him. "I'm not too surprised, either."

"Why is that?" Mark noticed a waiting customer out of the corner of his eye.

"With limited editions, we want to sell the matching pair, especially as they're collectible items." She tugged on her earlobe. "There are other stores in the area. Do you want me to find out anything for you?"

"No, thank you. I'm going to visit each one until I find my answer. Thanks for your help."

"Good luck."

Well, that was a strike. He crossed the store off his list. But the cashier made an interesting comment. Selling matched pairs of sneakers made sense if a collector hoped to eventually sell them to another interested buyer. What if there were *two* customers with different-sized feet? Was it possible one store might have sold a set to the suspect, knowing the second set would be bought by someone else? It was one hell of a long shot.

The next three stores on his list were within a two-block radius, and didn't give him any results. When Mark walked into the fifth one, however, he was impressed. It was larger, with more stock, and emitted a cozier, warmer atmosphere. He could see why this store was in his top five results when he had searched for cool sneaker shops. There were two security guards this time—one each at the front and back of the store—and it was even busier.

The young man behind the cash register was on the phone, and as Mark waited, he noticed something that offered promise—this particular store had four locations, and the pictures displayed behind the cashier were famous basketball, football and baseball players.

"Hey," the young man greeted him after he hung up the phone. "How can I help you today?"

Mark showed him his badge. "I'm looking for a customer who bought a pair of limited-edition sneakers from a few years ago, featuring a symbol that was offensive to a religious group." He mentioned the brand.

"Yeah, we had those." The cashier hit some keys on his computer. "I've got the list pulled up. There were only about fifteen sneaker stores that got these, all in the downtown core. Each store got fifteen pairs."

"The customer I'm looking for had different-sized feet. Right foot is a 14, the left a 12."

The man's gaze traveled down the computer screen. "Oh yeah, I know the dude. The only reason we offered to sell them that way is because we have a customer in Abu Dhabi who bought the other set."

Mark couldn't believe his luck. "Can you provide me his name, address and phone number?"

"Sure, let me print that out for you."

Several minutes later, he stood outside, looking at the sheet of paper. Henry Toussaint. His address wasn't far from Britt's bakery and Mr. Ferguson's building site.

The streetcar ride back to the parking lot took longer because of traffic and road construction, and he chafed at the delay. He finally got to his car and drove to Toussaint's address. Mark wanted to check out the house and neighborhood first before charging in with a team. He knew he had struck pay dirt finding the shoe owner so quickly, and he couldn't afford to mess it up by going in half-cocked.

About thirty minutes later, Mark cruised along Sierra Court. The houses were two-storied, with wide, deep lots and mature trees. Every house had at least two cars parked in the driveway. Nearby was a school and day care center, and as he continued driving, he noticed that the houses got bigger. The street ended in a cul-de-sac, and he turned around, continuing to mentally record the area while wondering how the hell he was going to arrest Toussaint without causing too much of a scene.

It made sense the suspect could afford those sneakers. This neighborhood was upper middle class, if not higher.

Henry Toussaint's house sat just south of Lomond Avenue, and Mark slowed his car down to get a good look.

Deep driveway—it could easily hold eight cars. Large two-story home, big front yard, several trees and a nice landscaped area filled with flowers. He could just see the security cameras, one over the front door and another covering the double garage. He was sure the backyard would be even bigger.

Mark decided to drive around the neighborhood, as he'd never been up here before. It was large, with Cunningham Pond and a park and play area beside it. Traveling north, he discovered another park, a huge spot with an off-leash area, with dogs barking and running in all directions. Behind it, a kiddie splash pad and a large stage made up the center of the park. It was certainly family friendly. Maybe he'd bring Mom up here once she was out of the hospital, to give her a new place to check out.

At the precinct, Mark turned to the computer to see what information he could dig up on Toussaint. There wasn't much—former soccer player for the Toronto team but had to retire due to an injury. There was some noise about offering him an assistant coach position, but as Mark read through the sport articles, he couldn't find anything else. He added these findings to his ever-growing folder and sat back in his chair, thinking. If he could get his hands on Toussaint tomorrow, he felt sure he could wrap things up by Monday night. However, there was something about Mr. Ferguson that nagged at him. He just wasn't sure what it was. Maybe paying the CEO an unannounced visit tomorrow morning would catch him off guard.

Mark liked that idea. He scheduled the two items into his work phone, alongside a visit to his mom in the hospital.

Suddenly, his personal phone pinged with a text. When

he retrieved it and read the message, he smiled—his Saturday night just got a whole lot better.

Hello, Mr. Detective, I wondered if you'd like to solve the case of finding a good meal? It has to be within a five-block radius of Konditori, fast and most important, tasty. Are you up for the challenge?-The Nordic Princess

P.S. I close up shop in forty minutes, just to give you added incentive.

Britt sat in her office, sipping a cup of tea as she reviewed emails. Today's order for an afternoon party had been a hit with the guests, judging by the three very happy messages from her repeat customer. Jacques and Thomas had Sunday's order well underway, with Betty, her full-time weekday employee, coming in to help them. Jacques had mentioned Betty possessed the instincts of a natural baker and wanted to foster that, to which Britt agreed. She wanted her employees to be happy, with ambitions to do what she and Jacques had accomplished. Nurturing dreams had become a mantra for her.

Her cell phone pinged. When she glanced at the message, a little thrill of excitement zipped through her.

Evening, *vakker*, mystery solved. I'll report to you in fifteen minutes.-Mr. Detective

Wait a minute. Britt read the message again, focusing on one particular word. *Vakker?* That was the Norwegian word for *beautiful*. Did he really just call her that?

Oh, Detective Hawthorne was really stepping up his game.

She shut down her laptop, stuffed it into her tote and headed into the store. "I'm going to start closing up," she announced to a few remaining customers who stood in line, and her weekend staff, Jasmine and Oliver. "Oliver, can you stand at the front door to let the customers out? I'm going to get the lights." Britt had learned the hard way that leaving the lights on was like a beacon. It was fantastic being so popular, but it had its annoying moments, too.

With the last customer finally gone, she and her staff cleaned up, pulled down the blinds at the front window and got everything ready for tomorrow. "Thanks, you two," Britt told them. "I'll see you tomorrow at ten."

In the kitchen, Jacques and his team were working steadily. "Are you sure there's nothing I can help you with?" she asked, looking around. It seemed chaotic, but her head baker had a method to his madness.

"Don't worry, *chérie*, we'll be fine. Another hour, ninety minutes tops."

"All right." Jacques knew she worried about her staff. "I'm heading out the front door tonight. I'm meeting someone. I'll see you all tomorrow. And don't forget to set the security alarm."

Betty picked up a large piece of dough and moved as if to throw it at her. "Would you get going already?" she demanded, laughing.

As Britt walked back to her office, she noticed a figure standing at the door and went to see who it was. Detective Hawthorne was waiting. She unlocked the door. "Hours are ten to five on the weekends," she quipped.

He kept a serious expression. "I was told there was a damsel in distress at this address. Said she would die from starvation if I didn't save her."

Britt's laugh turned into an undignified snort. "Oh my

God, look at what you made me do!" She hadn't laughed that hard in months.

His grin was wide. "Are you ready to go?"

"Let me get my purse." She let him inside, then ran back to the office to collect her stuff.

"Soo, what is tonight's mystery, detective?" she asked as she bolted the door behind her.

"About two blocks west and one street south. And the name's Mark. Only my mom loves calling me detective every chance she gets." He rolled his eyes.

"How sweet! I go by Britt, but I don't mind being called Nordic princess if the mood hits you." Man, that was a bold statement, even for her.

His smile looked sweet, almost shy. "Would you like to walk? If not, I brought my car…"

"No, walking's fine. It's nice to get outside."

They strolled toward the stoplight. "How was your day?" he asked.

Britt sighed. "Busy, as always."

"That's a good thing, right?"

"It is. I can't complain. And I have great staff, too. I wouldn't have gotten this far without them."

At the red light, Mark turned toward her. "It's rare to hear an owner compliment their staff like that. You have a kind heart."

This close, Britt noticed the dark stubble on his face and fought the urge to touch it. "Thank you."

People had started to cross when the light changed, but he held her gaze for a moment longer before following the crowd. She kept pace, her mind a whirlwind of untapped feelings.

The Korean restaurant Mark had chosen was small and brightly lit, with wide open doors letting in the evening's cool air. Several voices chattered loudly as Mark stepped aside to let her in first.

"Welcome!" a young man called out. "Please have a seat."

Britt stopped for a minute to look around. She'd never eaten Korean food before, but the smells were delicious.

He stood beside her and touched her back. "Let's sit near a window," he said into her ear.

She eased into a bright red wooden chair and plopped her tote on the table to one side. "I have no idea what to eat," she told him. "You've taken this mystery to a whole new level."

He inclined his head. "I aim to please."

That comment could be taken in so many ways, and she chided herself for going down a dirty-minded route. Although, looking at Mark, could she blame herself?

A waitress came over and handed them menus. Britt looked at the pictures and brief descriptions for each meal, unsure.

"Most of the food I've tried so far has a bit of a spicy kick to it." Mark leaned in close and pointed at a couple of items. "Since you haven't had Korean food before, let's stick with something less intense. Bibimbap is rice, mixed veggies, beef and an egg on top. They add chili paste for seasoning, but it's on the side. I like the *japchae*, that's glass noodles, vegetables and pork sautéed in soy sauce."

"That sounds great."

He placed the order, and she listened in wonder as he spoke a few words in Korean. "Do you know the language?"

He laughed. "No, just some words and a few simple phrases."

She was still impressed. "But you made an effort to learn, which says a lot." She wondered what else he could surprise her with. "How was your day at work?" Britt asked.

"Tiring… A lot of footwork today."

"Are you still trying to figure out what happened to Mr. Ferguson?" She bit her lip, nervous. "Sorry, I wasn't sure if that was classified…"

"It is, in a way. I can't discuss active investigations."

She nodded. "Gotcha. The mystery thickens."

He smiled at that. Britt noticed the dimple in his left cheek, which made his handsome face even more so.

Before she managed to say something embarrassing, their dinner arrived, along with a teapot and two small bowls. Britt admired her meal while Mark poured the tea. "This looks delicious," she murmured, then looked at his. "Those are noodles?" she asked, staring at them. "How are they so translucent?"

"I just know they're made from starch, like potatoes or beans."

"Oh, I see." Her cooking hat came on. "And probably mixed with water, then shaped into the noodles."

They ate in silence. Britt had used chopsticks when eating Japanese food, so she had no problem. Mark showed her how to mix the egg into the meal before taking her first bite. "Oh my God, this is so good," she exclaimed, talking around a mouthful of food. "How did you find this place?"

"During one of my investigations. There was an assault in the neighborhood. A respected elder got beaten up by a pair of teenagers who stole his money. Found them hiding in here, holding the owner as a hostage."

"Holy crap, they were armed?" This sounded like a thriller novel.

"No, but every kitchen utensil known to man was back there. I couldn't take a chance they'd use a knife."

"What did you do?"

He scooped some *japchae* into his mouth and chewed for a moment. "Basically, I told them don't make it worse. I had a neighbor translate my commands until they finally came out." He frowned. "The old man needed to go to the hospital for treatment. He didn't want to press charges, but I told him if you expect them to learn their lesson, they needed to go through the procedures." Mark's expression was sinister. "I had them locked up overnight and told them every possible thing that could happen. Next day, they were very apologetic. Last I heard from the waitress here, they were doing volunteer work for seniors and the homeless."

"So you had a positive influence on them. I like that."

All too soon, dinner was over, but Britt knew it would be another long, busy day tomorrow. "Thank you for dinner," she said as they made their way back.

"Thank you for inviting me. I loved your text."

She giggled. "Your mission, if you choose to accept it," she replied in a robotic voice, which had Mark laughing out loud.

He had parked his car close to Mighty Big Bakery. "Could I give you a ride home?" he asked quietly.

"Thank you." When she slipped into the passenger seat, Britt glanced up at the construction site, a stark building against the bright security lights. "Mark, I need to tell you something." Listening to him tonight, she knew she had to let him know about her first encounter with Mr. Ferguson.

He turned the car light on. "What is it?"

She felt foolish for not saying something during her

interview, but her mind had been on Mark. "Mr. Ferguson tried to buy my bakery."

He nodded. "I'm not surprised. When I talked to the other store owners on your street, they said the same thing." He frowned. "Did he threaten you?"

The question stirred up ugly memories she'd rather forget. "My neighbors and I got a peace bond against him. He wasn't allowed to come within one hundred feet of our stores."

His expression hadn't changed. Britt felt sure Mark picked up on what she didn't say, but didn't push it. "Seriously? That's some accomplishment." He got the car started. "Where to?"

She gave him the address, then eased back into her seat, watching the city lights pass by in their multitude of colors. Tonight had been the first night in a long time that she'd gone on a date, but it felt different with Mark. They had immediately clicked, like two pieces of a puzzle that fit, and she bit the inside of her cheek, pondering that thought.

The drive was short, surrounded by a comfortable silence until he reached her condo. "I had a really good time tonight," he told her as they walked to the front door.

"So did I. Are you up for doing it again?"

"Definitely." His voice had grown deeper. "Just say the word."

Britt suddenly remembered. "I need to know something. In your text, you called me *vakker*. Do you know what that means?"

"Yes." He stepped close, and she could smell the cologne she hadn't noticed at all until now. "And it's so goddamn true."

His eyes reflected her own emotions—how a chance

meeting evolved into the possibility of something they'd both been looking for.

He caressed her chin with a finger, and on a sigh, Britt touched her lips to his, tasting their texture and warmth.

Mark muttered under his breath, and she gasped as his arms wrapped around her. He tasted of hopes and promises, of a future that didn't feel so lonely anymore.

Chapter 4

Mark parked the car in front of Mackenzie Richmond Hill Hospital the next morning, knowing his mom was expecting him. He loved spending time with her, just not under these circumstances.

On the eighth floor, he turned left, then right, walking down a long hallway. He heard two voices laughing before reaching the nurses station.

"Mark!" Evelyn was a slim and fit woman in her forties. She'd been a nurse for close to twenty years. "How are you? How's your weekend been so far?"

He shrugged. "I'm on weekend shift and I have a case."

"Well, damn." She propped her hands on her hips. "I hope you get that solved soon. Come on, your mom just finished breakfast."

Evelyn sang a tune under her breath as she led the way, her voice enriched with a Barbados accent. Mark had immediately connected with her when they first met, and he was glad Evelyn had made herself the primary caregiver for his mother.

She swung open the door. "Ms. Hawthorne, I have a visitor for you."

Mom turned away from the television tuned to a talk show. "Mark! Sweetie, I'm so glad to see you."

"That makes two of us." He thanked Evelyn and grabbed

a chair to sit beside his mother's bed. "How are you doing today?"

"A lot better. The doctor said I could go home in about a week."

Mark grasped her hand and squeezed it. "That's great. You've always been a strong woman. It's one of the things I admire about you."

She smiled. "I've got you to thank for that. I had to keep you out of trouble."

He laughed. "You know I wouldn't risk my ass by hanging out with the wrong crowd. I was more scared of you."

"Got that right." She smoothed her hand over the bedsheet. "I'm glad you came by," she said quietly. "I'd love to see you more often, but I know you have your own life to live. And the detective work must keep you on your toes."

"It does, actually." He sighed.

"Are you working on a case?"

Mom was a puzzle-solver. She loved mysteries and putting the pieces together. Occasionally, he'd tell her about one of his investigations—leaving out names and certain information—and she would give him ideas that he never would have thought of. Some of her suggestions had panned out in the five years he'd worked at the precinct. "A man got beaten up pretty badly on a construction site this past Friday."

"Edward Ferguson? It was on the news." She made a face. "Asshole."

"Mom?" He sat back, surprised. "Do you know him?"

"I know of him. Owns Mighty Big Bakery. Odd name for a business." She snickered. "Maybe it's big to compensate for his small…ahem. You know what I mean."

Mark sat in shock for all of two seconds before he lost

it in a fit of laughter. "Did you just say that?" he asked between gasps.

She shrugged. "It's an ego thing, isn't it? He's a bully, too, from what I've heard."

"A lot of people are saying that." It seemed to be the CEO's reputation.

"Do you remember that little pastry shop we used to go to on Sundays?" Mom asked. "The French one where you liked the owner's daughter, but she ran away every time she saw you?"

He shook his head. Mom remembered the weirdest things. "They made the best chocolate croissants."

"That store was in the family for generations. Suzie, the girl you liked? She took over and ran it for several years."

He frowned, suspecting where this was leading. "Mr. Ferguson bought her out?"

"Mr. Ferguson threatened her—I was there when he showed up." She shuddered. "It was awful. I found out from Suzie he had bought the two properties next door to her and wanted her building, too. She told him where to stick it, and in French, too.

"Next thing I knew, I heard on the news that her store had been broken into several times that month. They trashed her equipment, broke things, spray-painted awful words…" Mom stopped to compose herself. "Suzie had no choice but to sell. She and I always suspected Mr. Ferguson had set up the vandalism, but we couldn't prove it."

Mark nodded. He wouldn't put it past Ferguson to do something like that. "I hope Suzie got a lot of money out of it."

"She definitely did. Enough to decide to move back to France and take her parents with her. They're living in a lovely village called Amiens."

Mom also had a knack for getting along with people. *When you're nice to them, they're nice to you* was her motto, and it worked every single time. "I'm glad to hear she's well," he stated. He squeezed her hand again. "Speaking of chocolate croissants, do you want me to sneak one in for you?"

Her brown eyes widened in surprise. "Have you found a bakery that would pass even my scrutiny?"

"I have. An amazing little place called Konditori. It's a Norwegian bakery. Best Danish and coffee I've ever had."

"That's amazing. Will you bring me something tomorrow?" Mom paused. "Only if you have the time."

"I'll make it work, don't worry."

"Wonderful!" She clapped her hands. "Let's hope that Ferguson man never discovers this bakery."

It was too late for that, but Mark didn't want to spoil the visit by telling her.

He chatted with Mom for about another hour and let himself be smothered with her hugs and kisses before heading out. At the nurses station, he waited until Evelyn finished her phone call. "Has Mom had visitors?" he asked.

She shook her head. "The nurses know to call me as soon as someone asks about your mom. Your father's photo is front and center on the bulletin board over there." She pointed at a large corkboard, and he sucked in a breath, staring at Dad's scowling expression. "Everyone knows they're supposed to call Security. One of my nurses knows self-defense. I've seen her in action at one of her competitions and I would not want to meet her in a well-lit alley. I also suspect a couple of the ladies have something in their bags, but..." She stopped.

"Let's just hope it doesn't come to that. Thank you for looking after her."

As he drove home, he thought about how his mom had ended up in the hospital—a freak accident, she said. She'd fallen down the stairs at home, broken her right leg and fractured her hip. She had managed to drag herself to the phone and call him, and he had summoned every emergency vehicle as he raced to her house, praying she hadn't passed out because she wasn't answering his frantic shouts. When he'd arrived, the police and ambulance were already there, her front door busted open, and Mom carefully strapped to the stretcher.

"She'll be okay," an ambulance attendant had told him while he fought back his tears and silently prayed for her to open her eyes. "She's unconscious but breathing normally. We're headed to Mackenzie Richmond Hill Hospital and immediately into surgery."

He had nodded, too stunned to speak. As everyone started to pack up and leave, Mark had a disturbing thought. "You two," he called out to the remaining officers on the scene. "I want to run a standard check through the house, make sure everything's as it should be."

They had stood guard at the front door while Mark looked around for...something. Mom wasn't the kind of person to just fall down the stairs—she was usually so sure-footed. While nothing seemed out of place, he'd called the best forensics investigator to beg for her help.

Cynthia Cornwall had been there in record time, and less than two hours later had the fingerprints in her lab. What she'd told him was disturbing.

His father had been in Mom's house, and more than once, if the amount of fingerprints Cynthia had found was correct—and she was almost never wrong. But was he there because Mom had invited him? Or had he decided to ignore the restraining order and sneak in when she wasn't around?

Mark had a lot of questions. But so far, his father hadn't been found, and his subtle inquiries with Mom resulted in her adamant replies that she'd had an accident, end of story.

"Well, *chérie*, your new, esteemed customer was more than thrilled to see us today, I think."

Britt nodded, her excitement so strong she almost squealed with glee. She had been starstruck when they arrived at the rap artist's mansion in the Bridle Path. "Can you believe he saw the lineup at the bakery one morning and sent his housekeeper to investigate?" She laughed at the image in her head—a middle-aged woman snooping around the store, asking customers questions and sitting in a corner, taking in everything. She could have worn a trench coat and fedora, and Britt wouldn't have noticed. "I guess he gave us a thumbs-up."

"But of course he did!" Jacques drove the company van around the block to get to their parking spot behind the store. "Why would you think otherwise?"

He was right, of course. Britt had a bad habit of not giving herself credit. In fact, she was her own worst critic. "Thanks for coming with me to help set up."

"*Avec plaisir*, with pleasure. Sometimes, it is good to get out of the kitchen."

He parked the van, and Britt stepped out, her mind on what to grab out of the back.

"I'll take care of the bags, Britt. Go inside and see how everyone is doing."

"Thanks, Jacques." He knew her mind was constantly on the bakery—that was one of the many things she had learned on her journey to becoming an entrepreneur. Her business absorbed almost all her waking moments, and she was constantly planning ways to stay one step ahead of her competitors. Moments of pure luck, such as attracting the rap singer's attention, helped; but it was increasing her steady stream of regulars that brought the money in, paid her staff well and kept her reputation in good standing.

She entered the store through the back and made her way to her small office located opposite the display counter and cash register. As she walked through the kitchen door, Britt was surprised at how many customers were inside. Jasmine and Oliver seemed to be keeping things moving, but she'd get out there and help as soon as she checked a few things.

Their website had been busy, too—orders were coming in for the next few weeks. Summer was their busiest time, but Britt refused to extend the store hours. She couldn't afford another full-time person yet, and Jacques and Thomas could only do so much, even with Betty's help. She had to think of their well-being, and not allow her staff to overextend themselves.

Right, better get out there.

She was greeted by enthusiastic people who sang praises about her bakery, the food and her staff. She grew embarrassed from all the attention and soon hid behind the counter, helping with orders and ringing up sales. At one point, she headed back to the kitchen, where Jacques was moving almost too fast for the eye to follow. Thomas was at the sink, chugging back a large glass of water. "How's everything back here, Jacques?"

He turned and gave her the okay signal with thumb and forefinger. "Thomas did a fantastic job with the prepping. We'll have more pastries in thirty minutes."

"Thank you." She smiled at Thomas, who had hurried back to his station. "Both of you."

She couldn't be happier with her little team, and especially Jacques—she'd really lucked out when she hired him.

The head baker brought out a tray of cinnamon rolls while Thomas carried one filled with Danishes, and a cheer went up from the crowd. She stayed out of the way as the chefs slid the desserts into the display case with ease before hustling back to the kitchen.

That was when she spied Mark standing by the window. He had a small paper bag with handles in one hand and a large takeout cup of coffee in the other, which he saluted her with. Smiling, she wove her way through a sea of people until she got to his side and wasn't ready when he suddenly kissed her full on the lips. She raised her hand to her mouth, surprised.

"It's more fun than just saying hi." His mouth curled up in a shy smile.

Damn it, how could Mark be so...well, damn cute?

He looked around the store in awe. "Do you play linebacker every time this happens?" he asked.

Britt leaned against the wall beside him. It had only been a couple of hours since arriving at the store this morning. She knew it would be busy, but this... "Pretty much. Usually it's more organized than this. I suspect we had more new customers today walking in off the street. My regulars aren't this rowdy."

"All of you handle it like professionals." He moved close enough that Britt felt the warmth from his body. He was a dangerous distraction, and if she wasn't careful, Britt could easily fall under his spell.

That was a sobering thought.

She tilted her chin at the bag. "Did you get what you wanted?"

Mark nodded. "I waited until there was a bit of a lull, then dived in. My mom wants to try your chocolate croissants."

"Oh, I hope she likes them."

"I would have brought her, but..." His expression clouded over. "She's in the hospital."

"Damn, Mark, I'm sorry. Is she okay?"

"Her doctor said another week to ten days. She's getting better, though, thank you for asking."

"Of course." Britt knew the importance of family. Her parents and younger sister still lived in Norway, and she missed them. "Did you want any other pastries? I can get something else for her to try. A cinnamon bun, maybe?"

"I'm good." He shook his bag. "But thank you." He sipped his coffee, but Britt noticed his eyebrows drawn into a frown as he looked across the tide of customers. "Oh, I wanted to tell you." He leaned in close. "I heard some customers chatting among themselves. It seems that there's some kind of event on social media to boycott Mighty Big Bakery."

She frowned. One thing Britt kept abreast of was news on the competition. Britt had nothing against another bakery opening nearby. No two stores were exactly the same, and in her studies, she found that customers in smaller neighborhoods loved the variety. But as for Mr. Ferguson's behemoth of a bakery... "I hadn't heard about that."

"I get the feeling people are upset that a Mighty Big Bakery is opening almost across the street from you, and someone did take their anger out on Mr. Ferguson, so..." He shrugged.

"Seems almost inevitable, don't you think?" Britt didn't

condone violence of any kind, but she did believe in karma. "He must have known that his...less-than-desirable business tactics would get him into trouble."

"Justifying the assault doesn't make it right, though."

Britt decided to tell Mark the story behind her peace bond. "When I decided to lease this property, there were no other bakeries in the area. It was a prime spot—lots of foot traffic, nearby neighborhoods, other stores. Mr. Ferguson's construction site was originally a fruit and vegetable store, a butcher shop, and a clothing store that also sold flowers." Her hands clenched in frustration. "Those stores had been here for close to forty years, and Ferguson bullied them into selling out."

"How did he do that?"

Britt closed her eyes. That incident had been nine months ago, but it felt like only yesterday. "I had arrived earlier than usual one day to get started on an order. Jacques was already waiting at the front door. He said he saw three teenagers come out of the butcher shop carrying baseball bats. The grocery store had already been vandalized the week before, but no one saw anything. He managed to get pictures of the kids and turned them in to the police."

He nodded slowly. "I think I remember that. It caught our attention because the boys confessed some rich man had paid them a lot of money to wreck those stores."

"It didn't matter, did it?" Britt felt the anger bloom within her body. "Those teenagers were only issued a fine and released to their parents. As for Mr. Ferguson, the police couldn't track the payment back to him.

"In the end, he got what he wanted. He paid the owners of those stores enough money for them to retire comfortably." Britt blew out a loud sigh. "A lot of the neighbors, including myself, hoped the owners wouldn't sell, but in the end, I couldn't blame them. They were older and their kids weren't interested in taking over. It just feels…" She stopped, thinking of her own situation.

"Like they gave up?"

She looked at Mark, his gaze observant. "It sounds harsh, doesn't it?"

"In the end, it was their choice."

She bit her lip. Mark's conclusion made sense, of course. Every businessperson that came into contact with Mr. Ferguson made their choices, whether they were bullied or not. She'd made hers. "I should tell you that he came after me, too."

Something changed in Mark's demeanor. Britt saw the tensed jawline and the frown that made her step back in concern. The air around her cooled considerably. "What?" he exclaimed.

"I couldn't prove it was Ferguson. I had to use the back door that morning, and I saw it had been forced open and the security camera smashed." That memory was still fresh in her mind. "I hid behind a dumpster and called the police and kept my phone out in case I got lucky enough to take pictures. The cops didn't find anyone, and some stuff got broken, but nothing else. I was lucky."

She blew out a breath. "The next morning, there was graffiti scrawled all over my storefront with the letters *MBB*. I couldn't prove anything. All I could do was re-paint." Britt smiled. "The pink basically screams *screw you* at him."

"Hey." Mark stroked a finger across her cheek. "In the end, you did what you felt was right. Not everyone has a steel backbone like my Nordic princess."

Man, he had a way with words, but he made her feel special each and every time. "*Takk.* Thank you."

"Listen, I have to run, but maybe we can talk later?"

"I sure hope so." This time, Britt initiated the kiss, and muffled a squeal of indignation when he pinched her backside. "I'll get you for that," she seethed between clenched teeth.

His expression gave her goose bumps. "I sure hope so," he said, his voice deep. He brushed past her, so close that their bodies touched from chest to thigh, and was out the door before she managed to collect her wits.

Oh yes, he was a very dangerous distraction.

Mark's second visit with his mom was short, because he had to make more progress on his case before his meeting with Captain Fraust tomorrow.

"I see work is more important than your own mother," she sniffed.

His body tensed in annoyance. "That's not fair," he growled. "I was here this morning, and I'm visiting you again because I wanted to bring a chocolate croissant for you. But my work shouldn't come as a surprise anymore."

Mom arched a brow. "And you should know better. Did you really think I was serious?"

Mark backed off, surprised and confused.

"Hmph, you did. Shame on you. I know you have an important job."

He blew out a frustrated breath. "Sorry, that wasn't like me."

"You're right. You sounded like your father."

Mark held his breath as his stomach twisted into a painful knot. He'd promised himself and his mother that he'd never be like that man. To hear her say those words...

"That hurts, Mom."

"I'm sorry, baby. But you did ask me to tell you if or when you acted like your dad."

Mark had worked so hard to burn his father's abusive tendencies out of his life. When he was growing up, it had never occurred to Mark that he'd been doing anything wrong. *Angry friends are weak friends*, Dad used to say.

High school had been his turning point. No one was afraid to tell him he acted like a jerk. Mom had never said anything, until he told her that he needed to change—and then she'd become almost a different person. Her encouragement and support helped him become a better version of himself.

"I'm sorry, too, Mom. I don't know why…" He stopped, racking his brain to figure out what caused his relapse.

"I think you're more stressed than you realize. How is your case progressing?"

"Slowly. I need to talk to a couple of witnesses today."

She looked at him, her brows raised. "What are your plans for the rest of the day? I hope you're going to relax. All this work…" She paused.

Mark wasn't going to tell her about his surprise visit to Mr. Ferguson then, that was for sure. Instead, he said, "I had a dinner date last night."

"What?" Her excitement filled the room. "Why didn't you start your conversation with this? Now I know why your visits are short. Another woman's taking my baby's attention away from me."

"Mom," he warned, but her mischievous smile stopped him. "My God, you're doing it again."

"You're going to have to get used to it. If not me, then someone else."

"I know." Mark remembered Timmins's jokes about

Jenny the construction worker, but he hadn't been upset, more annoyed.

"May I ask a question?"

He looked at her serious expression. What was wrong now? "Go for it."

"I'm just curious. Do you act so stoic at work?"

What was Mom getting at? "I don't believe so."

"No one teases you on the job?"

He nodded. "They do, but I try not to react to it. I guess I'm worried about…" He didn't look at her, suddenly realizing that his deliberate act of being unaware only masked the real problem. He shuddered. "I don't think I'm handling this the right way." He looked at her, hoping she'd see his concern. "Do you have any suggestions?"

She nodded, as if realizing something. "Maybe you should ease up a bit."

"With my case? Mom, that's not going to happen."

"That's not what I meant. I mean lighten up. Have fun but be humble, too. You say you want to be better than your dad, so I'm challenging you to open up a little. Who knows, maybe your date will be the one to stick that Cupid's arrow into your heart."

Ah, if you only knew. He smiled. "I didn't know you were a romantic."

"Always have been." She rubbed her leg, now out of its cast and secured with a metal brace. "Always will be."

Mark watched her expression, but she gave nothing away. He really hoped she wasn't talking about Dad. "I have to go. Enjoy your treats."

"Oh, I plan to. Thank you for bringing some for me." She patted the paper bag that sat beside her. "I'm going to have one now and save the others for tomorrow. I'll see you soon?"

"You bet." He smooched her cheek several times, gave her a tight hug and headed out.

Evelyn was at the nurses station and looked up when he approached. "Everything good?"

"Yeah, thanks. Mom's in a good mood." He hesitated, worried that Dad might have tried to see her.

"He hasn't been here. Don't worry, I've got it covered." She gave him an impish smile. "Christie's taught us some basic self-defense moves."

He grinned—when Evelyn said she'd be ready for anything, she wasn't joking. "You're something else."

"I do my best." She reached into a drawer, and her hand came back into view with an envelope. "This came for your mom."

He pursed his lips and took it from her. The envelope was empty. "What was in it?"

"A letter. Your dad's name wasn't on it, but then after I gave it to her, I wondered… Well, I thought, what if he faked his name, but your mom recognized the handwriting as his?"

Mark looked for that now, turning the envelope over in his hands. This wasn't Dad's writing. "Nothing to worry about," he said, tucking it into his jacket pocket. "But I'll have it scanned for fingerprints."

"What would you like me to do if another envelope comes in for her?"

He sighed. He had no right to hold back Mom's correspondence, but if there was a slight chance it *was* Dad… "Keep it in a plastic bag so it doesn't get touched by too many hands, then give me a call or send a text. I'll let you know."

Chapter 5

Edward Ferguson lived on High Point Road within the Bridle Path, a very ritzy and expensive neighborhood located in the north end of Toronto. Mansions were surrounded by wide lawns and high decorative concrete walls, and all were barred with thick metal security gates.

Mark turned right at the third driveway and stopped his car before a set of barred gates and beside an intercom embedded within a stone pillar. He opened the window and reached out to press a button. It took just over a minute before he heard an audible click, and then a woman's voice. "Yes? Who is it?"

"This is Detective Mark Hawthorne from York Regional Police 4 District," he announced. "I'm the lead investigator on Mr. Ferguson's case. I'd like to talk to him."

A short pause. "He's currently working in his home office. May I ask if you have an appointment with him?"

An appointment? On a Sunday? "No, I do not."

Another pause, and Mark wondered if the woman was discussing the situation with the CEO in the background. He drummed his fingers on the windowsill, refusing to let his impatience get the best of him.

"May I see your badge, Detective?"

"Of course." He dug it out of his pocket and held it up in front of the intercom.

"Thank you. I'd like to verify your identity. It'll take a few minutes."

"I'm not going anywhere."

Mark didn't understand why Ferguson didn't just let him in. It was obvious the intercom had a camera—the CEO could have looked out and told the woman it was okay to let him inside.

Oh well, it wasn't worth burning through brain cells to try and figure out what Ferguson was thinking.

A cool breeze scented with flowers wafted into his car, and Mark took a deep breath. He closed his eyes and listened to the sounds surrounding him—birdsong, the rustle of leaves, the buzzing noise of a lawnmower in the distance. Sometimes, he'd forget that a few minutes of quiet solitude was enough to ease his jostling thoughts. Work would always be there, but he also had to balance it with self-care. He felt his body relax, and he inhaled again, letting his breath out in a slow exhale.

The intercom clicked. "Thank you for waiting, Detective Hawthorne. Please come in."

The thick iron gates swung open, and Mark slowly drove along a curved driveway toward the front of the house. He parked the car and got out, letting his gaze scan over the manicured landscape. A large fountain with a Cupid statue at its center gurgled with water as it flowed from a stone pitcher into the basin. Hedges and tall trees planted in front of the surrounding walls bordering the property offered natural privacy and dampened any sounds from the main street. He imagined himself sitting out here reading a good book.

Mark approached the pair of huge dark-stained doors

and pressed the doorbell, curious as to why no one was already here to greet him. He stuck his hands in his pockets and casually strolled the length of the porch, spying the four security cameras—one over the front entrance and three others over the stretch of windows on the ground floor. He wouldn't be surprised if more surrounded the house. There was also another intercom embedded in the brickwork beside the door.

He blew out a frustrated breath, wondering if the CEO was deliberately making him wait. Mark would bet his next cup of coffee that Ferguson was looking at him even now through the security camera.

Annoyance bubbled through him, but Mark wasn't going to let it boil over. Instead, he stepped off the porch and walked across the impeccable lawn, stopping occasionally to smell the beds of flowers surrounding it. The lavender bushes that bordered the property were tall and lush with flowers, and he pinched several to release their heady fragrance.

Mark didn't experience a lot of moments like these— he was either buried in work, playing hard sports with friends or at home, trying to restore his energy after dealing with cases that tore at his emotions. He had few minutes to slow down, and he enjoyed these precious scenarios whenever he could.

His thoughts drifted to the woman who had entered his life, the stunning Nordic princess who had completely ensnared him with her voice, her looks, her eyes. Those eyes—such a bright, clear, sparkling green. He could stare into Britt's eyes all day and not notice the time going by. How could Mark ignore such beauty? He knew he was damn lucky that his reaction to her seemed to be mutual.

"Detective Hawthorne," a voice called out.

He turned around. A woman dressed in a housekeeper's uniform stood at the doorway, her hands clinging together. "I'm sorry for the wait."

He nodded, and walked across the lawn again towards her, noticing her anxious expression as she glanced down at his feet. Mark had deduced that Ferguson wouldn't like anyone touching his stuff unless they had permission. Stepping on his near-perfect lawn and manhandling his shrubbery would bother the CEO a lot. As soon as he placed a foot over Ferguson's imaginary boundary, Mark knew the man would get angry and put a stop to it.

The CEO should have just let him in, instead of testing Mark's patience.

As he climbed the stairs, the housekeeper, who looked to be in her late thirties, smiled. "I apologize. Ever since those robberies last year, Mr. Ferguson has insisted on extra precautions."

"Of course. I understand." Timmins and Solberg had worked on that case until they caught a woman impersonating a courier. For some reason, women often weren't suspected as criminals until it was too late. "Better to play it safe."

When he stepped inside, Mark let out a low whistle of appreciation. The foyer, covered in black and white tile, was almost the size of his condo. Marble statues were displayed in four niches, two on each side of the wide space. The walls were a pastel green, making the area feel bigger than it looked. A grand staircase led to the second-floor landing.

"If you'll come this way." The housekeeper turned right and opened a door that led into a large study. Books graced two walls, while a heavy mahogany desk dominated the room. A wide bank of windows looked out onto the front landscape.

She pointed to a pair of leather chairs in front of the desk. "Please have a seat. Mr. Ferguson is just finishing up his business. He should be here in a few minutes."

More waiting, but there was no use in getting mad about it. Mark sat in the plush high-back chair and crossed his legs.

The housekeeper seemed so nervous that Mark was worried she'd faint. "Would you like anything? Coffee, tea, snacks?"

He almost said no, then changed his mind. If Ferguson was going to make him cool his heels, he might as well enjoy it. "Yes, thank you."

Mark had finished his first cup of coffee and had popped a mini quiche into his mouth when he heard Mr. Ferguson's voice. Moments later, the bakery CEO strode in. "Sorry about that," he apologized. "If you'd let me know you were coming in advance, I would have made sure I had cleared my calendar."

"This is an impromptu visit." Mark stood and shook hands. "Everything good?"

The CEO looked surprised at the question. "Yes, yes, of course."

Mark watched as Mr. Ferguson settled in, grabbed a cup of coffee and a snack for himself, then sat down behind his desk. "So, Officer, how can I help out today? I would have thought you'd have Sundays off."

Mark hid his expression behind the coffee cup until he was sure he could keep a neutral face. "The law doesn't sleep, Mr. Ferguson, and my colleagues do rotations so that each of us can have a decent weekend off. It's called teamwork."

Mr. Ferguson pursed his lips but didn't reply.

"How are you feeling, by the way?"

"I saw the doctor yesterday and he gave me the all clear." He leaned back in his chair. "Thankfully, no concussion, broken bones or internal bleeding. Just a lot of bruises that'll take some time to go away. The swelling in my lip is already gone." He unbuttoned his shirt cuff and rolled up the sleeve to expose a large piece of gauze. "I don't remember it happening, but I got cut by something sharp. I had to get stitches." He rolled the sleeve back down and shot Mark a sharp look. "Any news on the scumbag who attacked me?"

"I have a couple of promising leads I'm looking into." He brought out his work phone, hit Record and placed it on the desk between them. "I wanted to ask some additional questions."

"Sure, that's why you're here."

Mark put his cup back on the serving tray and mirrored Ferguson's reclining posture. He wanted to observe the man's reactions without being distracted. "How long have you owned the Mighty Big Bakery?"

"Let's see." The CEO tilted his head back. "About thirty-five years. Well, I've been owner and CEO since that time. My father started it back in the 1950s."

"Was it called MBB back then?"

"No." He shook his head for extra emphasis. "Just Ferguson's. The original neighborhood loved the store—it offered a bit of everything."

Mark noticed the nostalgic expression on the CEO's face. "Why the name change?"

"The chain needed something more distinct, more powerful. I had plans for what I wanted to do—grow the business until everyone heard about it, bake the best of everything, beat out the competition."

"I've heard you had some problems considering that last statement." Mark decided to jump on that first, since he had an opening. "It seems that there are some people who aren't thrilled with your way of doing things."

Mr. Ferguson snorted. "What do you want me to do, huh? I'm running a business. My goal is to have a Mighty Big Bakery in every city and town of Ontario." He shrugged. "After that, I'll move on to bigger things. That's how business works, son."

"I get it, but you're steamrolling over small businesses using tactics that aren't, shall we say, ethical."

The CEO stared at him. "Are you pulling the bleeding-heart sob story on me?" He laughed. "Give me a break."

Mark linked his fingers together and rested them on his lap because he didn't want Ferguson to see the clenched fists he really wanted to show. This man sounded a little too much like his father. "Just saying what I've heard from others."

Mr. Ferguson sat up in his chair and leaned across the desk. "I offered the best deals when I bought out those businesses. If the owners turned it down, that was their choice."

"It wasn't their choice to be bullied when they stood up to you."

He sat back and blinked. "I don't know anything about that."

"Oh, I think you do, but you're too smart a man to admit to it." Damn it, Mark had to stop mouthing off before he got in trouble with the captain.

Mr. Ferguson frowned. "Are you accusing me of something, young man?"

"No, sir." Mark stood, knowing he wouldn't get any kind of confession out of the guy. He grabbed his phone from the desk and stuck it in his pocket. "Thanks for seeing me today."

"Of course." Mr. Ferguson followed him to the front door. "I'll help in any way I can. Maybe I'll put in a call to Captain Fraust, let her know how cooperative and efficient you've been."

Mark hoped the surprise didn't show on his face. "Thank you. Enjoy the rest of your Sunday."

Outside, Mark gulped mouthfuls of fresh air as he walked slowly to his car. His plan to catch the CEO off guard hadn't worked. If Ferguson was hiding something, he was doing a damn good job of it. Also, the man's discreet threat that he knew the captain threw Mark for a loop—he hadn't expected that. He knew he needed to finish up any leftover work on his case today before updating Captain Fraust tomorrow morning with his findings.

Mark hoped the second item on his list—bringing in the suspect with the different-sized feet—would go off without a hitch and make up for his lack of progress with Ferguson.

When Mark and Timmins pulled their car into Henry Toussaint's driveway, the older detective hooked a thumb towards his window. "I just noticed the curtains moving."

"Good, that means someone's home." Mark hopped out of the car and strode toward the front door. Similar to Ferguson's house, there was a security camera above the entrance.

Mark pressed the doorbell then stepped back, giving the homeowner a clear view of him. "Mr. Toussaint, I'm

Detective Mark Hawthorne with York Regional Police 4 District. We'd like to talk to you."

He heard a steady clicking as someone approached the front door. As it opened, a security chain blocked any entry, only allowing about three inches of free space to speak through. On the other side, a silver-haired woman almost as tall as him looked defiant. "What do you want?" she demanded.

It wasn't a greeting Mark expected, and it instantly put him on alert. "Good afternoon." He pulled out his badge, and Timmins did the same. "I wanted to ask if Henry Toussaint was at home?"

"I don't know where Henry is right now." It didn't seem like she was going to be cooperative.

"Does he have a day job?" Mark kept his voice pleasant-sounding. He hated going into situations like this when people immediately got their hackles up and became combative.

"What has he done?"

"We'd like to ask him some questions about an assault last Friday evening."

"He doesn't work." Her frustrated expression gave Mark a clue that she wasn't happy about Henry's lack of employment.

Mark pulled out a notepad and a pen. "And you have no idea where he might be today?"

"Henry's an adult. He does whatever the hell he wants. I'm not his secretary."

"I understand. We'll come back later on today to see if he's returned."

The woman frowned. "You can't come into my home unless you have a search warrant."

Interesting—was she hiding something? "We only want

to talk to Henry—I don't need a search warrant for that."
Mark glanced at Timmins, who gave a slight nod—time
to take it up a notch. "However, I can get one within a
couple of hours. The next time I'm here, I'm allowed to
come in, and you won't be able to say anything about it."

The woman looked surprised at that, but she didn't
back down. "Fine," she sniffed. "Bring your search warrant. You won't find Henry here, and he's done nothing
wrong."

"Fair enough. Have a good day." He turned on his heel
and walked casually back to the car, but inside, he trembled with adrenaline. He felt certain Henry Toussaint lay
hidden within the house.

He and Timmins would wait him out.

They drove onto Cunningham Drive, made a U-turn
and parked one block from the entrance to Sierra Court.
"I'm sure he's hiding in the house," Timmins stated.

Mark nodded. He didn't think Henry Toussaint would
be hiding unless he had done something. "I have no idea
how desperate this guy is," he murmured.

"We should call for backup just in case."

"Good idea." He listened as Timmins made the request,
telling the dispatcher to inform the officers to stay at a
distance so that the suspect couldn't see them until it was
too late.

Unfortunately, the waiting game gave Mark too much
time to think. Everyone he had talked to, including Britt,
suspected the Mighty Big Bakery CEO of illegal activities that should have gotten him arrested. The fact that
Ferguson still bullied victims to this day meant he'd never
been caught or received more than a slap on the wrist.
Was someone protecting his interests? Or did he just have

a team of shrewd lawyers that got the CEO out of any tainted situation he found himself in?

Mark wouldn't be surprised at all. The man was like an eel, slipping out of any dirty kind of muck that surrounded him. If he could find any kind of evidence that would stick...

The police radio crackled. "Detective Hawthorne, we're in position."

Mark glanced over his shoulder. A squad car was parked about half a block behind him.

"And not a moment too soon. There's someone coming," Timmins said.

Mark stared at a man who came to a halt on the sidewalk across the street. He was tall, taller than him, and very fit. He wore a red-and-white soccer jersey with Toronto's team logo emblazoned on the front, black track pants, and smart-looking red, white and black hi-top sneakers. He stood at the corner of Sierra Court and Cunningham Drive and looked around. His gaze lingered on the police car a bit longer than necessary, making Mark twitch with excitement.

After a few minutes, the man turned and walked in the opposite direction.

"I'll follow him." Mark was halfway out the car.

Timmins scooted into the driver's seat. "Don't do anything heroic."

Mark jogged across the street and walked at a fast pace until he was about half a block behind the man. There were few cars and fewer pedestrians at this time of day, so he knew if the guy kept an eye on him, Mark would lose the chance to take him by surprise.

They walked for a few minutes, Mark matching his pace to the man's. Suddenly, the guy made a left-hand turn into a field of tall grass. His pace had quickened.

"Damn it." Mark managed to keep the same distance between them. He didn't dare glance over his shoulder to see where Timmins was, but he was certain his partner was close. He spied the wide half-hidden path and got on it, spotting his target in the distance. Timmins and the others would have to follow him on foot.

He was sure this was Henry Toussaint.

Mark's cell phone rang, and he answered it.

"Where the hell is this guy going?" Timmins demanded.

"Don't know. Just the fact that he came this way where I can barely see him is already suspicious. There's a large pond to the right behind all this grass, and up ahead is a huge park."

"He's going to try and lose us at one of those spots." Timmins swore over the phone. "I'll follow you, but I'm sending the officers parallel to the pond, see if they can get ahead and cut him off."

Mark craned his head. The guy managed to get farther away—shit, he was fast. "Tell them to move like Olympic sprinters or we'll lose him."

There were more people here—mothers with children, joggers, seniors out for a stroll. Mark remembered the children's play areas. He wanted to take the guy down before they got too close to people. If the suspect became desperate...

He caught a flash of white to his right—the officers had just passed him, moving quickly through the foliage. Mark hurried as well, his quickened steps turning into a sprint as he heard one of the officers shout out a command to stop.

When he came around a curve in the path, both officers had the man restrained. "What the hell is going on?"

the suspect shouted. He didn't fight back and allowed the handcuffs to be snapped around his wrists. "Hey, I asked you a question!"

"Detective Mark Hawthorne with York Regional Police 4 District." He showed his badge. "What's your name?"

"I don't have to tell you shit!"

"Pat him down." Mark waited as the officers quickly checked the man over. Timmins had caught up, and was directing traffic, telling people to move on. A couple stood several feet away, recording the arrest on their phone— great, just what he didn't need.

"Here's his wallet, sir." One of the officers tossed it to him.

Mark caught it in one hand and opened it. Sure enough, it was their man—Henry Toussaint. Mark advised the man of his rights. "I need you to come with us to the precinct to answer some questions."

"And if I refuse?"

He had every right to do so and request a lawyer. Mark shrugged. "I'll talk to you one way or another. But it might seem like you saying no means you have something to hide."

"You've got nothing on me," Toussaint sneered. "I'll go with you, just to prove you're wrong."

Mark loved nothing more than a challenge. "Okay then. Prepare to be mistaken."

Mark, Toussaint and an officer waited while Timmins and the second officer brought their vehicles. The suspect was seated in the back of the squad car while Mark hopped in beside Timmins. Despite driving as fast as possible back to the precinct, Mark was impatient. "I can't wait to hear what this asshole has to say for himself."

"I get it, but don't get too cocky, either," Timmins

warned. "The suspect could pull a fast one on you and you'd have no way to dig yourself out of that hole."

"I know, I know." At a stoplight, Mark cracked his knuckles. "Did you see his feet? One is definitely bigger than the other."

"And if his fingerprints match those found at the crime scene, we've got him."

At the precinct, Toussaint was taken down to interrogation. Mark had called Myrna along the way, and she was waiting for him in front of his office. "Here's his wallet," he told her, providing the evidence nestled within a plastic baggie. "See if you can lift a viable fingerprint from any of his cards in there. Pray that we get a match to those at the crime scene."

"Gotcha." She ran off.

When Mark arrived downstairs, Constable Turnbull was sitting in the recording room. "Sir, all set when you are."

He nodded and watched as Toussaint was seated at the metal table, his wrists unbound. He decided not to handcuff the suspect to the table, on the very slim chance he wasn't their guy. If he was, however, Timmins would be in the room with Mark, and the two officers who had arrested him would be standing just outside the door.

He remembered Timmins's warning as he walked in and sat down. "Mr. Toussaint, I'm Detective Mark Hawthorne. Detective Walter Timmins is here as well to listen to your statement. As I said, I have a few questions for you."

"What's this about?" Toussaint wasn't quite belligerent, but his slouched stance in the chair said otherwise.

It did give Mark a chance to study the man's feet. "Your right shoe is bigger than your left."

"Yeah. What about it?"

"Just noticing. I haven't seen that before."

Toussaint shrugged. "An anomaly among many in this world. What's that got to do with why I'm here?"

"If I'm lucky, a lot." Mark had brought his notes with him and started shuffling through pages until he found the picture with the shoe prints. "Do you remember the story about the high-priced sneakers that got recalled because its symbol on the sole of the shoe resembled a holy Arabic word?"

"Man, I got the sneakers before they got pulled." Toussaint sat up. "I put them up on a sellers' website just to see how much I could get for them. The price got up to over ten thousand dollars. No one cared they were different sizes."

"That's a nice chunk of change for a pair of kicks. How did you manage to get different sizes? Most stores wouldn't sell shoes like that."

"I got lucky." He picked up a foot and brushed his fingers against his sneaker, as if to wipe away something. "Some guy in the Middle East has the same problem as me, but the opposite feet. Worked out perfectly for us."

It worked out perfectly for Mark, too. "That's some story."

"Sure is. The ladies get a kick out of it." He grinned. "Pun intended."

Mark laughed, but not at the bad joke. "Then you'll be fascinated with what I have to show you." Mark slid the picture across. "Imagine the coincidence of finding the same shoe prints at a crime scene. Oh, and the right foot is bigger than the left. And the print matches that infamous symbol."

Mark watched Toussaint's face become slack-jawed and tried not to grin in triumph. "How about telling us why you were trespassing at a construction site, and waiting for Mr. Edward Ferguson, CEO of Mighty Big Bakery, so you could beat the crap out of him?"

Toussaint licked his lips and looked around. His eyes, wide and dark, flickered from Timmins to the door and back again. Mark sincerely hoped the young man wasn't thinking of fighting his way out. "What makes you think it was me?"

"Please." Mark tapped the photo. "Like you said, an anomaly. Plus, some old-fashioned detective work."

"Excuse me, Detective Hawthorne." Turnbull's voice came over the speaker. "Walsh is here. She says the finger-prints found in the suspect's wallet are a match for those found on the piece of wood used to beat the victim. The same fingerprints also match those found on the gas can-ister at the construction site."

Mark smiled. "Another coincidence. Your prints match those at the crime scene."

Toussaint wiped his hands over his face—he knew he was cornered. "Look, it's not what you're thinking," he said quietly.

Mark eased forward in the chair, his body tense with anticipation. "Then how about explaining what happened that night?"

"If I do, will I go free?"

"Maybe you should think about whether to do the right thing and tell us why you were there."

Toussaint's attitude had completely changed. He looked defeated.

"Help me understand why you would take your anger out on Mr. Ferguson. And bring a gas canister to the site. You were going to burn the building down."

"Not with people still inside!" Toussaint got up and

paced a tight path between the table and Timmins. "Look, I know it's going to sound outrageous, but here's the truth, I swear."

He came back and sat down. "You know who Mr. Ferguson is. Big-name CEO of those bakeries. He hurt a lot of people when he bought out the small businesses. A real scumbag."

Jeez, Ferguson had really made a bad reputation for himself. "I've heard the stories," Mark said.

"A friend of mine told me about someone who was holding rallies to speak out against Ferguson's tactics. The first one I went to was about two weeks ago."

"A rally? Isn't that unusual?" And why hadn't Mark heard of it? Rallies were usually logged so that they could obtain police security. Unless… "Or do you mean a protest?"

"Does it matter? It was undercover, though. My friend picked me up, and we had to follow these weird instructions to get to the place."

"So that you couldn't report them to the police when the time came," Timmins chimed in.

Toussaint nodded. "All I know is that it was near the rail yard."

Mark frowned. "How do you know that?"

"I could hear the trains stopping and starting. You know, when they make those big clanging noises."

"Sounds like train cars being hooked together."

Toussaint nodded. "Yeah, like that. We went to a small building. The inside smelled of grease and metal, but I could barely see anything. There was a guy standing on a box, dissing Ferguson and saying that we should stop him."

"How many people were there?"

Toussaint shrugged. "Maybe a dozen? I don't know.

But listening to the guy talk, he had a way of getting us riled up, to do something against Ferguson, you know?"

There was nothing more dangerous than a leader with charm and incentive. Under the right circumstances, that leader could send a frenzied mob to do whatever he asked. "Did this leader provide instructions on what to do?"

"A few. A popular one was graffiti on the Mighty Big Bakeries, but someone yelled that spray-painting the stores wasn't enough. I heard another person saying something about torching the bakeries. Then some other guy shouted that we should beat up the employees." Toussaint shook his head. "It was getting out of control, but somehow the leader managed to calm everyone down."

"Could you see his face?"

"No, man, he wore a mask that covered the bottom of his face and a baseball cap."

Mark jotted some notes down. "So you decided to burn down the new Mighty Big Bakery store that's going up nearby?"

"No, that was my friend's idea. She was more excited than I was. She said she could get me onto the construction site with no problem."

A coil of anger wove up Mark's back until it hit him square in the face. If it was her… "How did she manage to do that?" he said through gritted teeth.

Toussaint gave him a weird look. "How else? She's a construction worker. Jenny was all for taking that bakery down. Now I want to talk to my lawyer."

Chapter 6

Britt read Mark's text and wondered what the hell had happened to him.

Have you ever wondered how it would feel to just stay home all day and IGNORE EVERYONE? Cuz I wish I had done that today.

Instead of texting back, she called. "Hey, Mr. Detective."

"Hi, Britt."

Okay, that did *not* sound like him. Work must have been especially stressful today. "Is everything all right? What's going on?"

A sigh. "Too much, but I think I have a handle on it now."

She didn't think looking for Mr. Ferguson's attacker would take that much effort, but what did she know about police investigations? "Excellent. That means we can have dinner together."

He was silent on the other end, and Britt mentally smacked herself. Mark must be exhausted. "I'm sorry," she started. "I shouldn't have presumed…"

"Are you kidding? Spending time with my Nordic princess is the perfect ending to a day like this."

"Mr. Detective, flattery will get you everywhere. Where would you like to go?"

"How about you make the choice? I'll be at your place to pick you up in about half an hour?"

"It's a date."

It was going to be a warm night. Britt chose her blue maxi dress, as she loved how it flowed around her legs. A small purse and comfortable sandals finished the outfit. She thought about leaving her hair down, but hated how it got easily tangled around things, so she swept it up into her usual ponytail. A bit of lipstick, and she was ready to go.

As she waited in the lobby downstairs, Britt thought of what she'd normally be doing right now, which would have been making dinner and watching another repeat show on television. Or work. She noticed she had picked up the bad habit of checking her laptop for customer emails during her downtime. Once, she had told herself it was necessary to stay one step ahead, but now she knew it was to fill in the long evenings until the next day arrived.

She had to be honest. Work had started to take up too much of her time. Oh, Britt loved it and wouldn't give it up, but she knew there was more to life than that. She had no problem being alone, but being lonely? That sucked.

Several times, she had thought about moving back to Norway. Her family would have been thrilled, and she could return to a familiar routine with no problem. Britt wouldn't be alone, but that was not what she needed. Independence was a critical part of her existence, supported by family, friends and work. She had all of that, but she'd realized something was still missing—a person to fill the remaining void in her heart.

Britt had been so busy building a life for herself, she'd forgotten about everything else. But she'd needed to do something—anything—to get her mind off the pain and humiliation she'd suffered before creating Konditori. She had built her dream from scratch—learning, failing and learning again had been the catalyst she needed to realize that she was capable of anything, and no one could tell her different.

However, Britt also believed in the Nordic Fates, that everyone's life was woven to follow one particular destiny. Was Mark one of the threads to be woven into her life's journey? Britt didn't know yet, since they'd only met a couple of days ago. However, their instant connection was something she'd never experienced before. It had been solid, never wavered, and if the gods were smiling down on her, it would last.

A horn beeped twice, and she mentally shook herself out of the past and into an exciting present. Mark was already out of the car and holding the passenger door open for her. "How are you, *vakker*?" he asked in a deep tone before managing to sneak a kiss on her cheek.

God, his voice... She smiled. "Starving. Oh, and happy to see you, too."

He raised a brow at that. "I'm not sure I'm convinced."

Oh, he needed convincing, huh? Britt grabbed his face and pulled him down so she could mold her mouth to his. Damn, he tasted good, like something rich and delectable. She backed away before she got too mesmerized. "I hope that helped."

His expression made her insides tie up in knots. "What's that look for?" she demanded.

His gaze traveled slowly down to her feet, then back up. Britt's nerves were lighting up and tingling. "Are you sure you want dinner? Or are you hungry for something else?"

She swallowed the lump that formed in her throat, knowing exactly what he meant and fighting to keep herself in check. "You are a very naughty boy," she whispered, "making suggestions like that."

"You don't seem shocked."

He noticed that? Damn it, Britt, of course he did—he's a detective. "You're very observant."

"With you? Yes, I can't help myself."

She didn't have a comeback. Instead, with a shaky smile, Britt slid into the car.

"Where would you like to go?" he asked.

"Do you like sushi?"

"Love it."

"I was hoping you'd say that. I found a great place on Yonge Street, just north of Highway 401."

They parked at a corner close to the restaurant. After Mark helped her out of the car, he didn't release her hand. With his fingers closed over hers, that strange feeling of belonging hit her again, along with something else—she was relaxed and content. And damn if that didn't feel wonderful.

The restaurant wasn't busy yet, and the hostess and staff greeted them in Japanese before taking them to a booth that offered a view of the sunset and the gradual uptick of nightlife.

"This is a nice place," Mark said. "I haven't been here yet."

Dark paneled wood covered the walls, which were decorated with bright prints of Japanese figures. The sushi kitchen was at the other end of the spacious room, with the chefs hurrying around each other as they made the meals. Soothing Japanese music played in the background. "Oh? Were you planning on trying it out?"

"Eventually. I worked a burglary case in the area a few months ago." He stopped as a waitress brought green tea and two cups, then poured for them. "I came in here to ask questions, and the hostess at the time had valuable information that led to the perp's arrest. She was very observant."

"That's amazing." They clinked their cups, and she took a sip. The tea was hot and refreshing. "So, how was your day? You sounded pretty stressed over the phone."

"Busy. But I'll have a final report for my captain tomorrow."

The only police procedures Britt knew were from the reality shows on television. They were real but didn't have the same impact as actually talking to a live person. "I don't want to sound nosy, and you can stop me whenever you want. Did you find Mr. Ferguson's attacker?"

"Yeah."

Short and to the point. "And the person will be charged?"

"There are a few steps in between, but yes, he'll be formally charged with assault."

Britt didn't think she could do Mark's job. It seemed like there was too much emotional back-and-forth. "I guess Mr. Ferguson could sue the attacker, too."

"If he wanted. I'd rather he backed off, but…" Mark didn't say anything.

Damn it, Britt, think of something else! "How's your mother doing?"

"Much better, thank you. She'll have months of physical rehab, though." His expression grew clouded. "I hope she's up for it."

"Why wouldn't she be? I'm sure your mom will have excellent help from the nurses." On an impulse, Britt rested her hand over his. "Maybe you can go to her follow-up appointments and encourage her."

He turned his hand over and laced his fingers with

hers. "Thank you, I needed to hear that." He grinned. "She loves your pastries by the way, and it takes a lot to impress her."

She smiled back. Britt sensed that Mark loved his mother very much.

The waitress had returned, and they placed their order.

Britt kept their conversation light and away from work as much as possible. "Do you watch cartoons?" she asked.

He gave her a weird look.

"You're kidding, right?" she demanded. "Everyone should watch cartoons. There's too much serious shit going on in the world, and I don't think that's going to change. I find watching cartoons makes me remember how funny life can be sometimes."

"Which ones do you watch? And if you say the coyote and weird-looking bird with the long legs, I might walk out."

She burst out laughing. "It's one of my favorites!"

Mark made a move as if to get up, but she grabbed his arm. "Hear me out," she demanded. "Since you know the cartoon, tell me—have you ever seen a more motivated individual? He goes after what he wants and nothing gets in his way."

Mark cocked a brow, which put her on the defensive.

"You know it's true," she insisted. "Okay, how about the two mice? The really smart one that wants to take over the world? That's what I call dedication."

Mark shook his head. "You sure are something else."

"And what's that supposed to mean?"

"I mean you're different. Your bakery is your job, but I sense it's a lot more than that."

Britt sat back, watching him. "It's my passion. I love what I do. And I think that's allowed me to look at life a little differently, too. Life's too short to, I don't know, worry about mortgages or what people think of me. If I enjoy it, that's what counts."

He nodded slowly, as if thinking.

Their dinner arrived—miso soup, salad, two different kinds of sushi rolls and tempura vegetables. "This looks delicious," she said in a singsong voice, moving several pieces onto her plate. She grabbed a piece of spicy tuna sushi and popped it into her mouth. "So good!" she groaned, as she chewed. "I never would have thought I'd love sushi until a friend introduced me to it."

"Have you tried a lot of different things?"

"Before I became an entrepreneur, yes." She started ticking items off her fingers. "I wanted to be a ballet dancer, but I hated the training and the eating lifestyle. I couldn't eat sushi if I kept it up. And I was in the army."

"Seriously?" Mark's brown gaze widened in awe. "How old were you?"

"Nineteen. All Norwegians are mustered at that age. Then I took the military's compulsory training. That was nineteen months of hard work."

"So, wait a minute. If there's a war, are you called back?"

She shook her head. "I don't know... I think it's possible."

"Shit." He looked upset.

"Hey, let's hope it doesn't happen. Trust me, if it did, I'd look for an administrative job." Damn it, she hadn't meant for the conversation to head in this direction. Maybe it had been her conscience telling her to warn him of the possibility? *Yeah, thanks, brain.* "Then I decided on politics. That didn't go so well." Just thinking about it made her a little sick to her stomach.

"What happened?"

Britt knew Mark would ask the question, but she wasn't ready to tell him. "A lot of crap that could have been avoided." She started eating again to keep her mouth busy—she didn't want to get into it. Except... "Now you see why I love cartoons. Oh! And anime. Japanese anime movies are just so beautiful."

He remained quiet but watched her while he ate, which made her squirm in her seat.

The restaurant started to fill with more customers, and the noise from their conversations got too loud. As the waitress returned, Britt had an idea. "Did you want to stay? Or maybe we could go for a walk?"

"Yeah, I'd like that."

The sidewalks were filled with people. It was a warm evening, and it seemed everyone wanted to take advantage of it.

Mark saw Britt glance back at the restaurant, as if she missed its atmosphere. "Come on, I know just the place." He grasped her hand and tucked it beneath his arm. At the next block, he turned right and entered the neighborhood just beyond the busy atmosphere of Yonge Street. He breathed in the scented air and felt himself relax as the quiet settled around them.

"I never knew about this," she murmured. As they crossed another street, a large park appeared between the stand of tall trees bordering it. The security lights came on as the sky grew darker, illuminating a group of kids playing soccer. Town houses and large older homes stood side by side and stretched out into the distance.

"You need to explore the city more often. I came through here because—what else? Another case." It felt like Mark only found out about hidden areas of the city when he was working. He led them into the park and walked to its edge, then stopped and offered her a bow. "Shall we take a turn, my lady?"

Britt giggled and curtsied. "You are too kind, milord."

Unlike on Yonge Street, the only other sounds here were songbirds and the children's laughter. They walked the length of the park in comfortable silence, not hurrying, and Mark suddenly realized this was what he needed—time to himself, not rushing headlong to his next case.

The thrill and excitement of his job was great—he had no complaints. He loved the adrenaline rush, hanging out with the guys during their downtime, or collaborating and throwing out theories over a complex investigation. But his colleagues had something else that, if he was honest, made him jealous. Solberg and Cynthia were dating now, and Timmins was married. Occasionally, the guys would talk about their significant others, their plans, their futures. Mark wanted that for himself.

He had no problem meeting women and had been on plenty of dates. However, there was always something missing. He couldn't explain it, but he felt it. Mom once told him he'd know when a woman was "the one." He had scoffed at the idea, but now…

He looked at Britt while she talked and pointed out things that interested her. Her body was warm against his, and Mark felt that same sizzle of awareness as when he'd seen her the first time. He knew it was too early to decide if she would be the woman in his life, but she'd certainly made one hell of an impression on him.

So far, so good.

They had almost reached the other end of the park. A

soccer ball rolled toward them, but one of the boys inter-
cepted it and kicked it back to his friends.

"Mark, could I ask you something?"

He looked down into her ocean-green gaze, those sparkling eyes that filled him with an emotion that ached in
his chest. "Only if you let me kiss you first."

"Ah, you're not above bribery then." She tilted her face
up to his, her full lips puckered and making smooching
noises that had him snorting with laughter.

"Will you stop that?" he told her.

"Make me."

That was a challenge he would not pass up. He molded
his mouth to hers, trying to get past the humor of her kiss
until she suddenly relaxed against him. Her lips parted,
and he gently delved his tongue into her warmth, exploring every bit until she groaned softly. The sound almost
had him begging for more.

He reluctantly backed away, and that's when he heard
the kids whistling, hooting and howling wolf calls.

Britt blushed a deep shade of pink. "Mind your own
business! I thought you were playing soccer!"

"This is a family park, lady!" a tall boy yelled out. "Go
find a room!"

Amid the jeering, Mark finally settled on her question.
"What did you want to know, Britt?"

They reached the second corner and turned right. Their
stroll took them past a small playground. Moms helped
their kids onto the swings, caught them as they reached
the bottom of the slide and called out when one got too
ambitious on the monkey bars.

"How did you become a police detective?"

He expected the question. He just wasn't sure how
much to say. "My family used to live in British Colum-

bia," he started as they walked back. "Mom and I loved it there, but Dad was too much of a nomad. He'd travel for work and leave Mom and me a lot."

That wasn't exactly how he wanted to start the conversation. "I got into a lot of trouble as a kid. Getting into fights, picking on the smaller kids. Mom tried her best and finally got me to settle down, but I didn't want to do anything. I didn't have an interest in school."

Mark remembered those days and wished he could take them back. "When I got to high school, I had a difficult time with my courses, and nothing grabbed my attention. I knew Mom was worried, and I tried to apply myself, but nothing worked."

He bit his lip against the pain and anguish swelling within him. He remembered hearing Mom crying one night in her room after a heated argument they'd had, and him storming out of the house. He had never meant to hurt her, but Mark had been too angry at himself to notice until that night.

"What did you do?" Britt asked quietly. They had reached the end of their walk and stood beneath the trees.

"Someone came to my rescue. My phys ed coach. He must have found out about my failing grades from one of my teachers. Gave me a swift kick in the ass first, then mentored me through high school. He was exactly what I needed."

Stanley Tucker had saved him from a life of regrets. "Next thing I knew, I got high grades and earned a scholarship. I studied law enforcement because I wanted to do what Stanley did for me, helping others." He looked at her. "Mom was proud of me, but I needed to be proud of myself or I was going nowhere."

"That's an amazing story, Mr. Detective. You've really impressed me."

Suddenly a voice yelled out. Mark approached the soccer ball bouncing in their direction and his competitive streak kicked in. He juggled it with his feet to the delight of the young boys, before kicking it out toward them.

"I see you like sports as well."

"It helps me release a lot of pent-up energy."

"Are you on any sports teams?"

He shook his head, looking out at the boys as they raced across the field. "Just too busy."

Britt moved up to him until their bodies touched. Jesus, he wanted to explore the woman beneath the clothing, discover her secrets and desires. Her flirtations were making it hard for him to concentrate on her as a person. "I think I did say that life was too short to not enjoy what you love." She caressed his cheek with her hand. "You should consider it."

He turned his head slightly and pressed his lips to her palm. "I will, *vakker*."

"God, I love how you say that. It almost makes me want to do anything."

He stared at her, thinking of the delicious things he'd love to do with her. "Really?"

"Mmm-hmm."

It felt like the air around them had stilled, as if holding its breath. His finger touched her chin, but he didn't move—he waited. He wanted Britt to be sure that this was a moment of no looking back, to know that he wasn't going anywhere, that he wanted her with every fiber of his being.

Her lips parted in a slight gasp. He wondered if she was

thinking the same thoughts, but then his brain shut down when she leaned in and brushed her mouth across his.

He uttered an unintelligible sound and wrapped his arms around her, dying to caress her body with his eager hands and fighting against the urge. Standing in a park with kids watching was not the ideal spot. But when her arms came around his neck and he felt her fingers grab his hair, he almost lost it. He gently grasped her bottom lip with his teeth and was rewarded with her soft sound of desire.

This moment felt right. He had no other way to explain it. His Nordic princess wanted him just as much, and when the time was right, he would lavish all his attention upon her like the true goddess she was.

Chapter 7

Sunlight was pouring through the window when Britt woke up, yawning and feeling refreshed. She'd slept through the night.

She stayed in bed, hugging the pillow to her chest as she reminisced about her dinner date with Mark. She imagined herself in one of those romantic movies, where the couple strolled around a city at night, looking at the bright lights and staring into each other's eyes. She wasn't one for clichéd plotlines, but now that she had experienced it for herself...

Britt stared at the ceiling. She hadn't wanted last night to end, and if she read Mark's actions correctly, he hadn't wanted to stop, either. But she wasn't quite ready to take the next step. Things were moving pretty quickly, and despite the swirl of euphoria that still rushed through her, she wanted to take things just a little easy.

Mark had more or less indicated the same thing, although while he was driving her home, his hand couldn't stop touching her arm and thigh. Which sure as hell didn't help. By the time they got to her place, she was ready to drag him upstairs, but she'd convinced her lust to calm down.

Maybe next time.

Giggling, she went to the bathroom to get a shower. Today was a new day. Mark had warned her about his busy work schedule, so Britt would have to daydream about last night until she could see him again.

But man, to have him kiss her like that...

She turned the tap to Cold to allow the water to wake her up and hopefully cool off the very sexy thoughts roiling around in her head. She had a business to run.

The bus ride gave her time to check her emails. She had received a couple more party requests for her pastries for this coming weekend. If this kept up, she'd need to consider hiring extra help. She hadn't wanted the bakery to grow too fast—she wanted to keep the small-business charm intact. It was something she'd need to discuss with her staff, especially Jacques and Thomas. She refused to overwork them.

When Britt arrived at her stop, other people were also hurrying to work. It was almost nine, but the bakery opened at eight during the workweek to take advantage of the early-morning crowd. As she approached the store, she noticed a couple of customers peering in through the window, and as she reached the door, Britt was shocked to discover how busy it was inside.

"Helvete." Hell. What was going on?

She hurried around the side of the store, intent on using the back entrance so that she could get inside and help out. However, as she turned the corner, she almost bumped into someone who looked like...

"Ms. Gronlund." Mr. Ferguson was almost unrecognizable, wearing blue jeans and a white shirt instead of his usual two-piece business suit. But it was his expression that made her take a step back—he was furious. "I couldn't get into your bakery this morning. You certainly have loyal customers and staff."

"What are you doing here? Have you forgotten about the peace bond and what it means?" He was the last person she expected to see. "It means stay away from my shop."

Britt glanced over her shoulder—she was about six feet from the sidewalk. The odd person glanced in her direction and kept going, not seeing anything wrong. But if she decided to scream...

Suddenly, his hand clamped over her wrist. "I can see what you're thinking," he growled. "I just want to talk."

"We've talked enough." Britt tried to wrench her arm free, but no luck. "Get your hand off me."

"Why didn't you sell your business? I offered top dollar. Do you want more? I'm sure we can come to an agreement."

"And I already told you where you could stick your offer." Mr. Ferguson was stronger than Britt expected, but she wasn't a lightweight, either.

"Name your price."

"Why?" She waved her other hand at the construction site across the street. "You got what you wanted. Leave me alone."

"No, I didn't. I've never had anyone refuse my offers. Tell me your price." He actually bared his teeth in a snarl.

"How about this?" She set her stance, then swung one leg up, aiming her foot at his crotch.

Mr. Ferguson howled in pain and let go of her hand to clutch his manhood with both of his.

"Stay away from me and my bakery!" She took off down the short alleyway. At the back, she scrabbled for the key that opened the back door, and after what felt like agonizing minutes, managed to grasp it between her shaking fingers. Moments later, she was inside, the thick metal door between her and that creep. She fought to slow her rapid breathing, but it was hard. The adrenaline had kicked in, and it would take some time before it wore off.

How dare he? Mr. Ferguson had some nerve, coming to her business like that. Competition she understood, but this—this smelled of desperation. She wondered about the CEO's comment of being refused entry into the bakery. Did he finally understand that trust and loyalty were the two things necessary to run a successful business?

"Nah," she told herself. He just resented it when a competitor was doing better than him.

As she walked through the large kitchen, she saw Jacques and Thomas moving quickly through the space like two synchronized partners. As she watched, Britt wondered with a bit of awe how they never bumped into each other.

"Ah, Britt, *bon matin*, good morning!" Jacques called out. He said something to his assistant, then hurried over to her, wiping his hands on his apron. "Our pastries are selling faster than we can bake them today! What has happened?"

"Konditori becoming popular is what happened. I couldn't get in through the front door. I had to come in the back way."

"*Mince!* Damn." Jacques wiped his sweaty brow with a dishcloth, then threw it into the laundry basket behind him. "This frenzied pace, *chérie*. I love the excitement, but…"

She grasped his arm. "I know. We'll need to have a meeting. I have a couple of ideas, but I want to hear from all of you, too." She'd also have to tell them about Mr. Ferguson threatening her in the alleyway. Her staff was going to be infuriated.

Britt joined Betty and Kevin in serving the customers, and about an hour later, it finally slowed down.

"Britt, you gotta stop with the billboard advertising," Betty said with a laugh.

This time, her fast breathing came from excitement. "Seriously, I haven't done anything different."

"It's word of mouth," Kevin said. "And those party pastry trays we set up. We hear what the customers are saying—they love this place. And it's getting around."

She nodded slowly, knowing Kevin was right, but she'd never expected this kind of popularity so soon. She'd have to decide on that fine line between expanding and keeping the coziness of the bakery.

Thankfully, the rest of the day was manageable. Britt finally had a chance to sit down in her office and let her body go limp. As she let her brain process the day, she realized she hadn't told her staff about her encounter with Mr. Ferguson. It was probably better this way.

"What have you got for me, Hawthorne?"

"Captain." Mark hadn't been able to get a read on Captain Michelle Fraust since she took over two months ago. Late forties, no-nonsense, and with a list of awards for her leadership and competency, she was one of the youngest officers to make the captain's list.

There had been speculation—and gossip—about her in the precinct. It was expected. But, Mark surmised, unless Fraust decided to suddenly open up about her personal life, all they had were guesses and theories.

He pulled out his notes from the thick folder he had brought with him. "After confirming that Mr. Ferguson was okay, Forensic Investigator Walsh and I collected evidence at the crime scene. Initially, the suspect's fingerprints were found and processed, but the database hadn't provided any positive hits. However, we found distinctive shoe prints in the area that helped to considerably narrow down our search."

"How so?" She sat on the other side of the meeting table, back straight in the chair, with no sign of emotion on her face. It was like talking to a statue, which creeped him out a little.

Mark summarized for the captain the work involved in locating the suspect who owned the limited-edition sneakers.

"And how did you find the right suspect? Shoe size?"

"Not just shoe size." Mark pointed at the left and right footprint. "Do you see the distinction?"

She frowned for only a moment before her blue eyes widened in surprise. "Different-sized feet?"

"Yes, ma'am. On Saturday I went to several stores until I got a hit. I found Henry Toussaint Sunday afternoon and brought him in for questioning. He didn't admit to the assault despite the evidence pointing to him. However, he told me that someone else came up with the plan to commit the arson." Mark still wanted to kick himself for missing that. "Jenny, the construction worker who first reported the incident."

Her ice-blue gaze riveted him in his seat. "Has Mr. Toussaint been charged?"

"No, ma'am." Mark thought carefully on how to phrase his next words. "I think Toussaint has been getting directions from Jenny. I also think Jenny knows pertinent information about these anti-Ferguson protests. If she's in hiding, I'll never find her. But with Toussaint out there..."

"He should lead you to her. A little unorthodox, but I understand your reasoning." She paused. "Mr. Ferguson may want to press charges against Toussaint and Jenny once they're arrested, but we'll wait and see if that happens. Was there anything else?"

Mark kept his expression neutral—he knew what she meant, but he was going to take a risk and feign ignorance. "No, Captain."

Fraust rose and slowly paced the room. "I received a call from Mr. Ferguson first thing this morning," she started. The captain looked over her shoulder. "He complimented you on being thorough with the investigation."

"I'm glad to hear it, ma'am." He was waiting for the other shoe to drop.

"However, you paid him an unexpected visit at his home Sunday morning." She came back to the table but remained standing. "Was there a reason for that?"

"More a gut feeling. I didn't feel that Mr. Ferguson had told me everything that had happened."

"I see." She sat down again. "What was the result of your surprise interview?"

"Not a damn thing." He should have known better than to think a shrewd businessman like Ferguson would accidentally disclose information about his business tactics.

"You should know that Mr. Ferguson is not a man to be taken lightly."

Surprised, Mark looked at his boss. "I understand, Captain."

"Do you?" Her smile was dangerous. "He didn't climb his corporate ladder with just grit and determination. He did so with a ruthless ambition that would scare off CEOs running the best-known global conglomerates."

Captain Fraust was giving him a hint, and Mark got it—if he was going to accuse Mr. Ferguson of his unethical business dealings with small-business owners, he'd better be damn sure he had everything lined up.

"I'm going to provide an update to the media, but you don't need to be there. My statement will be short, with some diplomatic phrasing that we're still investigating."

"Thank you, Captain."

"Good work so far, Hawthorne, both you and Walsh. Keep me updated. Dismissed."

Mark got on the elevator and hit the button for his floor. That had gone a lot smoother than he'd anticipated. He had felt sure Captain Fraust would browbeat him for suspecting a crime victim, especially a high-level CEO.

Maybe she knew something about Mr. Ferguson that shouldn't be known.

"Huh." Maybe, if he had time, he might poke around to see what he could find. There was no way Ferguson could threaten people and destroy property without suffering some of the consequences.

His personal phone pinged with a text, and Mark glanced at the short, humorous note from Britt.

Hey, how's it going? How was your meeting with the dreaded captain?

Mark couldn't get over Britt's choice of words. He texted her back.

I'm not walking the plank.

Chapter 8

Britt sipped her tea. "I'm telling you, Joyce, seeing Mr. Ferguson in the alley like that freaked me out."

Before the bakery had closed, her friend Joyce came in to say hi. Britt felt guilty for not keeping in touch with her, but between the CEO's threats, a busy bakery and Mark's sudden appearance in her life, she felt like she'd been stretched in too many different directions.

"Did you report it?" Joyce Mathurin had been hired to do the interior design of the bakery. In her thirties, she was a beautiful dark-skinned Torontonian with roots in Saint Lucia, and the two of them had hit it off almost immediately. Because of their busy schedules, getting together to socialize had been hard, so they made the most of each personal visit.

They were sitting in Britt's office. The bakery had now closed for the day, but she told Joyce to wait in the office while she and the staff cleaned up. The store sat in darkness except for the one lamp in the room, and the security lights located at the front and back of the building.

"No. I know I should, but it feels like I'm not getting anywhere with the police. I took it upon myself to let the man know how much I didn't like him."

Joyce's eyes widened with curiosity.

"I kicked him in the nuts."

Tea spewed from her friend's mouth as her laughter rang through the small office. Britt calmly handed her a napkin. "Are you kidding? Oh gosh, I wish I'd seen that!"

"I think it was more instinct than anything else. I just reacted."

"Hey," Joyce said suddenly, pointing at her. "Where's your bracelet?"

Confused, Britt looked at her left wrist. It wasn't there. "I'm sure I had it on today."

"I only noticed when you handed me the napkin. Maybe you forgot to put it on this morning?"

"Maybe." The rune bracelet had been a birthday present from her family—she rarely left home without it. "I've been distracted lately."

Joyce nodded and bit into a mini cinnamon roll. "I remember you saying you had a lot on your mind, and now this Ferguson guy is ignoring your peace bond. It's too bad you didn't have him in your security footage. I'll bet the police would have done something more."

Britt sat up. "You know what? I just might." Mr. Ferguson had told her he tried to get in the store, but the customers had blocked his way. Her laptop was still on, so she clicked on the security app and used the arrows to slide back to the time just before she arrived.

The scene she watched was chaotic. Several customers jostled in the tight space in front of the door, and in the middle, Mr. Ferguson was using his arms to protect himself from the shoving. Someone landed a punch on his chest.

"The bastard lied. He was actually inside my store," Britt whispered, her voice trembling with anger.

"Holy crap," Joyce breathed. "I can't believe that guy had the balls to walk in here."

"I admit to being more nervous that Mr. Ferguson might charge me with assault."

"You? But you didn't do anything—you were defending yourself!"

"It happened on store property." Britt sighed. "But, with the peace bond still in force, he shouldn't stand a chance if he tried to charge me."

They continued watching until Mr. Ferguson was forcefully shoved out of the store. He shook his fist and yelled something, then straightened his clothing. At that moment, a bus arrived at the nearby stop.

"I'm sure that's the bus I was on," Britt murmured.

The CEO looked over his shoulder, then hurried away and out of the camera's view. A minute later, Britt appeared on screen, opened the front door, looked inside, then left.

"That's when I realized I couldn't get in." She closed the app and shut the laptop.

"So it was coincidence when the two of you saw each other." Joyce wiped her hands on a paper napkin.

"A coincidence that I don't want repeated. How the hell am I supposed to keep this guy away from me and my staff if he deliberately ignores the peace bond?"

Joyce shook her head. "I honestly don't know. If you report it and provide this footage, the police should charge him with a criminal offense."

Britt snorted with disdain. "As if. With his slimy lawyers, Ferguson will only get another slap on the wrist."

"You've done the right things, Britt. The only other idea I have is moving your location."

"Like hell I will." Britt refused to be scared off.

Joyce laughed. "That's what I wanted to hear." She leaned forward in her chair. "So," she said, dragging out the word. "Anything else going on in your life?"

Britt looked at her friend's inquisitive expression and tried not to smile. "Just me and work."

"Mmm-hmm." Joyce picked up her mug. "Work must be more fascinating than usual. Other than dealing with Edward Ferguson of Mighty Big Bastard."

"Oh my God, did you just say that? That phrase is going to be stuck in my mind now." She laughed, enjoying the sound and how it made her feel. She could always depend on Joyce to find the humor in everything.

"So, tell me—what has made you look so glowy?"

"What?" Britt tried to act naive, but by the look on Joyce's face, that wasn't going to work anymore. "All right, you found me out. I met a guy last Friday."

"Oooh, good for you! Who is he? Give me all the deets."

"Well, he's a detective with York Regional Police."

"He's in law enforcement? How intriguing." Joyce propped her chin on her hands. "How did you meet him?"

"Would you believe me if I said our eyes locked on each other from across the street?"

Joyce frowned. "Sounds like something from a movie."

"Right? But that's what happened. I saw him as he was going to his car, and my eyes just went *boing*! You know, like how it happens in the cartoons when their eyes bug out?"

Her friend chuckled. "You and the cartoons...but I know exactly what you mean. Have you been on a date?"

"A couple, actually."

"Girl, you're not wasting any time—I love it! What kind of a kisser is he?"

Britt felt her cheeks heat up in a blush. "A thorough one."

"I'm liking this more and more." Joyce waggled her brows.

"That's as far as we got. I…" She realized that she didn't want to mess this up. Not because she hadn't been on a date in a long time, but because Mark meant much more than that to her. "I don't want to rush things."

"Totally get that. You're being smart. What does he look like?"

"Over six feet. Thick, beautiful hair—it's so soft. Brown eyes with these gold flecks I can see when I'm close enough. I'm pretty sure he's built, but I haven't had the chance to check out under the hood, so to speak."

Joyce laughed and clapped her hands. "Don't worry, you will. I'm so happy for you! I know the store has been your focus, but you need to live your life, too."

Britt couldn't have put it better herself.

"We should get going." Joyce looked at her watch. "Time flies when you're—"

The sudden noise of shattering glass reverberated through the office. "What the hell…?" Britt started to say.

"Someone's breaking in!" Joyce sprang to her feet and peeked out while Britt grabbed her laptop and stuffed it into her purse. Her friend shut and locked the door. "There's three guys, all with baseball bats," Joyce whispered urgently. "We need to hide."

"Joyce, they're going to destroy my bakery!"

"Better that than hurting you. Come on, where can we hide?"

Britt thought furiously. "Not in here, especially if they break the door down." She turned, trying not to panic as several loud voices traveled through the air toward them. "The window. It's our only chance. Hurry!"

Britt slid it open. Although she had installed security lights in the alley, she worried that one wrong move could spell injury for her and Joyce, or alert the intruders.

Joyce climbed out first, displaying her strength as she slid over the windowsill with ease. "Give me your stuff," she said, while holding her hands through the window.

Britt gave her the purse, then proceeded to perch her butt on the sill. Another loud crash, closer this time, caught her attention—they were destroying the display counter.

"Come on!" Joyce called.

She swung her legs over the sill and, grasping her friend's hands, eased down into the narrow alley. "If they get in the office and see the open window, they'll know I was here," Britt said, her voice trembling.

"I'll give you a boost up." Joyce linked her fingers together to form a makeshift step. Britt took her shoe off and stepped into her friend's hands, and held onto the sill while she was slowly lifted upward. Whatever Joyce was doing to stay in shape, Britt needed some of that.

She reached the edge of the window and pulled it down. She couldn't lock it from this side, but she wouldn't worry about that—she was going to call the police as soon as she and Joyce put some distance behind them and the intruders. Britt got her shoe back on. "We have to get out of here." She hurried toward the main street.

"Not that way." Joyce grabbed her arm. "They might have a lookout. Stay close to me."

They hurried down the walkway. At the back of the bakery, Joyce peered around the corner.

"Come on," Joyce whispered, taking the lead. Britt was

right behind her, trying not to imagine what those thugs were doing to her bakery.

They had to be careful in the rear alley. While several streetlights helped them to navigate the uneven surface, there were still pools of darkness to walk through. Add the broken, chipped concrete, and it made for a treacherous path. At one point, Britt cried out as she stumbled and fell to her knees on the hard surface.

"Shit, are you okay?" Joyce wrapped an arm beneath her shoulders and got her to her feet. "Give me your bag. We're almost there."

Britt leaned heavily on her friend, her knees burning with pain. Her feet dragged like lead weights, and she used all her energy to move one foot in front of the other. Her hands throbbed painfully from certain cuts. "Joyce, I don't know—" She gasped.

"Yes, you can. Just a few more steps. We're almost on Melville Avenue. We'll call the police then."

It felt like hours later before they finally sat on a sidewalk bench. Joyce had wanted to have at least a block between them and the burglars before stopping. "Hang on, I'll call them," Joyce told her.

"Wait." Britt was fighting to catch her breath. "Ask for Detective Mark Hawthorne if he's still at work. He'll bring the troops."

"The man who makes you go *boing*? Gotcha." Joyce hit a button on her cell, then started talking.

Beneath the streetlight, Britt assessed the damage. The skin on her knees was torn, and blood dripped down her legs. She tried to pick the debris out of her wounds, but it wasn't easy. Her palms were in better shape, just scraped a little, but they hurt like hell. She'd have to go to the hospital.

"They're on their way." Joyce sat beside her, then looked around. "Less than five minutes."

True to their word, three police cars sped toward them, their sirens off. Two vehicles raced by and turned the corner at full speed, while the third screeched to a stop in front of them. Mark literally jumped out of the car. "Britt!" he yelled, running toward her. "*Vakker*, are you all right?"

"Yeah," she said quietly, then hissed when the pain in her knees started to pulse up into her thighs. "I think so."

"Damn it. Hey, get me the first aid kit!" he yelled at the officer who was with him. "What the hell happened?" he demanded.

"Tried to run in heels down a dark alleyway." She smiled at Joyce. "But my friend got us out safely. That's what matters. Sorry," she apologized. "Mark, this is Joyce. She did the interior design for Konditori."

"Pleased to meet you." Mark shook hands. "And I'm glad the both of you are okay."

"That makes two of us," Joyce replied dryly.

Suddenly, a loud static noise came from a walkie-talkie on the officer's belt. "We're at the store," a voice called out. "No one's here. Repeat, the place is empty."

"Son of a bitch!" Britt's anger made her temporarily forget the pain. "They were just there!"

Mark looked at the officer waiting with him. "Tell them to make a sweep of the area, see if anyone's hanging around." He turned to Joyce. "Any idea what they look like?" he asked.

Joyce shook her head. "I managed a peek out the office door but didn't waste any time trying to see their faces. I locked it and got us out the window."

"Smart move." He broke open the kit and pulled out a tube and some gauze. "I'm taking you to the hospital," he mentioned. "But I want to at least get some of this on you and bandage it up." He popped the top off the tube. "I'm going to put this antibacterial ointment directly on your wounds. It's going to sting. You ready?"

Britt nodded, then bit her tongue as the cream burned her skin. "Holy crap, that hurts!"

"Sorry." His hands were comforting and gentle as he carefully taped gauze over both of her knees while the other officer held a powerful flashlight over them. He used the ointment on her hands as well, and after careful inspection, taped gauze over them as well.

Joyce insisted on riding in the front seat, giving Britt a coy wink as she slid into the police vehicle. Mark helped her inside, then sat beside her. "Check in with the others," he said, his voice demanding. "See if they found anyone."

As Britt listened to the officer's conversation over the radio, Mark shifted until he was up close and personal. "You're sure you're okay?" he asked quietly. Under the car's interior light, his worried expression made her heart thump hard in her chest.

She nodded. There was no way Joyce or the other officer could miss the intimate tête-à-tête going on behind them. "Yeah, I'm good. Just really mad that Ferguson sent more assholes to bust up my shop."

He raised a brow. "What makes you think Ferguson is responsible?"

"You mean besides the other time my bakery got vandalized?" She hadn't meant to sound sarcastic, but it was obvious to her the CEO was involved. But Mark also didn't know about her other unpleasant visit. "He was here this morning, trying to get into the store, but the customers kicked him out. I had the misfortune of running into him when I arrived."

She told him what had happened as the police car sped toward the hospital. "He's really pushing the boundaries," Mark growled. "Until we can prove Ferguson's responsible for the breaking and entering, the police can't do much."

"He's violated the peace bond Britt put on him. And Britt's customers are doing more than you guys," Joyce called out from the front seat. "If that Ferguson guy shows up again, something worse could happen. Shouldn't you all put a stop to it?"

"Trust me, I agree with you. But without hard evidence, I can't do anything."

"Mr. Ferguson is recorded on my security footage from this morning," Britt told him. "That should be enough?"

He nodded. "Yeah, that would do. But let's look after you first."

They arrived at the hospital within minutes, and Mark carried her into the emergency room. "I can walk," Britt complained, wiggling in his tight grasp. "You don't have to do this."

"What? Caring for you? What if I told you I want to?"

That shut her up. Mark had come charging in like a knight in shining armor and taken over. In the back of her mind, Britt quickly realized she didn't mind at all. She'd spent so much time doing everything herself that having someone else look after her made her feel comfortable, protected. And with Mark, she liked it—a lot.

An hour later, her knees and hands were thoroughly cleaned and bandaged. "I need to get to the bakery," she said as she slowly limped beside him and Joyce. The crutches felt alien in her hands. "I have to see what damage they've caused."

"I'll do that, Britt. It's a crime scene now. If you have

the security footage on Ferguson and the B and E, it would certainly help."

"I'll email that to you tonight. And I'll text my staff and tell them to stay home tomorrow." It was a serious blow, to both her business and her pride. If there was any shred of proof that Mr. Ferguson was responsible for the destruction of her store, she'd make sure he suffered for it.

"Britt, call me when you get in and settled, so I know you're all right." Joyce sent a meaningful glance in Mark's direction.

She almost laughed at her friend's expression. "I will. And thanks again for saving my butt."

"What are friends for? I'll call tomorrow to see how you're doing." She shook Mark's hand. "Thanks for getting us out of there so fast. Look after her." Joyce hurried to a nearby taxi parked at the curb.

It was just the two of them, and the tension built up in the air.

"Are you sure you're okay?" Mark asked her quietly.

His voice was a beautiful deep rumble, full of emotion. Britt couldn't help herself and turned to face him. "Yeah, thank you." She shook her head. "I can't believe I fell and skinned my knees, though. I know how to walk in my heels."

"You certainly do."

She knew her eyebrows went up at that. "What do you mean?"

"I've seen you walking in them." He leaned close and whispered in her ear. "And it's sexy as hell."

So, he'd been observing her from behind? Britt smiled. "I'm glad you noticed."

"I'd better get you home." He helped her to the police car and held out his arm as a brace while she hung on and lowered herself into the seat. This time, he rode in the front, talking to the officer and getting updates from the others still at the bakery. A jolt of disappointment hit her, but Britt understood the importance of Mark displaying leadership to his colleagues.

He did take her up to her apartment. "I'm sorry, I have to run."

"Mark, it's fine. You did so much more than I expected." She leaned the crutches against the wall and hobbled close to him, then grabbed his shirt collar to keep herself from falling flat on her face.

He prevented that easily enough, wrapping his arms tight around her. He rested his head against her shoulder. "I'm just relieved you're all right."

Britt relaxed against his warmth and inhaled the scent that was uniquely him. To be in his arms… It was so comforting, like sitting in a favorite chair with a wonderful book and a cup of hot tea. She didn't want it to end.

But Mark finally released her, slowly, and his hands rested on her hips. "I'll call you tomorrow and let you know what's going on," he said, his gaze intent as he stared at her. "And if you need anything—anything—call me."

"Sure." Britt caressed his face, feeling the slight stubble from a day's growth of beard. She leaned in and kissed him, her lips just touching his, hoping he sensed how grateful she was for his help.

He angled his head and molded his mouth to hers. Damn, he tasted good, and when his arms went around her again and tightened, she couldn't help herself. Her own arms encircled his neck as she melted into his embrace, her emotions weaving a spell around her that she didn't want to break. All this still felt like a dream.

Hmm… She reached down and pinched Mark's butt.

He backed away quickly, uttering a loud yelp of surprise. "What the heck?"

"Sorry. Well, not really. That was payback."

And confirmation that Mark was definitely real.

Britt didn't call Joyce right away because she needed to email her staff the bad news. As soon as she sat on her bed, she lay down and slept right through the night—she'd been that tired.

The next morning, she sent Mark a file of the security footage from the day before. Britt still didn't think Mr. Ferguson would be charged despite breaking the peace bond. As for the burglars, she saw they had worn masks—fat chance being able to identify them.

Finally, Britt called her friend after settling on her couch with a mug of tea.

"So, any news about the break and enter?" Joyce asked over the phone.

"Nothing yet, and I don't want to bother Mark, either. My staff wasn't happy about it when I emailed them last night."

"How are you feeling?"

"Much better. A little stiff in the legs, but I'll walk around to loosen them up."

"Awesome. So…that was the detective, huh?"

She laughed. "Yes."

"Very handsome. And attentive. I know it's none of my business, but what do you think?"

Britt knew what Joyce meant. "I want to be sure, so I'm taking things slow right now."

"Best decision to make. But I saw the way he looked at you. That detective gives me the impression he'll hang around if you give him half a chance."

Britt swallowed the sudden lump that lodged in her throat. "I thought that, too," she said quietly.

"I don't have to go into work until eleven, so if you want, I can come over and..." Joyce's voice trailed off into silence.

"Joyce? You there?" Nothing. "Joyce!"

"Yeah, sorry." A pause. "You'd better turn on the television."

"Why? What's going on?" She grabbed the remote and clicked the television to life. "What am I looking for?"

"Any national station. I'm sure all of them are covering the story."

"Joyce, you can be such a mysterious drama queen..." Britt's own voice stuttered to a stop as she watched the breaking news.

Edward Ferguson, Mighty Big Bakery's CEO, had been found dead in his backyard early that morning.

Chapter 9

*T*alk about being up shit creek without a paddle.

Mark stood on an expansive back porch made of fragrant cedar. Off to one side, furniture and a large BBQ dominated the space, while the other side was bare except for flowers that decorated the railing and roof beams. Directly in front of him, a set of stairs led down to a wide stone patio, and beyond, an in-ground swimming pool was surrounded by a spacious green lawn. More flowers and mature shrubbery bordered the high stone wall that he could just see between the slim gaps created by the tall hedge that offered additional privacy.

Edward Ferguson lay sprawled at the back entrance to the three-car garage, to the left of the porch. He was face down, his head resting against the flagstone. The back of his head showed blunt-force trauma. He'd been hit so hard that a trail of blood had oozed several feet toward the fence.

Mark couldn't say that he was surprised by what happened, but it still bothered him. The bakery CEO seemed to have made a lot of enemies, judging by what Mark had discovered during this investigation. He had hinted at something similar to Captain Fraust during his last update. Somehow, the media had gotten their greedy hands on the story before he arrived, and it had already been broadcast on the morning news.

Myrna was prowling the backyard looking for clues. Several officers were posted around the house to provide security.

He glanced over his shoulder. Ferguson's wife and the housekeeper were in the kitchen, and he could hear their grief echoing through the room.

This wouldn't be easy.

"Keep an eye out for nosy neighbors," he told the two officers that stood beside him. "The coroner should be here within the hour."

Mark had kept his arrival as low-key as possible. Along with his car, which he and Myrna had driven in, two police vehicles were parked on the curb about a half block away. It was possible that someone had spotted them going up to Mr. Ferguson's door, but he hoped that everyone would keep to themselves and not grow curious. As for the coroner van, Mark had asked that they drive straight in, and an officer would direct them to the back. He suspected the media would make another appearance and made sure the other four officers who arrived with him were advised to keep the gates closed and the area clear. It was the best he could do.

He approached Myrna, who was kneeling to one side of Ferguson's body. "Need any help?" he asked.

"I did a sweep of the backyard, but I'm pretty sure the attack happened around here." She lowered herself until she was almost at the level of the body. "I can see strangulation marks around his neck," she stated. "I can't tell if there are any fingerprints, but I'll check in with the coroner after he's finished examining the body."

Mark nodded. Mr. Ferguson was dressed in his usual

business suit, which could mean he'd been heading to work. One of the garage doors was open, revealing a dark green luxury sports car. Mark walked inside in a wide arc so as not to disturb anything, even though he had plastic booties on. Turning on his flashlight, he ran it over the car's gleaming surface. He saw some smudging, but nothing that looked like a print—still, he'd let Myrna know.

The other side had something interesting—a long scratch down the driver's side of the car. "I've got something here," he called out.

She looked up. "I saw that. Got pictures, too, but I can't find the keys."

Although he trusted his forensic investigator to be thorough, Mark knew he'd feel better if he reviewed the lay of the land so that it was clear in his mind. He did a slow walk around the perimeter of the backyard, stopping each time he thought he noticed something, then moving on. It wasn't until he almost reached Myrna on the other side that he noticed something between a pair of thick hedges. "Did you see the footprints?" he called out.

"What?" She jumped to her feet and hurried over. "Where?"

"They're actually behind that row of hydrangea." He only spotted them because he was particularly searching for footprints. "You have your kit with you?"

"Yep. Can't believe I missed that," she grumbled as she pulled out her tools, took photographs of the evidence in question and made a cast of the impressions. "How did you find them?"

"I was looking for them. I'm hoping they belong to Toussaint."

"With the different-sized feet? It would make our lives easier."

The cast had already dried, and Myrna carefully lifted it out. "Great," she said, placing it on top of a plastic bag. "And not so great."

"What happened? Did it crack?" Mark looked over her shoulder and swore in disbelief. "Those footprints don't belong to Toussaint. They're actually smaller..." He paused, his brain firing off a possible answer that made him want to throw something. "Son of a bitch!"

Myrna watched him, a quizzical expression on her face. "Care to clue me in?"

"Jenny."

She frowned. "The construction worker?"

He nodded. "She's been playing me from the beginning. Not anymore."

"Mrs. Ferguson."

The woman looked up from her pile of tissues. She was in her early fifties, with black hair and green eyes. She wore a silk pajama set beneath a thick, plush white robe.

"Do you think you can talk to me now?"

She nodded and blew her nose.

Mark sat down opposite her. She'd been crying—her eyes were red and swollen, and her mouth compressed into a thin line. He could tell she was trying hard to remain composed, but her trembling body spoke otherwise. "Can you tell me what happened?"

"Normally, I'd wake up before Edward around seven. But when the alarm rang, I didn't see him." She shrugged. "I thought he'd gotten up early to go to a meeting."

"Does he tell you his daily schedule?"

She nodded. "Or he'd have it written on a calendar in the kitchen." She frowned.

"Is that the calendar over there?" Mark pointed. She

looked over her shoulder. "I don't see anything written down for today."

"And he didn't mention anything to me or Gloria, our housekeeper. But he had his business suit on. The good one."

"What does that mean?"

"Oh." She waved a hand. "Edward wears the really good suits when he's taking over a business."

Mrs. Ferguson said that nonchalantly, but Mark could feel his temper starting to rise. He fought to control it. "He dresses up to take over someone else's company?"

"A weird habit, I know. It shouldn't matter what he wears. The ending is still the same."

Shit, she sounded just like her husband. "What did you do next?"

"I came downstairs. My housekeeper had already come in."

"Does she have a house key?"

"Yes, and she knows the security code."

He nodded to encourage her to continue.

"Gloria—my housekeeper—and I talked for a bit in the front hall while she put away her things, then we both headed for the kitchen. I turned on the television while she tidied up and made coffee."

"And Mr. Ferguson wasn't in the house."

"No."

His next question was critical. "How did you find him?"

Her hands scrunched the tissues, but that was the only movement he saw. "Gloria opened the kitchen blinds, then stepped out to look at the plants. She noticed the garage door was open, which was odd, and when she stepped down to the patio, she saw Edward lying on the ground." She shuddered. "Her screams were so loud they echoed into the kitchen. When I got outside and saw him…" She paused and dabbed at her eyes. "I pushed Gloria back into the house and told her to call 911. I tried to turn him over, but he was too heavy, and I—I couldn't…"

"It's okay. You did your best." Finding a critically ill or deceased loved one so unexpectedly was a fear Mark had lived with for too long. When Dad's abuse became more violent, he was scared that he'd find Mom on the ground every time he came home from school. Their divorce gave him peace of mind until that day when he'd found her at the bottom of the stairs with the broken leg and hip. "You can't blame yourself." But he knew she did—just like how he felt guilty every time he left Mom alone with that devil. "Did you notice anything odd about him? Or anything on the property?"

"No. I thought someone was trying to steal one of the cars since the garage door was open."

Made sense. "I'm going to talk to the housekeeper. If you need anything, let one of the officers know."

He found Gloria sitting on an ornate wooden bench in the hallway. Compared to Mrs. Ferguson, the housekeeper's grief seemed more palpable. He sat down beside her. "How are you holding up?" he asked gently.

In answer, her face twisted in pain, and a loud sob broke free. He gave her a few minutes to calm down before trying again. "What happened, Gloria?"

She blew her nose, then shook her head. "I don't know. Nothing seemed out of place."

"Tell me what you remember from this morning."

The housekeeper gave the same information as Mrs. Ferguson, except… "His briefcase was missing."

"Missing?" Mark pictured the area around the garage in his mind. She was right. "Did you look for it?"

"No. I was…" She waved a hand helplessly.

"Maybe it's in his car. We'll look for it. What does it look like?"

She blew her nose. "It's a metal briefcase. I think it's the fancy one that can withstand a lot of heat."

Damn, if it's the case Mark thought it was, it could do a lot of damage to a person's skull. On a hunch, he asked, "Any idea what might be in it?"

Something—a flicker of recognition—skimmed across her face. "Not at all."

He sensed a lie. "Are you sure?" he pressed. "It's possible whoever murdered Mr. Ferguson was after whatever was inside this briefcase."

"I don't know what you're talking about." The housekeeper rose. "If you'll excuse me, I'd like to tend to Mrs. Ferguson."

Mark got up as well. "Of course." As he watched her hurry toward the kitchen, he knew there was more going on than what the housekeeper was admitting to. He would need to question the ladies further anyway, and then he would sniff out the secrets Gloria was obviously hiding.

Back outside, the coroner had arrived. Mark mentioned the missing item to Myrna. "His briefcase?" She frowned. "I haven't seen anything lying around. Maybe it's in his car?"

"We'll need to see if the keys are in his pockets."

"Let me ask. I didn't want to turn the body over until they got here to supervise." She approached the coroner and after a moment, he and his assistant had deftly flipped Mr. Ferguson onto his back.

Mark grimaced. The CEO's face had turned an ugly shade of purple and blue and was horribly swollen. Which made him wonder… "How long do you think his body has been lying there?" he called out.

Both Myrna and the coroner looked up. "Judging by the body's state of rigor mortis," the coroner answered in a dull voice, "the male victim has been dead since very early this morning. Say, between one and five in the morning."

So, Mr. Ferguson would have gotten out of bed while his wife was sound asleep. The housekeeper wasn't a live-in, so he could sneak out and be back before Mrs. Ferguson knew. But what would prompt the CEO to go out at that time of night?

Mrs. Ferguson did say the suit her husband had on was only worn when he was about to conquer a business. What kind of business deal was so critical that he had to sneak out to complete it?

"Mark, here are his car keys." Myrna held them up with a gloved hand.

They opened the car door, but after searching the interior, didn't find the briefcase. Mark had just climbed out when he noticed a soft glint of something sitting on the dash. When he took a closer look, the blood chilled in his veins. It couldn't be…

Britt's bracelet.

"Myrna, can you collect that?" He pointed at the piece of unique jewelry, watching his hand shake. Confused, angry, hurt—he wasn't sure how he felt at the moment.

"It's pretty." She held it up and looked at it closely. "Huh. They're small Nordic runes, and it looks like they spell out a name. B, R, I…"

"Britt."

She squinted. "Yeah, you're right." Myrna looked at him with wide eyes. "And you know this because…?"

He chewed the inside of his cheek. "It belongs to someone I know."

* * *

Captain Fraust had her back turned to him as Mark updated her on his findings at the murder scene. "So you don't believe this Toussaint had anything to do with Mr. Ferguson's death." It was a statement, not a question.

"No, ma'am. The evidence at Ferguson's house doesn't support it."

"And this Jenny, the construction worker? Why did you bring her up?"

Mark tried not to bite his tongue in frustration. "Toussaint said she thought of the arson idea. I don't know if she's capable of murder, but the footprints we found were about her size, and the brand name stamped on the soles of the boots belongs to a well-known clothing company that specializes in construction gear."

She turned around, her brows raised. "You understand that you can't make that kind of assumption without additional hard evidence?"

"I know, ma'am, but it's one plausible answer. I'm going to bring her in on the premise that I have further questions. If Jenny gives any hint that she's responsible for the arson attempt or knows the identity of the murderer, I'll have her charged. Maybe sitting in a jail cell will get her to talk. I know it smells of desperation, but I think she'll provide the information I need."

Fraust cocked a brow. "This is highly unusual of you, Hawthorne."

"Yes, ma'am. But the two viable suspects I found are not talking." Mark paused, feeling unsure of himself. "I'm also afraid that if I let Jenny go after questioning her, she'll dig a hole so deep we'll never find her again."

The captain nodded. "Normally, I wouldn't endorse this kind of thing, and would recite all the reasons why it's wrong. But after listening to your theories, I'm going to let you go ahead. However," she warned. "Remember her rights."

"Yes, ma'am." Mark's gamble had paid off.

"What have you found out at the house?"

Mark felt like he was back in school, with the teacher singling him out to answer a particularly difficult question. "I believe the housekeeper knows more than she's letting on. I found out from Myrna—Investigator Walsh—that the coroner told her the method of death. The murderer strangled Ferguson first, then hit him in the back of the head several times. Approximate time of death was between the hours of one and five in the morning. We also can't find his briefcase."

She nodded. "The only way the murderer could even get close to Mr. Ferguson at that time..." Fraust let her voice trail off.

But Mark got the hint, and as he came to the most logical conclusion, he smacked the table, causing the papers to flutter. "Son of a bitch, the suspect arranged it. Must have called Ferguson and told him a lie so big that it made the CEO put on his best suit in the middle of the night to meet him."

"Agreed. We'll need to find out what business deal Mr. Ferguson had arranged that would make him go off schedule." She paused. "Anything else?"

Britt's jewelry burned a hole in his mind. For God's sake, why the hell was it even in the CEO's car? "We haven't located the suspects who pulled that B and E on the Konditori bakery," he said instead. "We received security footage, but the burglars were wearing masks. However, I believe they were hired by Ferguson to destroy it."

"It seems a moot point now. However, we can't let destruction like this go unpunished. Someone in Mr. Ferguson's small circle must know something. I want them flushed out."

"Yes, ma'am." Mark gathered his things and headed to his office. He should have thought of the suspect getting in touch with Mr. Ferguson. Honestly, he couldn't stop thinking of Britt's possible involvement. Her bracelet was a damning piece of evidence in the middle of this murder investigation.

Timmins was in the office when Mark walked in. "Hawthorne, you haven't told me what happened at the murder scene. How did the search go?"

He gave the older detective a rundown of his findings.

"Shit. An attack like that would need strong upper body strength."

And it was probable Jenny possessed that kind of power to cause lethal damage.

Mark couldn't stall any longer. Both women had a lot of explaining to do.

Mark just hoped Britt had nothing to do with the bakery CEO's death.

Chapter 10

Britt climbed out of the taxi, her injuries almost healed, though her knees were still stiff from not moving much yesterday. She walked the few steps to Konditori, her gaze scanning over the building. Her insurance company had been here since this morning, evaluating the property damage alongside the police, and they had called an hour ago to tell her they would help pay for the renovations. It wasn't as bad as it looked. Someone would be at the store tomorrow morning to give her the key to the padlock, and she could start cleaning up the pieces of her bakery.

The large picture window was completely smashed. Wooden boards had replaced it to keep the curious and the thieves at bay. The front door was sealed tight with a large padlock and covered in a crisscross of bright yellow tape with the words DO NOT CROSS.

The letters *MBB* were sprayed across the storefront multiple times with black paint, leaving only small glimpses of pink through the mess.

She hated to think what she might find inside and began to doubt her insurance company's reassurances.

She walked down the alley, remembering Mr. Ferguson's skulking form half-hidden in the shadows. His anger at her refusal to sell couldn't match the fury Britt felt deep in her stomach. That pretentious dickhead hadn't cared who he hurt—he had steamrolled over small businesses, families and innocent people to get what he wanted.

He wouldn't be doing that anymore.

Britt peeked around the corner before walking toward the rear exit—she didn't know if those jerks might still be around. There was no damage to the steel door or the windows here. It seemed that the police had arrived before the thugs could do anything else.

She completed her circuit, her emotions jumbled, but her anxiety was sitting pretty high. She would need to find additional money to make repairs. Even though her insurance said they would cover most of it, until she got inside, Britt didn't know what would need to be replaced. If the expensive kitchen equipment had been damaged…

She sighed. There wasn't much she could do.

Her cell phone pinged with a text. It was an officer from York Regional Police 4 District, advising her that their investigation was complete, and she could go into her store. Thank God for that.

Britt looked across the street to where Mr. Ferguson's latest bakery sat partially finished. Despite the CEO's death, she was sure his company would continue building, while she would scramble to make ends meet.

Her one consolation was the loyalty of her staff and customers. She had received emails that offered their condolences, reassuring her that they would return as soon as she got back on her feet. She had almost cried while reading those comforting notes, never realizing how she made an impact on strangers. Joyce had already insisted on helping her get Konditori back on its feet, and Britt could pay her back when she had the funds.

Britt sighed. Mark. She hadn't talked to him at all

today—he had to be busy working on Mr. Ferguson's murder investigation. She pulled out her phone, focused on calling to find out how he was.

He picked up on the second ring. "Britt, how are you?"

His voice sounded different—a bit strained, tired. "I'm fine. I managed to see my doctor this morning. My knees look good, just a bit raw and achy. How are you?"

"Okay. It's been a long day."

He didn't sound all right, though. In fact, he sounded like a stranger, not the warm, attentive man she had gotten to know over the last few days. "You don't sound okay," she said gently, hoping everything was fine. Did his mom take a turn for the worse? "Maybe you'd like to come over later? I could make us dinner." Those words came out of nowhere, but to her, they felt right. Mark had begun to bring out a portion of herself she hadn't seen in a long time.

"I'd like that, but..." He stopped.

This wasn't like him. In fact, this whole conversation felt wrong. "Mark, what is it? Talk to me."

"Are you home?"

She was sitting on a sidewalk bench near the store. Her knees weren't bothering her—Mark's strange attitude was. "I got restless. I'm at my bakery, assessing the damage from the outside."

"You are?" A moment passed. "You're not trying to sneak in to take a look, I hope."

"I did get the go-ahead from both the insurance company and the police. An officer just texted me with clearance, so I can finally get organized." Knowing this offered some closure. It meant she could move forward with plans, get her staff back up and running. They'd been anxious, worried they'd have to find other jobs to make ends meet.

She'd also toyed with the idea of renting out another, smaller space nearby to get Konditori back on its feet while repairs were being made to the original bakery. In fact, she might have to look into that, depending on what she found inside...

"I...need to ask you something, Britt."

All her senses were instantly on alert. Mark's voice sounded professional, almost distant. "Yes?"

"I have to ask you to come to the station."

Was that all? Did he want to give her a tour of his workplace, maybe introduce her to his colleagues? She rubbed her chin—Mark was taking their relationship a little too fast. "Mark, it's sweet that you want me to meet your fellow officers, but I don't think that's—"

"No, that's not what I meant." His voice had gotten quieter, and now he sighed. "I need you to come down to the station in order to ask you some questions about Mr. Ferguson."

Did she hear him correctly? "Mark, what are you talking about?"

She heard a car door slam. "Stay at the bakery. I'm coming now to pick you up."

"Mark, you'd better explain what you mean by that." She rubbed her stomach at the ache that flared inside. Something was horribly wrong, and Mark wasn't giving her any answers. "What's going on?"

"I'm almost there. Give me a minute."

The urge to run off and hide had Britt on her feet, even though she knew she hadn't done anything wrong. She could easily meld into the early-evening rush-hour crowd and lose him until she got home. Or maybe stay with Joyce until she could figure out why he needed to question her about a dead man who had threatened her hard-won business.

Too late. Mark pulled up in front of her. As he got out of the car, Britt moved to keep the bench between them. "What's this about?" she demanded, drawing stares from nearby pedestrians.

He stopped, his expression a mix of confusion and hurt, touched with a bit of anger. "Maybe you'd like to explain this to me."

He held up a plastic bag, and as she peered at its contents, her breath caught in her throat. It was her runic bracelet, a birthday present from her parents. "Where did you get that?" she asked, automatically rubbing her left wrist.

"Would you like to get in the car and I can tell you privately, or shall I announce it for everyone around us to hear?"

His anger sent a shock wave of trepidation coursing through every part of her limbs. She should have escaped when she had the chance.

Refusing to cause a scene, Britt came around the bench and quickly got into the car, slamming the door hard so that he got the hint she was frustrated with him. He climbed in, tossed the bracelet on the dashboard and gunned the motor. He waited until she got her seat belt on before driving off and merging with the busy evening traffic. Britt saw how tense his body was, from the white knuckles gripping the steering wheel to his clenched jaw. "Mark, talk to me. What's bothering you?" she asked.

His gaze hovered over her bracelet before he returned his attention to driving.

"My bracelet?" How did Mark find it anyway? She reached for the baggie.

"Please don't touch it, Britt."

Her hand froze in midair from the shock of his words. "Why not?" she whispered. "What does my bracelet have to do with Mr. Ferguson?"

She watched his expression, unsure what he was feeling. "Your bracelet was found in Mr. Ferguson's car."

There was a moment of pure disbelief before she burst out laughing. "Jeez, Mark, for a moment there you terrified me."

He frowned. "I found it in his car, Britt. I'll show you the evidence when we get to the precinct."

No hint of a smile or anything to portray that he was joking. And she suddenly realized he wasn't.

When they reached the precinct, Britt immediately got out of the car and walked to the front doors. Inside, she had to take Mark's lead and followed him onto an elevator at the back of the building. He hit a button two floors down, then turned to her. "Look, I'm sorry to do this to you…"

"No, you're not." During the ride to the police station, she had time to think about Mark's allegation. "You're doing your job—I get that. What I don't understand is how my bracelet ended up in Mr. Ferguson's car—it's not like I gave it to him. And in case you haven't noticed, you're making me nervous."

The elevator pinged. When the doors opened, they were in a brightly lit hallway, and stretching to either side were square rooms. She saw an officer open one of the doors and step inside. "Where are we?" she asked.

"These are the interrogation rooms." He guided her to the same room the officer stepped into. When she hesitated on the threshold, Mark said, "Step inside, please."

He indicated a chair. Jeez, he wasn't even going to be

a gentleman and pull it out for her as he usually did. With a huff of disdain, she dropped her butt onto the hard seat.

Mark looked at her for a moment, and she stared back, hoping he'd see her furious expression. He bit his lip, then turned back to the door. An older officer had come in and sat in a chair behind her.

Britt glanced over her shoulder, then looked back at Mark, willing herself to relax. She told herself again that she'd done nothing wrong, and this was just a simple Q&A Mark had to do as part of his job. She would wait until he started talking.

"Britt Gronlund, I'm Detective Mark Hawthorne with York Regional Police 4 District." His introduction was cold, unfeeling. "Behind you is Detective Walter Timmins, who is my backup."

She nodded and wrapped her arms around herself.

"I'm investigating the murder of Mr. Edward Ferguson, CEO of Mighty Big Bakery." He had a small pile of documents in front of him, and he shuffled through them until he pulled out a picture. When he slid it over, Britt looked at it and frowned. That was her bracelet, sitting on someone's car dashboard.

He then reached for the piece of jewelry, still in its plastic bag. "Does this item belong to you?"

She almost snapped at him. Of course Mark knew the bracelet belonged to her. However, she held back, and after taking a deep breath, she settled her emotions into a kind of calm detachment. "Yes."

He placed it to one side and wrote something down. "I need to advise you that during my investigation at Mr. Ferguson's home, your bracelet was found in his car."

She blinked, still not believing what she'd heard, but

remained silent, waiting to see if Mark would add any further context.

He looked at her, his brow raised. "Can you explain how your bracelet got into Mr. Ferguson's car?"

Mark wasn't seriously thinking... "I have no idea how my jewelry got into that jerk's car."

A small smile ghosted his lips before it disappeared.

"Are you saying you weren't in Mr. Ferguson's car at all, Ms. Gronlund?"

She turned to stare at the older man who had asked the question. "Not at all."

He gave her a look that had *I don't believe you* written all over it.

"Can you explain how it might have gotten into Mr. Ferguson's car?" Mark asked.

Britt kept her gaze on Mark. "On Monday morning, I arrived at my bakery, but it was filled with customers— I couldn't get in. I went around to the alley to go through the back door, and Mr. Ferguson was there." The angry look on the man's face still gave her the creeps. "He told me the customers threw him out when he tried to come in, and for some reason, he hung around until I showed up.

"He went through his usual spiel of trying to buy my business. I told him it wasn't for sale. He got angry and grabbed me."

A dark shadow crossed Mark's face. She hadn't told him that part because she knew she could handle the CEO. Besides, there were plenty of pedestrians at the time—a few high-pitched screams would have brought someone running to help her.

"What happened next?"

"I kicked him in the balls and left him there. I had a business to run."

This time, a full smile lit up Mark's features. "Very proactive of you."

Britt kept her professional stance up, despite the warm feeling seeping through her at Mark's grin. "I can only think that Mr. Ferguson pulled my bracelet off when he grabbed me. It makes the most sense."

"Do you think he planned on returning it to you?"

"I hope so. Although I wouldn't put it past him if he tried to bribe me with it. The bracelet has a lot of sentimental value."

"Can you tell us the rest of your day?"

Britt explained in detail up until Joyce had called the police. "The rest you already know, Detective Hawthorne. Thank you for assisting my friend and I last night." Being detached and polite worked both ways.

"We'll need to hang on to your bracelet for the duration of our investigation." Mark slid the picture back into his stack of documentation and placed her bracelet on top, then stood. "Thank you for your cooperation. We may need to call you in for further questioning."

She nodded, biting the inside of her cheek, only because she wondered what Mark was playing at.

He glanced over her shoulder. "I'd like to escort Ms. Gronlund outside, Timmins. Would you mind taking my notes to the office?"

Glancing at the other detective, who had grabbed Mark's stuff and was heading out, she finally surmised he probably had to be professional when questioning her. Still, he could have warned her.

When they got outside, he took her elbow and led her to his car, remaining quiet until they got in. He breathed a loud sigh of relief. "*Vakker*, I can't tell you how sorry I am for putting you through that."

Britt twisted her hands in her lap. "You're a real jerk, Mark Hawthorne."

He jumped in his seat, his eyes wide with surprise. "Britt, I mean it…"

"I get it. You were playing detective—can't get too close to the witness. Gotta keep it professional."

"Britt, that's not fair." He got the car started.

"No? Was treating me like a criminal fair?"

"I didn't do…" He stopped, his breath loud and harsh within the car interior. "We found your bracelet in Ferguson's car. How else did you expect me to treat it? And you?"

"You could have simply asked, instead of dragging me through a police interrogation and embarrassing me."

"No, Britt, I couldn't. Your jewelry was found at a murder scene. Think on that. If I treated you any differently to the other witnesses I'd brought in, Detective Timmins and the officers outside that room would have questioned my motives. I can't play favorites in this job." He drove out into the busy traffic. "If I'd given you any hint about what was going on, you wouldn't have been surprised or upset. That would have tipped off Timmins for sure. He's an old pro at this. He would have given me a world of grief."

Britt listened as Mark explained his actions. She understood the intent, but it didn't quite make her feel better. "Did you really think I killed Mr. Ferguson?"

"No!" His voice was firm, assuring. "You would beat him up, but not kill him. I knew you would think Ferguson wasn't worth going to jail for."

"You got that right." At least they were on the same page with that. She started to calm down, thinking through everything Mark had said, and coming to the conclusion that, yes, he was doing his job. She knew she was innocent and had nothing to worry about.

"Why didn't you tell me about Ferguson grabbing you in the alley?" he asked.

"Because I knew how you would react. Besides, he didn't expect me to know self-defense maneuvers."

"Wish I'd seen that." His smile was his own, filled with humor. "And how are your knees?" He rested a hand on one. "I noticed you didn't have trouble walking."

Britt had worried she'd flinch, considering what he'd put her through. But her anger had almost melted away, and the warmth from his touch felt good. "A lot better, thank you." She thought of something. "Have you found out anything about those jackasses that broke into my store?"

"No. Thanks for the security footage, by the way. Unfortunately, it doesn't help since the thugs were disguised. Myrna, my forensics investigator, did find some fingerprints, but she didn't get any hits."

"I wonder what they'll do now that Mr. Ferguson's dead."

"Best scenario? Stop trashing people's businesses."

For some unexplained reason, she didn't think that would happen. "Do you honestly believe that?"

Another sigh, but he sounded tired. "I don't know. Until I can collect more information, I can't do anything."

Britt noticed he was taking her back to her place. "Listen, do you want to grab a bite to eat? I'm starving."

"Great idea. So am I."

They found a well-known sandwich shop. It was empty, which Britt was glad for. In her gut, she felt that they needed to discuss some things—not just what had happened with Mr. Ferguson, but themselves, especially her.

She hadn't opened up about her past because she hadn't been ready to revisit the pain and humiliation. Britt knew that if she didn't get it out of her system, it would continue to fester like an untreated wound, and she couldn't move forward with her life. It seemed the best time to talk to Mark about it.

They sat at a table near the front window. Despite the noise of traffic, it was unusually quiet in the shop. "Other than interrogating me," she started, "how was your day?"

Mark frowned and twisted his mouth. "Frustrating."

"Can you talk about any of it? Or is it confidential? Maybe I can help."

His look was curious. "You have enough going on with the bakery. I don't want to add to that. Besides, it's part of my job to be pissed off when the clues don't come together."

"But you must discuss investigations with your colleagues, right? Just think of me as one of them." She imitated Detective Timmins's stance, crossing her arms and attempting to make a stern face. "Come on, Hawthorne," she growled in a deep voice. "Let's hear what you've got."

His widening grin burst into a loud snort of laughter. "That was almost perfect. Thank you for that."

Their meals arrived, and Britt stared at the smoked salmon and cream cheese specialty she had ordered—the sandwich was big, and it came with a salad and a chocolate-almond croissant for dessert. She could take half of it home to have for lunch tomorrow. She glanced at Mark's, inhaling the scent of steak, cheese and onions. "Oh my God, that smells delicious."

"I'll give you a piece." He used a fork and knife to deftly cut off a corner and put it on her plate. *"Bon appétit."*

They spent a few minutes enjoying their meal. By the time Britt came up for air, she'd finished her sandwich and half of her salad. "Crap," she mumbled, wiping her mouth with a napkin. "I didn't realize how hungry I was."

"I've heard that stress can increase one's appetite," he murmured.

"Oh, great." She eyed the croissant with disdain. Ah, what the hell. She took a bite of the sweet, flaky pastry. "Mmm, this is good. Maybe I should ask Jacques to come up with a similar recipe, Norwegian style."

Mark stirred his cappuccino. "How did you two meet each other?"

His question meant talking about her past, and it was as good a time as any. "I had Konditori all planned out. I found the perfect spot for it and hired Joyce to do the interior design. I started looking for staff, and Jacques answered me the day I posted the job, and I was honestly shocked at his experience. He worked at a Michelin-starred restaurant while living in France, before moving to Toronto."

His brows rose. "Why would he move from France?"

"He said better opportunities. He never talked about it, but my hunch is, he wants to open his own business someday."

Mark nodded. "You might lose a great baker."

"I know. But I'm not going to begrudge his ambitions. He'll do what's right for him." She paused, thinking of herself.

"How did you become a bakery owner, Britt? I don't think I asked you that."

Britt took a breath as her muscles wove into tense, painful knots. Here it was, her opportunity to clear out her past.

He grabbed her hand and squeezed it. "Hey, if you don't want to talk about it…"

"I have to." The words rushed out of her. "Because if I don't, I'll feel like I'm keeping secrets from you, which isn't fair to either of us."

His eyes widened, sparkling beneath the lights in the shop.

"When I was in university, I majored in economics with the goal of becoming a parliamentary secretary. My ultimate dream was to become a member of Parliament. I wanted to try to change some of the things going on in the country."

"A lofty goal."

"But achievable. I graduated with honors and was determined to find a position within a year." Back then, her ambitions were laser-focused. "I had my pick of various jobs everywhere from Fisheries and Oceans Canada to the federal security agency.

"I finally decided on working with the minister of international trade. That was five years ago. I loved it. I learned so much from Minister Frank Strathmore. But I started hearing strange rumors about the minister's mannerisms, especially toward women."

Mark's face darkened with anger, which she expected. "I found out the world of politics was still a man's domain, and of course, they like to do things their way. Minister Strathmore was no different. When he became a little too friendly, I accused him of assault. He just laughed in my face."

The awful, familiar feelings of humiliation and embarrassment reared their ugly heads, demanding that she acknowledge them. This time, Britt did, but chose not to let those emotions make her feel bad or ashamed. She fought them back, showing that she was in control, that she was sick and tired of feeling guilty for standing up for herself. "I learned quickly that every man and woman had to fend for themselves. After I reported the minister's actions, nothing was done. In fact, I was told to suck it up and be proud that Minister Strathmore was giving me 'personal support,' as Human Resources called it."

"Jesus," Mark breathed. He squeezed her hand. "One of my female colleagues at work talked about that. She had to prove her worth almost twice as much as the men. I used to think of her as aggressive, but when she told us what she went through…" He stopped. "Did you quit the job?"

"I thought about it—many times. But I wanted to put Minister Strathmore's head on a platter first.

"I collected evidence over a six-month period. Photos, calls, video, text messages, to support myself and the other women he'd been harassing. I called HR out on their crap, and next thing I knew, I was being summoned to defend my actions." She sighed. "Those were the worst five weeks of my life." Britt could see the scenes in her mind—the courtroom, the minister and his friends giving her the evil eye, the women who said they would support her instead looking at their hands while she testified.

"I had enough physical evidence to get him fired from his position, that's all. And the next time I heard his name, Minister Strathmore had somehow become an independent member in the Parliament of Canada." She chewed the inside of her cheek. "Just goes to show you what a person can do with enough clout."

Mark hadn't moved or said anything while she talked, but his being there helped to keep the demons away. "My ability to trust took a serious nosedive," she concluded. "I became introverted, closed myself off after the trial.

Thank God I was too stubborn to stay that way. So I pivoted and worked on my next dream job, which was owning my own bakery. Now here I am, making Nordic pastries and comparison shopping for supplies."

"But you love it. That's what counts."

"Sure do. And getting the all-clear from the insurance company to rebuild has taken a weight off my shoulders. My staff and I can start cleaning up tomorrow."

"That's great news, Britt." He finished his cappuccino. "Maybe I'll swing by to visit."

His cell phone pinged with a text. As he read it, she noticed his worried look. "Is everything all right?" she asked.

"Yeah." He raised his hand to get the waiter's attention. "It's my mom. She wants me to come to the hospital to visit."

"I hope she's doing well." They headed for the car.

Mark grasped her hand in his as they strolled down the sidewalk, and Britt could easily get used to this. To not just have a man in her life, but someone who was also in her corner, to provide support and encouragement. She'd love to return the favor. However, his line of work may not offer a chance to provide ideas or theories that could help in his cases. She could certainly ask. "You know, if you need a sounding board during your investigations, you can let me know. I won't tell anyone anything."

He raised her hand to his lips. "Thank you, *vakker*. That means a lot."

At the door to her condo, she wrapped her arms around his neck. "I'm not sure if I should even kiss you," she whispered, a breath away from his lips. "You thought I was a criminal."

He cocked a brow. "No. I thought you were up to something with that bastard."

"Ewww." She pulled at his ear. "I can't believe you'd think that!"

"No, I didn't mean it that way. I meant..." He paused. "I was worried you had changed your mind about selling your bakery."

"If there's one thing you should remember, Mr. Detective, it's that I'm stubborn. I get what I want, but not by hurting others."

"Yup, that's my Nordic princess." His kiss was thorough, lingering. She didn't want it to end.

Another ping from his phone. He groaned as he slowly released her. "I'd better get going before Mom sends a hunting party out looking for me."

She grinned. "Your mom sounds like fun."

"Great sense of humor. I think you two would like each other." With a wink and another kiss, he disappeared down the hallway.

Britt had plans of her own to organize. She emailed her staff with the good news and told them to wait for her by the rear door so she could let them in. Then she called Joyce, who screamed with delight, and said she'd be there by ten o'clock tomorrow morning to assess what needed to be done.

All in all, a good day despite the vandalism hanging over her head. Britt was taking baby steps to move her life forward again, this time with Mark at her side.

Chapter 11

Mark had never felt so scared. He could handle mouthy dickheads with ease as he dragged their sorry asses to jail. No problem at all.

Britt, on the other hand… The drive to the precinct yesterday to interrogate her about her bracelet had him on pins and needles. He had no way to know how questioning her would turn out.

What hurt the most was remaining silent. She may not have noticed, but he heard the increasing note of panic in her voice as she demanded answers. Answers he couldn't provide until he got back to the police station.

Perhaps there was a better way of handling the situation. Mark certainly hadn't been thinking straight when he'd found her bracelet in Ferguson's car. Considering all that had happened these past few days, how else could he have viewed that damning piece of evidence?

But his instinct had told him how wrong he was. And while instinct was a great indicator, it was hard to ignore what was in front of him——Britt's bracelet, in the car of Mighty Big Bakery's dead CEO.

He remembered how the weight lifted off his shoulders when the interrogation was over, although he still had an angry Nordic princess chewing him out when they'd left the precinct.

Mark sat at his desk, piecing clues together, thinking on theories. The footprints at Mr. Ferguson's home and the fingerprints found on the CEO's body didn't match Henry Toussaint's as he'd first hoped, but he had to be sure. As for Jenny the construction worker, she had already lied to him once, so he'd have to be ready for any tricks, including that flirtatious manner of hers. If she was the killer, she would do everything possible not to get caught.

Mark still believed he hadn't received all the truth from Toussaint, either. He thought the young man might know who the protest leader was, but scratched that idea. Since it was Jenny who drove them to the secret protest site, Mark might have a better chance of obtaining that information from her.

Now all he had to do was locate her.

As for the housekeeper and Mrs. Ferguson… Well, something definitely smelled fishy about Gloria. He would explore that after talking to the construction worker.

His first visit, to the partially built Mighty Big Bakery, yielded no results. Mr. Smith, the supervisor who was still in charge of the site, told him that Jenny got called to another location. "Damn pain in my ass," he grumbled. "How the hell am I supposed to stay on schedule when I'm down a person?"

"Is that normal?" Mark asked.

"No, it's not. And with Mr. Ferguson dead, I don't know who's taking over this project."

The comment made Mark's ears perk up. That was right—there should be a succession plan in case the owner couldn't direct anymore. He'd have to pay a visit to the MBB head office. "No one called?"

"Not a peep. I'll keep going until I hear otherwise."

"Thanks." He headed back to his car, thinking. Toussaint no doubt told Jenny about his interrogation with the police, and she was probably in hiding. He had her address, which wasn't far from the sushi restaurant he and Britt had gone to.

It was an old duplex apartment, which blended in with the large houses on the street. He hit the buzzer twice, and when he didn't get an answer, tried calling her cell phone. It went immediately to voice mail. He left a message, asking her to call as soon as possible, then slowly went down the stairs. He turned around to look up at the apartment. The blinds were shut—maybe she was sleeping in and had turned her phone off.

Maybe...

Mark hopped back up the stairs and hit the buzzer for the other apartment. This time, a dog barked furiously but went quiet when a stern voice hushed it. The inner door opened to reveal a man in his late fifties. "Yes? You looking for someone?"

"Good morning." He showed his badge. "I wanted to ask if you'd seen Jenny recently."

"The young lady lives here, but I haven't seen her today. Might be with that boyfriend of hers."

Mark felt like a first-class douchebag—why hadn't he put two and two together? "Don't tell me, Henry?"

He nodded. "Yeah, that's the name. He came by around five or so yesterday. Jenny gets home about that time. Did the horizontal mambo for a couple of hours before taking off. I don't know where."

Mark had his suspicions. "Thank you, sir."

This time, no more Mr. Nice Guy.

With a search warrant in his pocket, Mark pounded on

Henry Toussaint's door. "Open up! York Regional Police 4 District! I know Henry Toussaint's in there!"

Timmins, his hand resting on a stun gun, glanced at him. "What do you think?"

"I think they'll make a run for it. Ergo, officers watching the back door and windows."

The front door finally opened, and the woman he had met a few days ago appeared. "Oh, it's you again," she sneered. "Henry's not here."

"Now you're just bullshitting me." Mark's temper was getting hot, but he wasn't going to lose it.

The woman's surprised expression morphed into anger. "How dare you talk—"

"Where's Henry?" He pushed against the door, but the woman held her ground. "Look, Mrs. Toussaint, I have a warrant to search the premises and bring Henry and his girlfriend in for further questioning."

"Henry doesn't have a girlfriend," she spat.

"Well, you're in for a surprise." The woman was strong, but not enough to keep him and Timmins out. "Unless you want my partner and me to thoroughly search through the house for your son," he warned, "I suggest you tell him to make an appearance." He took the warrant out and waved it in the air. "Your call."

The expression on her face would have scared off a grizzly bear. "Henry!" she yelled out. Damn, she had a powerful voice. "Henry! Get down here, now!"

No answer. She frowned, then turned back to him. "He's not home. What's this about anyway?"

Mark knew his brow went up at that. "He hasn't told you?" He glanced at Timmins, and at his nod, barged in and raced for the stairs.

"Hey! What are you doing?"

Mark got on his walkie-talkie. "This is Hawthorne. Anyone show up?"

"No, sir, the windows are clear."

"One of you get to the garage. Bust the back door down if you have to."

With the older detective at his back, they checked each of the rooms on the second floor but couldn't locate Henry or Jenny. "Team, tell me you have them!" he said into the walkie-talkie, running back downstairs.

"Negative, sir. No one's out here."

He and Timmins checked the rooms on the main floor before Mark stepped up to Mrs. Toussaint. "If you don't tell me where Henry is, I'll arrest you for obstruction," he growled out.

"As if. Henry hasn't done anything wrong."

"Your precious Henry beat up the CEO of Mighty Big Bakery," Timmins chimed in. "And now the man is dead."

Whoa, Mark hadn't expected Timmins to be so blunt. But maybe it would get Mrs. Toussaint to open her eyes and help them find her son and Jenny.

She grasped the front of her blouse, and Mark watched with growing concern as her face turned a ghastly shade of white. Her mouth trembled, but nothing came out.

"Mrs. Toussaint," he said gently. "We need to find your son and take him and Jenny in for questioning. We believe they haven't given us their full story."

Every minute the woman remained quiet was another minute that Henry and Jenny could escape. Mark snapped his fingers in front of her face, concerned that she'd gone into shock. "Mrs. Toussaint."

She blinked slowly, as if waking up from a dream. But then her face screwed up in anger, and he was now worried she wouldn't help at all.

"Follow me." She headed toward the back of the house.

He eyed Timmins, who shrugged, then hurried to catch up to Mrs. Toussaint. "This is Hawthorne," he called over the walkie-talkie. "Maintain position. Repeat, maintain your posts."

They followed her into a spacious kitchen. Wide, ceiling-high windows let in plenty of sunshine and offered an amazing view of the expansive backyard, with a swimming pool and BBQ patio. She veered to the left, then stopped in front of a door. "This leads to the family room in the basement," she told them. "He's down there."

"Is there any way for him to escape?" Mark asked, eyeing the entrance.

"There's a door that leads into the backyard. I guess if he was desperate, he could crawl through a window that faces the front."

"Would you mind calling him out, Mrs. Toussaint? I'd like to conduct this with the least resistance."

"If you need to knock him about the head, I don't mind."

Mark kept his surprise in check as she indicated to him and Timmins to stand around the corner. Mrs. Toussaint opened the door. "Henry! Get your ass up here!"

Timmins gripped his stun gun in one hand. Mark had debated taking out his weapon but held back—this could get ugly really quick. "Stand by," he whispered into the walkie-talkie. He noticed two officers at the back door and hurried over to quietly slide it open. "Stand with Timmins," he told them. "Suspect's coming upstairs from the basement."

They remained silent, the tension building.

"I'm busy, Mom," Henry called out.

"I don't give a shit. Just get up here. I need you for something."

Mark indicated to the officers to have their stun guns ready.

"I told you I didn't want to be bothered," Henry told her. His voice held a hint of frustration. "Come back later."

Wow. He saw Timmins rolling his eyes.

When Mrs. Toussaint glanced at him, Mark nodded in encouragement.

"Henry, we've talked about you living here, remember? If you don't pay rent, you have to help around the house, that was the deal. Now I need your help with something."

Mark backed away and radioed the rest of his team. "Keep an eye on the garage and backyard for the female," he whispered.

Footsteps stomped on the stairs. Mark motioned for Mrs. Toussaint to stand away from the door so that she didn't get caught in the middle. "You had to bring that up, huh? I've been trying to find a job for weeks."

"Which tells me how much effort you're putting into it," she retorted. She appeared at the corner and continued backing up, keeping her gaze on Henry.

As soon as he stepped into view, the two officers jumped him. Henry yelled out in surprise and fought, kicking out and landing a bare foot against an officer's knee. The officer's grip loosened, and Henry pushed him away, before turning his attention to the second cop, throwing punches into his face.

"Henry!" Mark shouted. He managed to grab and pin the man's arm and held on tight as the first officer cuffed him. Damn, this guy was strong. Mark kept his legs together as Henry tried to kick him in the balls. "Hey, calm down!"

The young man continued to struggle. "Get your hands off me!" he yelled.

It wasn't working. "Henry, if you don't calm down you'll leave me no choice but to stun you," Mark warned. "Do you want me to Tase you in front of your mother?"

That seemed to do the trick. Henry finally stopped thrashing around. "Get him in the car," Mark demanded. "And read him his rights."

He moved to stand at the top of the basement stairs. "Jenny, I know you're down there," he called out. "We've got Henry. Don't make this hard on yourself."

A couple of minutes went by. "Detective Hawthorne, I didn't see anyone come in with Henry," Mrs. Toussaint said.

"He might have sneaked her in through that back door you told me about." He tried again. "I'd better not have to come down there to flush you out. The house is surrounded. You won't get away."

He tensed at the sound of a door. He was about to call in to the officers when a person appeared at the bottom of the stairs—Jenny, with her hands raised in the air.

"Get up here," he shouted, and backed away as she reached the top. "Turn around."

She complied, and an officer slipped the cuffs on her. "Aren't you going to read me my rights?" she asked, sounding cheerful, for the love of God.

"The officer taking you to the police car will do that." Mark was still trembling with adrenaline after the scuffle with Henry.

As the construction worker was led out of the house, he turned to Henry's mother. "Mrs. Toussaint, I need to find Henry's sneakers."

"He keeps them lined up downstairs in the closet. Second door to your left."

When Mark opened the door, he couldn't believe his

eyes. There were eight pairs of limited-edition sneakers, as clean as if they'd come out of the box. He pulled on a pair of gloves and grabbed the ones he needed, noticing smudges of dirt in the creases and more stuck to the sole. He dropped them into an evidence bag and headed back upstairs.

He and Timmins were the last to leave. "I'm sorry, Mrs. Toussaint," he apologized. "I had a feeling Henry might have resisted the arrest, but I didn't think he'd actually start fighting. Are you okay?"

She nodded, her expression sad. "Henry never said anything to me about this. It happened last Friday night?"

"Yes." How did she know?

"When he came home, there was mud on his clothes and his best sneakers." She frowned. "He treated those shoes like they were his pets. When I asked him what happened, he ignored me and hid in the family room for most of the weekend until you showed up on Sunday." She shook her head. "I don't know what's gotten into him recently."

"That's what we hope to find out. An officer will call with an update." Mark didn't know what else to say, so he nodded at her before leaving.

At the precinct, Mark was all business. "Henry and Jenny in their own interrogation rooms," Mark demanded. "I'm getting tired of the bullshit."

A cheer went up when Britt turned the corner. All her staff were waiting at the rear entrance. "Good morning, everyone."

"Chérie." Jacques grasped her shoulders and kissed both cheeks. "We heard what happened to you. Are you all right?"

"Yes, thanks to Joyce." His worried expression tugged at her heart, and she placed her hand on his cheek. "I'm fine, Jacques. See? The scrapes have almost healed. My calf muscles are just a little stiff, that's all." She moved past the rest of her employees. Betty gave her an impromptu hug, while Kevin, Jasmine and Oliver gave her big smiles. Thomas, Jacques's assistant, tilted his head in a nod—he'd always been shy and quiet around her.

Inside, everyone was silent as Britt led them to the kitchen. As she went through the swing doors and took one look at the room, she breathed a sigh of relief.

Everything looked to be in place. The door leading to the front had been knocked off its hinges, but as they moved farther in, she didn't see anything out of place or smashed on the floor. "Thank God they didn't get in here before the police arrived," she breathed. "Jacques, can you and Thomas go through everything carefully and let me know?"

"*Bien sûr*, of course." He took off his jacket and talked to Thomas about how to inspect the kitchen properly.

The front of the bakery was where the most damage had occurred. The display cases were destroyed, tables and chairs thrown about, the bookshelf shattered on the floor. Some of the books had been torn to shreds and the pages strewed everywhere. The office door had been kicked but had held in place.

It had been a scary night—Britt was so glad Joyce had been with her. Without her friend's support, she might have done something unthinkable, like confront the jerks.

"I honestly thought it was going to be a lot worse than this." Britt turned in a slow circle, glass crunching under her feet. "Let's get this cleaned up," she announced. She got her key in the lock to the office, but it took a bit of persuading before it opened. The room was undamaged.

She put her things in the desk drawer and got her laptop fired up to check for messages. Other than Joyce reconfirming her arrival, her new emails were from customers, reiterating their support and good wishes.

Britt wanted to cry she was so happy. This was what she loved the most—the loyalty and trust from almost perfect strangers. Many of them stated they would wait until Konditori reopened, as they didn't want to spend their money anywhere else.

She called everyone into the office and read some of the emails out loud. "Wow, now that is something," Betty exclaimed. "I hadn't realized how much our customers loved the bakery."

"And the staff," Kevin added. "Without Britt, I think we'd just be another bakery like MBB."

"Bite your tongue, young man." Jacques trembled. "That will never happen."

"How does the kitchen look, Jacques?" Britt asked, worried there might have been damage that she'd missed.

He kissed his fingers. "The criminals didn't have a chance to destroy the appliances, but everything is covered in dust and debris. The power had been turned off, no doubt during the police investigation, but *merde*, they could have turned it back on when they were finished. Everything is spoiled in the fridge and freezer."

"The food is the least of my worries, and honestly, I'm glad everything was turned off. Heaven help me if a fire started in here."

They got to work. Britt grabbed a large broom and carefully swept the glass to one corner while Kevin and Oliver stacked the broken pieces of the bookshelf in another. Betty managed to stack the chairs, then Britt, Oliver and Kevin helped manhandle the tables until they, too, were stacked on top of each other.

Suddenly, there was a loud knock on the door, followed by the sound of the padlock being opened. The makeshift door swung open. "Good morning. Is Britt Gronlund here?"

That must be the insurance representative. "Hi, that's me."

The representative stepped inside carefully and put the padlock down on the windowsill. "I've brought an extra key for you," she said, holding it out and giving it to her. "I'm glad my insurance company was able to help you."

"So am I. The payment will cover everything that needs to be replaced."

"Oh, speaking of which." The woman opened her purse and pulled out an envelope. "You'll receive two insurance payments instead of four. You're a longtime client, and we want to help get you back on your feet as soon as possible."

Frowning, Britt opened the envelope and stared at the number on the check. "Seriously?"

"Uh-huh." The rep smiled. "I'll have to come down one day and try your pastries. I've heard a lot of wonderful things about the bakery. The second payment should arrive in the next two to three weeks."

Britt squeezed her eyes shut to keep the tears from flowing. "Thank you," she whispered.

"You're most welcome. Good luck." And just like that, the rep was gone.

Joyce arrived about a half hour later. "Shit, the storefront looks like it got hit with a bomb."

"I'm glad those assholes didn't come up with that kind of plan." Britt swept her arm around the room. "The kitchen is in one piece—I have the Fates to thank for that.

Jacques and Thomas are cleaning it up now. As for here, well, you see what we're dealing with."

Joyce swept her gaze around the room. "Honestly, sweetie, this won't take long to fix up. I'm glad it's just this space. Replacing the kitchen would have cost you a pretty penny."

"Tell me about it." She showed her friend the check.

"Whoa, I didn't expect that much."

"The insurance company decided on giving us two payments within a month. I can get the bakery up and running in that time."

"Then we should go shopping. I brought my laptop, so I'll show you the latest styles I have in furniture, paint and fabrics." She looked at the walls. "Do you still want to keep the same colors?"

"Absolutely."

For the next hour, they worked out a plan for rejuvenating Konditori. "I can have a team here in a couple of hours. We can start work on replacing the display cabinets and front door, getting glass for the windows and giving the walls a power wash and a fresh coat of paint. I still have all the original measurements, so it won't take as long."

Britt nodded—she couldn't speak she was so grateful.

As Joyce made her calls, Britt went into the kitchen to see if Jacques needed any help, but her staff was already there, working under Jacques's exacting demands. The back door was open to let in fresh air, and it looked like everything was under control.

Britt returned to her office and dropped into her chair, mentally exhausted. Things were moving faster than she had anticipated, all because of a few people who cared about her bakery. She wanted to call Mark to give him the good news. Instead, she grabbed her phone and sent a text, knowing he was probably busy with Mr. Ferguson's murder.

Goose bumps prickled her arms as she thought about her reaction when Mark had held up her bracelet. Joyce had noticed it was missing, and for the life of her, Britt hadn't remembered whether she'd put it on or not that morning. The simple move of clasping it over her wrist was so automatic, she never thought about it. She had never noticed it coming off during her scuffle with Mr. Ferguson, and because she'd been so upset with everything else, she'd completely forgotten about it until she got home and started looking for it. She was only glad that it had been found—it was a custom-made birthday gift from her parents.

There was another loud knock at the front door to the bakery. She rose and watched as Kevin scooted across the space and opened it. "Yes?"

"Hi there." It was a woman in her fifties, and Britt recognized her as a regular customer. "Will Konditori be open again soon?"

"We're hoping in the next few days."

"Thank God!" She waved at someone. "I told you I saw someone coming in here!"

Britt watched in fascination as several people crowded around on the sidewalk. "What's everyone doing here?" she asked.

"We hadn't heard anything about the bakery since that horrible break-in," the woman told her. "And we were worried that Mighty Big Bakery had bought you out."

"No, that won't happen." It felt good to say that with certainty, although horrifying that Mr. Ferguson had to pay with his life. She shook her head at the senseless loss, wondering if he had a wife, family, friends.

"We're glad you're reopening," a young man called out from the crowd. "I miss my morning Danish!"

Everyone laughed, and at a gentle push from Kevin, Britt stepped into the animated crowd, shaking hands and answering questions. As she turned, Mighty Big Bakery's construction site across the street came into view, but now, she wasn't worried. With an incredible staff, wonderful friends and customers who stood by her, Britt believed she had turned a page in her life. The next chapter held new opportunities, including a man who had literally swept her off her feet, and the future looked glorious.

Chapter 12

Mark had left Henry and Jenny to cool their heels in separate interrogation rooms while he sat at his desk, thinking. Some of the clues he had found didn't make sense, such as the footprints behind the shrubbery in Ferguson's backyard, the missing briefcase, and the fingerprints that didn't match Henry's or Jenny's. Evidence that had been found at the construction site only led to Henry, despite the young man's admission that Jenny was the mastermind behind the attempted arson.

"You okay, Hawthorne?"

He glanced at Timmins, who was leaning back in his chair, hands clasped behind his head. He knew the older detective would help him if asked, but sometimes, Mark's stubborn streak got in the way. "Just trying to sort everything out."

"Let's hear it. I know you're eager to get at those two downstairs. But go over what you've got out loud, and I'll chime in if necessary."

Mark rehashed everything from the beginning, starting with Mr. Ferguson's assault. "The one thing that has remained consistent is everyone's hatred for the CEO, and someone took it far enough to kill him." He looked at his list of potential suspects. "That could be anyone listed here."

"Who stands to gain the most from this?"

"Mrs. Ferguson, definitely. But she already has everything. Of course, if his business personality was the same as his personality at home..." Mark knew he had to get back out there to question her and the housekeeper.

"What else?"

Mark was glad to have Timmins hit him with questions—his mind had been a jumbled mess even with his notes all neatly organized in front of him. Too many pieces were not fitting together. "The housekeeper gave off a weird vibe when I asked about Ferguson's missing briefcase."

"Then you can ask the ladies to come in later today. As for those two downstairs, do you think they're capable of murdering Ferguson?"

He shook his head, more out of confusion. "I think Henry's capable of it, but not on his own."

"Agreed. What about Jenny?"

"I don't get the impression she'd get her hands dirty, but I can totally see her guiding someone into doing it. I'm not sensing that here, though."

Mark closed his eyes, a trick he used to block out everything around him and concentrate on one item. Henry and Jenny were his immediate focus. They had lied to him to cover their butts, that was now obvious. But why? To avoid being tied to Ferguson's murder or just avoid jail time for the beating and attempted arson? He believed it was the latter, but he would ask Myrna to reconfirm that the fingerprints found at the murder scene did not match either Henry's or Jenny's.

Mrs. Ferguson and the housekeeper were on a different level, being much closer to Mr. Ferguson. He couldn't see them attempting anything as risky as murder, but he couldn't rule them out either. Mark was sensitive to the fact that Mrs. Ferguson would be mourning, and bringing her to the precinct for questioning felt wrong. A visit to her home would be more sympathetic, and might yield better results.

It only took a couple of minutes. When Mark opened his eyes, he felt clearheaded and had a direction. He hit a button on his office phone. "Myrna, sorry to bother you. Can I ask you to compare our two suspects' fingerprints again with those at the murder scene? Yes, I do trust your results, just humor me, okay? Thanks. I'll be in the interrogation room with Jenny."

Five minutes later, he sat across from the construction worker with Timmins in the background. "You've already questioned me," she snapped, leaning forward in the metal chair. "What the hell am I here for now?"

So, she was going to be like that? "I'm waiting on confirmation that fingerprints found at Mr. Ferguson's murder scene match yours. My forensics investigator got clear fingerprints from your purse."

Yep, that got a terrified look out of her—even Timmins's jaw dropped. "No, no! There's no way. I didn't kill him!"

"Guess we'll wait and see." He kept his tone and stance professional, refusing to let her try to bait him into anger. "In the meantime, let's talk. You never mentioned that you and Henry were an item."

"More like friends with benefits." Her smile was crafty. "I was more into you."

He let that comment slide. "You're already implicated, in case Henry hasn't told you. Why did you want to burn down the new Mighty Big Bakery location?"

"I'm sure you already know the answer to that," she spat out.

"Humor me."

She sat back in her chair. "You saw what Mr. Ferguson was like. Arrogant, a bully, a first-class asshole. If he didn't get his way, he'd threaten, cheat and steal to get what he wanted. I never understood why the *police*—" she emphasized the word "—never arrested him."

"I don't know about the other precincts. As for us, we never had enough evidence to charge him."

"That's horseshit!"

Mark let that one go, too. "You haven't answered my question."

Jenny blew out a loud breath. "My friend and her family got caught in Ferguson's vicious net. That jerk sent his goons after them and trashed their store. When that didn't work, they upped their game and burned the business to the ground." She shook her head, upset. "I'm sure you've had your share of grieving witnesses. It was tough on them."

Mark knew exactly where Jenny was coming from, since he had seen what had happened to Britt and her bakery. His fury almost had him hunting down Ferguson, except that Britt's needs came first. "I know how you feel."

Her eyes blazed with rekindled anger. "Then you know why I did what I had to do. Get revenge. An eye for an eye. Why should my friend and others suffer the loss of their life's work, while that dickhead acted like he'd done nothing wrong?"

"If Mr. Ferguson had any involvement with the arson and B and Es, we haven't found any proof. We need facts, Jenny, not theories."

She shrugged. "Guess it doesn't matter anymore. He's dead, and good riddance."

Jenny explained how she got Henry inside the construction site by leaving the gate unlocked. She had provided him with a hard hat and a high-visibility safety jacket so that he'd blend in. The idea was to hide the container until everyone had left, then go back, spread the gasoline around and light it up. Unfortunately, when Henry saw Mr. Ferguson, he let his anger do the talking and gave the CEO a thorough beating.

Mark digested her story as he wrote his notes. "What about the leader of these anti-Ferguson protests? Do you know who he is?"

"Like I'd tell you if I knew. You'd just arrest him and do nothing about Mighty Big Bakery's abusive takeovers."

"Not true, but I know you don't believe me. For now, I'm charging you with attempted arson."

Jenny jumped up so fast, the chair went flying. "Are you shitting me?"

"Nope. If you want a lawyer, I'll arrange your phone call. You already know your rights." He stood up. "Be glad it's not worse. If I find out you had anything to do with Mr. Ferguson's murder, I'll make sure you won't get out."

The young woman screamed a litany of curses as he and Timmins left the room. Two officers who had been guarding the room hurried past them to subdue Jenny and take her to a cell.

"Well, Hawthorne," Timmins said as they approached the second interrogation room where Henry waited, "I didn't quite expect that."

"It got results. That's all I wanted."

Their talk with Henry didn't reveal anything new, other than his relationship with Jenny. He did blame her for coming up with the arson idea. "I had nothing to do with that," he complained.

"You went with her to a secret protest to find out how to piss off Mr. Ferguson," Mark told him. He jabbed a finger onto the table. "You impersonated a construction worker and carried a gasoline container onto the site. You deliberately hid it with the intent of burning down the building. But when you saw the CEO, you also beat him up because hey, why not." Mark wasn't going to waste any more time with the young man and rose. "You'll be charged with attempted arson, as well as assault."

"How can you charge me with assault if the man's dead?" Henry yelled.

"You'd better hope I don't find out you had anything to do with Mr. Ferguson's murder as well."

This time, Mark was ready. When Henry jumped out of his chair and dived over the table, Mark grabbed the young man's arm and put a knee into his back.

Henry yowled in pain. "Get off me!"

Timmins had let the officers inside, and they deftly took over, cuffing Henry and getting him on his feet.

"If you had hit me, that would have been a charge of assault on an officer," Mark told him in a flat voice. "Get him out of here."

So far, Mark had solved a part of the puzzle, but he worried it wouldn't be enough for Captain Fraust. He knew the captain wanted a murder suspect captured as soon as possible—hell, so did he. He dropped into his office chair and blew out a frustrated breath.

A knock on the door, followed by Myrna. "Hey," she called out. "Sorry to say, but my analysis still stands."

He scrubbed his face with a hand. "Thanks, Myrna. It was a long shot, but I was hoping. I hadn't meant to insult your work. Sorry."

She shrugged. "There's nothing wrong with double-checking."

"What's next?" Timmins asked.

"I need your help," Mark said. "Can you go to Ferguson's head office and find out who's next in line to take over?"

"Any reason why?"

Mark knew Timmins was testing his methods, and he appreciated it—it kept him on his toes. "It's possible the head office didn't like Ferguson's methods. Maybe someone there wanted to get rid of him?"

"Now you're thinking." Timmins rose and grabbed his satchel. "No time like the present. It'll throw them off if I suddenly show up."

Mark smiled. "Good idea."

His phone pinged. As he read the message from Britt, his body tingled with pleasure. She mentioned that she and her staff were inside the bakery, cleaning up. She then sent a second text.

If you'd like something sweet, why don't you come over and see me.

How could he ignore that invitation?

"What's got you smiling so big?" Myrna asked.

Startled, he put the phone back in his pocket. "Good news from a friend."

"You mean the blonde beauty you rescued a couple of nights ago?" Timmins chimed in with a wink.

"'Blonde beauty'?" Myrna demanded. "Who? What did I miss?"

"She's just someone I met last week." It was bound to happen that one of the guys would pick up on something, but Mark had hoped for a bit more time.

"I'll bet she is. Don't get distracted, Casanova. Let's get this case solved first."

Mark couldn't help himself, though. As soon as he got in his car, he drove straight to the bakery. He wanted to spend a few minutes with Britt to show his support before driving over to talk with Mrs. Ferguson and the housekeeper.

He parked a block away and walked quickly to the front door, which stood open. Inside, it was a chaotic blend of work, chatter and laughter as debris was cleaned up and furniture moved to one side. A couple of employees swept the floor.

One of the staff noticed him. "Hey, aren't you the guy that asked for Britt last weekend?"

Mark stuck out his hand. "Good eye. Yeah, I am. Is she around?"

"I'll grab her. Just be careful. There's glass everywhere."

Mark took a good look around. Anything that wasn't nailed down had been smashed to bits. Even the display case had a couple of holes where someone had kicked it in. The bookshelf was nothing but a pile of firewood, and even the books hadn't survived—they were torn to shreds. The letters *MBB* were scrawled on the bright storefront. It almost felt like…this was personal. The vandals had managed a lot of damage in the short amount of time they had.

"Hi, Mr. Detective."

He turned and smiled as Britt approached, wearing jeans and a white T-shirt. "Hey. I see you've already started getting things back together."

She nodded and looked around. "I was lucky. No one got into the kitchen. That's where the most expensive stuff is."

"Did your insurance pull through?"

"With flying colors."

She told him how much she received, and he whistled. "That's a healthy chunk of change."

"It'll go toward buying foodstuffs and replacing the glass in the windows and a new door." She looked around. "And giving the inside a good makeover. We'll hang on to the salvageable furniture until we receive the second payment."

"Sounds like you have everything in order, *vakker*." He stepped closer but watched her carefully. He was suspicious that Britt might not want to get too intimate in front of her staff, but he couldn't resist teasing. "How about a kiss before I go?"

Her eyes widened in surprise, but their color darkened as well, a deep emerald. He kept his gaze on her, waiting, because she hadn't said yes—or no.

"Damn you." She licked her bottom lip, and he drew in a sharp breath. How could he back away now? "I want to, I think a little too much, but..." She glanced over her shoulder and gasped.

He looked up and saw her friend Joyce standing at the doorway to the office, arms crossed and the biggest smirk on her face. "Hello, Detective Hawthorne." She came over. "I want to thank you again for saving us."

"Don't mention it." He glanced at Britt until her cheeks flushed a light pink—damn, she looked adorable. "And I have to commend you on your fast thinking. To go out the office window and through a dark alley? That's gutsy."

"No, that's desperation. I wasn't going to let us sit in the office and wait for those shitheads to break down the door." She paused, and Mark noticed her clenched hands. "Any news?"

"I haven't heard anything, but I'm not on the case. I'll follow up and let you know what I find out."

"Thanks, Mark." Britt raised her hand as if to clasp his, then let it fall.

Joyce made a noise. "Could you two go outside and, you know, make out? I'll hold the fort."

Britt led the way—she hadn't hesitated at all. Feeling encouraged, he was right behind her until they stood at the entrance to the alley. "Joyce knows you well."

She laughed, a joyous sound that rang free and happy. Britt seemed more at ease. "I didn't have to tell her anything. She figured it out before you came to rescue us."

He reached for her hand, and her fingers wrapped around his. "I might have been too protective that night," he whispered, kissing her hand.

Her smile was bright. "I loved every moment, even when you cleaned my knees."

He laughed. "Jeez, I felt like a guy trying to hold on to a condom, my hands were shaking so bad." He sobered. "Are you still mad at me about bringing you to the police station for questioning?"

"No. But you really caught me by surprise."

"That makes two of us. I'm sorry, Britt, but I had to be an officer. I didn't know what to expect."

"I get it. I'm just ticked that Mr. Ferguson had my bracelet, instead of me finding it in the alley or at home. Will I be able to get it back?"

"As soon as everything's over. Speaking of which, I have to go." Although he didn't want to—he wanted to drag Britt away and spend the night with her. "Duty calls."

"I understand." She came up to him and wrapped her arms around his neck. "Maybe you and I can do something fun when duty finally stops calling?"

"Oh, you mean I can have that sweet treat you teased me about?"

Her surprise lasted only for a moment. "Haven't you heard? Norwegian treats are the best."

He crushed his mouth to hers, trusting that his intent was clear. *I'm here for you,* vakker, *no matter what.*

Chapter 13

Mark hit the buzzer beside the main gate. At the same time, he got a text from Timmins.

Call me as soon as you're finished.

Intriguing.

"Yes. Who is it?" The housekeeper's voice echoed through the intercom.

"Detective Hawthorne." He held up his badge to the security camera. "I'd like to talk to Mrs. Ferguson."

"Well… Mrs. Ferguson has had a long day preparing for her husband's funeral."

"I'm really sorry, but I wouldn't be here unless it was urgent."

It remained silent for so long that he thought the housekeeper had hung up on him. Then she said, "Please enter through the small gate to your right."

He heard a faint buzz, then walked through and shut it behind him. It locked with a loud click.

The housekeeper was waiting at the door when he reached the front steps. "Detective, good evening." They shook hands. "Please come in. Mrs. Ferguson is waiting for you in the library."

"Thank you. Oh, and I'd like you to join us as well."

That got a reaction. "Oh? Well, I'm trying to get last-minute preparations ready for tomorrow."

"I won't be long, I promise." He indicated to her to lead the way.

She clearly wasn't happy about it but walked down the hallway and stopped at a door to their left. She knocked twice, then entered. "Detective Hawthorne is here, Mrs. Ferguson."

The widow sat in a plush high-backed chair. She wore a long-sleeved black dress and black slippers. Her hair was tied back into a fashionable bun. She seemed calm, poised, but on a closer look, Mark noticed the swollen red eyes and a faint trail of black smudge down one cheek. She'd recently been crying.

"Mrs. Ferguson, I'm so sorry for your loss."

She remained silent, but waved her hand at the seat opposite her.

"Actually, I've asked your housekeeper—Gloria, is that right?—to join us. Please." He pointed at the other chair.

Both women glanced at each other before the housekeeper sat down, back ramrod straight, clenched hands on her knees. She seemed nervous.

Mark had thought about what to say to the ladies, and finally decided he'd be blunt in explaining what he was looking for. "I want to thank you for seeing me unannounced. We've cataloged everything from the scene—" he wanted to be careful in his choice of words for Mrs. Ferguson's sake "—and we're working on some leads. There are two things I'm curious about." He paused, watching their faces.

The housekeeper refused to look at him. Mrs. Ferguson glanced up. "What is it?"

He slowly paced across the width of the room. "Mrs.

Ferguson, do you know who will inherit Mighty Big Bakery with your husband's death?"

"I do. I would have thought that was obvious."

He glanced at her. "I thought perhaps you had children, a son maybe, to run Mr. Ferguson's business."

"Oh." She paused. "No. We don't have children."

"So, as heiress, you'll take over?"

"I'll have Edward's leadership team continue with the day-to-day business operations, of course. I don't plan on changing any of that."

"And they'll hire a new CEO as well?"

"Yes. I'll need a crash course on understanding how to elect, but I'll be a part of that process with them as well."

"Thank you." Mark stopped in between the women. "My second concern is your husband's missing briefcase. Would you know if he had any important documents in it?"

Mrs. Ferguson shook her head. "Leaving the house at that time of night in one of his best suits, I think it might have been contracts to sign over whatever business he planned to buy. That's the only thing I can think of."

"I see. And what about you, Gloria?"

When she faced him, her frightened expression raised a red flag. "What about me?"

"Well, you were the one who told us about the missing briefcase. Did you look for it? It's possible he didn't take one with him. Maybe it's in his study or in the bedroom?"

"I—I don't know. I didn't search for it."

"You didn't?" Mark stared at her, another red flag waving in his face. "Why not?"

She shrugged. "It didn't seem important at the time."

"So here I am, under the impression that the briefcase was stolen, when in fact, it might be here? It's a crucial piece of evidence, Gloria. Now I'll have to bring the police in to look for it."

"Gloria, you told me Edward's briefcase wasn't in the house." Mrs. Ferguson's hands were wrapped around the armrests. She was shaking and angry.

Gloria glanced from her employer to him, then back again. "I'm sorry, Mrs. Ferguson. I didn't want you to worry about it."

"You're not in a position to tell me what to worry and not worry about! Because of you, Detective Hawthorne will be bringing in officers to search my home! While I'm grieving! And everyone in the neighborhood will see this! All because of your incompetence!" She started crying, loud sobs that filled the room and tore at Mark's feelings. Mrs. Ferguson no doubt had kept her emotions in check, but Gloria's admission broke it. "How can I trust you now?"

"Mrs. Ferguson, I'm sure Gloria meant well." He knelt by her chair and rested his hand on hers. "I'm probably breaking protocol, but how about I wait until after the funeral? And I'll only bring in about five officers. I'm sure with Gloria's help, we can get this done in about a couple of hours. And we'll be discreet—no police cars, no flashing lights, I promise."

She held a handful of tissues to her face as she struggled to calm down. It took a few minutes before she looked up. "Thank you, Detective. That means a lot to me."

"Of course." He glanced at Gloria. Her expression betrayed the guilt she felt, which was part of the plan. He wanted her to confess what she knew, but the housekeeper wouldn't do it in front of Mrs. Ferguson. He got to his feet. "I'll leave you alone, and I apologize again for coming at this difficult time. I'll call in a couple of days, and we can arrange a suitable time."

Gloria led him out, leaving Mrs. Ferguson crying quietly in the library. As they reached the front door, the housekeeper turned on him. "How dare you pull a heartless stunt like that!" she seethed through a clenched jaw.

Mark feigned surprise. "Heartless? You're the one who lied."

"So that Mrs. Ferguson wouldn't worry!" She placed her hand to her forehead. "And now she doesn't trust me."

"She will if you find the briefcase. Where is it?"

Her innocent wide-eyed expression had him on alert. "I don't know."

"I think you do. You either hid it in the house, or maybe…" The thought struck him. "Maybe you know the murderer and let him take it."

"That's preposterous!" she yelled, then quickly lowered her voice. "I had nothing to do with Mr. Ferguson's murder."

"Then prove it to me. Where's the briefcase and what's in it? You know something, Gloria. Talk to me, or I'll have to bring you in for questioning and still search the house."

"No, not that, please. It'll tear Mrs. Ferguson apart."

Mark waited and watched while the housekeeper seemed to struggle with a decision. "I know where the briefcase is," she said quietly.

"Why didn't you say something when my team and I were here?"

She tangled her hands together and looked over her shoulder where they left Mrs. Ferguson. "Because of what's inside it."

Silence. He waited while she fidgeted, but she didn't say anything more. "Gloria…" he warned.

"I can't get the briefcase now. If Mrs. Ferguson saw..." She stopped and took a deep breath. "Can you come back tomorrow morning, around eleven? I'll give you the brief-case then."

He frowned. "Isn't the funeral tomorrow?"

"Yes, but I'll get out of it. Mrs. Ferguson will have her two sisters and brother with her." Gloria pinched her lips together. "Besides, she doesn't trust me right now."

That had been a productive, though emotional, evening. His unexpected visit with Mrs. Ferguson filled him with mixed feelings of guilt and accomplishment. The only other good thing that came out of this was that he wouldn't need to bombard the woman's home with officers turning everything upside down to find that briefcase.

In the car, he checked his text messages. Timmins had obviously found something out, but that could wait a few minutes. He texted Britt, letting her know he was fin-ished for the night and asking if her offer still stood. As he waited for her to reply, he called his partner. "Hey, it's me. Before you start, just letting you know the house-keeper had the briefcase all this time."

"Say what?" Timmins yelled into the phone. "You're kidding me."

"Nope. She was acting strange, so I was expecting some-thing. Threw me for a loop. The housekeeper deliberately said to Mrs. Ferguson and me that she hadn't searched for the briefcase. When I told the ladies I would have to come back with officers to look for it, Mrs. Ferguson lost her cool and chewed out Gloria.

"The housekeeper and I had a private chat. Gloria fi-nally admitted to hiding the briefcase and said to come back Thursday morning to grab it, as she won't be going to Ferguson's funeral. I hope Myrna can lift some viable prints from it." Mark paused, reabsorbing the unexpected turn of events. "What did you find out?"

"Edward Ferguson's head office is a well-oiled engine," Timmins began. "His board of directors had instructions that in the event of his death, they would hold a vote among themselves, their shareholders and Mrs. Ferguson to see who would become the new CEO. That's ongoing, and they know Mrs. Ferguson will inherit the business. No surprises there.

"What caught me off guard was a couple of security guys. My guess is they were hired after Mr. Ferguson was assaulted. As I was leaving, one of them asked about the investigation. I told him it's moving along. Then he had the nerve to say that if we were doing our job, Mr. Ferguson would still be alive."

"I'll bet you weren't expecting that," Mark told him.

"Nope, but I took a page out of your book and kept quiet. But what concerned me was that these two had the smell of *bad guy* on them."

That caught Mark's attention. Timmins had been doing this job for years, and his instinct was never wrong. "What are you thinking?"

"Possible mercenary."

Whoa—that was taking it to a whole new level.

"The guy also had a strong accent. I couldn't place it. Then he says if he was looking for the killer, he would do whatever it took to find the bastard. When I got back to the precinct, I asked Myrna to run all the fingerprints from your love interest's bakery and the murder scene through Interpol's Automatic Fingerprint Identification System database. It's just a hunch, especially after listening to that muscle-head jerk, but—"

"No, that's a good call, spread the net wide. Thanks for checking it out, Timmins."

"You bet, but my day got even weirder. Found out that Jenny wants to cut a deal."

"What?" How many strange things could happen in one day? In this case, a lot. "Tell me."

"She said she could get you into one of those secret protest meetings she'd talked about. Get you close to the leader."

"What's the point of that? Ferguson's dead—that should be the end of it."

"Not in this leader's eyes. Mighty Big Bakery is still here, and as long as they continue to run over the little business, Jenny said her leader won't back down."

"Goddamn it." For every answer Mark found, two more questions popped up. He'd have to find a chance to sit down and get all of his shit together and rethink probabilities. Captain Fraust would be asking for an update, too, and he'd need to be ready for that. "All right, thanks, Timmins. I'll see you tomorrow."

When he checked his phone, Britt had sent a text.

You'd better show up or I'll hunt you down, but you might already know that.

He coughed out a laugh and replied.

There's that Nordic warrior coming out of you. I'll bring dinner as tribute.

Her reply was short and promising.

Just bring yourself.

* * *

"Thank you for bringing takeout," Britt said, licking her fingers. "That was delicious."

Mark had an odd look on his face. "My pleasure." His voice was deep, almost rough.

Nervous, she grabbed the dishes and headed for the kitchen. Britt knew what to expect—she had invited him over for goodness' sake—but the anticipation and awkwardness made her feel like a teenager.

A very excited teenager.

She rinsed the dishes and placed them in the dishwasher. "Mark, would you like anything to drink?" She turned around and squawked in surprise. He stood inches away, hands in his pockets, his dark gaze traveling slowly over her. "You startled me."

"Sorry." He reached out his hand.

She could almost see the wheels turning in his head. Honestly, she wondered if her thoughts matched his. Britt grasped his fingers and watched in wonder as he raised her hand to his lips. The touch was warm, but her whole body burned inside.

When he looked at her, his brown eyes held a light of their own. "What are you thinking, *vakker*?"

His question, though innocent, wrapped itself around her, a force she couldn't fight against. She knew exactly what she thought, what she wanted, and was sure Mark picked up on it.

The past four years after the debacle with Minister Strathmore had been difficult and lonely, despite building a new life around her bakery. But finding Mark… She closed her eyes, because staring at him made her heart ache.

Movement, and then the warmth of his body against hers. "Britt."

She opened her eyes and looked into the depths of his own. "I was thinking that I shouldn't have been such a chicken Friday night."

He touched her cheek, a soft caress. "I figured you had your reasons."

She nodded, trying to form her next words. "I was scared, I think. I was sure you were married or in a relationship or something."

"Nope. You have me all to yourself." He leaned in, his mouth barely brushing against hers.

She trembled, the force of this moment intense and electrifying. Without thinking—Britt didn't want to think, just go for it—she wrapped her arms around his neck, pressing her breasts against his hard chest. She was tired of tiptoeing around her uncertainty.

Mark's grip was so tight she could barely breathe. He picked her up and managed to get them into her bedroom. He let her go and grabbed her hands. "Are you sure?"

"Just shut up and kiss me."

Mark didn't hesitate, kissing her so thoroughly Britt thought she would pass out. His hands slipped beneath her T-shirt and massaged her breasts until she groaned into his mouth.

"Damn it, *vakker*, you're driving me crazy. Lift your arms."

She did so, and Mark had her top and bra off in moments. His hands rested lightly on her skin, skimming over her nipples until they hardened with a will of their own. "Absolutely gorgeous," he whispered in a hoarse voice.

Undaunted, Britt reached for his shirt, her fingers shaking as she unbuttoned it. She pushed the material off his shoulders, letting her hands travel over firm muscle. His upper body was wide and defined, and Britt trailed her fingers across his chest and down his abs.

He hissed. "If you keep this up, I don't know how much longer I can hold still."

Mark was fighting to keep his desire in check, and hearing that made her feel mischievous. "You mean I can't tease you?"

He arched a brow. "There could be consequences."

She bit her lower lip, and his gaze focused on the movement. She didn't want to tease—she just wanted him.

Britt reached for his belt, unhooking it while keeping her eyes on him. He glanced down at her busy hands but slowly raised his head, his gaze dark and focused as he studied her body. He rested his hands over hers as he pushed his clothing down to his ankles before kicking his pants and underwear off with a swift movement.

Britt held her breath. Now that Mark was completely naked, she could ogle to her heart's delight. His body was covered in thick, dense muscle courtesy of the sports he enjoyed playing. She ran her hands over his arms again.

He moved close enough to let her feel his manhood against her stomach. "Let's get you out of those leggings, shall we?"

He kneeled in front of her and grabbed the waistband, pulling both tights and panties down in a slow, torturous movement. Britt couldn't look, but she felt his warm breath on a spot just below her belly button. She lifted her feet to remove the clothing, but Mark hadn't gotten up yet. The tension built up within her as she realized he wasn't in any hurry. "Mark…"

"Shh."

His hands caressed her legs, moving up until he grabbed her backside in a firm grip that made her bite her tongue. She held her breath, wondering what he would do. "I think you're teasing now," she managed to say.

Silence, but then she inhaled sharply when his lips kissed just below her belly button. Without thinking, her hands grasped handfuls of his hair to steady her shaky legs.

He rose, and in one movement, swept her into his arms and laid her on the bed. He hovered over her, his mouth trailing hot kisses across her body until she squirmed, desire flushing her skin with heat.

He reached the delicate skin between her legs, and her body tensed, emotions conflicting with each other. He massaged her with firm, slow movements that finally allowed her body to relax. When his tongue touched her sensitive folds, Britt arched off the bed, crying out in surprise at the strong reaction. Heat pooled in her lower body, and fast breathing turned to quiet cries as Mark relentlessly probed at her. He touched a spot that sent her over the edge, and Britt gave in to her orgasm until she fell limp against the pillow.

He propped himself above her and kissed her face. "How are you, *vakker*?"

"Mmm, I'm not sure yet." She flicked her tongue along his mouth.

"Hold that thought." He scrambled off the bed and reached for something in his pants pocket—a condom.

"I might need to keep a few of those handy around here," she quipped as he rolled it on.

He gave her a heated look as he crawled into bed beside her. "That sounds like a hint."

It did, didn't it? Britt didn't want to dwell on that, not now. "Come over here," she whispered, reaching for him.

Mark held his body above hers, and she didn't need

any prompting, wrapping her legs around his waist as he pushed slowly into her. She hadn't realized she had held her breath until he looked at her, his expression concerned. "Are you all right?"

"Yes." Without thinking, her body rocked to its own beat, pushing away all thoughts until she only saw him, smelled his scent and tasted his sweat. Her soft whimpers in Mark's ear encouraged him, his own pace increasing until with a loud drawn-out cry, her body spasmed, leaving her no choice but to ride the waves of desire that overtook her.

Mark wasn't far behind. His grip around her tightened as he shook from the force of his own orgasm, his deep groan loud in her ear.

He rolled onto his side and kissed her so hard she thought she saw stars. His hand gently caressed her as he stared into her face, remaining quiet.

Britt wondered what he was thinking but didn't ask. "I've heard that the first time is always the best."

He frowned and propped himself up on an elbow. "And?"

"It doesn't make sense if you have the right person in your life."

He stroked her hair, damp from their lovemaking. "Is that what you believe, *vakker*?"

"Yeah," she whispered, her chest swelling with unknown emotions. "Yeah, I do."

Chapter 14

When Britt woke up, sunlight had eased into her bedroom, a gentle warmth against her bare skin. She yawned and reached over, ready to caress Mark's body. But he wasn't there.

Alert, she turned onto her side. An empty, wrinkled spot on the bed was all she saw.

For a moment, a sharp pang of bitter disappointment hit her chest. He'd already left, probably going back to his place to shower and change before work. Logically, it made sense, and yet...

A toilet flushed, and a minute later, Mark appeared, dressed only in his boxers. "Morning, *vakker*," he called out.

"Good morning." Glancing around her bedroom, she finally spied Mark's clothing neatly arranged on a chair, and felt a little embarrassed at thinking that Mark had taken off during the night.

"What's wrong?" He sat on the bed beside her.

She shook her head, not wanting to admit her rash thought.

He frowned, his brown eyes not leaving her face. "You didn't think I'd leave, did you?"

Britt shrugged, refusing to meet his gaze.

His finger touched her chin and gently tilted her face so that she was forced to look at him. "I was kicking myself when I didn't follow you that night. You think I'm going to screw up now?"

She swallowed the lump in her throat. Mark had a way with words that made her insides tie up in knots.

His smile was devilish. "Besides, how can I resist this hot body of yours?" He whipped the bedsheet aside before she could hang on to it.

"Mark!" She covered her breasts with her hands.

"Oh, no, none of that." He kissed every bit of skin he could reach until he stretched his body over hers. She giggled at a ticklish spot above her navel, and he hovered around it, taking advantage until she gasped from laughter and tried to fight him off.

"Stop, please!"

When he raised his head, his brow was cocked up at a high angle. "I hope you won't doubt my intentions again."

Her throat constricted so much she could hardly breathe. "I'm sorry," Britt whispered, fighting to hold back a sob. "It's just…well…"

"Hey." He kissed her nose, her forehead, then her lips. His gentleness pulled at her heart until she thought it would shatter into a million pieces. "I plan on hanging around. You won't get rid of me that easily."

Their lovemaking this time was slow, filled with whispered endearments and gentle caresses. Mark's gaze never left hers as he explored her body again, his hands smoothing over her skin until the heat built up inside and her body trembled with excitement. His encouragement and urgent desire mirrored her own and then, with a shudder, Britt's orgasm burned through her body until she felt turned inside out.

A peaceful bliss settled over her. She was relaxed, her skin still warm. She yawned and stretched her arms over her head, thinking she'd like to stay in bed with him all day.

But it wasn't meant to be. A cell phone rang, and with a muttered curse, Mark jumped out of bed and dug it out of his pants pocket. He talked quietly for several minutes, and Britt heard the word *case* a couple of times—it was work. She gathered the bedsheet around her and headed for the bathroom while Mark watched her. Just as she passed him, he reached out and wrapped his arm around her waist. "It's seven now," he said into the phone. "I'll be at the station in about an hour."

He hung up, then kissed her on the cheek. "Sorry—work," he apologized.

"That's okay." Smiling, she returned the gesture but kissed him full on the lips.

"Damn, I wish I could stay with you." He wrapped his arms around her waist and grabbed her ass. "I'd like nothing more than to ignore work and love you all morning."

Her heart smacked against her chest. Hearing Mark say that he'd rather be with her than doing his job... She swallowed, but didn't say anything.

He released her and got dressed, putting his keys, phone and wallet into various pockets. She followed him out of the room and to the front door. "Talk to you later?" he said.

Britt smiled. "You bet."

He gave her a lingering kiss, his lips warm, gentle. With a squeeze of his hand, he was gone.

She locked the door, then turned and leaned against it. If she had told herself two weeks ago that she would meet the man of her dreams on a busy street, she would have laughed so hard she'd scare her staff.

* * *

Mark found it hard to focus on work with Britt constantly on his mind.

He'd gone home to shower and change, and arrived at the precinct just after eight to add yesterday's surprising revelation to his notes. The captain would want another update for sure.

He wanted to think about Britt, spend time dreaming of what they could possibly have together, but right now, the job called out to him to defend the less fortunate, including a man like Ferguson. Work was his balm, his comfort. Mark wanted to excel—he loved solving his investigations and bringing closure. He knew he was good at his job. Dad was finally out of the picture, and his and Mom's relationship had become tighter. Mark had a good life, and when he was ready, he'd hoped to find a woman he could love unconditionally.

To say that karma had blessed him when he saw Britt at Konditori was an understatement. The chances of ever finding someone like his Nordic princess seemed slim to none. If she hadn't stopped to check him out, he never would have recognized her at the bakery.

He blinked, refocusing his thoughts. Britt was here, he had spent a passion-filled night with her and she hadn't pushed him away or told him it couldn't work. This was real—*she* was real, and Mark wanted to find out how far they could take their journey.

He sat at his desk, coffee mug in hand, and pulled out everything from his work bag. As he waited for the computer to boot up, he read through his notes again, looking for areas he could link together. They hadn't found the weapon used to kill Mr. Ferguson. It was possible the briefcase was used to hit the CEO over the head, but he'd have to wait until he got the item from Gloria, the housekeeper.

Mark also remembered Timmins's remark about using the international database to see if there were any hits on the fingerprints found at the murder scene and Britt's bakery. He buzzed Myrna.

"Good morning," she said in a cheerful voice. "I figured you'd want some answers to that age-old question, who-dunit."

He smiled at her bad joke. "It sounds like you got some-where."

"I certainly have. I was waiting on Timmins, but you're just the guy to see what I've got."

At that moment, Timmins walked in. "He's here now," Mark said. "We'll be down in a few."

As he and Timmins walked into Myrna's lab, the forensics investigator waved at them from the other end of the wide room. "Over here," she called out.

She sat in front of two large computer monitors. Blown up in detail on one of the screens was a fingerprint. On the other monitor were three pictures of a man from the chest up in various mug-shot poses.

"Did you get a hit?" Mark stared at the picture. The man looked to be in his early thirties, with a full black beard and thick curly hair tied back in a ponytail. His dark eyes were unfeeling, bottomless. "Who's this?"

"Now, that's a good question. He has so many aliases, I don't think anyone knows. What we do know is that he's one of the men who broke into and destroyed that bakery across from Ferguson's construction site. His fingerprints were all over the place."

"You don't say." He leaned in to get a closer look. This

dude did not look friendly at all. "Did you find an address?"

"No, but here's the interesting part. He had to provide fingerprints for his current job." She hit a few keys, and the picture of a high-level security card appeared, with the suspect's picture and current name. Beneath it was the name of the company he worked for.

"Mighty Big Bakery Inc.?" Mark said, incredulous.

Myrna smiled. "I knew you'd get a kick out of that."

"Do me a favor and print that for me." It was a small step forward, and Mark was cheering inside. "Any other surprises?"

"Why, yes." Myrna pulled up the second set of fingerprints found at Britt's store, then called up the corresponding picture. This second man was younger with a blond crew cut, thick eyebrows and a permanent scowl.

"Hey, that's the jerk who talked to me when I finished my interview with the MBB board of directors," Timmins exclaimed. "Nice, we're getting somewhere."

"And behind door number three…" Myrna retrieved the information on the third suspect.

"That was the other security guard," Timmins told them.

"We could collect their work records, just to see what they wrote down to get a security job at MBB," Myrna advised.

So, one part of the puzzle solved. Myrna provided him with pictures of the men and their prints.

"Thanks, Myrna. Great job."

She got up and offered a curtsy. "My pleasure."

Upstairs, Mark laid the additional information on top of his other papers.

"When are you grabbing the briefcase?" Timmins asked. "Want me to go with you?"

"No need. I'm just getting it and bringing it right back. However…" Mark wasn't sure that Gloria had told him everything. "I think I'll bring the housekeeper in as well for further questioning. Are you going to pick up those three security guys today?"

"Damn right I am."

Mark checked his watch. "I'm going to head out. It should be a full house when we get back."

"Oh, don't forget Jenny's offer."

He swore. "I'm wondering how much we can get out of it. I guess I'd better talk to her first."

He headed toward the jail cell and talked with the officer on duty. "Is Jenny awake?"

"Oh yes, and very impatient to see you. She's in the last cell on the left."

"Did she use her phone call?" Mark asked.

The officer shook his head. "She didn't want to—at least, not yet."

Jenny was pacing the small cell when he stopped in front of it. "Good morning."

She glared at him. "Easy for you to say. You're standing out there."

Mark refused to let her bait him. "My partner told me you wanted to cut a deal."

She smiled, but he sensed an underlying malice behind it. "That's right. You guys want to arrest the protest leader before he does more damage. I know where he's going to be today. Got a text from him before you busted Henry and me."

When she didn't continue, Mark crossed his arms. "And?"

"What do I get?"

He shrugged. "I don't know. I'll need to talk to Captain Fraust."

"Shit, maybe I should have asked for your captain instead." She approached the cell door and wrapped her hands around the bars. "How about a reduced sentence? And you haven't allowed me my phone call. What's up with that?"

"Not true. The officer who brought you in yesterday said you didn't ask for it, despite reading your rights. And I just asked the officer on duty. He said you didn't call your lawyer."

"Fine, I want that and a reduced sentence."

"You'll get your phone call. As for the sentence, I can't do anything. Maybe it'll depend on what you've got to offer." Mark knew she was playing a game, but he was all over that—he had no idea if Jenny's information would be any good.

"Mr. Ferguson's funeral is today, isn't it? At eleven?"

Mark fought not to react, but a cold finger of dread ran down his spine. "What about it?"

She walked to the other side of the cell. "The protest leader is going to show up there. I have no idea how many followers will be with him, but I don't think it's going to be pretty."

"Christ!" Mark ran down the hallway. "Call in every officer on duty!" he yelled at the startled cop. "Find out where Mr. Ferguson's funeral is being held and call it in!"

"Hey, what's going on?" the officer shouted as Mark raced past him.

"The protesters against Mighty Big Bakery. They're going to cause a riot!"

* * *

Timmins had already left for MBB's head office to arrest the three suspects whose fingerprints were all over Britt's bakery.

Two police cars had already raced off by the time Mark jumped into his car. He got on the radio. "All units, this is Detective Mark Hawthorne. The funeral is at Mount Pleasant Cemetery on Bayview Avenue. Sirens and lights on until we reach Bayview and Eglinton, then go silent. We'll reconvene at Bayview and Sutherland Drive to assess the situation."

He got moving, speeding through traffic as he raced with the others to their destination. Suddenly, his radio came alive. "Hawthorne, it's Fraust."

He picked up and gave her a quick summary of what was going on. "I want us to get there before the protesters," he told her. "Surround the area without anyone knowing. As soon as they show up, we'll take them down."

"This is going to be a large memorial—at least a hundred mourners. You'll need to keep your eyes and wits sharp."

"Yes, ma'am."

"How many officers are with you?"

"I won't know until I get there."

She cursed under her breath. "It may not be enough by the time you pull in. I'll send more but do the best you can." She signed off.

The cemetery encompassed a massive amount of land, surrounded by tall mature trees, condos and large, expensive homes. They parked on Sutherland Drive, and Mark quickly counted his men—nine officers in total. That was all he had to work with. He pulled everyone together into a tight circle. "I don't know what to expect," he told them.

"I've heard these protesters wear masks, but they might take them off and try to blend in with the crowd. If you spot the leader, try to arrest them or follow their movements at a safe distance and call for backup."

"That's going to be hard if we don't know what the leader looks like," one of them grumbled.

"He'll be the one up front. I know, it feels like a guessing game, but it's what we've got right now." If they messed this up, the protesters would scatter. "We've got one chance at this. Team up and arrest anyone who endangers the mourners."

Mark instructed them on the go, telling them to sneak toward the church located at the center of the cemetery and to stay hidden. He saw a couple of workers preparing a burial site and went to speak with them. "I'm with York Regional Police," he said quietly to the startled men, displaying his badge. "I understand Edward Ferguson's funeral is this morning. Do you know where he'll be buried?"

"Over there." The older man pointed at a small mausoleum located at the edge of a wooded area. "The service already started." He looked at his watch. "The procession to the mausoleum is supposed to start at eleven—about twenty minutes. What's going on?"

Mark looked around—the officers had surrounded the church at a safe distance and kept mostly out of sight. "We might have unwanted company." At the man's confused look, he added, "Protesters."

"Those anti-MBB bastards." The man spat on the ground. "I'm all for stating my opinion, but they take it too far. Are they really going to show up here?"

"I don't know. I hope not." He scanned around him—no one was in sight.

"You want us to help you with anything?" the other employee asked.

He shook his head. "Just stay out of the way."

Mark hid within the shrubbery close to the mausoleum and talked to the officers via walkie-talkie. No one suspicious had appeared so far, and he surmised the protesters would start something as Ferguson was being entombed.

The mourners had started filing out of the church in small groups. Mrs. Ferguson was in the center, wearing a wide-brimmed hat, a black veil pulled over her face. Two ladies stood on either side while a large man shadowed them; no doubt her siblings.

Mark's radio crackled to life. "Sir, there's a group of people heading this way, moving quickly."

It had to be them. "There's a mausoleum about two hundred feet east of the church," he advised. "Ferguson's to be buried in it. I'm just behind the building."

The coffin was finally brought out, carried by six pallbearers. The priest came next, and Mark watched as everyone slowly proceeded toward the mausoleum. The next five minutes were going to be tense.

As the procession came to a stop, he saw several people marching on the wide path, their faces covered in masks, heading straight toward the mausoleum. Several of the officers appeared from behind, forming a semicircle around the protesters.

As the priest intoned a final prayer, the leader of the protesters started shouting. "Your husband doesn't deserve a funeral—he deserves to rot in hell! He's got a lot to answer for!"

That was their cue. "Move in!" Mark shouted into his radio, then scrambled out of the bushes to confront the protesters. "York Regional Police! Stay where you are and get your hands up!"

Damn it. Instead of everyone holding still, a mass panic ensued. Mourners and protesters alike ran away in several directions, and in the confusion, Mark lost sight of the leader. "Go!" he shouted to the officers.

As planned, they teamed up in twos. Two officers ran west, the next two hurried east, the third pair traveled south and the last two went north. Mark and his partner surveyed the crowd in front of them. Mrs. Ferguson stood by her husband's coffin, with her family flanking either side. Meanwhile, the priest was trying to calm everyone in a loud, commanding voice.

Mark ran the crowd's perimeter, his partner encircling the opposite side, hoping to spot the man who had made the threat. But by the time he managed to find an opening and look around, the protesters were either too far away to chase down or had disappeared among the tombstones and large trees. Masks were scattered across the grass. "Son of a bitch!" he shouted and got on his radio. "All units, report."

"In pursuit of a protester," an officer yelled back, sounding out of breath. "Proceeding south on Bayview."

"Stay on it," he ordered.

The other officers reported in, stating they had lost their targets in busy pedestrian traffic.

"Get to your cars and follow the chase on Bayview," Mark demanded. "Don't lose them." He radioed the officers chasing their suspect. "We have backup coming. Stay on course."

Mark turned to face the mixed emotions of the mourners. He walked straight toward Mrs. Ferguson. "Are you all right?"

"What the hell was that about?" a middle-aged, large-boned man yelled at him. "You've ruined what little peace my sister managed to salvage. When I get back to—"

"Stop." Mrs. Ferguson grabbed the man's arm. "Just stop."

The big man glared at him but backed off.

Mark breathed a mental sigh of relief. "Are you okay, Mrs. Ferguson?"

"Yes. Those are the people who hate Edward?" She shook her head. "Jealousy and anger won't stop the business from running. I wish they would learn that. Now, if you'll excuse us."

"Of course." Mark retreated, silently paying his respects to the grieving family before running to his car. "Status," he commanded as he got in.

"Still in pursuit. Heading west on Moore Avenue. Shit, this guy can run."

There were neighborhoods the suspect could hide in. "You have to grab him before he gets to Moore Park Ravine or we'll lose him. Box him in, mount the curb if you have to." It was too late for him to join in the chase. Glancing at his watch, he needed to get that briefcase from Gloria before Mrs. Ferguson and her family returned to the house.

Mark got the car started and drove off, periodically receiving updates until he heard, "Suspect in custody."

"Yes!" He did a fist pump. "Excellent work. Bring him in."

Mark arrived at the Ferguson house just after eleven thirty. The gates were already open, and he drove up towards the front door. When he got out of the car, Gloria opened the door, as if she'd been sitting beside it. "You're late," she accused. "They'll be back soon."

"The protesters against Mighty Big Bakery showed up at the funeral. We have one in custody."

If Mark only had a camera to take a photo of Gloria's expression. Surprise, mixed with fear—she couldn't be more obvious. "Do you know who?"

"Nope, haven't questioned them yet. Where's the brief-case?"

She headed toward the kitchen. "I haven't touched it after hiding it in the garage."

The housekeeper opened one of the garage doors. "The briefcase was lying here." She pointed at a spot between two of the luxury cars. "I kicked it under the Jeep."

Mark wanted to knock his head against a pole. He'd been so distracted by Ferguson's corpse and finding certain clues, he hadn't thought to search in other areas beyond the crime scene. He got down on his knees and looked under the vehicle. Sure enough, a silver metal briefcase sat between the front tires. "Do you have a plastic bag?" he asked. "And something with a long handle."

In a few minutes, his evidence was out in the open. As he inspected it, Mark saw dark red stains on one corner—blood. He wrapped it carefully in the green garbage bag Gloria provided him, believing he was close to finding the answers he needed. There was still one problem...

"Gloria, why did you hide this?"

That fearful look again. "I'm not sure what you're—"

"You know exactly what I mean. Obstructing a crime scene, hiding evidence and lying to an officer."

She looked around, as if expecting someone to appear. "No, Detective. It's not like that."

"It is, and you're coming with me."

Gloria backed away. "I can't. Mrs. Ferguson will need me when she returns."

"You should have thought of that before pulling this stunt."

The precinct was full. Between Timmins's arrests, the officers' capture of one of the protesters and Mark bringing in the housekeeper, Mark didn't know which way was up. On top of that, Britt had left him a couple of voice mails, and he hadn't yet found time to answer her, not with everything else going on.

He immediately took Gloria to an interrogation room and handed an excited Myrna the briefcase and its combination code on a piece of paper. "Give me a miracle," he told her.

"I'll let you know in an hour." She practically ran to her laboratory.

"I think we'd better divide and conquer," he told Timmins when they met up in their office. "I'll question the housekeeper. Who can help you with those security guards and the protester?"

"I'll get Solberg to talk to the protester and one guard. He's in between cases at the moment. I'll handle the other two."

Ten minutes later, Mark sat opposite the housekeeper. "I believe you were read your rights," he told her, setting pen and paper before him. "You refused your phone call, but if you change your mind…"

"I won't. Let's get on with it."

Her demeanor had changed, and now Gloria looked defeated. "Why did you hide the briefcase?" he started.

"I wanted you to think it'd been stolen." Her voice was calm.

"Why?"

"Because I needed to get something out of it."

"What did you think was inside?"

The housekeeper paused. "A contract to buy a business from…someone."

She hesitated on the last word, and Mark pounced on it. "Who? The more information you provide, the better I can help you."

She chewed her lower lip. "A relative. They own a place called Levi's Bread & Bakery on Bathurst and Lawrence Avenue. It's been there for over fifty years."

Mark knew the area. It had been run-down for the past ten years before the city started renovating it, tearing down derelict buildings and putting up condos and multimillion-dollar homes. He also knew the bakery—three generations of the family worked there, fighting against the rapid change of their neighborhood. "Did Mr. Ferguson offer to buy the bakery out?"

"He didn't offer—he threatened. Someone else wanted to buy the business, and Mr. Ferguson wasn't going to give up without a fight. My uncle didn't want to sell."

Mark sensed a *but* somewhere. "What made your uncle change his mind?"

"No one would tell me. I was frantic, worried that something bad happened. I'd heard about those criminals that attacked businesses who refused to sell to Mr. Ferguson." She wrung her hands. "My uncle is a proud man, and he wouldn't give up anything belonging to him. That bakery is his lifeblood."

Mark was still missing a piece of the puzzle but decided to forge ahead. "We need to talk about the briefcase—what's in it?"

"I'm pretty sure the contracts to sign over my uncle's

bakery. Mr. Ferguson bragged that evening about how he was going to purchase one of the best properties in the Lawrence and Bathurst area. I knew he meant my uncle's business."

He frowned, staring at the housekeeper. Was it possible…?

She gave him a hard look. "I didn't kill Mr. Ferguson, if that's what you're implying. He's not worth going to jail."

He'd still check her fingerprints against the database to be sure. "What *did* you do?"

"Nothing. I couldn't do anything at all. I went home and called my uncle to try to talk him out of it, but he wouldn't listen, wouldn't tell me what Mr. Ferguson offered. He said it was no one's business but his own." She covered her face with a hand and cried quietly. "That man had no right to destroy my uncle's work, or anyone else's."

Mark waited a few minutes to give Gloria a chance to compose herself. "And you didn't know anything else until you saw Mr. Ferguson's body Tuesday morning?"

She shook her head. "I saw the briefcase and believed it had the contract for my uncle to sign. I kicked it under the Jeep and prayed no one found it. I thought with Mr. Ferguson dead, his company might forget about buying my uncle's bakery."

Well, this was an interesting turn of events. Tampering with evidence usually meant covering up a crime, but the housekeeper didn't hide the briefcase because it was the murder weapon. She wanted to avoid selling her uncle's business.

Man, what a tangled net. Ferguson was like a spider, and anything caught in his web was doomed. "Is there anything else you'd like to tell me?" he asked gently.

"I wanted to know about the protester you caught."

She sighed. "My male cousins talked about joining the anti-MBB protests. I hope it's not one of them, but they're adults—they knew what they were getting into." Gloria shook her head. "I'm sorry. I was scared. I didn't know what else to do."

"I'm glad you told me what you know. I have a couple more inquiries. What you've done would normally result in a criminal offense charge, but I'll try to have that rejected. You won't lose your job and you won't have a criminal record."

She smiled through her tears. "Thank you, Detective."

"Oh, and tell your uncle not to worry about anyone destroying his business if he changes his mind and doesn't want to sell." He winked.

Gloria was a smart woman—her look of surprise changed to relief, and she nodded while fighting back tears.

Mark felt better about himself. He hadn't thought she'd done anything as horrifying as murder, and his instincts proved him right.

She was escorted out while he headed to his office and organized his notes yet again. He saw that Captain Fraust had called and buzzed her. "Captain."

"Tell me you have good news."

He updated her on the housekeeper, the MBB security guards and the one protester they had managed to catch. "We have the briefcase, ma'am, and it's stained with blood. I'm waiting for Walsh to provide me with her results."

A short pause, then she said, "Good work, Hawthorne. As soon as you get something, let me know." She hung up.

He had a few minutes, so he called Britt's cell. No answer, and it went to voice mail. "Hey, it's me," he announced. "Sorry I couldn't call you sooner. The case I'm working on is growing intense, but I'm finding answers. I'll call you or drop by later. Talk soon."

Mark could feel a headache coming on. When this was over, he was going to take a vacation. Maybe Britt would join him.

He let that thought roll pleasantly through his mind as he headed down to the forensics lab. Timmins and Solberg hadn't returned, and he was getting antsy.

Myrna was hurrying from one end of the room to the other when he paused in the doorway. She looked stressed, so he waited a few moments until she sat down in front of a large microscope. "Hey, how's it going?"

"Oh, Hawthorne, you're just in time. Have a seat." She gestured at a chair opposite her.

"What have you got for me?"

"Good news and bad news." She jerked her thumb at the briefcase lying on an examination table, along with a small stack of legal papers. "The good news is, the bloodstains belong to Mr. Ferguson. And there's a good-sized dent in the briefcase, too. The murderer must have hit the CEO hard several times. The bad news, no prints."

Mark swore with a few choice words that had Myrna's eyebrows go up. "What was inside?" he asked.

"A contract for a Levi's Bread & Bakery. I know that place—they make the best bagels in Toronto."

He nodded. "Do me a favor. Keep that contract locked someplace where I can't find it—for now."

She gave him a look. "Because?"

"I want the owner to have time to think about whether selling his life's work is what he really wants to do."

"Well…yeah, I could do that and sort of forget where I've put the documents."

"Thanks." It's not something he would normally do, but Mark knew he'd feel horrible if he didn't at least try to reverse a situation that shouldn't have happened in the first place.

"So, let me provide you with better news," Myrna told him. "The coroner found hairs in Mr. Ferguson's clenched fist and sent those to me for analysis."

Just then the database pinged, and Myrna rubbed her hands together. "Let's see what we've got."

Mark came around the wide table and stood behind her as information flowed onto the computer screen—a name, face in three poses and information he hadn't expected.

"This guy has an international warrant?" he exclaimed. He scanned the charges—domestic terrorism, uttering death threats, aggravated assault, possession of illegal weapons. "How the hell are we going to find him?"

"Like we always do—we have one of the best teams, Hawthorne. We'll get it done."

Myrna's confidence was stronger than his. A tendril of doubt trickled into his consciousness, but he slapped it away. "Print everything for me," he told her. "After I update the captain, I'm pulling everyone in on this."

She hit a couple of buttons, then sat back. "I heard over the intercom this morning you needed officers. What happened?"

He gave her a rundown of what had occurred at the funeral. "If everyone hadn't panicked at once, I might have caught the leader."

"Well, you caught someone, so it's a start."

He gathered everything and headed out, then stopped. "Myrna, I want you in on the meeting with the captain. Can you make it?"

"I'll come up now." She grabbed some additional paperwork and followed him.

In the office, Timmins and Solberg provided their findings.

The protester knew nothing about the leader and insisted he had only joined because he wanted to impress his girlfriend, which made Mark throw up his hands in frustration. "What about those three heavies?" he asked Timmins.

The older detective propped his hands on his hips. "They couldn't talk fast enough. Said that Ferguson paid them under the table to rough up anyone who resisted his buyout offers." He shook his head. "That dude was a piece of work. The CEO sounded like a mafia leader, for crap's sake."

"Those guys are bad news. Keep them locked up—I'll have them charged and sent to prison for the B and E at least. Personally, I think there's more to them than they're letting on."

Mark buzzed Fraust, who told him to come up. With Myrna at his side, they entered the captain's office. "Ma'am."

"Have a seat."

They arranged their investigative work on the meeting table.

"I don't have to tell you that after the melee at Ferguson's funeral, the media and populace are demanding to know what we're doing, among other things," Fraust stated.

Fraust's words made him unreasonably nervous. She had backed him up on everything he'd done so far. Still... "I'll provide a rundown of our findings, and Walsh can interrupt if I'm missing anything."

Mark condensed his detailed notes into a fifteen-minute speech, summarizing everything that had occurred, up until his conversation with Myrna today in the lab.

"What are your conclusions?"

He nodded toward Myrna. "Walsh has been in contact with the coroner, as we couldn't find any prints on the briefcase. The footprints found in the flower bed are a size 10 for a construction boot. Unfortunately, they're the wrong size. Jenny wears a size 7, so the footprints don't belong to her. Our next best chance was finding something on Ferguson's body. Foreign hairs were clenched in the CEO's fist and provided us with a solid hit." He slid the photo across to the captain. "The suspect is dangerous."

Fraust picked up the photo, her gaze scanning across the page. "Agreed." She looked at him, eyes sharp. "What do you suggest?"

Mark knew his face held surprise—he had expected the captain to provide ideas, especially now with the knowledge that the case had developed into a high-profile investigation. "Originally, I would have said to get this perp's face on all the news channels, but…" He stopped, knowing now that wouldn't work. "It's not a good idea. As soon as he sees that he's on the news, he'll go underground. We'll never find him."

"Very true." The captain paused, waiting, her gaze intent.

"We could advise all law enforcement officers, but I think…" He was taking a big risk on this theory. "I think the perp is still in our area. I also believe he's the protest leader, but that's only speculation."

"But a solid one. Excellent call on making that decision." Her smile was brief, but he noticed it. "I'll put out an all-points bulletin and give the media a general summary of our progress. Like you said, we can't afford the perp seeing his face on the news. Let's catch the son of a bitch first."

Chapter 15

It had only been a day, yet Britt was surprised and happy at the progress made on Konditori. It was as if someone had lit a fire under their butts.

No, that wasn't it—everyone was determined to resurrect the bakery. Her staff had stayed last night, cleaning up and deciding what to keep or toss. Today, Joyce came in with a contractor and a small team, and Britt stayed out of their way as they measured and discussed ideas.

"I want to run something by you," her friend said as she sat down in the other office chair. She plunked her laptop on the desk. "You've been saying how busy it's been, which is never a complaint in my books, but I think a bit more space would help. Have you thought about relocating to a larger building?"

Britt shook her head. "I can't move. I have a lease for another four years. Honestly, I never expected the growth to happen so fast, but I don't want to overextend myself or the staff, either."

Joyce nodded. "Smart. So this is what I'm thinking. Could we make your office a little smaller? The wall between it and the front room isn't load-bearing, so we could knock it down and shave off…" She glanced around the office, her gaze calculating. "About a foot?"

Britt did the same thing, carefully looking about the room. She only used it when she needed privacy, and if she was honest with herself, she wouldn't mind an update, either. "A foot should be fine. It makes the room a bit narrow, but I don't need the built-in bookcase in the corner. Just one set of fireproof metal drawers with a lock, a sit-stand table and a comfy office chair. The window brings in plenty of light, which was always a plus."

"Trust me, sweetie. I'll make this room look nice. The extra foot will also let me add some additional recessed storage behind the cash register. There'll be more space for people to come inside. And you can still have your little area for tables and chairs, but the furniture will be built in a way that'll take up less space. Even the bookcase you used to have out there? The contractor mentioned we can build that into the wall. No more fears that it might tip over."

Britt gave her friend a tight hug. "What would I do without you?"

"That's why I'm here. I'd like to do some last-minute measurements while you and the others continue cleaning, if I'm not in the way?"

"Never."

Just then, someone knocked, and Kevin poked his head around the door. "Hey, Britt, your friend Mark is here."

"Thanks." She glanced at Joyce, who had an unapologetic grin on her face. "What?"

"Girl, if this isn't a hint, I don't know what is."

"Oh, Mark's been throwing clues around." Britt thought of a movie character for her impersonation. "The force is strong in this one, Mistress Joyce," she said in a booming voice.

Joyce rolled her eyes, then laughed. "How do you feel about it?"

Britt got up from the chair. "Let's just say I'm leaning in his direction."

In the front room, Mark walked the perimeter of the space, his gaze taking in their hard work. "Hello, *vakker*," he said softly as she approached, and kissed her on the lips. "You've made some great progress here."

"We did. The staff has been fantastic. I want to give them a bonus or something to show how happy I am."

"You'll think of something."

She mentioned the new layout, and he asked some questions, showing his interest. This feeling of having him in her corner made Britt think she could conquer the world.

"Do you need any help with tidying?" He rolled up his sleeves and glanced around. "Anything heavy that needs moving?"

She opened her mouth when an amused voice chipped in. "Hey there, Detective Romeo."

Oh God, why did Joyce keep embarrassing her? Mark grinned, as if reading her thoughts, then turned to her friend. "Joyce, how are you? Oh, since you're here, I can give you ladies an update."

Britt knew her mouth hung open in surprise when he had finished. "So all the rumors *were* true. Mr. Ferguson hired those creeps to wreck my bakery."

"I'm just glad you got those assholes off the streets," Joyce grumbled. "They were as bad as their boss, except Ferguson didn't want to get his hands dirty. Scumbag." She stepped closer. "I guess you can't say anything about the CEO's murder investigation, can you?" she whispered dramatically. "Clues, updates?"

"Joyce!" Britt exclaimed, but truthfully, she was curious, too.

Mark winked. "All I can say is we're getting somewhere. My captain held a media conference earlier. It should be on the evening news."

"Thank God for that." Joyce hid a yawn behind her hand. "I'm going to head out. Britt, I'll be here tomorrow morning with the contractor to start the renovations, so it'll be best if you give your staff the day off tomorrow. They should be able to finish the wall in one day, then start installing the display cabinets and shelving."

"Maybe I could hire you to renovate my condo," Mark said with an innocent look.

"As long as you could afford me!" Joyce called out as she left.

Mark helped Kevin with the remaining pieces of the broken bookshelf and took the tables and chairs out back by the garbage bins. "That's done," he said, brushing off his hands. "Anything else?"

"No, thank you. I'm going to close up. Everyone, thank you as always. We'll need to close the store tomorrow so Joyce can work on the wall, but I'll keep all of you up to date via email." She turned to Mark and gave him a big smile. "Let me see if Jacques and Thomas are ready to leave, then I'll get my things."

"I'll be here."

In the kitchen, Jacques was putting on his jacket. "I think another day, *chérie*, and we'll be back in business."

Britt couldn't contain her joy and clapped her hands. "You have been amazing! I can't thank you enough. I admit, I was worried you or the others might have started looking for other jobs."

"Of course not! You treat us very well, Britt. You stood

up against that horrible Ferguson man, and with everyone's love and support, you and I shall be ready to give pastry comas to our loyal customers."

She laughed—she loved Jacques's play on words. "Joyce needs to work her magic tomorrow, so you won't need to come in."

"Do you think we'll be in the way if we do?" Thomas asked unexpectedly. "She doesn't need to come into the kitchen. Nothing has been touched."

"Thomas has a point. We'll need all the time required to be ready for our grand reopening," Jacques added.

She pursed her lips. "I don't see why not. I'm just concerned that the dust will get in here. But if Joyce puts a thick piece of plastic over the entrance leading to the front room and tapes all the edges down properly..."

"*Voilà*, that should work. Thomas and I will use the back door, if that is all right."

Britt nodded, her decision made. "I'll talk to her tonight and let you know." She grasped Jacques's arm. "Thank you again."

He placed his hand over hers. "Anything for you, dear boss."

After Jacques and Thomas left, Britt locked up and set the alarm, then returned to where Mark was waiting. "Almost done."

In the office, she grabbed her stuff and made sure everything was secure. She was excited about the plans Joyce had shown her, and she couldn't wait to see how it progressed.

Outside, the early-evening rush hour had already started—the sidewalk was getting crowded. She manhandled the large padlock into place to secure the front and closed it with a loud click.

"What do you want to do, Britt?"

Startled, she looked at him. "I thought you had to get back to work."

"Nah, not right now. I need to clean up some paperwork, but I want to spend some time with my Nordic princess first."

How did Mark always manage to say the right things at the right time? She didn't want to go home yet—she was too excited about reopening the store—but spending time alone was never fun. It had been okay when she started planning Konditori because it kept her busy. But now with Mark in her life, she realized how much she craved having another person to share in her triumphs and challenges. "I feel like celebrating," she told him.

He arched a brow as he moved in close enough to brush against her. "I can think of a few ideas," he said quietly.

Britt couldn't move, couldn't speak. It was as if a bubble had surrounded them and everything else disappeared. She didn't hear people talking or cars honking—it was only Mark. She fought to get air into her lungs.

His hand clasped hers, warm and strong. "Tell me what you'd like to do."

If Mark had started walking, she would have followed him without a second thought. That scared and excited her at the same time. Yet here he was, asking her what she'd like to do, and Britt could feel herself falling for him just a little bit more.

A chorus of screams suddenly caught her attention, and Britt looked around until she spied the top half of a Ferris wheel. She pointed. "Let's go to the carnival."

He looked to where she indicated, then turned back, his expression skeptical.

"What?" she asked.

"Are you sure?"

She gave him a look. "Of course I am! Why are you asking?"

He grinned. "Because I love getting on the wildest, fastest rides they have. You don't have a problem with that, do you?"

She glanced again at the Ferris wheel. It looked like the tallest ride, and she enjoyed riding those. Everything else should be a piece of cake. "Lead on, brave knight," she told him.

Twenty minutes later, they stood in line to get in. The upbeat music and the kids running around in a frenzy lifted her spirits.

"So, what do you want to go on first?" He held up a batch of tickets.

"Let's walk around a bit, then maybe I'll see a ride I'd like to try."

It wasn't packed with people, but children bounced around them like Ping-Pong balls. "I'm scared I'm going to step on one!" she yelled out as another child zipped between them.

Britt paused in front of a ride consisting of huge tea-cups that sat four people each, and as she watched, they spun in circles. It also stayed on the ground. "How about this one?"

Mark gave her a cautious glance. "Do you get sick easily?"

She looked at him. "No, why?"

He got to the front and handed the employee several tickets. "Guess we'll find out."

There were no seat belts, just a circular bar in the middle.

"Make sure you hold on tight," he warned.

"Mark, it's an oversize teacup spinning on itself."

His grin was evil as he grabbed the bar. "Don't say I didn't warn you."

The ride started out innocently enough, but as it spun faster, she kept sliding around the teacup. Finally hanging on to the bar helped a bit but not enough. "What fresh kind of hell is this?" She had to scream over the suddenly loud eighties music blasting through the speakers around them.

"I said you needed to be sure!" Mark yelled back. "The ride isn't called Mad Teacup for nothing!"

It was a wild ride, all right. While the kids were screaming with glee, she was screaming to be let off. "Oh my God, how much longer?"

"Don't know. Just hang on!"

After what felt like an eternity, the spinning ride finally slowed down. When Britt managed to step out, her vision started spinning like those damn teacups.

Mark grabbed her arm. "Are you okay?"

"I need to sit down." They walked slowly until he grabbed both of her arms and lowered her to a bench.

She covered her face with a hand. "How could a teacup be so menacing?"

He laughed out loud. "I'm a detective, and I view everything with a critical mind. I honestly didn't think those teacups could knock us about like that."

His laughter, so full of life and contagious. She couldn't help but giggle along with him. "Wasn't there a mystery story by a famous author called *Murder in a Teacup*? Did she mean this?"

"Who knows?" He was still laughing as he wiped tears from his face.

Now that Britt knew what to expect, she eyed every ride with suspicion. The kiddie roller coaster looked okay, and it was a snug fit for the two of them. "I think I like this," Mark told her with a wink and sexy smile.

"Until I throw up on you," she retorted.

The highest peak was about twenty feet off the ground, so it didn't gain enough momentum to turn into a heart-dropping dip. But as the ride reached the end of the line, something happened that she'd never have suspected. The damn thing started to go backward.

"Oh, come on!" she yelled out, while Mark busted a gut, laughing beside her.

The ride was more disorienting, since she couldn't see where she was going, and the sudden dips and twists made her body ache in places she didn't know she had.

"You knew about this," she accused him when it was over. She felt like a pretzel, trying to untangle herself from the seat.

"Honestly, I didn't!"

No more rides. Instead, she told Mark they should play it safe with the games and walking through the attractions. One of them caught her attention—a maze of mirrors. "Let's try that one."

Bad choice. She got turned around so badly she had no idea how to get out. Britt tried not to panic as she slowly refocused, managed to get her bearings and finally made it outside.

"Hey." Mark wrapped her in a hug. How he knew she needed one, she didn't know and didn't care. She leaned into his embrace, inhaling his scent. "I guess that wasn't a good idea, either," he said.

"You think? How can this be called fun if all it does is scare people half to death?"

His body shook as he chuckled. "The kids seem to love it."

"The little tyrants have a warped sense of the word *fun*."

They walked through the carnival as the sun set and the bright, colorful lights were turned on. The atmosphere felt electric, and as more people arrived, the air around her came alive as a multitude of voices spoke in different languages. Britt stood in the midst of this diverse populace and loved every moment.

Although maybe not as much as standing beside a man who accepted her for exactly who she was.

Britt paused on that thought. Was she falling in love? This past week had seen some strange incidents, enough to last her a lifetime. Through it all, Mark had remained her constant rock, despite the unexpected and nerve-racking interview at the police station. He hadn't disappeared when her situation got rough—he'd been there to support, advise and protect. And in her world, that was saying a lot.

"I want to stay with you tonight."

Despite the frantic day he knew he would have tomorrow, Mark didn't want to leave. He stood just inside Britt's condo, his arms wrapped around her waist. He kissed her soft lips, losing track of time within her warm embrace.

She caressed his cheek. "Mark, I want that, too."

Something in her tone made him pause. He'd been absorbed in discovering all he could about his Nordic princess, but he was worried that he might have missed something important. Was he moving too fast? Being too demanding? He searched her face, and it was the small movement of her licking her bottom lip that told him she was nervous. "I'm overstepping, aren't I?"

She frowned now. "I'm not sure what you're talking about."

"I think I'm pushing your boundaries." He'd promised himself that he would let her take the lead between them, but the last few days had been so amazing, spending time with her, just chatting, touching, understanding how she ticked. He'd been enveloped in her scent, drowned every time she looked at him with those ocean-colored eyes, and he had wanted more—so much more.

Yet he kept forgetting that Britt might not be as eager.

Oh, he knew she liked being around him. She hadn't hesitated when they'd made love that first time—in fact, it was as if she couldn't get enough, and Mark had plenty of energy to satisfy her. But her slight hesitation now reminded him that she might want to take things slow, and she was right. With their busy jobs, they needed to make sure any relationship would work.

"No, you're not," she said softly. "Meeting you has pulled me into the light, so to speak. I've had my head buried in the sand for too long with work and ignoring my emotions. It's about time I enjoyed myself with people who want to be with *me*, instead of me using my bakery as a crutch.

"Having said that…" She sighed. "I do have a business to fix, and it couldn't happen at a worse time."

His heart did a funny thump in his chest. It sounded like Britt was ready to take the next step. He wanted to shout his joy but kept a tight leash on his excitement. "Oh, so you're saying you don't mind having me around."

Her smile was sweet. "Yeah, I guess I am saying that. Just…not tonight, Romeo."

He groaned. "Are you going to call me that now? I'm not sure I'm going to like it."

"What's wrong with Romeo?"

"He was a kid with family issues." He bit the inside of his cheek. *Ouch—like me.*

"He was also a romantic. Sort of like you."

"Okay, okay. Compliment it is." Speaking of family, he would have just enough time to see Mom before visiting hours were over. "I'll talk to you tomorrow?"

"You'd better."

He kept their kiss going as long as possible before Britt pushed him away, laughing. "You're stalling."

He waggled his eyebrows. "Of course I am."

That didn't work. Britt firmly turned him around and gently pushed him out. "Sorry, Romeo, but this Juliet needs her beauty rest."

"Like my Nordic princess needs to improve what's already perfect."

She smiled. "Smooth move. Not going to work, though, at least not tonight."

With a final kiss and a glance, she closed her front door.

Mark jogged downstairs, adrenaline flowing through him. Things couldn't get any better between them. He would surprise Mom with a quick hello and a chat before heading home.

Evelyn was off duty, but she had told him she'd updated all the nursing staff who worked on Mom's floor. The envelope she had given him a few days ago didn't get any hits on the AFIS database either. If the letter Mom had received wasn't from Dad, then who?

He stopped in front of the nurses station. "Hi there. I know it's late, but I'd like to see Mrs. Hawthorne before she goes to bed."

Mark had never met this nurse before—he'd never come to the hospital this late. She gave him an odd look that sent chills down his spine. "She has a visitor. But it's not Mr. Hawthorne—it's someone who comes at this time to see her for a few minutes."

He felt his blood start to boil. "And no one thought fit to tell me this?"

He ran down the hallway, the nurse calling after him, but he refused to listen. He slowed down to a stealthy walk as he approached the door, then stopped when he heard laughter.

Mom's laughter.

He pushed the door open without knocking and stopped dead in his tracks at what he saw.

Mom was sitting up in bed, chatting with a man who looked vaguely familiar. When he saw Mark, he stood up quickly, his face flushing red. Mom turned around and gasped, actually raising her hand to her throat. "Mark! What on earth are you doing here so late?"

Not her usual greeting. He stepped inside and let the door swing shut. "I was in the area and decided to come up and visit." He kept a hard glare on the stranger. "I hadn't realized you were entertaining other people."

"Oh, Mark, stop scowling. It makes you look like an ogre." She turned to the man. "Don't you remember Stanley?"

Mark couldn't breathe. It felt like he'd been hit with a baseball bat. Stanley Tucker—coach, mentor and the father figure Mark had desperately needed. This man had saved him from spiraling into a morass of hatred, revenge and depression. Stanley hadn't put up with Mark's shit and had coached him with prompts and a firm hand until Mark became the human being his mother deserved.

"Hi, Mark. Wow, your mom's right—you really have grown into a fine man." Stanley came around the bed, his hand extended.

"Mr. Tucker," was all Mark could manage to say.

"There's no need to be formal, young man." His coach gently grasped his hand and shook it. "Damn, it's good to see you."

Past memories flooded Mark's mind, the ones that meant something, recollections that he'd never forget. Someone else other than his mom had cared for his well-being, stamping their imprint on his conscience. The handshake wasn't enough, and Mark enveloped his mentor in a rough bear hug. "It's so good to see you, too," he whispered in a choked breath.

"Well, there goes my little secret," Mom said out loud, with a sniff for added emphasis.

He released Stanley with a couple of slaps on the shoulder. "Why was this a secret?" he asked, confused.

"Because I wanted to surprise you when I was home from the hospital." Her glance at Stanley was tender.

"That wasn't going to work. I asked the nurses to—" Mark stopped, changing his words at the last moment. "I asked them to keep an eye on you."

"You mean spying. You're letting work take over."

Mark changed the subject. "How did you two find each other?"

"I was scrolling through social media a few weeks ago and found your mom's profile. I was actually looking for yours," Stanley added. "But you don't have anything."

"Too busy to have one."

"I get it. Your mom and I chatted, then next thing I knew, she posted a picture of herself in the hospital." Stanley had a worried expression on his face, but Mark sensed these two weren't telling him everything. The dozen roses sitting on the side table was another hint. "I work late, but I've managed to squeeze in visits."

"Thanks for checking up on her." He meant it. Stanley was a great guy, and Mark felt more comfortable knowing there was someone in Mom's corner he could trust. "I'll leave you two lovebirds alone."

"What—Mark Hawthorne, what's wrong with you?" Mom's voice gave it away, even though her words didn't.

"Oh, nothing." He walked over and planted a big smoochy kiss on her cheek. "I'll try to come visit tomorrow. Work has ramped up, and I've got to be around when an arrest is made."

"I've been watching the news," she said, her voice filled with excitement. "Did you find Mr. Ferguson's killer?"

Mark glanced at Stanley, but his former coach held up his hands. "Nothing will leave this room. To be honest, I don't even watch the news."

He grinned. "We've identified a potential suspect. Now it's just getting our hands on him."

"I knew it! I knew you'd crack your investigation." She held out her arms. "Let me give my detective son a big hug and kiss before he goes."

"Mom," he groaned, but he let himself be fussed over while Stanley watched in amusement.

"Didn't I tell you Mark was doing well?" she said.

Stanley nodded. "Better than well." He grabbed Mark's shoulder. "I'm proud of you."

Mark left the hospital in good spirits. Not only did he manage to see Mom, but Stanley had reappeared at the most opportune time. He had suspected his mentor had a crush on Mom after her divorce, but he couldn't prove it. But watching them just now gave him hope that it was true.

It seemed like his life was filled with second chances, opportunities and love again.

* * *

Britt was mentally floating on air, and she couldn't concentrate on anything. Except for a pair of golden-brown eyes that made her feel like she was the only woman in the room. How the heck could she get anything done when Mark talked and looked at her that way? But he'd warned her he would stick around, so she'd have to get used to it.

She made a light dinner and placed that and her work laptop down on the kitchen table. She started to eat as it powered up, then paused while scrolling through some messages. Customers knew Konditori was closed, so she wasn't expecting anything important.

So when she saw the email labeled Please, it's urgent! Britt, can you help?! she hesitated, wondering if it was spam. However, looking at the email in Preview mode, she saw the message was from the very rich client who had sung her bakery's praises to her circle of high-class friends.

Britt, I hope you're well, and I hope you might help me—I'm desperate!

My husband and I are hosting a very important dinner Friday evening for the Defense Minister of Canada. I know, it's an honor for us!

It's only ten guests. I heard your bakery was wrecked during a break and enter—so sorry!—but I wanted to ask if there was any way you could supply some of your delicious treats? If you can't, is there anyone you could recommend? I really hope you can help me!
Thank you,
Angela Weinstein

Mrs. Weinstein was married to a powerful CEO who provided materials to build aircraft. She'd been to the store and asked exclusively for Britt's assistance in choosing the best pastries for her women's club meeting. Ever since that day, Mrs. Weinstein would place an order every week without fail. Even though she knew Britt's business wasn't functional at the moment, she had emailed anyway.

Under other circumstances, Britt would have made the painful decision to say no to the lady's request. However, Britt had to wonder if Mrs. Weinstein was entertaining more than a defense minister. Was it possible one of her guests could also be the prime minister?

"Damn it!" The opportunity was too good to pass up, but it would all hinge on Jacques.

She grabbed her phone. "Jacques, it's Britt."

"*Chérie*, you're calling later than usual. Is there something wrong?"

"Sort of." She hoped he understood her excitement behind this. "What do you think of providing an order for tomorrow evening?"

Silence on the other end. "Jacques?"

"My apologies. Your request stunned me for a moment."

Britt swore under her breath. "I'm sorry, Jacques, but this one is really important. Mrs. Weinstein will be entertaining ten very high-level guests tomorrow." She paused for emphasis. "I think one of them is the prime minister."

"*Merde!* Are you certain?"

"No." She wouldn't lie to him. "But Mrs. Weinstein let it slip that the defense minister will be there."

"That's good enough for me. There are only ten guests, so it will not be difficult to bake some specialties for Madame Weinstein. Thomas and I have finished cleaning and sorting the kitchen, and we've purchased the supplies. As long as your friend Joyce provides adequate protection from the debris, we shall be fine."

She wanted to squeal with delight. "You're amazing, Jacques, you know that? I could kiss you."

He laughed. "I will hold you to that promise, *chérie*. I'll be in the bakery about seven thirty tomorrow morning. I will contact Thomas to come in as well."

"*Merci beaucoup*, Jacques. I'll come in, too, and help keep the contractors' mess to a minimum. See you tomorrow."

Britt didn't know how much better today could be. If Mrs. Weinstein's guests offered even one compliment about Konditori, she would be overrun with customers. She would seriously have to consider a bigger space if that happened, and more staff...

She got up and grabbed today's mail, then turned on the television. As she flicked through the channels, she stopped on the twenty-four-hour news, listening to a female officer describing the progress on Mr. Ferguson's murder. She kept the information vague, and as reporters clamored for more details, she ended the news conference and walked off. She must be Mark's boss.

Britt flicked through more channels until she settled on an action movie, then slowly sifted through the envelopes. A couple of bills, something from her insurance company—probably a letter formalizing the activation of the renovations—a flyer insisting she vote for her MP candidate in her region. The four nominees, offering their best smiles, didn't interest her, but she guessed she'd better make time to find out what promises they were throwing out to voters.

The last piece of mail was a plain white envelope with her name and address. There was no return address on it. She cut the top with her mail opener and pulled out a single sheet of white paper. As she read it, the air around her seemed to turn ice-cold, and her body trembled, her hands shaking so badly the paper fell to her lap. Britt couldn't tear away her frozen gaze from the terrifying sentences typed in cap letters.

YOU ARE MAKING A MISTAKE THAT YOU'LL REGRET. I URGE YOU TO RECONSIDER.

Chapter 16

Britt didn't sleep for half the night—her mind poked and prodded that elusive message until she thought she'd pull her hair out in frustration. She finally managed to fall into a restless slumber, but her alarm clock rang much too soon.

She got in the shower and turned the nozzle to Cold, letting the icy water wash over her, dissolving the cobwebs in her head. She needed to think clearly, which she sure as hell hadn't managed last night.

The only person she could think of who would send such a note was Mr. Ferguson. His verbal intimidation toward her that past Monday morning was definitely reflected in that letter. What an asshole, sending her another threat after he was dead. Seriously?

She finished getting ready, putting on a pair of flared yoga leggings and a short-sleeved T-shirt. It would be hot in the kitchen, so she packed her duffel bag with three reusable two-liter bottles filled with water for herself and the guys.

At the last moment, she stuck the unknown letter in her purse. It was probably a good idea to call Mark and let him know about it. Not that she thought it would matter—the bakery CEO was dead.

"Ah, whatever," she mumbled. She had other important things to concentrate on.

The bus ride to the bakery was uneventful, but as she stared out the window, that letter came back into focus. The sooner she got rid of it, the better.

She thought she may as well text Mark and let him know. Maybe he could meet her at the bakery and take it off her hands.

Less than a minute later, her phone rang—it was Mark. "Britt, when did you get that letter?" he demanded. "What does it say?"

She repeated its contents. "It was in yesterday's mail. I assumed it was Mr. Ferguson being a jerk and threatening me again."

"What do you mean, *again*?"

She sighed. "Sorry, my mind is… I meant when he grabbed me in the alley and I kicked him."

"And he retaliated by sending those criminals to your store!" His voice rose on each word, but he suddenly stopped. "Damn it, I'm sorry, *vakker*. But you knew what Ferguson was like. You could have gotten hurt, and I'd never forgive myself."

She sighed again. Mark was right—she probably should have handled the situation differently, but Britt believed she gave Mr. Ferguson a very good hint on how she felt about his financial offer. "I'm sorry, too."

The bus arrived at her stop. "I'm at the bakery now," she told him. "I need to help with a special order I received last night."

"That's not a good idea. You don't know if that letter came from Ferguson or someone else."

"Who else could it be?" She blew out a breath. "Look,

if you want to grab it and check for fingerprints or whatever, I have it with me."

A pause. "Fine. I'll be there in about twenty." He hung up.

He was angrier than she expected.

She walked around to the back and entered the kitchen, where Jacques was prepping ingredients for tonight's event. "Do you need help with anything?" she asked, then looked around. "Where's Thomas?"

"He's a little late, but he promised he will come in."

"Okay, I'm going to get settled in. Joyce should be here between nine and ten, and I'll make sure the doorway to the front room is taped up tight before she starts the renovations. I'm just waiting for a friend to come by to pick up something first, then I'll help."

By the time she dropped her stuff in the office and got the padlock off the front door, Mark was strolling toward her. "Hi," he said in a short tone.

His stance spoke volumes—he *was* angry. "Mark, there's no need to get huffed up about this," she told him as he walked in.

"Britt, I have to. Do you have proof that letter came from Ferguson?"

She made a face. "Of course I don't."

"Then until I know for sure otherwise, I have to treat that note and envelope as criminal evidence. Do you have them?"

"They're in my office." Britt didn't wait for him, just turned on her heel and headed to the room. She plucked the envelope out of her purse and held it out.

He produced a plastic lunch bag. "Drop it in here for me."

She did as she was told, feeling a bit flustered at his

attitude. He was in work mode, which she now recognized after his treatment of her when she'd been questioned about her bracelet being found in Mr. Ferguson's car. "Was there anything else you needed?"

He tucked the evidence and bag into a jacket pocket. Now he looked at her, blinking. "What's that?"

"Do you need anything else? If not, I have a special order to make for a prestigious client." She left the office, but halfway to the boarded door, Mark grabbed her arm, and she stumbled. "Hey!"

"I'm sorry," he apologized. He released her and ran a hand through his hair. "I don't mean to sound like a bastard, but I'm worried."

"About what? The only person that note could have come from was Mr. Ferguson."

He stared at her, his expression growing more concerned. "Has Ferguson ever sent you a threatening letter before?"

"He's—" Britt stopped, uncertain. She let her mind travel back to when she first met the CEO. "No, he hasn't." She looked at him, the fear she fought and won against last night threatening to overwhelm her. "Mark…"

"There's a first time for everything. I won't know for sure until my forensics colleague analyzes the letter and tells me the prints belong to Ferguson. I'd ask you to stay home until I figured this out, but I know you won't." He moved close and brushed his fingers against her cheek.

"Any other time, I'd do whatever you asked, but tonight… It's really important."

"I get it." He took out his phone. "Where are you going?"

She gave him Mrs. Weinstein's name and address and the reason for the unexpected delivery.

"The defense minister will have plenty of security, but I'll be there as well. Find me when you arrive, and I'll drive you home after you're finished."

"Mark, do you really think…?" She stopped when she saw the stubborn expression on his face. "I don't have a choice, do I?"

"Nope."

She nodded, feeling a bit better about having him around.

"Hey." He brushed a thumb across her lips. "Don't worry. If you go in, get everything set up and then leave, things should be okay." He frowned. "You're not catering, are you?"

"No, Mrs. Weinstein hires help for that. We do it exactly as how you just described it."

"As soon as you're finished, come out to the car, okay?"

"Mark…"

This time, he shut her up with a kiss that left her speechless. "You were saying?" he asked, smiling.

Despite the late arrival of Joyce and the contractors, and the constant noise they created, the last batch of specialty pastries—a secret recipe from Jacques—was almost finished. Britt helped to get the boxes assembled, labels printed off and pasted on each container, then gathered a small stack of business cards to leave on the table where the pastries would be displayed. This was the adrenaline-induced excitement she loved—cooking, preparing, organizing. She loved fitting the pieces together until they created a masterpiece filled with pride, love and, of course, sweet deliciousness.

Jacques and Thomas even managed to bake a couple of cakes, both covered in icing the same colors as

Konditori—they even wrote the store name on each one with blue icing. She looked around in wonder at what her team had created—along with the two cakes, there was an assortment of Nordic and French tarts, Danishes, cinnamon rolls and cream-filled croissants. "Jacques, Thomas, you truly outdid yourselves. Bravo."

Jacques bowed. "*Chérie*, you and Konditori are in a class of your own. I'm proud to be part of your staff."

Thomas nodded. "I really like working here."

"Thank you both. Shall we get going?"

They carefully loaded the pastry-filled boxes onto special built-in shelves in the van. "Thomas, Jacques and I can handle it from here," Britt told him. "Thank you so much again for coming in on short notice. I'll lock up—I think the contractors have already left."

Britt hurried around to the front and went inside to grab her things—the plastic and tape still covered the door to the kitchen. She made sure the boarded-up front door was secure, then walked back down the alley to Jacques. Britt punched in the code for the security alarm and locked the back door. "Ready to roll," she announced as she got into the van.

Mrs. Weinstein's residence, located in the exclusive Uplands, was a twenty-minute drive east. They decided to get on the toll highway because the other routes would be busy with cars coming home from work. As they got off the ramp going south on Bathurst, traffic on this major street was packed.

"We can turn left here onto Flamingo Road," Britt said to Jacques, checking a map on her phone. "Then onto Golfer's Gate to Callaway Court."

Ten minutes later, they halted in front of an imposing set of black iron gates guarded by four security men. The enormous two-story stone mansion within the grounds was ablaze with light. Britt rolled down her window. "Britt Gronlund. I'm with Konditori Bakery," she announced. "Mrs. Weinstein is expecting us."

The guard repeated the information into a radio and was given the go-ahead. "Take your vehicle over there," he said, pointing out the direction. "There's a York Regional officer parked back there, too, a Detective Mark Hawthorne. He informed us that he's here to escort you home afterward."

"Yes, that's right. Thank you."

They were instructed to park next to a side entrance. As Britt got out and looked around, all she saw were luxury cars in front of the five-car garage located beside the home. Others were parked in an empty lot across the street, and surrounded by several security guards.

"Your new boyfriend must be worried about something if he's here," Jacques said.

She turned around, wondering about her baker's choice of words. "I guess he wants to make sure I get home safely."

"*Chérie*, I could drive you home."

"You've been up since six in the morning, Jacques. I'm sure you're exhausted. It just saves you an extra trip."

As she approached Mark's car, he climbed out, smiling. *"Vakker."*

"Hey." She wasn't sure if kissing him in front of security was a good idea.

Mark didn't seem bothered and pressed his lips to hers, firm and insistent. "All ready to go? Anyone else with you?"

The security lights were bright in the parking area, with waitstaff, security and valets jostling around each other to get to their destinations. "My head baker is with me." She turned and pointed out Jacques, standing by the front of the van. "My van is the bright pink one."

He laughed. "Why am I not surprised?"

When she turned back to him, though, Britt noticed Mark's gaze had narrowed as he glanced over her shoulder. "Is something wrong?" she asked.

"Everything's fine." He kissed her again. "I'll be here. Good luck with tonight."

As she and Jacques started bringing in their desserts, uniformed staff surrounded them in a chaotic, but organized manner.

Jacques whistled. "This will be a night to remember, I think."

"Over here!" a young woman called out to them. Her uniform was different from the others, with a name and her position printed on it—Sylvia, Head Caterer. She held a clipboard. "You are?"

"Britt Gronlund, Konditori Bakery." She nodded at Jacques. "And my head baker, Jacques Baudin."

"Ah yes, yours was a last-minute order." She smiled. "Mrs. Weinstein loves your pastries. I'm glad it worked out. This way."

She led them to a small butler's pantry off to one side of the huge kitchen. "The other pantry is being used for the dining ware and service," she told them. "Thank God it's a small number of guests, but it's a very exclusive dinner event. The serving trays are in the cupboards above you—choose whatever you require. You can leave it all in here—the waitstaff will bring everything out when ready. They've just served the hors d'oeuvres, so it'll be about two hours before the desserts are served. You have some time."

"Thank you."

"If you need anything, I'll be in the hallway where you found me." With a bright smile, she was gone.

Britt and Jacques took turns bringing in their food-stuffs until everything was stacked on the wide counters. "I think we should just get our desserts on the serving plates and call it a night," Jacques said quietly.

She nodded. "Good idea. It's not like we'll get close to Mrs. Weinstein to thank her."

They arranged everything accordingly. Britt heard detailed instructions shouted through the back rooms, all timed down to the minute. "You know, I thought about hosting catering events in the future, but if they're going to run it like a military operation, it's going to be a big nope in my books."

Jacques laughed. "For diplomats such as these, there's no choice. They have their schedules, and everything else works around them."

She glanced at him while he arranged the cakes on stands, then covered them with glass domes. "It sounds like you've catered something like this."

"Oui." He fussed over the Danishes. "Back home, my events were all planned. It made things easier."

Britt checked her watch—fifteen minutes to spare. "Looks like we're done. Honestly, I'd like to get out of here before we're descended upon by the waitstaff."

Just as they left the pantry, a contingent of servers hurried in their direction, and they flattened themselves against the wall as the horde went by. "So glad we're not staying," she muttered.

Once outside, Britt inhaled a deep breath of the cool summer air, scented with roses and other flowers. She stretched her arms over her head, looking out into the vast backyard lit with solar lighting and lanterns and bordered by tall hedges and colorful foliage. A stone pathway led from the extensive back porch to a small gate at the opposite end. Britt was curious as to what lay beyond. "Jacques, I'm going to take a walk around the backyard."

He raised a brow. "Do you think that's wise, Britt? What if a security guard finds you out there?"

She laughed. "We're at a party. They must expect guests to come outside and admire the scenery."

"Then let me join you before we leave. I just need to use the bathroom, if you don't mind waiting?"

"Of course not." She wished Mark was here to enjoy such a lovely sight with her.

Mark stood just within the open door leading out to the parking area. His body was on full alert, adrenaline pumping through his veins as he studied his immediate surroundings. The long, wide hallway before him was filled with staff, and as he tried to angle himself to look at the various faces that hurried past him, he realized it was impossible to pick out an individual person.

But something—or rather, someone—had triggered an internal red flag.

When he had been talking to Britt outside earlier, he noticed a man that looked vaguely like Ferguson's murderer—Mark had memorized every detail from the picture Myrna provided—but he wasn't sure. And if he wasn't sure, he couldn't alert security and cause a panic.

A young woman approached him. "Excuse me, are you a guest? The entrance is that way…"

He pulled out his badge. "I'm here to assist security. I'd like to take a quick look around, if you don't mind."

"Yes, of course." She passed by without another word. Mark walked casually down the hall, listening to the shouts and clatter of a dining service being prepared. Britt would be in the midst of that, which meant she'd be far away and, more important, safe from anything that might happen.

The end of the hallway revealed an enormous dining room. Everything had been set up, but the room was currently empty. Beyond, he saw several guests in another room, holding champagne glasses as they chatted. That had to be the reception area.

He walked quickly to the other side, his gaze searching. Here, Mark had to be more careful, as his presence would certainly be noticed among the bejeweled women and men in tuxedos. Bodyguards stood at strategic points around the room, their scrutiny taking in everything around them. He stood just behind the grand archway and studied the room, looking for any sign of his adversary. Nothing.

He turned around, intending to backtrack and try another hallway, when he heard several ladies laughing. He wasn't sure why it attracted his attention, but Mark looked over his shoulder...

Damn—it was him.

Before Mark got his wits together, the murderer left the reception via another door. But shit, that was the guy.

He went back the way he came, knowing that discretion was critical. He got outside and hurried to his car, then grabbed his walkie-talkie. "This is Detective Hawthorne!" he said urgently. "Get every available unit to Callaway Court. Ferguson's murderer has been spotted. No sirens and park at the corner of Callaway and Golfers Gate. The house is directly across, with all its lights on. Head for the main gate—I'll meet you there. We don't want to spook him."

He dialed another number on his work phone. "This

is Detective Mark Hawthorne with York Regional Police 4 District," he said. "I had a request for the Emergency Response Team to be on standby to assist with the arrest of an international criminal. He's been located."

He gave them the address, and then called Britt, but there was no answer. It was possible she was still busy with setting up, but...

Mark sent her a quick text instead, telling her to get in his car when she was finished and lock the doors. He knew she would freak out when she read the message, but hopefully she'd just do it and wait until he returned.

Now he had to alert security. If the murderer tried anything during the party...

Jacques remained in the guest bathroom for a few extra minutes to freshen up. The work he and Britt had done left him feeling sweaty and unfit for such esteemed company.

He checked his clothing, making sure he wasn't dabbed with icing or fruit, swiped away a few flecks of pastry and looked at himself in the mirror, thinking it would do. He needed to hurry as Britt was waiting for him in the gardens. He sighed. This detective was a very lucky man to be dating his boss.

When he opened the door, he stared in surprise at the familiar face before him. "What are you doing here, *mon ami*? I thought—"

Thomas slammed into him, knocking them both into the powder room, and locked the door.

Jacques's brain clicked into overdrive. He held his hands up, palms facing forward. "Now, now, there's no need for this..."

"Why do you have a cop following you?" he snarled.

"An officer? He is not following us. He's here to escort Britt home. He's waiting in his car."

"Not anymore. He came into the house and was hanging around in the hallway."

"I—" Jacques thought fast. If he wasn't careful... "There's no way the police can trace anything back to me. I've played my part leading the Ferguson protests, but I did not expect the police to make a surprise appearance at the funeral. I was lucky to get away. How do I know *you* haven't done something stupid?"

"Because I'm not in jail. But if we're not careful, we will be."

Jacques considered the situation. Thomas was agitated for some reason. "Where is the police officer now?"

"I don't know."

"Mon Dieu." Jacques knew he hadn't been spotted at Ferguson's funeral—he had kept himself well camouflaged. As for Thomas... "We must be very careful as we leave," he warned. "We cannot be seen together, and Britt will ask questions if she notices you."

Thomas stared at him. "I'm leaving the city tonight."

Jacques knew his brows went up at that. "What are you talking about? Why would you go?"

Thomas's expression held a chilling quality that made Jacques nervous. "Because I killed him."

Jacques felt his body grow still with dread at the terrifying response. "You killed an officer? What is wrong with you? Why would you do...?"

Thomas slashed his hand in a downward motion. "Not the cop. I wasted Ferguson."

Jacques's mind couldn't keep up with the horror story Thomas was telling him. The young man had twisted all of Jacques's hard work until he felt like he couldn't escape. "Why?" When Thomas didn't answer, he slammed his palm against the wall. "Why?" he demanded.

"Because he deserved it." Thomas spat on the ground.

Jacques swore. Their plan to terrorize Ferguson into backing off from buying neighborhood businesses had gotten messed up. Somehow, young Thomas had turned it into some kind of personal vendetta, and he didn't know why. "Is that it? Because he deserved it? You need to provide a better reason than that."

"You told me what he's done to you—to other small-business owners. His death could be a warning to Mighty Big Bakery to back off."

"Or it might spur them on, to continue his legacy." Jacques shook his head—where had he made his mistake? His own revenge against Ferguson and Jacques's business partner—who had sold him out behind his back—had gone horribly wrong. It wasn't supposed to go this far... not all the way to murder. He'd have to figure out how to extricate himself from this mess. "*Mon ami*, I think we need to back up and reassess our situation."

"Too late for that." Thomas pulled a gun out from behind his back. A silencer was attached to it.

"*Merde.*" Jacques weighed his options—all of them looked bleak. "There's no need for that," he said gently, keeping his hands out in the open. "I'm not going to say anything to anyone. Just leave—leave the city, the country even. Please, don't hurt a friend."

Thomas hesitated, and Jacques saw his chance, grabbing the young man's weapon and smashing it against the wall. It went off with a muffled pop. Suddenly, Thomas dipped low, and Jacques howled in pain, his eyes watering from the excruciating blow to his crotch. His grip loosened, but before he could regain his balance, hot, searing pain burned in his leg and stomach. Jacques slumped to the ground, his vision darkening as Thomas pushed him out of the way to make his escape.

Britt glanced at her watch again—Jacques had been gone for over fifteen minutes. Then she realized he must have found an opportunity to schmooze with the guests. "What a guy," she said out loud. She'd take her stroll through the beautiful garden, then head to Mark's car and go home.

She walked down the few steps into the sunken space and stayed on the main path. The grass was a lush green beneath the lights, and on an impulse, she took off her sneakers and walked through it, the soft blades tickling her toes, the earth cool beneath her feet. It felt amazing.

She reached the other end of the garden. Here, the tall gate led out onto small undulating hills with sandbanks in between—a golf course, and to either side of her, the blackness of a forest.

Odd, the gate didn't have a lock on it. She assumed the course and surrounding area were possibly so secure that a lock wasn't needed. It must be nice to live in this type of luxury.

She heard footsteps from behind. "Holy crap, Jacques, you took your time," Britt called out to him as she turned. "Did you score an opportunity to talk with Mrs.—" She stopped.

Thomas stood a few feet away. "Hey, Britt."

"Um, hey." She glanced at the house. "Why are you here? I thought I mentioned Jacques and I wouldn't need you tonight. We're already finished."

"Oh." He laughed, but it didn't sound right. "Sorry,

I guess I thought…maybe you and Jacques would need help cleaning up."

"No, we're done, thank you. You can go home. You've had a long day." She had no idea how she kept her voice steady—her body was ready to bolt because something didn't feel right in this conversation.

"Would you like a ride home?"

Her stomach was turning into knots of fear. There was no reason for Thomas to be out here—none. And the way he was acting in front of her was not the same young man who worked in her bakery. "No, thanks. Jacques said he'd take me home," she lied.

"Oh." Thomas scratched his head. "I thought your detective boyfriend was driving you back."

Thomas couldn't know that—there was no way. Britt swallowed the large lump in her throat. "He's supposed to, but he hasn't come back from wherever he is. Actually, I think I'll go wait for him at the car." Her laugh was forced. "I don't want to have an officer waiting on me."

She almost screamed when her cell phone pinged with a text. She dug it out of her bag and looked at the screen— Mark. He had called and texted several times, but she had turned the phone off when she and Jacques were in the house.

She glanced at Thomas, who had remained still. Something very spooky surrounded him, like a bad aura, and if she didn't get away, Britt was scared she'd be sucked into it. "It's Jacques," she lied again, hoping it sounded convincing. "He's wondering where I am." She started typing a reply.

HELP. IN BACK GARDEN!

"Don't do that."

Startled, she looked up. Thomas was swaying from side to side, as if listening to a song only he could hear. "Come on, I'll take you home."

"No." She backed up until she bumped into the iron gate, slipping her phone into her pocket. "I told you, I have a ride."

"Not anymore." His voice had gone quiet, menacing.

"Thomas, what the hell do you want?" she demanded in a loud voice. Despite the fear coursing through every limb, she had to ask the question.

"I did something bad, and the police are after me." He took a step forward. "If I kept you as a hostage, your boyfriend would back off. I just want to get out of the country."

That was a big OH, HELL NO in her mind.

Britt didn't think, just reacted. She threw her shoes and bag at him, scoring a direct hit in his face, then raced out the gate, turning left and rushing into the depth of the trees.

She immediately slowed down, wincing as her bare feet stepped on small rocks and stubbed against tree roots. She looked over her shoulder but couldn't see Thomas.

She hunkered down against a tree, her breaths panting out in short gasps. Her instincts had taken over, allowing her to escape a potentially dangerous situation. As she fought to gather her wits, she heard shouting. "York Regional Police! Remain where you are and get your hands in the air!"

Mark's voice. "Oh my God." Britt started crawling in the opposite direction, desperate to stay out of sight until he came for her. Bile rose in her throat, her fear a tangible thing as it wrapped around her ankles to slow her down.

"It's okay. You're okay," she whispered to herself. She used her hands to feel her way around tree trunks and thick bushes. A noise caught her attention, and turning around, the glare of a flashlight wove erractically behind her. Britt heard a shout—was that Mark? She wasn't sure, and decided to keep going.

Britt looked around, hoping to spot something for reference. She knew there was another house beside the Weinsteins' and carefully crawled in the general direction. She needed to gain some distance before attempting to call Mark.

Suddenly, a bright light illuminated the forest in front of her, the trees a stark silhouette of dark angles. Glancing behind her, a portion of the golf course appeared. Several officers ran by, but she didn't see Thomas.

And that flashlight continued to dog her steps. Damn it, was it Thomas? "Shit!" She got to her feet and stumbled through the undergrowth, using what light she could navigate by to get away from the mayhem unfolding behind her.

She desperately wanted to call Mark but was terrified that if she hesitated for too long, Thomas might find her. On that thought, she took her phone out and placed it on Mute—if Mark called, it'd vibrate instead, alerting her but not Thomas.

Several agonizing minutes later, Britt spied a square of light some distance away—a window. Sobbing quietly with relief, she got down on her hands and knees again to save her feet, and crawled as fast as she dared, occasionally bumping into a tree trunk, or swearing under her breath as she pulled her tangled hair out of an errant bush. She stopped, noticing the darkness around her had receded—it looked like all the security lights at the golf course were turned on. The police should be able to catch Thomas.

Unless he had escaped through the forest like she was doing and was following her. With all the illumination, he could easily find her if she didn't get her ass moving.

Britt focused her waning strength on that square of light, which meant a house, and people inside who could keep her safe.

God, she hoped Mark was okay. Chasing Thomas like that when he could be armed with a weapon...

Suddenly, she stopped and crouched down beside a large tree as crashing noises caught her attention. It was difficult to tell how far away it was, but as Britt listened, she realized it was getting closer.

"Britt!"

She heard her name, but with fear coursing through her body, it could be Thomas trying to draw her out of hiding.

She'd have no choice but to make a run for it.

Tucking her hair down the back of her T-shirt, she worked out a path of least resistance and got moving, trying to be careful where she placed her feet. A couple of minutes later, she slapped her hand over her mouth to muffle a cry of pain—she had stepped on something sharp that pierced her foot. Not missing a beat, she scrambled to find what broke her stride—a piece of broken branch. She bit her tongue as she yanked it out quickly, then half hobbled, half hopped the rest of the way.

Her phone vibrated. *Damn it, could this be a worse time?* If it was Mark, he'd have to wait while she made her last dash to safety. It felt like every piece of plant life was trying to ensnare her, but fear gave her the strength to fight through the foliage that blocked her escape.

And then, nothing. Britt stumbled to a stop in a clearing

and looked around, breathing hard. The ground seemed level beneath the faint illumination of the golf course security lights. She took hurried, though careful steps through the knee-high grass. Her foot throbbed in pain, punctuated with sharp stabs that almost had her crying in frustration. She knew it was bleeding, and no doubt infected as well. Sparing a few precious minutes, she stripped off her T-shirt and bound it around her foot, feeling the thick stickiness of blood along her fingers.

Just a little farther—at the edge of the clearing, a thick hedge stood like a sentinel, and there, in the middle, a gate.

"Almost there, almost there," she chanted softly. She used her toes on the injured foot to propel herself forward until her hands brushed against the textured leaves, then moved to her left until cool metal replaced the natural border.

The light from the large picture window was bright, a beacon that called out to her. It stretched far into the backyard, which allowed her to find the gate's latch. She carefully lifted it and looked over her shoulder. No one was behind her, but Thomas would easily see her silhouette from the edge of the forest if he made it this far.

Haunted by the thought, Britt slid inside. She moved to the side so that the hedge hid her from view and looked around. Several feet in front of her, a swimming pool lay covered in a dark tarpaulin. Thank God she hadn't charged straight ahead—she would have fallen in. Around it was a stone patio and beyond, the unbroken darkness of grass—a lot of it. The backyard was huge. She had a lot of space to walk through before getting close enough to yell for help.

She gritted her teeth and started limping, spurred on

by the distant shouts behind her. As soon as she managed to get inside, she'd call Mark and let him know she was safe...

Britt hesitated, listening. Above the shouting, she also heard a dog barking. Was it a police dog? Or something else?

When she looked at the window, she froze in her tracks. The large shadow of a canine danced across the grass, and at the window, she spied a German shepherd. It was going wild, jumping up and down, teeth bared, its baleful stare locked on her.

Damn it. Britt needed to weigh her options. If the homeowner released the dog into the backyard before she made it to the door to explain her situation, she didn't stand a chance. It was possible the police had informed anyone living in the area to keep their doors locked and be on the lookout.

"Shit!" She looked around quickly, then took a closer look at a tall square object just beyond the window's light. As she hobbled toward it, she realized it was a garden shed. Perfect, she could hide in there until Mark got her.

A small light winked on when she opened the door. It was a good size, large enough for her to stand in. On the walls, various garden tools hung neatly in rows. Britt grabbed a long-handled aerator, its numerous spikes a couple of inches long. If Thomas opened that door, he'd get a face full of sharp metal.

Mark stood in the middle of a group of security guards and police officers. "I need your help. The police have been hunting a dangerous criminal the past couple of days, and I saw him in this house." Mark gave them a brief summary of the Ferguson murder case. "We can't have a panic on our hands." He pulled out a picture. "This is the man we're looking for."

Several more security guards had hurried over. "I saw that guy," one of them said. "I don't know how he got in, but I saw him hanging around that pink bakery van."

"We have to find him." Mark's anxiety went up with every second that passed without hearing from Britt. "My men will cover the exits. Go inside and take a look around—"

His phone pinged. When he read the message from Britt, his adrenaline skyrocketed. "The back garden! Move!"

He took off at a full run, his officers and several security guards trailing behind him. In the distance, he saw a flash of white and Britt's terrified expression before she bolted. A man was about to give chase.

"Goddamn it!" He ran faster. "York Regional Police!" he yelled. "Remain where you are and get your hands in the air!"

The murderer he'd been hunting sped away, running straight onto the golf course. If they didn't catch him in time, he'd disappear into the darkness.

"Go after him!" he shouted. "Radio for help to block off the course and get some lights on!" Mark turned to the man beside him. "I heard you guys are one of the best ERT units in Canada," he said to Staff Sergeant Victor Moore.

The commander smiled, but it wasn't a friendly expression. "My boys are already circling around the course, detective. I'll follow your men. Don't worry, we'll find him."

As Moore raced off, Mark noticed something white in the grass that worried him—Britt's sneakers, and nearby, her bag. He veered left, following her course. Somehow, she'd already reached the blackness of the forest beyond.

"Britt!" he yelled. He dug a flashlight out of his pocket and switched it on. Thick stands of tree trunks and undergrowth hindered his progress as he pushed through. How the hell did she manage to get through this stuff?

Just then, the remaining security lights at the golf course turned on, illuminating everything in a bright white glare. It didn't quite reach back here, but it offered Mark a little more light to see by.

Several anxious minutes later, his flashlight picked out a gaping hole. The branches were recently broken, still hanging by pieces of bark. He kept going, turning one way, then the other, trying to see through the bush and wondering if she was hiding somewhere.

Something glistened wet on the ground a few feet ahead, and Mark bit back a cry when he realized it was blood—*shit*. "Britt! Where are you?" he yelled out. No answer.

Swearing, he pulled out his phone and dialed her number, hoping she'd pick up or he could hear it ringing in the undergrowth. Nothing.

He continued following her path, shoving at anything that got in his way. He stopped when his walkie-talkie went off. "Staff Sergeant Moore reporting." The ERT commander possessed a thick British accent. "Perpetrator has been captured. Repeat, perpetrator captured."

He hit the send button. "Good work, all of you. Take him to the precinct. I'll be there shortly. The rest of you, get back to the Weinstein residence and make sure everyone's okay. I'm looking for someone—I'll radio when I'm done."

The golf course security lights barely penetrated this far into the forest. Britt must be terrified, hunkered down somewhere and staying quiet until she thought it was safe.

The trees thinned out into a meadow, but before he continued, his trembling fingers wrapped around long, silky strands of blond hair caught on a bush. He was on the right track, but he was frightened for her, wondering what condition she'd be in.

Mark ran across the meadow, following a faint beaten path through the long grass until he stopped at a thick border of hedge reaching almost ten feet in height. As he panned his flashlight, he spied the half-open gate.

Britt must have gone through here.

He opened the gate wider so that he could slip inside. It was eerily quiet, as if the air held its breath.

He jumped at the sound of a dog barking. He looked towards the mansion and saw a large German shepherd thrashing against the glass doors and baring its teeth. The homeowner was nowhere in sight.

Mark started walking the length of the extensive back-yard, being careful not to get too close to the edge of the pool. Under his flashlight's glare, he spied a garden shed.

He stopped and looked around. There was nowhere anyone could hide unless they buried themselves beneath the thick hedge.

As a precaution, Mark hunkered down low and swept the flashlight's beam around—nothing.

He rose and blew out a tense breath. With a bloodied foot, Britt wouldn't get too far. And a very angry guard dog would make her think twice about going to the house for help.

He glanced back at the garden shed and started toward it. If he were in Britt's position, he would pick this place to hide and choose a sharp weapon to defend himself.

However, Mark hesitated with his hand on the door handle. He couldn't hear anything, even when he placed his ear to the cool metal. He chewed the inside of his cheek, thinking.

"Britt, it's Mark. Are you in here?"

Silence.

"*Vakker*, it's okay, you can come out. We've caught Ferguson's murderer."

Still nothing.

If Britt was as scared as he guessed, she wouldn't trust anyone right now. She could attack first without realizing it was him.

He looked at the door, noting the hinges—it would swing outward.

Mark stepped to one side, keeping his flashlight up. "Britt, I'm going to open the garden shed door." Tensing himself for a violent reaction, he yanked the door open.

Suddenly, a garden tool with spikes stabbed the air, followed by a pained scream.

"Britt!" He backed away, dodging as she swung her weapon wildly. "Britt, it's me! *Vakker!*"

She stopped, her green eyes wide and unfocused in the flashlight's beam. "Mark?"

He pointed the flashlight at himself so she could see him clearly.

With a sob that tore at his soul, she dropped the garden tool and reached out for him.

Mark snatched her into his arms, crushing her to him, crooning nonsense words as she cried, loud, wracking sounds that broke his heart. He hid his face in her hair, inhaling the sweet scent that was only hers, then kissed her, hoping she'd forget everything until it was just him in her mind. "Britt, shh, it's okay. I'm here, *vakker*. I'm right here."

He swung her into his arms and cradled her against his chest. She had buried her face into the curve of his neck, and thank God, her sobbing had quieted down—he'd almost become a gibbering mess when he heard it.

Mark carried her through the backyard and to the front of the neighboring house. The dog had continued its frenzied barking while he walked past the home, heading to the Weinstein house so that Britt could get much-needed care before being transported to the hospital.

Chapter 17

The sound of rain.

Britt slowly became aware of other noises, although her eyes remained closed—footsteps, low voices. Her hands touched something cool and soft, and when she moved her fingers, she realized they were bedsheets. Was she at home? Had it only been a nightmare?

She cracked open an eyelid and squinted at the bright light slamming into her eyeball. She groaned softly and raised her hand to block it out.

"Vakker."

His deep voice, strong yet tender at the same time. She took a breath and winced at the various aches and pains. Her right foot throbbed, and in a moment, she remembered what had happened—Thomas's uneasy appearance, the escape through the woods, hiding in the garden shed…

Britt slowly opened her eyes and held still as her vision adjusted to the well-lit room, and the first thing she saw was Mark. He leaned over her, his brown-gold eyes filled with concern. "How are you feeling?"

"Sore." She didn't recognize her surroundings. "Where am I?"

"At the hospital. The way your foot looked scared me, and you were pretty scratched up. I wanted to be sure you hadn't picked up an infection."

Damn. She moved her limbs, reassuring herself that nothing had been broken.

"Did you want to sit up? Have some water?"

She nodded, not taking her eyes off him as he raised the bed to an elevated position, then lifted a glass of water with a straw to her mouth. "Not too fast."

She took a few sips, the cool liquid quenching her dry throat.

"Girl, what on earth have you been up to *now*?" Joyce appeared in her line of vision.

"Hey. Um, I'd say nothing, except..." She paused, feeling confused.

"We all know that isn't true. You look like something the cat dragged in."

"I certainly feel like it." Britt was relieved that Joyce was here—right now, her friend offered a sense of balance. Mark, on the other hand... Well, he'd been her anchor in a storm of fear and loneliness. But it didn't feel steady right now... More like it wanted to cast off, and she fought to keep it in place. "Joyce, could I have a few minutes with Mark, please?"

Her friend's eyes widened, almost as if she sensed what Britt was thinking. "Of course. I'll be right outside."

As soon as the door closed, she wrapped her hand around his. "What the hell happened? Why was Thomas there?" Her mind snapped on to another troubling thought. "Where's Jacques? I haven't seen him."

Mark raised her hand to his lips, and she gasped at seeing bandages covering her palm. "You need your rest, but let me try to explain it. It seems that Jacques and Thomas were more than just bakers."

"No." Britt didn't want to believe Jacques had anything to do with Mr. Ferguson's murder.

"Jacques Baudin led the protests against Mighty Big Bakery. Seems he owned his own business for a long time with a business partner. Unfortunately, Ferguson convinced the partner to sell and bought it under Jacques's nose. By the time Jacques found out, he'd lost everything." Mark tilted his head. "He never said anything to you?"

"Nothing." Poor Jacques.

"He took matters into his own hands. Raised quite a crowd of rebels, too. Jacques used scare tactics to slow down construction or force employees to quit."

"Jacques, damn you." She squeezed Mark's hand. "Is he going to jail?"

"I don't know. Thomas shot him at the Weinstein house, but I haven't found out why. Jacques is all right, and I'm hoping he can fill in what happened."

Britt nodded. "What about Thomas? What's his story?"

Mark swore. "He's not talking, but we discovered enough criminal evidence against him that will earn him jail time here or extradition."

"Are you saying I hired criminals?" Britt raised herself from the bed as her voice cracked on the last word. "How did— Thomas had all the paperwork!"

"Documents can be deceiving." He gently grasped her shoulders. "It's okay, lie back down."

She rested back on the bed.

"I'm just glad you're all right, *vakker*." He leaned down, and she felt his warm lips on her forehead. "I'd never forgive myself if anything happened to you."

She looked at him. Mark's eyes were suspiciously shiny. "This wasn't your fault. Why are you blaming yourself?"

He swiped at his face with his other hand. "I should have caught him before he got to you. If I had been better at understanding the clues, maybe I could have prevented…"

"Hey, hey!" She reached over and grabbed his face, then pulled him down until he was level with her. "You did your job. You caught the men responsible, and that's important. Maybe I shouldn't have run off, but you came after me and brought me back safely. And I adore you for that."

His eyes widened in surprise, and she bit her lip, realizing what she'd just said. But she knew it was the truth, and she shook his head gently to emphasize it. "Did you hear me, Mr. Detective?"

Something changed in his expression, a look that made her skin tingle with goose bumps. Britt shivered, but heat flushed her face until she knew it was bright pink.

"Say it again," he told her, his voice rough.

"What? That I shouldn't have run away from you?" she teased, but the look in his eyes shut her up.

"Try again."

Britt hesitated, feeling suddenly shy. Somehow, her perception of Mark had recently shifted. A part of her recognized a kindred spirit, a man who cared for and had protected her without question during one of the scariest moments in her life. She wanted to tell him her feelings, and she had the perfect way to do it. "Ah, Mark," she crooned in her best French accent. "Do you know how much I adore you? *Mon cher*, talk the language of love to me."

His look had her laughing so hard her stomach hurt. "It annoys me that I know you're imitating that lovestruck cartoon skunk." He groaned out loud. "It annoys me even more that I like it."

She giggled. "I'll have you know I don't talk about my

favorite cartoons with just anyone." She paused. "You're pretty special."

He kissed her for a long moment, his mouth insistent and filled with promise. "And you are my Nordic princess."

"Mark, you're absolutely wonderful! Have I told you that?"

He tried not to roll his eyes as he smiled. "Yes, Mom. Several times, actually."

Britt was in the same hospital as Mom, so after making sure she was comfortable, he'd ridden the elevator to his mom's floor for a surprise visit. He'd stopped short when he'd seen Stanley standing over Mom, combing her hair. "Sorry," Mark apologized, backing up. "I'll come back later."

"Don't be absurd." She patted Stanley's hand. "We were watching the news. Congratulations on catching your killer."

He always appreciated her enthusiasm. "How are you feeling?"

"So much better." She looked at Stanley. "And Stanley's been a sweetheart. He's been looking after the house and watering my plants."

Stanley touched her chin with a finger. "It's the least I can do."

Wow, these two. He and Britt were very close to that level of relationship, and he couldn't wait until she decided to take that next step. "Thanks for helping out, Stanley. I really appreciate it."

He waved a hand. "Anything for—" He stopped, his surprised expression flushing a deep red. "You're welcome."

"I gotta run, but I'll come around tomorrow, okay?"

"Where's my kiss?" she demanded.

"Mom." But he obliged her as always, presenting his cheek to be noisily smooched.

He finally managed to escape and headed back to Britt's room, but she was sound asleep.

"She just drifted off," Joyce said quietly, closing the door behind them. "Poor thing's been through a lot."

He nodded, his mind on work, thinking on finishing up some loose ends.

"Are you in love with her?"

Startled, Mark stared at her. Her dark eyes danced with amusement. "We've only been seeing each other a week."

"Okay then, do you care for her?"

He stopped. "I'm not sure why you're so curious about us."

Joyce halted beside him, her demeanor now serious. "Britt is a dear friend, and I don't want to see her get hurt. Emotionally speaking."

"I'm not going to do that." This felt like an interview. "I mean, she's a big girl and can handle herself."

"She certainly can." He crossed his arms. "Where are you going with this?"

"I just wanted to be sure if you were the right guy for her."

Mark couldn't figure out where Joyce was going with this, but he was going to put a stop to it. "I know you're her friend, and I'm glad you're in her life. I'm mature enough to understand my feelings and how to act on them, but in the end it's for Britt to decide if she wants a relationship with me."

Joyce suddenly smiled, her teeth bright against her dark skin. "Well said." She grabbed his arm. "Gotta run, I have a bakery to finish. Grand reopening is planned for next week, and Britt should be on her feet by then."

This past week had been a roller coaster of tension involving...everything. Now that he could take a breath, Mark collapsed into his car, his body limp and boneless. Captain Fraust had run with the final points of his investigation at this morning's news conference, sparing him the spotlight and the thousands of questions he knew would bombard him.

He wanted to go home, but he was too wired despite the exhaustion. Joyce's words rang in his head. He assumed she was being protective, and he got that. But her conversation sounded like she had her doubts, which of course didn't make sense. Obviously he cared for Britt; nothing had changed in that department. If anything, his feelings had only grown stronger in the short time they'd known each other.

But he also understood the merit of not rushing into things—he had learned that lesson the hard way in his early twenties. And Britt had displayed that same caution, which he had no problem with. Mark would respect her thoughts and fears, just as he was sure Britt would do the same thing for him. And when it was time for them to talk and take the next step, they would do it together.

Restless, he drove to the precinct and headed for his office. After his computer booted up, he started working, feeling his mind get into the flow of providing proper documentation. About an hour later, he had an organized file folder containing everything he'd collected.

Mark hadn't found the chance to thank Myrna properly for her hard work on this case—it had been nonstop since yesterday. He sent her a text and wished her a good weekend.

Ten seconds later, his cell phone rang. "Hey," she said. "How's it going? Is your girlfriend all right?"

He'd never said anything definite about being in a relationship, but it seemed everyone thought that way. "Yeah, she's fine. I'm in the office cleaning up."

"Seriously? I'm downstairs. I called because I have news for you, so come down and I'll show you."

Curious, he took the stairs and walked down the hallway, his footsteps echoing eerily in the empty space until he knocked on her door and stepped inside. "What's up?"

Her head appeared from behind a screen. "I'm surprised you're here. I'd thought you would take a day off."

"I wanted to finish up." He grasped her shoulder. "Seriously, thanks for all of your help. You've been outstanding."

"We make a great team, Hawthorne. And this was an interesting case." She pressed a few keys. "So, two things. That envelope and threatening letter you gave me to check? Mr. Ferguson's fingerprints were all over it, so it must have come from him."

Mark nodded. "I figured as much, but thanks for confirming it." He watched as information scrolled across Myrna's computer screens. "And the second thing?"

"Cynthia finished working on that other investigation you asked for help with."

What the hell—she was talking about Dad. His body shook with trepidation. "What did she find?" he whispered in a hoarse voice.

Myrna typed something and several photos of fingerprints appeared, along with a picture of Dad's brooding expression. "She's not sure if he was there when your mom fell down the stairs."

"For God's sake." Either way, Dad had breached his bail conditions by entering Mom's home.

"However, with some of her famous ingenuity, Cynthia discovered his workplace." Another moment of typing, and another photo appeared. "He's been working on a farm north of here. He's been arrested for assaulting the farmer and his wife. Cyn made sure to provide every bit of criminal evidence so that he stays behind bars this time." She glanced up at him.

Mark felt light, as if a terrible weight had been lifted off his shoulders. After all this time, he could breathe easier, knowing Mom was safe. Having Stanley in her life again was an added bonus. "Thanks, Myrna. I needed that."

"I thought that would make your weekend better." She shut down the computer.

He had an idea. "I'm starving. Do you want to grab something?"

She smiled wide. "Sure. I've got just the place. You can update me on last night. Man, I wish I had seen the ERT in action."

Britt stood by the front window of Konditori, looking out onto dozens of customers who had been waiting since the crack of dawn.

She turned in a slow circle, taking in the wonder that Joyce had created. The front room was larger, allowing more guests to come inside. The walls were a pale shade of muted gray, a stunning contrast to the vibrant pink on the outside walls. New furniture that allowed more space, a wider display counter and plenty of hidden storage cupboards made the room look brighter and bigger.

"What do you think?" Joyce asked, standing at the office doorway.

She laughed. "You could tap me with a stick and I would fall over, that's how stunned I am. The bakery…"

She paused, searching for words. "It feels like an extension of me."

"That's exactly what I was going for."

Britt watched as her friend unbuttoned and rolled up her sleeves. "What are you doing?"

Joyce gave her a look. "Did you think you could handle this mob with only the staff and you? Betty's going to help Jacques, so I'm helping behind the counter."

Britt shook her head. "Joyce..."

Her friend wagged her finger at her. "No *but*s. I'm happy to help."

The first pastries had already been stocked in the display case. Kevin, Betty, Jasmine and Oliver were all smiles as they approached. "This looks amazing!" Betty exclaimed, wrapping her arms around Britt's waist. "I'm so proud of you."

"I'm proud of everyone. Honestly, without you all, this wouldn't have happened."

"No, *chérie*, all of this is because of your hard work." Jacques, in his usual apron and baker's hat, stood by the kitchen door. Fully healed, he had provided evidence that resulted in a hefty fine but no jail time. He was more than happy to pay that.

"And your delicious concoctions. Which reminds me— we'll need to think of some new recipes."

"But of course. Now, if you will excuse me, there is baking to be done!" He disappeared into the kitchen, with Betty running after him.

Today would be a zoo, but she wouldn't have it any other way. As she watched everyone making last-minute preparations, she wished Mark was here. Maybe work had gotten in the way...

The sudden loud wail of a police siren startled her—it

was close. As she looked out the window, two police vehicles pulled up to the curb and three officers stepped out. But the fourth...

Mark.

She ran to the door to unlock and open it, then stood there, watching as he flashed his badge so that he could get through the crowd. A collective groan emanated from the customers.

"Don't worry, we're here to help. You all look like a hungry bunch," he yelled.

Britt could only stare as he came up to her, a big smile on his face. "I—I assumed you'd be at work."

He wrapped his arms around her waist. "And miss this most important day for you? Oh ye of little faith."

The officers who came with Mark organized the boisterous crowd into a semblance of a lineup.

"Come on, let's get Konditori open for business," Mark shouted.

A collective cheer rose from the crowd, but Britt only had eyes for Mark as he melded his mouth to hers.

Oh, how sweet life was going to be.

* * * * *

Romantic Suspense

Danger. Passion. Drama.

Available Next Month

Guarding Colton's Secrets Addison Fox
Her Private Security Detail Patricia Sargeant

....

Murder At The Alaskan Lodge Karen Whiddon
Safe In Her Bodyguard's Arms Katherine Garbera

LOVE INSPIRED

Cold Case Tracker Maggie K. Black
Her Duty Bound Defender Sharee Stover

Larger Print

....

LOVE INSPIRED

Yukon Wilderness Evidence Darlene L. Turner
Hidden In The Canyon Jodie Bailey

Larger Print

....

LOVE INSPIRED

The Baby Assignment Christy Barritt
Uncovering Colorado Secrets Rhonda Starnes

Larger Print

Keep reading for an excerpt of a new title
from the Intrigue series,
THE RED RIVER SLAYER by Katie Mettner

Chapter One

They shouldn't be here. Mack Holbock had had that thought
since they were first briefed on the mission. The hair on
the back of his neck stood up, and he swiveled, his gun at
his shoulder. The area around the small village was silent,
but Mack could feel their presence. Despite what his commander said, the insurgents were there and ready to take
out any American at any time. The commander should
have given them more time for recon. Instead, he executed
a mission on the word of someone too far away to know
how the burned-out buildings hid those seeking to add to
their body count. Mack knew the insurgents in this area
better than anyone. He'd killed more than his fair share
of them. They didn't give up or give in. They'd put a bullet
in their own head before letting you capture them. If you
didn't get them, they'd get you. Survival of the fittest, or
in this case, survival of their leader maintaining his grip
on terrorized villages.

That said, the first thing you learn in the army is never
to question authority. You follow orders—end of story. No
one wants your opinion, even if you have intel they don't
have. His team had no choice but to go in. Mack still didn't
like it. He didn't join the army by choice. Well, unless you
consider the choice was either the military or prison. He

*chose the army because if he had to go down, he would
go down helping someone. In his opinion, that was better
than being shivved in a prison shower.*

*The kid with a chip on his shoulder standing in the
courtroom that day was long gone. The army had made
him a man in body, mind and spirit. He'd learned to contain his temper and use his anger for good, like protecting
innocent villagers being terrorized by men who wanted
to control the country with violence. As long as Mack
and his team sucked in this fetid air, they had another
think coming.*

*"Secure one, Charlie," a voice said over the walkie at-
tached to his vest. His team leader, Cal, was inside with
their linguist, Hannah. They needed information that only
Hannah could get.*

*"Secure two, Mike," he said after depressing the but-
ton.*

"Secure three, Romeo," came another voice.

*Roman Jacobs, Cal's foster brother, was standing
guard on the opposite side of the building. So far, all was
quiet, but Mack couldn't help but feel it wouldn't stay that
way. They needed to get out before someone dropped
something from the air they couldn't dodge. He shrugged
his shoulders to keep the back of his shirt from sticking to
him as the sun beat down with unrelenting heat. The one
hundred degrees temp felt like an inferno when weighed
down with all the equipment and the flak jacket.*

*"Come on, come on," he hummed, aiming high and
swinging his rifle right, then left of the adjacent buildings. There were so many places for a sniper to hide. He
checked his watch. It had been ten minutes since Cal
checked in and thirty minutes since Hannah had gone*

into the complex. She would have to sweet talk some of the older and wiser women in the community to cough up the bad guys' location. Sharing that information would be bad for their health, but so was not rooting the guys out and ending their reign of terror. If Hannah could ascertain a location, their team would ensure they never showed up around these parts again. There was far too much desert to search if they didn't have a place to start.

"Charlie and Hotel on the move," Roman said. "Entering the complex veranda, headed to Mike."

"Ten-four," he answered before he backed up to the complex's entrance. With his rifle still at his shoulder, he swept the empty buildings in front of him, looking for movement.

A skitter of rocks. Mack's attention turned to a burned-out building on his right. A muzzle flashed, sending a bullet straight at the courtyard.

"Sniper! Get her down!" Mack yelled, bringing his rifle up just as another shot rang out. The "oof" from the complex hit him in the gut, but he aimed and fired, the macabre dance of the enemy as he collapsed in a heap of bones, satisfying to see.

"Charlie! Hotel!"

"SECURE ONE, CHARLIE."

"Secure two, Romeo."

"Secure three, Echo."

"Mack!" Cal hissed his name, and it snapped him back to the present.

"Secure four, Mike," he said, using his call name for the team. His voice was shaky, and he hoped no one noticed. Not that they wouldn't understand. They'd all served together and they all came back from the war with memories they didn't want but couldn't get rid of. Sometimes, when the conditions were right, he couldn't stop them from intruding in the present.

At present, he was standing behind his boss, Cal Newfellow, dressed in fatigues and bulletproof vest. Was that overkill for security at a sweet sixteen birthday party? Not if the birthday girl's father was a sitting senator.

"Ya good, man?" Cal asked without turning.

"Ten-four," he said, even though his hands were still shaking. It was hard to fight back those memories when he had to stand behind Cal, the one who lost the most that day. "Something doesn't feel right, boss."

"What do you see?"

"I don't see anything, but I can feel it. My hair is standing up on the back of my neck. My gut says run."

"We're the security force. We can't run." Cal's voice was amused, but Mack noticed him bring his shoulders up to his ears for a moment. "Keep your eyes open and your head on a swivel. Treat it like any other job and stop thinking about the past."

Mack wished it were that simple. Cal knew that not thinking about the past was tricky when you'd seen the things they had over there. War was ugly, whether foreign or domestic, and Mack was glad to be done with that business. He liked the comforts of home, not to mention not having to kill people daily.

He glanced at his boots, where the metal bars across the toes reminded him that his losses over in that sandbox were his fault.

At least the loss that ended their army careers for good was his fault. Mack had missed a car bomb tucked away in the vehicle he was tasked with driving. He was carrying foreign dignitaries to a safe house that day, but nothing went as planned. In the end, Cal had lost most of his right hand, Eric had lost his hearing and Mack had suffered extensive nerve damage in his legs when the car bomb shot shrapnel across the sand. Now, the metal braces he wore around his legs and across his toes were the only thing that allowed him to walk and do his job. Something told him that tonight, he'd better concentrate on his job instead of worrying about the past.

"What are the weak points of the property?" Mack asked, fixing his hat to protect his ears better. It was early May, but that didn't mean it was warm in Minnesota. Especially at night in the rain. Sometimes working in damp clothes with temps hovering near forty-five was worse than working in ninety-degree heat.

Cal swept his arm out the length of the backyard. "The three hundred and fifty feet of shoreline. This cabin is remote, but anyone approaching from the road would be stopped by security. If someone wants to crash the party, it'll be via the water. We need to keep a tight leash on the shore."

A tight leash. That had been the story of Mack's life since he'd been four. His mother was the first to make helicopter parenting an Olympic sport. When his dad died in a car accident, and Mack survived, she became obsessed with keeping him safe. His mother would have kept him in a bubble were it possible, but she couldn't, so she kept the leash tight. Sports? Out of the question. He could get hurt, or worse, killed by a random baseball to the head! As much as Mack hated to say it, he was relieved when she'd passed of cancer when he was seventeen. She was more a keeper than a mother, and it had to be a terrible way to live. It wasn't until she was diagnosed with blood cancer when he was fourteen that she started living again. The sad truth was that she had to be dying to live. When she passed away after three years of making memories together, he was relieved not for himself but her. She was with her soulmate again, and he knew that was what she'd wanted since the day he'd passed. Mack was simply collateral damage.

When he was seventeen, he'd stood before a judge after breaking a guy's arm for talking trash about a female classmate. He was told there were better ways to defend people than with violence. If you asked him, the military personified using violence to defend people. He joined the army to find a brotherhood again. He'd found one in Cal, Roman, Eric and his other army brothers. They were Special Forces and went into battle willing to die to have their brothers' backs. Until the one time that he couldn't. It had taken Mack a long time to understand he shouldn't use the word *didn't* when it came to what happened that day when Cal's soulmate was taken before their eyes. It wasn't that he didn't. It was that he couldn't. His mind immediately slid down the rabbit hole toward the car full of people he didn't save. Mack shook his head to clear it. Going back there would result in losing sight of what they were doing here.

Mack eyed his friend of fifteen years and reminded himself that Hannah hadn't been Cal's soulmate. He used to think so, but then Cal met Marlise. Hannah had been a woman Cal loved in youth. Her death opened a path for Cal to start a successful security business and eventually find the woman who centered him. The moment Cal's and Marlise's eyes met while the bad guys bombarded them with bullets, time stood still. Cal used to think he started Secure One Security because of Hannah, but not anymore. They all believed Marlise was the reason. The tragedy that started years before was the catalyst to put Cal on that plane when Marlise needed him.

It had been three years now since they met. They were engaged one month and married the next, which hadn't surprised the team. Marlise had shown Cal that he could love again, but Mack never thought he'd see the day. Not after the scene that spread out before him in that court-yard. Then again, Cal never saw that scene. He never saw his girlfriend with a fatal shot to the head. He never had to drag his friend's body out of the square, stemming the blood oozing from his chest to keep him alive until help got there. Cal hadn't known any of that. It was Mack, Eric and Roman who lived that scene. They were left with the worst memories of a day when they could save one friend but not the other. Whether he liked it or not, Cal had been spared those images, and Mack was glad. There weren't many times you were spared the gruesome truth of war.

Not all wars are fought on foreign soil. The new team members of Secure One had taught him that three times over. Roman's wife and partner in the FBI had been under-cover in a house filled with women who had been sex traf-ficked and forced to work as escorts and drug mules. Mina had been injured to the point that she lost her leg and had come to work at Secure One when she married Roman. Their boss at the FBI, David Moore, was responsible for her injuries by putting her undercover in a house run by his wife, The Madame. Because of the deception, Roman and Mina could retire from the FBI with full benefits.

Marlise was one of The Madame's women in the house with Mina, and when she arrived at Secure One, she was broken and burned but determined. She wanted to help put The Madame behind bars. As she healed, Marlise worked her way up from kitchen manager to client coordinator, but not because she was Cal's girl. She had earned her position by observing, learning and caring about the people they were protecting.

His thoughts drifted to the other woman at Secure One who sought shelter there not long ago. About six months ago, Charlotte surrendered to Secure One under unusual circumstances. She was working for The Miss, the right-hand woman of The Madame in the same house Marlise and Mina had lived. The Miss had left Kansas and moved to Arizona to start her escort business, funded by drug trafficking. Charlotte was one of the women she took from Red Rye to help her. The Miss had made a mistake thinking Charlotte was devoted to her. She wasn't, and she wanted out. Last year, she'd helped them bring down The Miss by providing insider information they wouldn't have had any other way.

Charlotte took over the kitchen manager position when Marlise moved up to client coordinator and fit in well with the Secure One team. She had healed physically from the illness and injuries she'd suffered while living with The Miss, but her emotional and psychological injuries would take longer to scab over. She'd been homeless for years and then went to work for people who used and abused her without caring if she lived or died. There was a special kind of hell for people like that. Mack hoped The Miss had found her way there when he put a bullet in her chest.

Had he needed to kill her that night in the desert? Yes.

Her guards had had guns pointed at his team, and there was no way he would lose another friend to her evil. As it were, Marlise took a bullet trying to protect Cal. Thankfully, it had been a nonlethal shoulder wound.

On the other hand, the gaping chest wound he'd left The Miss with was quite lethal and well-deserved. Mack had learned to channel his temper in the army, but he couldn't pretend he wasn't angry at the atrocities that occurred in a country that was the home of the free to some, but not all. He would defend women like Charlotte until his final breath so they would have a voice.

Mack rolled his shoulders at the thought of the woman who currently sat in their mobile command center on the other side of the property. The mobile command center offered bunks, food and a hot shower to keep the men warm and fed when they were on jobs away from their home base of Secure One. A hot shower and warm food were on Mack's wish list at that moment.

The hot shower or seeing Charlotte again?

His groan echoed across the lake until it filtered back to his ears as a reminder that he didn't need to concern himself with the woman in the command center. He could protect her without falling for her. He noticed how his team raised a brow whenever he helped Char in the kitchen or took a walk with her. He didn't care what they thought. She needed practice in trusting someone again without worrying about being hurt. It was going to be a long hard road for her, so the way he saw it, he'd be the one to teach her that not all men were bad, evil or sick. Sure, he'd done some bad things, but it hadn't been out of evilness or demented pleasure. He had done bad things for good people in the name of justice or retribution, making the world a better place to live. She didn't need to know that, though.

His gaze traveled the lakeshore again, searching for oncoming lights and listening for outboard motors. It was silent other than the call of the loons. The hair on the back of his neck told him it wouldn't stay that way for long.